SO-AIF-316

# Praise for
# *Chronicles of M'Gistryn:*
# *Core*

"Anastasia M. Trekles takes readers on an epic adventure in her debut novel Core. Told from the perspective of multiple characters, Core borrows familiar elements of our world to create a thrilling fantasy filled with intrigue, action, and romance. The characters are engaging with witty banter and personalities that sprawl across the page. Trekles masterfully guides readers through worlds rich with lore, but never bogs down the prose with too much description or exposition. She has a keen sense of a modern reader's imagination and deftly transports us through time and space. Trekles has a deep understanding of the fantasy genre and weaves a tale that will satisfy anyone who appreciates a great story told well. This novel establishes the foundation for a series of books and invites a reader back for more."

-S.E. White, author of *A Murder of Crows*

"Wondrously imagined! M'Gistryn is a realm rich with possibilities. The characters are rich in detail, and the plotting just complex enough to grab your interest and not let go!"

-Jay Erickson, author of *The Blood Wizard Chronicles Series*

"Simply amazing! Characters who actually behave like adults! This novel is highly recommended!"

-J.P. Strohm, coauthor of *Exactors: Tales from the Citadel*

# Books by Anastasia M. Trekles

## THE CHRONICLES OF M'GISTRYN

*Core*
*Ascent*

# CHRONICLES

## OF

# M'GISTRYN

# BOOK II

# ASCENT

Anastasia M. Trekles

Halsbren
Publishing, llc

All text and front matter images
Copyright © 2018 Anastasia M. Trekles

All characters in this book are fictitious. Any resemblance to actual persons, living or dead, is purely coincidental.

This book is protected under the copyright laws of the United States of America. Any reproduction or unauthorized use of the material or artwork herein is prohibited without the express written permission of Zelda23Publishing, Halsbren Publishing LLC. and the author.

ASCENT

First Edition Printing
(2018)

Published By: Halsbren Publishing LLC  La Porte, IN. 46350
ISBN- 13: 978-0-9964311-2-5


Cover design and layout by Jay Erickson.
Photography by Anastasia M. Trekles.
Ajna Mandala by Morgan Phoenix
Ajna Mandala used under the Creative Commons Attribution-Share Alike 3.0 License


Made in the United States of America

# DEDICATION

To the Wordcrafters of LaPorte, and "word-crafters" all around the world. Keep believing in yourself, and all things are possible.

Anastasia M. Trekles
-Author

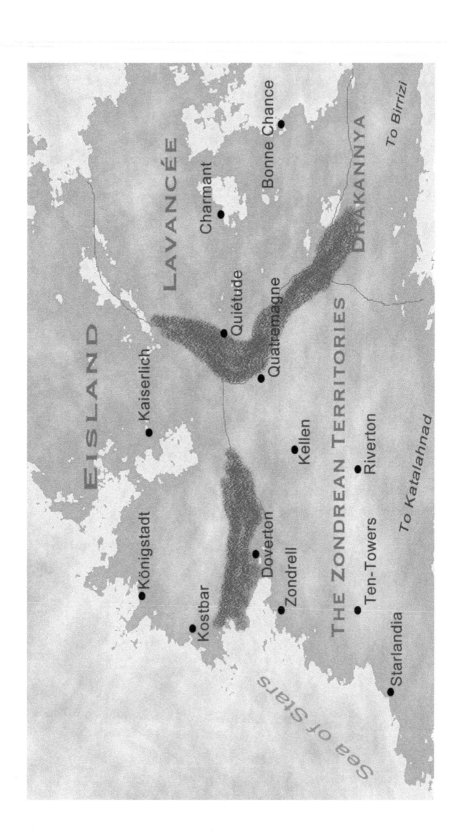

# Heraldry of Zondrell - the Eight Ruling Houses

Kelvaar V (reigning King of Zondrell)
Wife: Mariana
Children: Larenne, Beatrix, Katarina, Edin

Andrew Avery Piers
Wife: Diana
Children: Hann, Leon, Amis, Davies

Percival Tyr Anthony
Wife: Therese
Children: Victor, Peter

Cen Marcus Lyster
Wife: Dona
Children: Corrin, Frederick (Fyr), Elena

Jonathan Colywyl Michael
Wife: Gretchen
Children: Tristan

Alexander Marcus Xavier
Wife: none
Children: none

Morvaine Gallus Stephen
Wife: Rosa
Children: Melody, Squire

Alastair Aric Percy
Wife: Tirana
Children: Birann, Tressia, Milena, Gregory

# TABLE OF CONTENTS

# PART ONE

I am not sure I disagree with those that believe that this world is not "ready" to understand the grander subtleties and true nature of magic. Half the time, men only find ways to use it to kill each other.

From *The Research of Archmage Tiara Chandler:*
*Lectures and Essays*

# CHAPTER ONE

## At the Gates

*19 Spring's Dawn, 1271*
*Andella Weaver*

Somehow, I kept finding my way back to Zondrell. I graduated from the Magic Academy half a year ago, and then, I thought I was more or less done with the place. Not that it was a bad city – Zondrell was pretty, actually, especially the great sand-colored stone cliffs overlooking the sea on its western shore. The Academy, too, was fantastic, with the most amazing library where I could spend hours poring through books. But, the city was also crowded and noisy and much too hectic for my tastes. I liked the slower pace of my native Doverton, and even though it was colder there, it was just... nicer. Cleaner, too.

I might never go home again. The realization hit me with unexpected force as our caravan wagon bumbled up to the entrance gate, awaiting inspection. It had not been what I'd call a comfortable ride all the way from Doverton, especially since the caravan moved at a snail's pace and we had spent nearly three days on a trip that should have only taken one. Not that I was complaining – much – though my bottom certainly was.

"Andella? Are you all right?" Tristan Loringham fixed his sky-blue gaze on me and put a large, warm hand on my arm.

"Hm? I'm fine," I said, managing a smile. Did I feel a little moisture at the corners of my eyes? "I'd just really like to get out of this wagon."

"By the Lady, me too. Let's get this over with." Seated across from where Tristan and I sat was Alexander Vestarton, Tristan's best friend, and I supposed a friend of mine now as well. He had been quite good at carrying the burden of complaining for all of us the entire trip, often punctuated by very creative cursing. I never had any idea that noblemen could be so foul-mouthed, though sometimes he tried to rein it in. This was not one of those occasions.

"Just be ready," Tristan said, tone as flat and serious as ever. I actually liked that about him, crazy as that sounds – he was conscientious, focused, genuine. My sister warned me before we left not to get too wrapped up, but my heart was definitely ruling out over my head the more time we spent together. The speed and ease with which it happened was a little disturbing, truth be told. "You know what could happen."

"I'm telling you, don't worry. I'm a Lord. They *have* to listen to me."

"Yeah, they don't have to listen to me, and I'm the one they want."

It was a risk to come here – I knew that much. He and Alex knew it, too. Yet, here we were, but what was the alternative? Could we run and hide for the rest of our lives? Zondrell was a big city-state with a powerful army, and we were... well, fugitives, in a sense. They would find us eventually, and we all knew it.

Good Catherine in Paradise, how could a simple little Pyrelight from Doverton become a fugitive in the span of just a few days? The thought made me shudder, and I had to wipe my eyes to keep any additional wetness from spilling down my cheek. This was not how I envisioned my life after graduation. I was supposed to help people send their dead up to Paradise, performing the rites that only a Fire mage can perform. That was what I trained to do, what I thought I was meant to do. I came from a family of priestesses and acolytes, after all. Now, not only was I no longer a Fire mage, but I was no longer welcome in my own hometown. We were too "dangerous," they said, as if *our* magic was what had injured a number of city guards and caused a huge ruckus at the temple. The King knew it was the people from Zondrell, not us, and yet, he cast us out anyway. Honestly, it made me more angry than sad.

Of course, I didn't have to come here, with Tristan and Alexander. I could have let them do whatever they wanted to do and never seen them again, but we were all... connected, somehow, in a way I didn't really understand. And I wanted to know more. Maybe it was just Fate. Or it might have been part of some prophecy in an old book, if one believed in those sorts of things.

> *Seven elements comprise the energy of this world – the Greater Three are lost, but not gone. They live and wait for a new dawn, this, the dawn of Prophecy. Time stops, half a hero's blood soaks the land to bring forth new Life, bearing with it the Light of a new age.*

I did believe in it – any self-respecting scholar would have a hard time refuting the evidence. Tristan was half-Zondrean and half-Eislandisch, and the poor man had bled plenty in the last few weeks. Alexander was... well, a Time mage. It was bizarre, unheard of, and yet, he could stop time and speed it up and do all kinds of interesting things. He seemed to get better at it every day, even though he claimed to hate everything about it. And me? I could heal people. Oh, I know, I know – that's not natural. Healing someone just by touching them is something only found in storybooks... but I can do it. I had a hard time just summoning this power on command, and it seemed to have erased four years of training with Fire magic from my body completely, but if healing magic didn't exist, then Tristan would almost surely be a dead man. Instead, he was sitting next to me trying his very best not to look nervous, his hand still reassuringly resting on my arm. His right hand, as a matter of fact, now worked quite well and he didn't seem to strain to move around or anything. It was the closest thing to a miracle I had ever witnessed.

So, this prophecy, as translated from the book I found buried in our roadside church back in Doverton, had come true, as far as I could tell. And yet, I did have my doubts. There was no new age happening. No gods were coming out of the skies, the hills were not shifting, and the seas were not boiling. Nor were people suddenly smarter, or even just a little nicer. None of the ideas of a "new age" that one typically finds in books or hears about in sermons were happening – at least, not that I could tell.

In fact, people seemed even less charitable than normal in Zondrell, as we started to hear a good deal of mumbling and fussing and shouting as the line for gate inspections had ground to a halt. I didn't know how long it normally took to get into the city, but apparently this was out of the ordinary. Our wagon was covered to shield us and our things from rain and wind, so I couldn't see much beyond the little window in front, which revealed the feet of our driver, the rear ends of the two horses pulling us, and not much else.

"This is not good," Alex said, digging into his pack for something, and I could hear the jingling of coins. "I've got about... a thousand here and a couple of gems. What do you have?"

"Maybe a thousand, and a sapphire," Tristan said. "I told you, I didn't bring a lot of money with me when I left."

"A thousand Royals isn't a lot of money?" I asked. That was more money than my sister's church would make in months, though the two of them had left a sizable donation before we left Doverton. I suppose, if I never get to see my sister again, I will at least be able to remember the look of sheer joy and gratitude she had when they handed her a pile of Catherine knew how many Royals. Again, I wiped at my eyes with the back of my hand.

Alex chuckled. "It goes fast when you have to, ah, explain things to city guards."

Suddenly, the corner of the cover right by my head flew open, and I jumped with a sharp breath. A fresh-faced young man in heavy armor tore back the rest of the cloth, letting it hang loose by the rear frame. He looked to be in his early twenties, same as all of us in the wagon, and he looked very troubled, maybe even conflicted about something. "Look, guys, I tried," the man said.

"Corrin! What's going on?" Alex asked, leaning in to shake the man's hand. The man called Corrin took Alex's hand in his gauntleted one, but didn't hold on very long.

"They read the manifest and someone ran to get a commanding officer. I tried to talk them down, but no luck. By the gods, guys, did what they're saying happened really... happen?"

"Depends on what you heard," Tristan said, unable to look this apparent friend in the eye as he also leaned over to shake his hand.

"I heard a lot of things, my brother, not a lot of it good."

"I... I'm not going to lie. I did some things I'm not proud of."

Corrin cursed as he looked over his shoulder, then back at us. "I was hoping you wouldn't say that. The General's coming – you have to wait here."

My eyes widened. "Sir, are you in charge here?" I asked the soldier.

"Yes, ma'am, Captain of the Gate Watch." He offered a brief salute, striking his left shoulder with his right fist. "That's as far as my command goes, I'm afraid."

"Corr, it's fine," Alex said. "We'll deal with it. We came here willingly – you'd think that counts for something."

"Maybe. I don't know. Look, I'll do what I can, but..." He trailed off as something caught his attention – the sound of a dozen men in armor marching toward us, and swords ringing as they left their sheaths. The two at the front of the pack pushed Corrin out of the way as if he were some street urchin.

Alex stood up and hopped out of the wagon, motioning for Tristan to stay where he was. This didn't go over very well from the way Tristan squared his jaw, but he did as instructed. "Well, it's not often General Torven himself scouts the gates. An honor to see you, Sir." Despite his low bow, Alex's voice dripped with annoyance.

Two men in silvery armor flanked another without armor, but wearing a long black coat upon which hung a number of medals, most in the shape of the falcon symbol of Zondrell. With the gray scattered in his beard and at his temples, framing a strong face and intense steel-colored eyes, he had a regal air about him. I knew he was not the King, though – this was the General they had been talking about, and he did not look happy to see Alex, or Tristan, or anyone else for that matter.

"Lord Vestarton," he said, "I assume you understand why I'm here. And I expect your cooperation."

Alex offered little in reply, and as he straightened, he made a point not to look at the General or the guards for too long.

His magic, as it is for all mages, had manifested in his eyes quite a lot now, even though there was still a peek of his original chestnut brown in there. The rest of his irises had erupted into something like quicksilver in an alchemist's jar. He had tried to hide it for years, as I understood, by smoking Katalahni tobacco of all things. But he'd run out of his supply, and his emotions were running too high, anyhow. Everyone knows that magic intensifies when under stress, which makes it such a dangerous weapon when used in battle – Alex had seen his share of stress in the past week or so. All of us had.

The General turned away from Alex and leveled his steely gaze at Tristan. "Lieutenant, I expect you understand the gravity of your situation?"

When Tristan failed to answer right away, he got three swords pointed at his throat. I let out a tiny sound and without thinking, clutched at his elbow. What I thought I would do in this situation, I really had no idea, but my protective instincts kicked in anyway.

"I expect you to stand and salute when in my presence," the General said, and even though Tristan did move to comply, he didn't get to do it under his power. The silver-armored men began to reach in and haul him out of the wagon, and they were not kind about it, either. Even though Tristan didn't resist them in the least, one of them poked him in the back with the butt end of his sword while another spat on his boots. How barbaric! I had half a mind to tell them exactly what I thought of all this, but thought better of it. Why? Because they were now peppering Tristan with questions, the General and his guardsmen. What did he think he was doing? Did he understand how many men he'd gotten killed? What happened in Doverton? And on, and on, and on. Tristan really never got a chance to answer because before he could gather his thoughts, they were on to another topic. If their real goal was to scare him, they seemed to be doing a fine job of it.

The General gestured and someone came forward with a set of wicked-looking manacles, the kind with little barbs on the inside so that the prisoner wouldn't try to wriggle out of them. I held my breath, unable to take my eyes from them even as the General began to speak again. "I don't have time for this, Lieutenant. You're going to Interrogation."

"Whoa! What do you think you're doing, General?" Alex barked, moving to get in front of the General and not apparently caring that some of those drawn weapons were now trained on him.

"We need to get to the bottom of this, Lord Vestarton. If you choose to stand in my way, you can go to the front of the list. As it is," he said, turning toward me with a look that chilled me to the bone, "the girl comes next. Gentlemen?"

A rough metal-covered hand reached in and pulled on my arm to get me out of the wagon, too. "Wait, look, you don't understand," I started, but it wasn't any use. No one was listening to my weak protests.

"Young lady, I understand from witnesses that you were in Doverton on the day of the incident. Do you care to explain what happened?"

I took a deep breath and looked into the General's eyes and their total lack of emotion. His anger might have come out in his tone, but to look at him, he might as well have been having an inconsequential conversation over tea. "Sir, I... no," I said with every ounce of courage I had. It wasn't much, but it forced those words out. "No, I don't care to explain, Sir. We've traveled a long way, and we haven't had a decent meal, and..."

My voice trailed off, but rather than bash me with a sword, the bearded man's expression softened, just a little. Did he see the magic in my eyes? It presented as lavender, not orange, white, blue, or green like normal mages, but with unusual white flecks and swirls. He couldn't know what that was, could he? "Very well," was all he said as he turned away from me again and back to his guards. "Gentlemen, escort them. Lieutenant Loringham is not to leave his home without explicit permission until further notice."

Alexander scoffed. "House arrest? Are you serious?"

"It's either that, or the dungeon. Consider this a favor to the Council. Lieutenant, tell your father I'll be calling on him shortly. Lord Vestarton, I'll expect to see you in the Council Chamber." With that, he took his leave, though only the guardsmen that followed put their swords away. The rest just eyed us with menace.

It was odd to be led through the streets of Zondrell by armed guards, and even odder was the reaction we got.

People darted to the other side of the street as we approached. Mothers held their children back, and merchants and noblemen looked away. Alex muttered about the embarrassment of the whole thing most of the way down countless blocks through the maze-like city, while Tristan just walked along in silence. At least they never did put him into those evil barbed manacles.

"Are you okay?" I whispered to him as we turned onto the next street.

"I'm fine," he replied, voice also low and soft. It was hard to hear him in the clamor of Zondrell at midday. "Look, I don't know where this will all lead, but I won't... I won't let anything happen to you. You'll stay with my family; you'll be safe and well cared for."

I didn't know what to say. It might have been gallant or even sweet if I had read it in some trashy novel and wasn't living it.

"Just don't answer any of their questions," he went on. "My father and I will handle this." His teeth seemed to grind at the mention of his father, but he remained steadfast.

In fact, through the days to come, I never once saw him back down from any of the men who came to talk to him. I never once saw him break under their constant questioning, their mind games and general torment. I paid close attention to all of it, but from a distance, often locked in an opulent upstairs bedroom where they all talked in a private study or in the grand dining room of the Loringham manor. Tristan – and his father, too, to some extent – made absolutely sure that none of them ever accosted me, or even so much as breathed on me wrong. In some ways, it was frustrating, I'll admit, but I understood why. This new Life magic I seemed to have discovered was precious, and that meant I was precious, too. Funny, I didn't really feel that way about it myself.

What was more frustrating, though, was knowing that throughout that entire time, while Tristan appeared fine on the outside, I knew it hurt. All the questions, all the grief, all the accusations – they cut him as sure as any sword. He would spend long hours alone, lost in thought, and he slept hardly more than three or four hours a night. A few times, I went to him, to try to provide some kind of comfort, but it didn't seem to help.

Finally, after two weeks, came the final day of torment – the day of the trial. I refused to believe that when he walked out the door, it might be last time I saw him, but still, I wished I could have gone along. At least then, I could testify. I could help in some way. Instead, I had to stay behind, helpless, even though I was as much a part of what happened as Tristan or Alex or anyone else.

# CHAPTER TWO

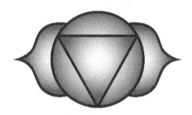

## The Trial

*40 Spring's Dawn, 1271*
*Tristan Michael Johannes Loringham*

*I should have told her I loved her.*
At the very furthest point before the great city of Zondrell dropped off the rocky cliffs upon which it perched lay the Great Palace, a monstrosity of stone and glass and metal that had housed kings since the Early Age. Once, before Zondrell was even a city at all, it was said to be a fortress, a perfect location with the sea to protect its back, and the wide sweeping countryside before it. From its watchtowers, one could see for miles around, everything from the caravans shuffling along down the roads, to the ships coming in from the Sea of Stars, to the farmers tending their crops and cattle in the fields outside of the city walls.

However, from the balcony of the Council antechamber, where people waited for an audience with the noble Lords who advised the King in all matters, one could only see the sea crashing against the jagged rocks just below. An endless, merciless sea, with no end in sight and a distinct, vibrant, salty smell. Far out in the distance, dark clouds shed long streams of rain-tears, but Zondrell's sunny sky was safe from them for now. Somewhere to the south lay the docks, where fishermen and tradesmen from every city along the Western Coast came to hawk their wares and make a living. Every once in a while, a ship would pass by the Palace on its way there – an hour ago, a crimson-bannered ship from Starlandia, and just now, a silvery-blue one from Königstadt.

*Why didn't I? What if that was the last time I'll ever see her? I'm an idiot.*

I watched the Königstadt ship move out of sight, and I thought of the letter I'd handed over along with my reports. Stamped on it was the same seven-pointed star on that ship's sail, the symbol of the nation of Eisland. I'd been told King Keis Sturmberg put it there himself. Even if I wasn't sure, they had to believe it.

"Lieutenant?"

I hadn't even heard the footsteps or the gentle clinking of steel buckles on polished Royal Guard armor. I turned, trying to look less surprised than I actually was.

"They're ready for you, Sir."

My joints ached as I followed the soldiers back through the antechamber. Truth be told, I hadn't had a good night's rest in months, going from sleeping on the cold ground in the Eislandisch-Zondrean borderlands, to laying in bitter convalescence in a strange church, to coming back to a place that should have felt like home, but didn't. Nearly every day, I woke with a headache that burned straight into the center of my forehead, like the one that plagued me now. In spite of all that, I was grateful for one thing: I was whole. I could wield a sword in the proper hand. I could move without feeling faint or weak or sick, even though there was still plenty of pain. I could write and eat and… well, breathe – all of the little things that people often take for granted. That I could do all of those things again was truly nothing short of a miracle. That's why I wasn't shocked when someone said so, as I stood there, joining two other sons of Lords before the Zondrell Council, awaiting judgment.

*Just stand by your truth.* Far easier to say than to do.

The three of us stood before seven men, as well as the General of the Army, Jamison Torven, all seated in that opulent chamber. They went through the same battery of questions we'd written endless reports about. Yes, I was aware of the consequences of my actions. No, I did not know the girl I decided to let live was a spy. Yes, I knew my orders were that any of the captives that we took during our mission were to be killed after interrogation. But no, I did not know the Eislander who cornered me alone was a General, or that we were related. And I most definitely did *not* know that he had set an ambush for my men at the village of Südenforst.

Was I naïve? Absolutely. Did I intend for good men to die that day? If I could trade my life for theirs, I would have done it – gladly. The story never got less unpleasant no matter how many times it was told, and it never failed to send flashes of gore and grief across the battered landscape of my psyche.

By the Lady, my head hurt. *Please, let's just get this over with.*

At the table, I could see the stirrings, hear the muttering as the Lords all tried to decide what to ask next. In a different situation, with men of lesser blood standing before them, things would be different – I was not so naïve as to think otherwise. And I also knew from the silent, piercing stare of the General that things might be different still if I had taken the pardon he'd offered me. I still wasn't going to get the same kind of trial that a nameless sergeant would get. The reason I wasn't already dead was because someday, whether they liked it or not, I would take a seat at that table in place of my father. And, of course, they still thought I knew *something important.* How wrong and yet how right they were.

Even in all their finery and resplendence and power, when it came down to it, the Council was still just a group of men, men who bickered over all manner of details. This they did, to no end. I wondered if it was worse because the King wasn't there, but then again, King Kelvaar V was not the kind of man who commanded a room. I doubted he'd ever had much luck controlling this bunch.

"We should never have been there in the first place," Lord Alexander Vestarton interjected. At twenty-three and just a few months older than I, he was the youngest man at the table. Something like that hadn't happened since Cen Shal-Vesper's grandfather had to take his seat at twenty-five, after his father fell to some manner of poisoning. In spite of his age, Alex made serving as a Councilor look natural enough, including the posturing. He crossed his arms behind his head and leaned back in his chair with an annoyed grunt, staring out at all of them from behind dark, stained-glass spectacles. They were the same type that most magic users wore when they preferred not to be recognized by everyone around them, even though the spectacles themselves were more of a dead giveaway than the distinct colored whirls and lights that lived within the eyes of the average mage. Still, hiding behind that smoke-colored glass seemed to give my oldest friend a bit more confidence in going out amongst the public as of late.

"Boy, your father supported that mission. If I recall, so did you, Loringham." This was Lord Percival Wyndham, a fellow that never failed to remind me of a bloated old goat.

Alex shook his head. "If *you* recall, my father was nearing his deathbed then. If you think he was making good decisions, think again. This was the stupidest thing I've heard of Zondrell doing... ever."

"Really, saying that right in front of the General, are we?" Wyndham snorted. "Your father should have taught you to watch your tongue."

"Gentlemen! Please!" the Head Councilor, Lord Andrew Miller, shouted over them enough to calm the group down for a moment. The large, bearded gentleman had a very tenuous grip on the peace in that room, but he seemed determined to keep it.

General Torven cleared his throat before letting anyone else get ahold of the silence. "The point is irrelevant. If you recall, the Council's support was requested, not required. The investigation of the Kaeren item was ongoing and under the direction of the King."

The Kaeren... I still couldn't believe they all sat there and agreed to send men off to find it. I thought it was a joke when I learned about my actual mission. At worst, it was a cruel one. But the King wanted to show the world the extent of the power of Zondrell with that legendary weapon in his hands. Not even the possibility that none of it was true at all seemed able to deter him.

Seated between Lords Vestarton and Shilling, gaunt, lanky Cen Shal-Vesper crossed his arms over his chest, scowling. "But the letter that General Jannausch wrote is right – it does violate the Second Treaty of the Northlands, and I *told* you this when we discussed it. I distinctly remember this. It was only a few bloody months ago."

"You are correct, Lord Shal-Vesper," Torven said, shifting in his seat but never looking the least bit truly uncomfortable. For him, such a thing wasn't possible. "His Majesty was made aware of this when he ordered the campaign."

Various mutterings flew across the table, but Miller put up his hand. "So, Lieutenant, let me ask you this: if you had figured out that this young girl was a spy, would you have killed her then?"

Words caught in my throat. I had rehearsed the answer to this question, because I knew it was coming. No matter how many times that particular scene replayed itself in my subconscious, though, I could not come up with any but one real answer: *We are not barbarians. I am not a barbarian.* Finally, I got my wits about me enough to speak my lines. "Sir," I said at length, "I would have questioned her differently. After that, I cannot speak to what would have happened."

Percival Wyndham stood up, beating his withered hands against the table. "Bah! Please, you're a sympathizer, boy – like father, like son. An Eislandisch sympathizer, and one of them to boot. We all know it."

A sympathizer? Maybe so. Half of my heritage came from there, and there was no denying it. With my blond hair and blue eyes, I looked far out of place in that room full of smaller, darker people. But the slaughter of women and children went against every code of ethics I'd ever been taught. Zondrell's progress, or whatever was going on, wasn't worth losing what little soul I had left – not then, not now. Treason be damned.

Several glares with mixtures of confusion, agreement, and even hatred all bore down on Wyndham at once. Shal-Vesper got in the first word. "Wyndham, are you a seer now? Do you honestly think we should convict based on what might have been? You read that letter. The enemy already knew the location of our camp. Isn't that what it says?"

From the center of the table where all of the other evidence had been gathered, Alexander grabbed up the letter adorned with the blue star seal of Keis Sturmberg and waved it in the air. I had been given that letter not even knowing if it was real or a spectacular fake. The Council didn't seem to question its authenticity. "The spy was confirmation. They knew where the camp was for almost three weeks. Says so right here." For effect, he tossed the letter back onto the table.

"The Eislandisch know their land better than we do," my father added, shaking his head. "Trust me – I know. And so should you. Why should this be a surprise? We're lucky at least some of our men made it home at all."

"That doesn't matter, Jonathan, and it doesn't change the facts," Wyndham pressed on, with Lord Morvaine Silversmith sitting next to him bobbing his head in blind agreement. This, I imagined, is how Silversmith spent every Council meeting – everyone knew those two families were so close they ought to hold only one Council seat instead of two. "He let them right in and let them get comfortable. Unbelievable. I cannot believe in hearing this testimony that any of you would vote for anything *but* treason. This boy should be hanged today. Sorry, Jonathan, but it's the Lady's truth."

"If you'd *ever* actually picked up a sword in your life, Wyndham, maybe you'd understand a few things." Father's words dropped like lead onto the table.

For much of the day so far, the General had remained expressionless, offering little except a cold stare. But at this, his hawk-like features grew animated. "I would agree with Lord Loringham. Living by the blade it not an easy road to follow."

Wyndham let out a disgusted chuckle. "It doesn't change anything, and you of all people, Torven, should agree."

Always willing to say what no one else would, Alex tapped his fingers in time with his words as he shot them out across the table. "Wyndham, just shut the fuck up. We all know you're not here to be reasonable, so let's just get through this and let justice be served. How about we ask *your* boys a few questions, shall we?"

Again, Wyndham scoffed, beady dark eyes narrowing in his round and cantankerous old face. "You are the most insolent child. Your father would be ashamed to see you at this table."

"All right! Gentlemen, please." Miller rapped his meaty knuckles with great force against the table as he turned his attention on one of the other men standing next to me. "Let's get through this. Lord Vestarton has a point, and there are some other questions that remain unanswered. Captain Wyndham, three weeks ago, you went toward the north border after a report came back that our men were ambushed. We read your report, but how did you wind up in the city of Doverton?"

A pause, a long deep and shuddering breath. I could barely bring myself to even look in his direction as he spoke. "My

Lord, I was doing my due diligence to find any lost men. So I led the remaining troops over to Doverton to see if any had gone there for healing or sanctuary, since it was so close."

As Victor Wyndham, Percival's older son and a Captain of Magics, prattled on in a weak voice trying to sound smarter than he was, I found my focus wandering off. I had been in the Council chamber a few times before with my father, but it had not lost its stunning luster. Along the walls of the vaulted chamber, lit by torches in gold sconces, were various tapestries illustrating the glory and wealth of the great families in Zondrell. They hung in the order of succession, from Blackwarren to Miller and all the way down to Shilling, who currently held the last slot as apparently, three hundred years ago, theirs was the ruling house. Now Blackwarren had adopted the silver falcon symbol of Zondrell itself as its banner, and no one seemed to remember what its original symbol was. If all the Blackwarren men died tomorrow, though, then the honor would go to the family of Head Councilor Miller, whose stonecutter tools set against the peak of the Great Temple was by far one of the most ornate tapestries there. The banner of my own family – House Loringham – hung at fifth place, with its prominent sword, shield, and wheat scythe. We still owned most of the wheat farms around Zondrell, collecting the profits while employees did the hard work. I'd never even seen half of those fields myself.

"Lieutenant Loringham?"

It took longer than appropriate to realize they were talking to me. "Yes, my Lord," I said in my best, most stoic tone. I had been standing at attention the whole time, never moving, staring through them rather than at them.

"Is it true what Captain Wyndham says? Did you approach him in Doverton with the intent to attack?"

What a fucking liar! This is what I wanted to shout, but instead I just shook my head. "No, Sir. I was not armed. I went to him and his men in an attempt to give myself up, so that we could leave Doverton peacefully."

Out of the corner of my eye, I could see Victor let out an annoyed huff and shift his weight on the cane he now hobbled around on. I refused to look him in his magic-tinged blue eyes even as he addressed me directly. "So, why am I like this then, if *you* weren't armed? Why can I barely stand and you can walk around freely, hm?"

"There's never a minute when I am not without pain." This was true; I was starting to tire more with every minute that we stood up there. Of course, I could have been much worse off – I could have been buried on a hill somewhere near Doverton instead. But that was another matter, and one I couldn't explain. I *wouldn't* explain it here, not to them. Above all, the question of the strange magics that Andella and Alex both had displayed that day was not one I wanted raised.

"You didn't answer my question." When I said nothing more, he turned back to the table. "My Lords, Lieutenant Loringham tried to kill me that day in Doverton – me, the commanding officer at that time. This confirms this man is a traitor to Zondrell and brings shame to our Army."

Now Alex was out of his chair, which was probably not that wise. At best, it was inappropriate – all of the other Lords turned to look at him with various levels of disapproval written on their features. At least he could get away with what I could not. "Yeah, when was that, Victor? Was that before or after you tried to level half a town with magic? Let's not lose track of our facts here – you lost your mind and got a lot of people hurt before Tristan was able to stop you. From what I've seen, there's only one person who deserves name-calling."

"I don't recall it that way," Victor replied though a weak cough. "Besides, *Lord* Vestarton, I'm sure you've left out some important details yourself. Otherwise you'd have more to say about that so-called magic you're trying to hide. Gentlemen, perhaps you should look within your own ranks before casting aspersions."

If Alex could have leapt across the room and strangled the gaunt-faced elder Wyndham brother, he would have. It took everything within me to resist doing it myself. "How does any of that have *anything* to do with the fact that you neglected your officer's post, went against any sense of decency, and damn near started a war with an allied state?" His voice rose with each word. "Can you tell me that? Because that's the part that I find most fucking intriguing."

This was not going the way I'd pictured it, not a bit. But I wasn't prepared for Victor to just flat-out lie, and hold to his story with such... a lack of shame. Even more so, I didn't think the Council would entertain it. I had hoped we could skip talking about Doverton all together, but of course that was just a wish. From the Council's standpoint, this was probably the best part of the story. After a few more words and curses were shot around, Lord Miller put his hand up.

"Gentlemen, please," he said with a sigh. "Lord Vestarton, take your seat. And Captain Wyndham, hold your tongue. Don't forget that you're under investigation here as well. Who we have not heard from yet is Lieutenant Wyndham."

Peter Wyndham, someone I'd fought both against and alongside quite a bit over the past year or so, stood at his brother Victor's shoulder, ready to keep him from falling over at a moment's notice. Up to this point, Peter had been silent, barely saying a word even when the Council did address him. When I looked over at him, following the gaze of everyone else in the room, his big round eyes were glassy, still, staring off into the distance. He looked a bit pale, too, but when he finally spoke, the room quieted. "We went against the will of the gods."

"What?" Victor looked at him with something between disdain and confusion.

"We were wrong, what we did." His voice sounded as if it were coming from far away. "I've been thinking about it. I don't know what happened, but I know what I saw. I saw magic that was... miraculous. And we were punished – that's the only explanation."

Lord Miller spoke up before anyone else could. "Do tell, Lieutenant. What do you mean by that?"

"We attacked a church."

"We didn't *attack* anything," his brother jumped in, but Peter shook his head. I think it was the first time I had ever seen them disagree. Although, most of my formative years had been spent trying to avoid any member of the Wyndham family, most of all Victor and Peter.

"Yes we did. We argued with their King, and when that didn't go well, you decided to go back to the church. And the gods were angry. The Great Lady Catherine, someone... doesn't matter who. That magic, that's where it came from."

The Lords' table devolved into chaos. I heard everything from accusations of conspiracy to insanity and everything in between. But through it all, Peter's manner never changed, even when his brother started berating him under his breath, and even when some of the Lords began peppering him with more questions. Did he see anything that would make him think that? Why would he say such a thing in the first place? He didn't answer most of them with any more than vague replies, deferring to his brother. Victor *was* the commanding officer, after all, but hiding behind that seemed quite weak, even for Peter. What had changed in his mind to make him go from the rather arrogant, headstrong ass that I knew to the quiet, fearful man I now saw, I'll never know.

Some of the questions inevitably made their way to me and Victor as well, and in true form, Victor tried to protect himself with even more fervor. Sure, he took twelve priestesses hostage in their own church, and a number of Doverton guardsmen were killed or injured by his magic, but he was only doing what he could to protect himself and his men... what he thought was right. Funny, I thought that was my line.

"All right, all right, look. I know what you all want." Alex was back on his feet again, and six curious, unhappy Lords stared him down. "You want answers. You want to know what all this fuss is about magic and whatnot. Lieutenant Wyndham makes an... interesting observation, but I was there, and I'm here to tell you, there was nothing divine about what happened in Doverton. But, a bad situation was stopped from getting worse. That's what I know. That man there did that." He pointed at me. "Why? Because that's the kind of man he is. The King of Doverton called him a hero – you read his letter. You people should be giving Lieutenant Tristan Loringham a commendation instead of trying him for treason. I'm sick of this, and we're not going to learn anything new here. I call for a vote."

"You can't call for a vote," Silversmith snarled.

Across the table, Shal-Vesper also got to his feet. "Yes he can – any of us can. And I'll stand with that call. We've heard enough here."

"We can't vote until we get some answers on this magic situation," Wyndham said, slapping his hand on the table so loud it sent reverberations through the room.

My heart sank, my blood going cold. That trepidation must have been written into my gaze because when Alex looked back at me, he had something not unlike the same expression. But, he hid it much better than I, with bravado. *Trust me*, his face told me. Sure, Alex, I trust you. Just don't get us both killed.

Alex took a deep breath and reached into his jacket pocket, pulling out a small, rolled piece of paper. Insurance, he'd called it – I didn't think we'd have to use it. "You want answers, eh? Here's your answer, Wyndham. Lord Head Councilor, if you would, please?" He offered the paper to Miller, who gave him a sideways look as he took it.

"I want to hear answers from *him*." Next to Silversmith, Wyndham folded his arms across his chest, nodding.

"He's not a mage."

"Neither *were* you, boy, and yet here you are." All eyes fixed on me again, except for Miller's, who simply put his hand up again.

"Are you quite serious about this, Lord Vestarton?" Miller asked, narrowing his gaze at Alex.

"My Lord, I've never been more serious. I will move forward if this conversation is not dropped this instant. A vote's been called. Let's do this now, or stop wasting the time I'll need to start my investigation."

Everyone's faces had questions on them, but Wyndham said his aloud. "What are you talking about?"

Miller shook his head. "He's calling his own charges against Victor. I hope you realize, Percival, that this complicates matters."

Next to me, I could almost feel Victor tense as he leaned on that cane. He said nothing, though – what could he do? He was as trapped as I was. And as Alex had predicted, it wasn't unpleasant to watch him squirm.

"What?" Victor's father was now red-faced, doing all the shouting for the both of them. "Are you out of your... unbelievable. Just unbelievable! Your father would be devastated if he could see you now. You are a disgrace to this entire city. I should have you..."

Alexander peered over his spectacles enough so that everyone could see just a sliver of the strange light in his eyes. "Have me *what*, Wyndham? You know, criminal neglect and attempted murder of a ruling Lord is in the same category as treason, I think. So, you may want to be careful with your words there." But Wyndham had no words – they were stolen right out of his mouth. Alex snorted derisively and ran a hand through his dark brown hair, catching some of the sweat before it dropped off his brow. "Let's vote and get this over with, shall we?"

With that, he took his seat. At least he *could* sit – I felt like I was about to collapse. My heart pounded so loud I barely heard Miller put this whole situation to an actual vote. Weeks of reports and questions and accusations all came down to one word from seven men. It could have been just down to five men instead of seven. They decided to allow Wyndham and my father to vote here, despite the obvious conflicts of interest. What that had cost them, I had no idea – I wasn't about to ask.

"Fine. The vote has been called. The discussion is over. Gentlemen, stand and be counted."

And they did – Wyndham and Silversmith immediately bolted out of their chairs. No one else did, however, not even Alastair Shilling, who had been calm and mostly silent the entire day. His brother was my commanding officer up there in Eisland... old Cedric surely had plenty to tell him about everything that happened, including my performance – or lack thereof. Every time I had given him the same basic report, day after day, he grew more and more flustered. Cedric would ask me if I was trying hard enough, if I asked the right questions. The longer we were up there, patrolling, interrogating the captured... well, I wouldn't have been surprised if he'd blamed me for everything. But perhaps he didn't after all.

Miller nodded. "Four votes of no, two votes of yes. The Head Councilor does not need to vote."

At this, General Torven stood, medals of distinction and battles won jingling on his chest as he did so. I thought he might say something, but instead he calmly handed a small piece of paper to Miller and walked out of the room without another look at me or the Wyndham brothers. His narrow, steely eyes and squared jaw said volumes, though.

Miller reviewed Torven's paper for a moment, then looked up. "Lieutenant, at the recommendation of General Torven, you are to be... ah, relieved of your rank and command starting immediately. You will report to Headmaster Janus to begin your next assigned duty this coming Queensday, to serve the Military Academy as an Instructor."

*Free? I don't deserve this.* It felt like a dream. My head swam, that point buried in the center of my forehead throbbing with an almost audible rhythm. I was sure I didn't just hear him say what he did. There had been a time when I looked forward to the chance to teach at the Academy, but that was a lifetime ago. Besides, why would they want the so-called traitor out there corrupting the young officers of Zondrell? Of course, deep down I knew why – Torven wanted to keep an eye on me.

A thousand disjointed thoughts stormed through my mind. I could hardly begin to speak, let alone move or even look at Miller, who had come to stand before me, offering one large hand out. "You're free to go, son. We appreciate your candor here." Still in my stupor, I reached out and shook the big Lord's meaty hand. I still couldn't find any words, though. "You're free to leave," he said again. I started to do just that until I heard him call out the next part of the Council's agenda. Somehow, I felt riveted in place. "Now, on the second matter, the punishment for Captain Victor Landis Percival Wyndham and Lieutenant Peter Kest Anelican Wyndham – the Council must vote."

"Victor is in no shape for..."

"Thank you, Lord Wyndham. But this is a matter that cannot be put off any longer." He glanced back at the paper Torven had given him. "The General has offered the following for your consideration, gentlemen: removal of command and rank for Captain Wyndham, and indeterminate leave for both men. And before you say anything, Percival, Victor was clearly the one making the decisions. Peter did not have the same hand in what transpired at Doverton."

I glanced over at the Wyndham brothers; Victor seethed while Peter continued to stare ahead, expressionless. I was quite surprised that neither of them had anything to say – a protest, a call for pity, something. Peter felt my gaze just long enough to look up, and there was nothing but an emptiness there. I wondered if he lived with nightmares like mine.

When I turned back to the Council table, the Lords had already voted – almost the exact same way they had voted before. Except this time, Alex, my father, Shilling, and Shal-Vesper were all standing, while Wyndham and Silversmith sat straight in their chairs, faces dark and eyes narrowed.

Wyndham's cheeks were crimson. "The Council has voted," Miller said with a resigned sigh, turning to the brothers. "You will both be on leave until further notice. You're free to go."

With that, the meeting broke up, the Council's business ended. Several Lords came up to me and congratulated me. For what, not getting sent to the gallows? For successfully defending what I still was not sure was defensible? Nonetheless, I accepted as if I were standing outside of myself, watching everything but yet detached. As Alex gave me a big hug and a triumphant grin, the headache began to spread, creeping across my temples, and I wanted so badly to go lay down somewhere. It hadn't even yet dawned on me that getting stripped of rank and command was nothing short of an enormous black mark on our family name. My father, to his credit, seemed to be taking the whole thing in stride – when I caught his eye, the look there was one of relief, not anger.

"Come on, son – everyone will be waiting at home," he told me.

Meanwhile, neither Wyndham brother acknowledged me as Peter cautiously started to lead Victor and his heavy cane away. "Hey Peter," I said, then trailed off. I didn't quite how know to say what I wanted to say. And he didn't know how to answer, either, but the distraction caused him to lose hold of his brother's arm. Victor crumpled to the floor too fast for anyone to stop him.

The former Captain of Magics grunted and groaned and Peter struggled to help, but their father's sharp voice cut through the whole scene. "Let him rot. Peter, did you hear me? I said leave him. He can find his own way home." Ever obedient, Peter stood back up and started to follow his father out the door. I could hardly believe it.

As everyone else began to filter out around us, I did not. Instead, I felt a pang of remorse. Victor Wyndham was an ass, yes, but I never wanted him dead – not really. Yet, it was my dagger in his chest that had turned him into this tormented mess of a man. Had he done the same thing to me, and tried to do worse to many others? Absolutely. And yet, there was only one reasonable response now.

I reached down and helped the struggling former Captain back onto his cane; we both strained like old battered veterans with the effort.

"I don't get you," he rasped, staring at me with his alien, magic-blue eyes. They pulsed in time with his breath, but they were dim, like a candle starting to burn out.

"There's nothing to get."

"That's horseshit and you know it."

"It's over, Victor. It's just… over."

"Yeah, it is." He paused, letting his heavy rasping slow. "You know, my brother's right. I – we – saw some magic there. Can't even begin to describe it, what Alex did? Then whatever happened to you?" Strangely, there was none of the usual malice in his tone.

"I don't know anything," I told him. "I know I'm no hero, and I know I'm retiring a bit earlier than expected. That's all I know."

"Yeah, retirement. Ha. Well, at least *your* father's likely to speak to you again." Victor spat out a wad of blood, marring the pristine marble floor below. "Congratulations." He started to shuffle off, slowly, but with his head held about as high as it would go.

# CHAPTER THREE

## The Deal

*42 Spring's Dawn, 1271*
*Brinnürjn Jannausch*

I hate Zondrell. I will always hate Zondrell. The brutality and arrogance of its people knows no limits, and never has. Why I found myself there twice in less than a few months was beyond my own comprehension. Yet, there I was, though this time I had a fancy carriage to bring me there, and no trouble with bureaucratic guards thinking they were beyond their years.

"Sir?" One of them in polished platemail ducked his dark little head into the carriage after exchanging some words with the driver. I imagined him to be some sort of noble by his bearing and good straight teeth. "I've been instructed to bring you to the place where you'll be staying."

"Lead on, *Hauptmann*," I replied, pushing my way out. It felt good to stretch the legs. He started to take my pack and blade from the driver, but I was too quick for him. "Not necessary."

We did not go far. My arrangements had been made at a small inn just within the city gates, and the inside was dim but smelled of good beer and better meat. It felt like many places in Doverton and Quatremagne and other Zondrean cities I had been to over the years, a warm and cheerful place with a big hearth in the floor and serving girls who smiled when you looked at their chests and paid them for another drink.

"Enjoy your stay, Sir," the boy soldier said to me before moving on to other duties.

Even though the sun had newly risen from behind the city walls outside, there were few people in the place. Indeed, there was only one aside from the girls and the barkeep, a lone figure seated at a far table. I noticed how old his face looked to me when in the light of those hearth flames. He looked little like I remembered from long ago, but it had been, what... twenty-five years?

"I'm glad you accepted my invitation," he said. "To be quite honest, I didn't think you would."

My tone was bitterly sarcastic. "Anything for family, *ja*?"

"Hmm, indeed. Have a seat. Please."

Sitting with this man, at this table, in this place? My younger self would have laughed at me – or struck me down. But things were not what they once were, and perhaps we were both different men. As soon as I rested my sheathed sword against the wall and sat down, a girl was there with a mug of beer so dark it was almost black. At least the people here were not complete barbarians, as this beer was good. Very good, in fact. I allowed the rich flavor to linger while I stared at him and his graying hair and the tiny wrinkles setting in around his eyes. Steel-dark, almond-shaped eyes, very, very familiar.

"I trust your ride was comfortable?"

"Comfortable, *ja*. Slow. I could have walked here faster."

"Sorry about that, but I'm glad you're here." He paused as I took another long sip from my mug. If he was waiting for me to talk about the weather, he was going to be disappointed. "So... you got all the way to the rank of General, eh?"

"Retired. For about ten years. I assume you used my letter?"

"Yes, yes we did. You have my thanks for that." If he had noticed the... truth-stretching in that particular letter, he made no indication of it.

"A promise I intended to keep." Perhaps old Johann remembered the one I made to him so long ago? Maybe not. That was one I hadn't kept, though – he was still very much alive. "What happened to your boy, then?"

"There was debate, reports, finally a trial – yesterday, in fact. Tristan was, ah... stripped of his rank." I could tell it hurt him to even speak those words. "They did give him the assignment he wanted – he'll be teaching at the Academy."

Imagining any half-breed *Halben* boy teaching these people how to be soldiers made me laugh out loud. "He has great talent, but being talented is different from being a teacher. Someone just wants to know where he is."

Johann – Jonathan, I suppose he was called, though if he wanted to pretend that he was part of *my* family, then I would call him whatever the hell I wanted – leaned forward in his chair, and took a deep breath. "I'm well aware of that. Look, Brin, this is why I asked you to come here. The war drums are beating louder and louder every day. It needs to stop, and I have associates that want to stop it. But we can't do it alone. I heard all about Quatremagne, the rebellion. I know what you're capable of, and we need that skill here."

My eyes narrowed over the rim of my mug. What an *Arschkriecher*. "What, you wish to start rebellion here? This place is *not* Quatremagne, and that was years ago." I was starting to regret coming out to this forsaken hole of a city in the first place.

"Hear me out. I know you. I know you don't want another war."

"How do you know me, Johann? Maybe I would like the chance to send more *Zondern* to the Great River. Besides, this *Hurensohn* King of yours is an idiot. At least the last one had enough sense to sign a treaty."

"That's what I mean." Johann grew intense, animated. "He taxes the people beyond what they can endure, and spends the money on luxuries. He makes ridiculous demands of the Council and the Academies, and doesn't even bother to see them through. He wants to see Zondrell unite the other Zondrean states again and make them one, and he'll go to war to do it. And he is obsessed with the faery tale of the Kaeren beyond what is sane. It's time for things to change, before they get worse."

"How do you know Kaeren is a tale?" I asked. He knew something, otherwise he did not know his own son, or what he almost died for – what, three times now? Young Tristan was lucky, that much was certain. On the other hand... maybe I made too many assumptions, as old Johann just shook his head and reached into his jacket for a small leather pouch, setting it on the table before me.

"It doesn't matter, Brin. Stories are stories, and they're best left in the past. We need things to change, for Zondrell's sake, and everyone else's. You're not doing this for me. Do it for your people. Do it for Gretchen. Do what I can't do myself."

"Of course you cannot. You are a *Milchtrinker.*" He understood that, as I knew he would, but he seemed indifferent. Too bad. "Tell me this, do you think that I would have come here just for a holiday? Stop trying so hard."

He nodded and pushed the leather purse a little closer to me. "In here is an advance and more information. You can start on your tasks right away. Of course, your room and board are completely covered."

The pouch was as light as it was small. Too light for this kind of work. Indeed, why *was* I doing this at all? Certainly not for him, and not even for Gretchen, my sister who I would still do anything for... including not kill her *dummkopf Zondern* husband. But, this wasn't about family, no, it was about curiosity. After all, I had told young Tristan I would tell him more when he was ready, did I not? I would have to watch to know when that might be.

The note inside was detailed, with names, places, and needs spelled out in words even an Eislander like me could understand. "This could take many weeks. I expect payment after each of these tasks you want is complete," I told him flatly.

"When it is done, there will be plenty of coin for you, if that's what you're most concerned about. You have the backing of the Council of Lords here."

"Then you should be able to provide payment when I ask for it."

Johann did not share my amusement at the situation, only sneered at me in a very familiar kind of way. This was more the "Captain Loringham" that I remembered from my youth. "Just... if you'll do this, attend to the tasks, and keep a low profile. It will pay off for all of us mightily in the end, I promise you. Do you have any questions?"

Questions? I looked back at my blade resting against the wall, as if I could ask it. Oh there were many questions, to be sure, but when I searched Johann's face again, he still had no answers after twenty-five years.

That sword was not always mine. It used to hang on our hearth wall at home in Kostbar, unsheathed so that we could read the words etched in fine script upon it every time we walked by. *Bewahrung über Eisland, vernichtung der Feinde* – protection over Eisland, destruction of enemies. It stood taller than I for many years until I was about ten, and finally able to pick it up without falling over. With my father long dead by then, to touch it meant I would incur the wrath of my mother, and sometimes my sister as well. They liked peaceful things – they did not want violence in the house. That sword was a reminder of him, a monument, not a weapon. Anytime I thought I would take it outside and practice – just a *little* – I got a rap on the head and an extra chore to do. Still, every day I looked on that sword and imagined what it would be like to carry it into battle the way Father did when we were almost too little to remember.

It came off of its hallowed perch for good when the *Zondern* pushed their way toward Kostbar. I had just turned fifteen. The minute I heard about the fighting getting closer and closer to our town, I stopped caring about what my mother and older sister said, and started to teach myself how to use it. For short, I called it Beschützer – Protector – but it was not fun, this practice of mine. Instead, it felt like desperation. The *Zondern* could be here at any moment! I had to be ready. No one else believed me, of course, and no one saw it coming until those very same *Zondern* they never thought would break through the gates were marching through our very streets.

I watched as dozens of black-and-silver men led a small group of our warriors, heads low, shadows of themselves, toward the center of the city. Among them were our *Hauptmann* and two of his elite guard, and on seeing the defeat in their eyes, I was enraged in a way I never had been before. How could these men – good, strong men that I had admired – surrender and fall to these people? Where was their bravery? Their honor? People would say that what I did next was reckless and stupid, but at least I can say that even at fifteen, I held onto my honor.

"There must be a hundred of them," Gretchen said, peering out of a tiny corner of our front window. I stood behind her with my mother clutching me at the elbow – she knew what I was about to do even before I did.

Mother hissed and held me tighter as she reached for my sister, too. "Stay away from the window! They'll see you."

"What will they do? Are they going to... are they going to hurt us?"

I shook my head. "Not without a fight." Beschützer was in my hand. All I had to do was walk out that door and use it. So what if there were a hundred men out there? I started to move but Mother dug her nails into my flesh so hard they left tiny welts.

"Stop it, Brin! What do you think you're doing?"

"I have to – this is war."

"They'll kill you on sight with that thing in your hands. You're just a boy."

Just a boy? True, yes, but I was the man of that house. As the soldiers continued their march, I finally unlatched myself from her and bolted for the door, ignoring their angry screaming behind me.

I marched up to the invaders with that sword flashing its brilliance. Somehow, I thought this would be enough to make them stop and run the other direction, but it did not. Some continued walking right past, but a small group of Zondern with perfect, clean silver falcons on their chests drew their own weapons. Piddly little longswords, yes, but they had skill enough to use them. I thought I had skill, too, and I was almost as tall or taller than most of them.

One of them said something. Then another said something else, now impatient. I understood none of it, and cared even less. I wanted their blood to run through the streets of my city – I wanted them to pay for disgracing our soldiers, for destroying our lands. And I told them this in a string of Eislandisch curses the likes of which I had never spoken aloud, all the while swinging that big blade around to look threatening. I would like to say this worked, but it did not. All it got me was several angry Zondern ready to bear down on me. All around, I heard more steel drawn, and some of the Eislanders they had as prisoners telling me to let it be, that the battle would not be won here, to go back to my mother. Cowards. This just fueled my rage, but my feet were held fast. Somewhere in that fifteen-year-old brain of mine, I realized that to attack meant death. The rest of me – the stupid, childlike part – just wanted to make a stand and scare those *Zondern* into leaving Kostbar forever.

I should have known better. At least I never made the same mistake again.

The moment Beschützer stirred in my hands, they were ready. First came a swipe from the side that made it very hard to hold my weapon with both hands all of the sudden. The pain seeped in as the blood seeped out of a fresh wound running along my upper left arm. I turned to face my attacker, clumsy and heavy on my feet, only to have my face meet the butt of one of those longswords. Crimson poured from my nose and filled my senses with the taste of copper.

I dropped to my knees in a heap, my father's sword crashing to the ground next to me. Desperate, I reached for it, but someone's boot was already there to fix it in place. I looked up into a sea of pointed weapons with pure hatred. I do not remember what I shouted at them through the blood, but it was not pleasant.

At some point, I heard someone running up behind me and turned to see my sister... dear sweet Gretchen. "Stop, please! Don't hurt my brother!" she yelled at them in Eislandisch, putting herself between me and the wall of enemies. I reached out to pull her aside, but she was too strong and shook me away. "He means no harm, truly! Please don't hurt him."

No, I meant *plenty* of harm, and even though they were *Zondern*, they were no fools. They laughed at her, and at me crawling on my knees in the dirt.

"Get out of the way, Gretchen," I growled, but was ignored.

"You have to stop. He does not know what he does," she continued to plead. It seemed to make little difference.

"Hold," I heard someone say, and the pointed blades before us parted. They called him "Captain." Young, though, not much older than my sister, fresh-faced with shiny dark eyes that looked so strange to me. Up until that moment, I had never looked at a *Zondern* up close before. They were just as ugly as I pictured, with their olive-tanned skin and brown hair and short bodies. They had none of the grace and stature of the Eislandisch. "Stand down," this man knelt down to speak to me, his Eislandisch broken and accent almost unintelligible.

I spat at him. "Fuck you, *Hurensohn Zondern*. Get out of my city." If he understood me, I was not sure, and did not care.

The story could have ended here – I was "just a boy," after all. They could have put me down like a dog there in front of my sister. In fact, I was ready for it; my father would have been proud to know I died trying to defend our home. But instead, he wiped the spittle from his cheek and repeated his plea. Still, even broken and on my knees, I would not surrender. If I could just get my vision to clear and pull my weapon from under that *Zondern's* boot...

"You are crazed, Brin. Stop this!" Gretchen's clear blue eyes met with mine and there were tears in them. She turned back to this man they called Captain, grabbed him by the arm. "You have to stop this!"

The *Zondern* officer nodded and spoke to me again in his terrible Eislandisch. "Boy, you will have your chance – today is not that day. Listen to the girl." It would only be much later that I would realize that the Captain's kindness was mostly about the fact that he was enthralled with my sister and her pretty golden braids. If I had known that, I would have made one last stand and run him through.

Ah... regrets.

Now, years after they sent me bleeding back to my mother with a good hearty laugh, I was looking at that same man. He had that same veiled expression of kindness on his much less fresh face... and I still wanted to run him through. Then again, things were different now, and in some ways, I suppose we both had gotten what we wanted.

I looked through the list of tasks he had given me one more time. My reading of their language may not have been good, but it was good enough. "Consider it done." I would like to say that the noble idea of stopping a war was why I agreed to it, and I would tell anyone that if they asked. But in truth, sending a few more *Zondern* to the River... it seemed like a better way to spend retirement than being an errand boy for the Doverton crown, or rotting away under a sea of liquor back home in Kostbar.

The good Captain Lord Loringham, or whatever he wanted to be called, rose to leave me to my drink. "Very good then. I must say, your command of Zondrean is impressive now."

"Sure. I will fit right in," I said with a smile. *Hurensohn...* what an ass. I was sure he didn't forget why I learned the language in the first place – to spy on their people while we toiled under their watch. "Give Gretchen my regards."

"Come by and see her. You're welcome at the house anytime. You know where it is."

As he took his leave, I looked back again at Beschützer – my father's loyal blade – resting there next to me. I imagined it happy to be tasting *Zondern* blood again, and the day was still quite young. The two of us... we had work to do together once again.

# CHAPTER FOUR

## Visions

*43 Spring's Dawn, 1271*
*Lord Alexander Marcus Xavier Vestarton*

*K*nock, knock. "My Lord?"
Go away. Honestly, Dennis, how many times…?
"My Lord? It's urgent, Sir."
It's also too fucking early. What could he want? I rolled over in bed and bumped into something heavy and unmoving and dark and lovely. Great – now she was awake too. Because the sun wasn't even up yet, I couldn't see much except the faint light of her eyes as they fluttered open. "*Ya Habibi?* What is happening?" she whispered.

*Knock, knock.* This time, not as polite. "Nothing," I told her. "Go back to sleep. I'll be right back." Fumbling around, I got my wits about me enough to find some pants and a bit of patience so that I did not tear my butler's head off the moment I opened my bedroom door.

"M'Lord, I am sorry," dear old Dennis said with his customary bow.

"Dennis, do you know what time it is?"

"Yes, m'Lord." Another bow. "But the Council has been summoned to the Palace for an emergency session."

My heart took a dive off a cliff. "Right now? I'm supposed to be at the Academy this morning."

"I'm aware, Sir, but it would appear this session takes precedence." He knew my next question before I even asked it. "They did not state the reason – at least, not to me. I understand Lords Loringham and Shal-Vesper will meet you outside."

"Fuck. All right, I'll be down in a minute." As he left, I turned around to look at two sparkling little eyes staring at me. "Zizah, I'm sorry. I've got to go."

"I hear this. Do you think this is because of *Tanin*?" Since one of her artistic sisters had put that tattoo on his shoulder, she had taken to calling my friend Tristan *Tanin*, which meant "dragon" in her native Katalahni. At least she didn't call me and the white rose on my chest "Flower."

"No, all that's over, settled it the other day. The case is closed," I said as I started rifling through my closet in the dark for something to wear – something *appropriate*, of course, for the Council table. My best attempt an hour before sunrise would just have to do. "I don't know what the fuck they want now." And if I found out it *did* have something to do with Tristan, I had a feeling I'd wake the entire city up screaming in frustration. I wanted to scream then and there as I felt all manner of things go bump and jostle around in the closet.

A tiny click from a flint and a low glow from the oil lamp at my bedtable filled the room. "This helps?"

It did. I huffed and kept rifling until I came out with my good black silks and silver vest. A clean-up at the washbasin, a quick comb of the hair... done, presentable. Except for the eyes, of course. And that horrible, burning sensation crawling under my skin that I'd lived with for... well, for years now. I still wasn't used to the magic. It felt weird and wrong, and always had since the minute I knew I had it. To make matters worse, it got much more intense under stress, adding to my annoyance at even the simplest of irritating situations. It flared during every Council meeting to a level that was almost unbearable – talk about wanting to scream. I shook my head at the image of the rumpled lout with the quicksilver eyes staring back at me. "Good enough for a Council meeting?"

When I looked back at her, wrapped in my blanket as she sat on the edge of the bed, she gave a wry smile. Oh, that smile! I don't care what anyone says – there is nothing better than a bright smile from a bronze-skinned Katalahni girl. "You need to let the magic out more. I can see it on your face. It hurts?"

"Yeah, a little. I know, I know about all that, but this is not the time. I'm supposed to go up the Magic Academy later today, or something. I'll deal with it then."

"Hm. I think you fight it too much. Practice more." The blue-white sparkle of magic in her eyes grew just a tiny bit. She was better at hiding it than I, had even shown me how to hide the magic, too. But that was a long time ago, and a few puffs on special Katalahni *tsohbac* sticks every day was no longer enough. I gave it up weeks ago, though that didn't keep me from longing for the sweet, heady smell of that smoke every so often. "So," she said, changing the subject, "the King is there, yes?"

"Not always. This time, maybe."

"Fix your buttons, then." I shook my head as I fixed the horribly askew buttons on my vest. "There, that is good. And the glasses?"

Right, can't leave without those. She had gotten them for me – "mage spectacles," they called them. They kept people from knowing what your eyes really looked like. Sure, the *tsohbac* didn't work anymore, but I wasn't ready for the whole world to see me as I had suddenly become. Everyone knew something was "different" about me, and there were lots of rumors going around, including Peter Wyndham's fantastic thought that I was involved in some sort of miracle. If so, the gods had quite the sense of humor. Either way, I didn't need to feed the rumors one way or the other, and I certainly didn't need the attention I'd get if everyone saw how absolutely odd I looked now. My eyes, once a nice rich brown, had become this strange silver with swirls and light all their own. It looked like nothing anyone had ever seen, nothing like any of the four elements of magic. In some circles, I might pass for a white-eyed Air mage, but anyone who knew anything about magic would know better. I couldn't take any chances, so I wore the glasses. Despite having to get used to things being an awful lot darker than they usually were, they weren't so bad.

The wire rim rested on the bridge of my nose, and I peered over the top of the smoked glass to try smiling back at her. "Sorry about this, really. I'll see you later?"

"I will let myself out, *Habibi,* but I do think I will sleep some more first. Your bed is very comfortable." So it was, and I wished I was still in it. Whatever this emergency session nonsense was, it had better be fucking worth it. "Do not worry – I will not talk to your mother on the way out."

Mum's opinion on my taste in women was just about the furthest thing from my mind. "Ha, yeah... Sorry. Look, I'll see you later, all right?"

Downstairs, Dennis offered me only a scone and hardly another word – Catherine bless his kind soul. The buttery pastry was gone before I even made it to the parlor, where my sister was already up, reading by the glow of a small candle.

"What's going on? Lord Loringham came by a few minutes ago," she said, hardly looking up from her book. Even first thing in the morning, her long chestnut hair was neatly combed and braided, although she had yet to paint her lips and cheeks for the day. It didn't matter – she always looked the same to me.

"I'm well aware. I've got to go." I turned to go then stopped, and looked back at her. "Are you always up this early?"

"Yes. Some of us actually like seeing the sunrise. You know, you're lucky Mum's still asleep. You know how she is. That girl's still here, isn't she?"

The way she said *that girl* made the hairs on the back of my neck stand on end. "Yes, Zizah is her name, actually. She's still here, and she'll leave when she's good and ready. Who cares?"

"Mum cares."

"Uh-huh. I'm pretty sure it's my house and my rules now."

"That's a lovely attitude to have. Seriously, Alex, think about it. Are you going to marry that girl? Or *any* girl? Are you seriously going to have an heir with a Katalahni who runs *a bazaar stall*? I think you might need to start thinking about those sorts of things."

This coming from the woman who was almost thirty and had yet to have any serious relationships. Most men were scared half to death of her, even though almost every one of my friends couldn't get enough of looking at her. If only she wasn't... well, such a shrew. "Yeah, look, it's too early for this conversation. I've got things to do."

"I get it, but listen, Alex. What if something happens to you? What happens to the family then?"

"Then you and Mum can run it." Hell, if I thought I could get away with it while still breathing, I would have happily given up my seat on the Council to my sister in a minute. *She* could go deal with whatever fresh horror awaited me in the Palace at such a miserable hour, and she'd be good at it.

"You know that's ridiculous."

"Who says? The same people who made the rule that I can't spend my time with a Katalahni girl who runs a bazaar stall?"

"Just think about it, please?" Alice's features softening just a little. "I'll make sure Mum doesn't see when your little *friend* – ah, Zizah – leaves. All right?"

"Yes, do that. Thank you." I hurried out the door without another word. By the time I got halfway down the block, I found Jonathan Loringham and Cen Shal-Vesper talking in hushed tones with another, much stouter man. Oh my, it was the Lord Head Councilor himself.

"If you do this, Wyndham will go mad," Andrew Miller was saying as I approached.

"Why? What does he care?" Loringham's voice was sharper than steel. "He has as much stake in this as anyone else. And in light of the possibilities to the contrary, I'm sure Wyndham and Silversmith will sign this as well."

Miller made that grunt he made when thoroughly unconvinced. "You know how he is. You need every signature."

"If everyone but those two have signed, they'll have to. No choice."

I hated walking into the middle of conversations anymore. Before my father died a few months ago and left me in charge of one of the most powerful Houses in Zondrell, I could have cared less what nobles spoke about in the darkest hours. But now, every time I turned around, it seemed like something new was happening. Important things, too, not just loose talk about who made off with who's sister the previous evening. Cen Shal-Vesper noticed me before anyone, and nodded his acknowledgement.

"Alex, good." In his hand, the stately middle-aged Lord held some kind of a piece of parchment. "We need you to sign this."

"What? You do all realize that the sun hasn't even risen yet? What's all this about?"

Lord Jonathan Loringham – my father's best friend, a man I'd known since I was a child – turned to regard me with a dark, intense gaze. There was a sort of calm confidence there, too, like nothing I'd seen in him for weeks, or longer. Maybe having Tristan's trial done and over with had put a new gleam in his eyes... or a fire under his ass. "They found High Captain Walrich in his bed this morning with a knife in his chest. You need to sign that to keep the King and General Torven from preparing for war."

I could not find words. I looked up, searching for them, and saw only the twin moons above. Sarabande and Larenne so close together, at this time of year? And was Sarabande always so red? Well, I supposed Peaceday Festival was right around the corner... my, how time marches on. For just a moment, I thought I could see their soft blue-red light in pieces, waves, particles, moving in slow motion as they came down from the heavens to illuminate our path. No, I *could* see it, every piece of everything captured in a moment like a painting, but in the next instant, it was gone. Back to normal. I shook my head with a frown.

With still nothing useful to say, all I could do was grab that piece of paper and read it through... Council against the declaration of war, we insist on something, something, something, signed, the Council of Lords. It already had the flourishing scrawls of Loringham, Shal-Vesper, and Shilling at the bottom. My name would make four, but something like this still needed all seven. This wasn't a simple vote, after all – it was a declaration. "Couldn't you have just brought this to the house? What are we doing out here? I don't have a quill."

Just my luck. Cen had one of those too, with a tiny vial of ink. "You just need to sign, Alex."

I thought about it. Yes, war was bad – no doubt about that. But who was saying we're going to war? "So... isn't this all a bit preemptive? We don't even know who killed the poor sod yet." Cen and Jonathan narrowed their gazes; the Head Councilor just cocked his big head, at a loss for words. "It's not like I won't sign, but what's the difference? I'll sign when we get to the palace."

Cen's disapproval was written all over his tight, thin little face. "The more signatures we have, the more support we garner."

"Okay, but it's only a ten-minute walk. Think about it – we don't know who did this. Could be a bad business deal, some ex-convict... for all we know, Walrich could have been fucking the General's wife. Right? Starting a war over the whole thing seems a bit of a stretch."

Cen started to say more, but the Head Councilor butted in. "The investigation is forthcoming," Miller said. "That's part of what the meeting needs to determine."

"Right, so...?"

"Right then, let's just get going. I've got other business this morning." Old man Miller started moving as fast as his legs would carry him down the street, and the rest of us followed suit.

"Alex," Jonathan said, pulling me back a bit from the other two as we strolled with purpose up the road and around the corner. "Let me give you some advice. You need to start paying closer attention to how you conduct yourself."

"Yeah, I've heard that one before." And... I honestly did not care. Ever since coming back from Doverton, all of the business of appearances and politics seemed rather trivial next to life and death and magic and such.

"I'm serious. We're supposed to have an alliance here, and more importantly, it needs to *look* like one. Particularly to Miller."

"Does it matter what that fat fuck thinks?"

The sneer on his face indicated that such an observation was probably not proper lordly conduct. "Yes, it does. He's already watching you after what you pulled the other day at the trial."

Now I was pissed. I moved in front of him and stopped, forcing him to stop as well. "What I 'pulled'? You know, Tristan is *your* son. You should be thanking me. I had insurance; I used it because it had to be done. It was ironclad, too. That Drakannyan lawyer drew those charges up – cost me a lot of money."

"You don't get it." John Loringham shook his head and stalked off past me, heading down the street once again.

"What don't I get?" With no answer forthcoming, I turned and sped up to catch him. "What don't I get?" I asked again.

We turned the corner before he responded. "They were never going to put Tristan to death."

"Could have fooled me. They seemed pretty serious about it."

"He knows things the King and the General want to know. About this magic you all found. They're willing to wait to find out, and they're convinced they eventually will." Before I had a chance to protest, he continued. "Don't think you're safe, either. They're watching you, too, now. You really need to get yourself settled in with a wife and an heir to that estate."

This again? "Why, planning on putting a knife in my chest sometime soon?"

"Very funny. Best to be prepared, Alex – I'm quite serious. If something happens to you, Vestarton House could be no more."

"We'll see about that. Got the Drakannyan lawyer working on that issue, too."

"Pavel's good, sure. But if you want my advice," Loringham looked right at me, one graying eyebrow raised, "start putting your House first. We need you thinking and acting straight, please."

I could think of nothing other than rude and inappropriately witty replies, so I kept my mouth shut as we made our way up toward the Palace.

**

The steel, chop-style blade skittered across the Council Table with a heavy screech, leaving a smear of half-dried crimson in its wake. It stopped about an arm's length from me, and I found that I couldn't pull my gaze from it. Such a simple thing, no carvings on blade or handle, no decoration other than a few grooves along the grip, most of which were obscured by drying gore. It was fascinatingly gruesome.

"Gentlemen, this is the blade that killed my friend, the High Captain. I should hope that you would join me in finding justice." General Jamison Torven hovered over the table, seemingly the pure embodiment of the silver falcon crest of Zondrell.

Head Councilor Miller spoke for the rest of us. "Do you have any leads yet?"

"No. No signs of forced entry, no struggle, nothing. I sense the work of professionals."

Behind Torven, sitting at his grand throne that was far more gilded than it needed to be, King Kelvaar V himself made sort of a disappointed *humph* sound. Even at dawn's first light, he was decked out in lavish robes, though his skin seemed a bit more ashen than usual. He was one of those people who looked far older than he actually was, despite a lifetime of leisure. The man couldn't have been beyond his forties, but he looked to be closer to sixty. "Indeed," said the King, shifting in his throne so that he now slumped over the other arm. "Doverton is the most likely culprit."

"Doverton? To what end?" The various Lords erupted into pointless rhetoric. Though Kelvaar might have had a point. We'd pissed off Doverton royally just a few weeks ago, and they knew their assassination methods quite well. I'd seen that for my own eyes. Except...

"They're not that stupid," I offered, and all eyes settled on me. "Seriously, I've been there. It's small; their army is half the size of ours. They know better."

The General shook his head, and some of the medals adorning his jacket jingled in turn. "You should also know how well-trained they are, Lord Vestarton. They're among the best, and we've opened up discourse with them that has not been... positive, of late."

"I hope you're not blaming *me* for that, Sir." Ah, but he was – I could tell, even though it was Wyndham's crazed kids that created havoc in the Doverton streets. I just tried to stop it.

Torven changed the subject before I had the chance to say much more. "We need to investigate this situation and devise a strategy immediately." As he continued going on and on about his strategy with details I failed to pay much attention to, Loringham tapped me on the shoulder. That piece of paper I was supposed to sign was pushed in my direction with some insistence.

Whatever. I signed my name. He was probably right — if they were so quick to assume it was some Doverton operative that killed Walrich, then war wasn't far out of reach. But why was this their assumption in the first place? What could Doverton have that they could possibly want? No doubt, that's what it all came down to — no one starts a war for free.

The rest of them prattled on for a bit longer until someone mentioned the murder weapon, still resting there, cloaking its secrets under a mask of sticky crimson. "Yeah, where do you think it came from, anyhow?" I asked. Again, I felt their stares boring a hole into me. "If you find out where it came from, you might find your killer, right? It's brand new, you can tell. Look at it. So there's what, about a dozen smiths in the city, maybe a few more outside the walls? Assuming, of course, it came from around here. But if I was going to kill someone, I'd probably go buy myself a new blade from somewhere I don't normally go, so they don't know who I am."

Percival Wyndham snorted. "Think about this sort of thing much, do you?"

Ha, more than you'd think. "Doesn't take a scholar, Wyndham. I don't see how you can skip straight to the war table before you even know the first thing about what happened. That's all I'm saying."

"He's right," Alastair Shilling said. "We're not here to start a war, and that document there states as such. Your Majesty, we must insist that you get some facts in order before you come to us accusing another city of assassinating one of our highest officials." Some others at the table mumbled, but no one disagreed.

Torven turned an expressionless gaze back at the King, then at us. They both seemed a tad unhappy, but Kelvaar spoke first. "Wise to be cautious, yes. I appreciate your thoughts on this matter, gentlemen." He wasn't a big man, or a bold one, and he certainly didn't have a way with words. Nonetheless, all listened, patient, as he searched for words to continue. "Hmm, Torven? Would you arrange to have King Eric of Doverton and his general come here for a visit? I shall speak with them and assess our relationship."

Now Miller perked up. "Is that wise at this time, my Lord, given the recent incident?"

"What other time would you suggest? In the time it takes for Eric to arrive, our men may discover more about the fate of our esteemed High Captain, yes? Yes, of course, I'm right. General, please attend to this immediately and begin your investigation." With that, Kelvaar rose and dismissed himself, stalking off with those grand robes that hardly seemed to fit his thin form flowing behind him.

I thought that was the end of it, but Torven did not follow. I'd noticed he had a habit of not following Kelvaar's orders right away. Apparently, he would do it when he felt like it. For the time being, he continued to posture and talk about strategy and the investigation and such while the Council grumbled their dissent. With nothing much to say over the noise, I turned back to that bloodied blade on the table. It was so plain, it could have come from anywhere, even Doverton... or about four thousand other places. Thinking there might be a smith's mark on it somewhere, I reached out and touched it, ever so gently, just to get a better look at the hilt.

And I was immediately somewhere else.

What the...? I could see nothing but darkness, a darkness that shimmered in a somewhat familiar way – a darkness where I could see all of its infinite little particles, glimmering and moving about. It was like I'd entered a world made of black silk. I looked down to see that I had not just fainted with my face somehow buried in the collar of my jacket. No, actually, I couldn't see anything below me at all, not the table, not myself, nothing but darkness. Holy fucking Catherine on a pike... what was going on?

Then I saw something stir in all of that nothing. Figures and shapes began to take form, and I was in a tavern. A tavern I didn't really recognize, but I felt it was in Zondrell somewhere. Why, I had no idea. It was mostly empty and dark save for two men, seated at the far back. They appeared deep in conversation, and though I could hear nothing, I got the sense that they were planning something. Something important... and probably illicit. I couldn't get their attention, though I did try to wave my arms about and say something. But I wasn't really there, was I? I didn't know where I was anymore, but when one of the men before me turned to scratch his shoulder, I saw his face.

No. It can't be.

Then it was gone. I was back in the Council room, looking at the same face I saw in that... whatever it was. Bittergum hallucination? No, I knew what that felt like, and I was still in the Academy the last time I took any of that. Hell, for once I was actually quite sober. Yet, that was more vivid than anything I'd ever seen while drunk, high, or otherwise. And I had no doubt that whatever I saw had actually happened – when, I had no idea, but I knew it. The magic told me. Fucking hell, this Time magic was getting to be far more trouble than it was ever worth.

Jonathan Loringham looked back at me with some confusion. "Are you all right?" he asked, voice low under the din of everyone else going on about Doverton and High Captain Walrich and war.

"Yeah, sure." What else do you say to the man you just saw colluding with a stranger in some dark tavern in a vision? "It's ah... all a little too early for this."

"You look pale."

No surprise there. Suddenly, I wanted to be anywhere but in that Council chamber. I didn't even care what they said after me as I pushed my chair away, rising on unsteady legs. I think I told them I'd be right back, but that wasn't a promise. I just had to get out of there, and as soon as I did, I ripped off those stupid mage spectacles and rubbed at my eyes so hard they hurt. It felt good, though, the kind of pain that could quell the confusion and strange thoughts rolling around in my head.

When I finally stopped, the dancing lights in my vision came together to form the figure of a young boy. Wait a minute. No, it definitely was a boy, staring up at me with a fascinated look on his face. "Don't tell me you're spying on the Council?" I said, trying to sound authoritative.

The little prince just cocked his head – this was Edin, Kelvaar's only son after previous child-rearing attempts netted him only princesses which were mostly nice to look at, but overall quite useless in terms of royal continuity. Then I realized what he was staring at. Damn it all... I almost poked my eye out trying to get those spectacles back on my face and put myself back in the land of shades of darkness. I was not fast enough, though, and the boy's interest was piqued. Who could blame him? I'd be interested too if I saw a guy who wasn't supposed to be a mage running around with glowing eyes like molten silver. Actually no, scratch that – I'd be terrified.

Edin, though, was quite the opposite. How old was he now? About eight? He was still a bit on the small side, though – there wasn't a posting in the First Cavalry and a great big spear with his name on it in this one's future, it seemed. He looked up at me with a curious, boyish innocence, a far cry from the sort of dim light of consciousness that I associated with his father. If things went well, the boy might have much greater presence than Kelvaar ever had.

"Prince Edin? I asked you a question, I believe?"

"Lord Vestarton, can you take your glasses off? I want to see that again." I'd had approximately three interactions with this boy in my whole life, but he was a smart one. He knew what title to use and everything, even while whining like a kid half his age.

"No."

"Please?"

Desperate to change the subject, I folded my arms across my chest and tried to look stern. "What are you doing out here? You're spying on the Council. Do you always do that?"

The little prince shook his head, insistent. "I'm not spying. Everyone got up so early today. Father told me to stay in my room, but I want to know what's going on. It's hard to listen through the door, though."

That door was reinforced specifically so people couldn't listen in, unless they were trying really, really hard. I had a feeling this kid had spent a fair bit of time trying to figure out the best method. "So you *are* spying."

"Everyone seemed upset." Edin shrugged, as if spying was no big deal. And maybe it wasn't – who was I to scold the crown prince, anyhow? "Why, Lord Vestarton? Why are they all upset?"

"I think that's a conversation for adults. See? They even kicked me out."

"Father's mad at you, anyhow. You won't tell him about your magic."

Mad at me, eh? Perhaps this little meeting in the Council antechamber was a blessing in disguise. Time to take advantage of the situation. "Here's the secret," I told him, lowering my voice to a whisper. Edin leaned in to listen. "It's not magic."

"No way. It's all in your eyes. I saw it!" He stood on his tiptoes to get a look over the glasses, and I admit, I hesitated. He was awarded just a peek before I stepped back and out of his reach. "It's pretty, too. I've never seen magic like that."

Pretty? Please... "Yeah, well, you know what it is? Really?"

"What? Tell me!"

"A disease. Yeah, I picked up this weird disease. Don't know what it is, but I can't use magic. I know that for sure."

"That's not what General Torven says. He said you used magic in that town up in the north."

"General Torven wasn't there, now was he?" I held fast to my tactics, but the boy was quickly draining my strength. What the hell, kid? Can't a man just have a moment to himself?

"Yeah, but General Torven knows a lot of things. He's teaching me about how to be a great General like him."

Good thing – don't take those kinds of lessons from your weakling father. Even though in his own right, Torven was... "A great guy, that General. You'll learn a lot from him."

"So you admit it! He knows lots. Maybe he knows about your magic, too."

"You've got me there, kid. But really, it's not magic. I don't know what it is. I think I'm sick. You probably shouldn't get too close – you might get it too." Oh, if only that would have worked. But it didn't. The prince didn't even flinch, but he did finally take a deep sigh.

"Okay, okay. Maybe you shouldn't tell if it's a big secret anyhow. Father might get more angry."

"Why do you say that?"

"He says secrets are like weapons. They can be really dangerous, I guess. I'm not allowed to keep secrets."

"Well if that's true, you better stop spying on the Council, or you might get caught keeping a secret, yeah?"

*This* was the winner. Edin crinkled his little nose in a frown. "I guess so. Don't tell?"

"On my honor, my Prince." I put my hand to my heart and took a little bow, which seemed to perk the boy up immensely.

"Okay," he said as he bounded off. "Hope you feel better, Lord Vestarton."

Yeah, me too, kid. Me too.

I got to stand out there contemplating the sheer oddness of the day so far for maybe two more minutes, until Loringham ducked his head out of the Council chamber door. "Alexander! What's wrong with you?"

"I need a minute, please."

The incensed flush in his cheeks meant there were no minutes available at present. Whatever was going on in there, it must have gotten interesting fast. "Get back in here. You can be ill later."

I wondered if he thought I was drunk. Well, wouldn't be the first time, but if only he knew why my heart wouldn't quite stop racing and my head was blazing. No matter, this wasn't about me, was it? So I smoothed my jacket, took a deep breath, went back into the fray, and did my best to pretend everything was fine.

# CHAPTER FIVE

## A Day in the Life
*44 Spring's Dawn, 1271*
*Tristan Loringham*

*I* *cannot believe I'm doing this.*
I said this to myself many times as I prepared to leave the house that morning. I said it as I got up before the sun to make sure I had plenty of time to get to the Academy. I said it as I bent over my washbasin and splashed some cool water on my face. I said it as I shaved and made sure my hair was just perfect for the day ahead. I still couldn't believe it.

Part of the problem was that the person staring back at me in the mirror seemed a stranger. What I saw there was a searching, sorrowful sort of man, a warrior with scars across his chest, including one great big pink one. Shaped a bit like a star, it almost looked like some treasure being guarded by the ornate, serpentine gold dragon tattooed on my shoulder. The golden dragon, said the old stories, was a symbol of strength, something to be both respected and feared. I chose it for that very reason. But the look in that face I saw staring back at me was far from worthy... in fact, it was not so unlike the expression I'd seen in Peter Wyndham the other day. The gods were angry, he'd said. They brought forth a miracle, he'd said. Maybe that was true, but it didn't change the fact that the man in the mirror seemed no more a proper Instructor than some vagrant they'd given a sword to get him off the streets and into the barracks.

Luckily, the Academy wasn't that far away from the Gods' Avenue where we lived, and I got there just as the sun had finished its ascent over the tremendous archway that marked the entrance to the Academy grounds. The great structure was carved with scenes and figures that spoke of more ancient, bloodier times, of times when Zondrell was part of the nation of Zondrea, the capital and crowning jewel in a large kingdom constantly at war with itself. As its own state, Zondrell had shaken off a past of tyranny, but artifacts like that great arch still stood, reminders of what once was... of what some wished would be again someday.

The last time I had passed under that arch was six months ago. It felt like six years. Some of my time amongst this grand ring of buildings – four for the Military Academy and four for the Magic Academy – I would have liked to have forgotten. Hell, some of it I *had* forgotten in a blur of studying and training for hours each day, living on the bare amount of sleep and food necessary to sustain myself. But there were other times, good times. As I walked past the Sciences hall, I thought of how Alex and Corrin Shal-Vesper and I quizzed each other on math and history facts so we could pass that awful Instructor Quensbury's class. Further down, near the entrance to the dormitories, I remembered those few occasions when we'd snuck out late to go meet girls and drink and do all the kinds of things young men did when their parents weren't around. Next to that was the Instructors' Hall – my hall now, I supposed. I had actually never been inside before; cadets did not enter the place where many Instructors and the Headmaster himself spent their time outside of classes. Now, the mystery of what lay inside would finally be revealed.

"You're early. Good." Headmaster Janus rose from his seat in the entryway, a lobby with bookshelves and some places where the Instructors could share tea and chat. There was nothing ornate about the décor here, no paintings on the walls, no tapestries or trophies or statues. That sort of thing they saved for more public view, in the classroom buildings and the Grand Stadium. No, this was a place of business – the business of making men into officers.

The lobby was empty for the moment, all save for the two of us, and every move we made echoed tenfold across the bare stone and marble that made up the place. I gave a salute, right fist against left shoulder. "Sir."

The salute was returned, but halfhearted. Janus's dark eyes gleamed, cloaked under graying brows and withered, gruff features. "No need for that. You're not a cadet anymore."

"Yes, Sir." But I couldn't make myself drop the at-attention stance – I just *couldn't*. I had stood at attention in front of this man for four years of my life. I had attempted to follow every order, obey every command. I had been whipped by this man on more than one occasion. To stand in front of him now as some sort of an equal seemed... unimaginable.

"I'm not kidding. Save the formality for your students, Instructor." Was that a smile? From Headmaster Janus? "And let me tell you, you've got a tough group. I'm putting you with the second-years."

"Yes, Sir."

"You know that group – they could hardly keep themselves together last year. This year isn't much better. Just don't be soft on them. I don't expect that from you. You know why I wanted you, don't you?"

I shook my head. I'd applied to teach after graduation months ago, but even when I first heard I'd been accepted, I had a hard time understanding why Janus would want me anywhere near any cadet, even the "bad" group. Now, I was just completely dumbfounded.

"Let me tell you something. Don't go repeating this, but I always expected you to succeed here."

I blinked. Wasn't this the same man who seemed to want me to fail more than anyone? "Sir, I... didn't get that impression, Sir."

"I was hard on you, wasn't I?" The old soldier chuckled as he clapped me on the shoulder. "I'll tell you the truth – you're the best fighter I've ever seen, no question. You've got a lot of potential, and I didn't want to see it wasted. Greater trials make for greater men, as they say. And... I hate Eislandisch. You, though, you're all right, boy." If that was supposed to make up for four years of torture, I supposed it would have to do. I had no wish to keep this man as a permanent enemy. If he liked me, fine. Don't expect too much in return, though, old man. "But you know, it doesn't matter about your potential or your medal or your exam scores or any of that. What matters is what happens on battlefields, what you do when a man raises a sword against you. None of those privileged idiots they send here understand any of this. Now you do. Those kids won't hear it from me, but I think they'll listen to you."

I had to search to find something to reply to Janus' questioning dark stare. "Look, I don't know how to say this. I was tried for *treason*."

"Yes, and you're still here, aren't you? Stupid trial, that." Janus turned his head and spat on the floor – the trademark of a grizzled veteran who rose to his station not because of blood ties, but because of the way he could mold brash kids into sturdy soldiers.

"I just don't know how you expect any of these cadets to listen to me. I'm not even in the Army anymore."

"Like I said, you're still here. Besides, those cadets think you're a god in a man's body. You won that Medal; you know damn well that's all they care about."

"That may be, Sir, but –"

"But nothing. If you had it to do over again, would you do it different? All the things you did up there in the mountains?" A few blinks and a blank stare was all I could muster for a response. "Thought so. You know, you can put yourself aside and not think about what you're doing, but it eats at you. Eats at your soul. Smart soldiers know that. It's only the idiots that follow with their eyes closed. Now, I may have said a lot of things to you over the years, son, but I never once called you stupid."

*Who are you and what did you do with the asshole I used to train with?* This was what I wanted to say, but instead I just nodded. "I... ah, I appreciate that, Sir."

"Just think about that as you go over to your class. And, of course, you'll be evaluated from time to time. Though, I haven't seen the General around for a few days, so who knows when that might be."

"General Torven evaluates all the Instructors himself?" Of course, I knew he didn't, and the shadow that passed across Janus' face confirmed it.

"Just keep your eyes open."

*Thanks for the warning.* "Anything else, Sir?"

"No, get over to your cadets, Instructor. Oh, I just gave three of yours a week in the smithy for being late, so hopefully they got the message. If not, give them another week. After that, punish them accordingly. They're doing shield work right now, but they need more weapons training. All of them are like children with clubs out there."

I gave my salute then headed out without another word, even though Janus' shift in temperament still ran through my mind. Was I supposed to feel vindicated? Inspired? Or perhaps the Headmaster just wanted to earn my loyalty. At any rate, I had more important things to think about, like what I was going to do with a class full of second-years who, by all accounts, were trouble.

And there they all were, waiting in the second-year training hall of the Armory. The cadets nearly fell all over one another as they scrambled to find their places and stand at attention. I noticed a few uniforms not cleaned well, one tabard going threadbare on one of the silver falcon's wings. A few of them had hair that looked like they'd just rolled out of bed. Then there was that last one, standing alone from the rest with her haughty sharp chin thrust out. Yes, *her.*

Janus was right about this lot. *Where to begin?*

"Cadets," I said, and they straightened even more, even though most of them couldn't help but stare, their eyes following me as I paced up and down the row of the eight of them. A small class, but that was fine. Each face showed a mixture of fear, hope, and fatigue. "I'm sure you know I'm to be your new Instructor, and I'm sure that you already know who I am. So, you may call me Instructor Loringham." I stopped before the first man in the row, someone I knew well enough – the youngest son of the Head Councilor. "Cadet Miller, yes?" I asked him.

"Cadet Davies Miller, Sir," he said. He was not imposing, but he tried his best. Even standing as tall as he could, he had to angle his head up quite a bit to look me in the eye.

"What's your favored weapon, Cadet?"

"Sir?"

"If I told you to go over there and choose a weapon off the racks, what would you pick?"

"I'm trying to specialize in the dual-hander, Sir."

This sounded a bit suspicious. "Trying?"

"I like it, you know, but it's just that…"

"What, Cadet?"

Before Davies could answer, someone else piped up for him. "They're too heavy. I told him he should try a smaller sword."

"Yeah, he can't block," another voice offered from further up the row.

I put up a hand. "All right, thank you, Cadets, but I believe I was only speaking with Cadet Miller. Miller, go get your weapon of choice, please, and bring it back here." He did, bringing back a big two-hander that was indeed much too large for him. He'd learn in time.

I did this with each man in the row. Most of them were members of minor noble houses or common folk who had passed the tests to get in. All of them had that same look of fright and anticipation in their eyes. Then there was my friend Corrin Shal-Vesper's younger brother, Frederick – or "Fyr," as he liked to be called, since it rhymed with "fear," and of course, he fancied himself quite fearless. It always struck me as odd that he could be so… well, *Fyr*, while his brother was always the opposite – quiet, reserved. With his penchant for crazed stunts and talking nonstop, I was actually a bit surprised that he even made it into the second year. "Cadet Fyr… er, Frederick Shal-Vesper, Sir," the younger Shal-Vesper said with a beaming smile when I addressed him. "I'm good with spears and axes, Sir. But I have a question."

"Go on."

"Are you going to tell us how you won the High Honor?"

*What kind of a question was that?* "Did you see the graduation tournament, Cadet?"

"Yeah, it was amazing! The way you got up after that one hit – incredible." Some of the others bobbed their heads in agreement. "Oh, and that one move you use, with the turn and then the backhand?" More agreement, now verbal and laced with excitement.

"Getting a concussion is not something to aspire to, Cadet." There were still about three days after that tournament I couldn't remember at all – not exactly a good feeling. "But if you pay attention and do the work, you'll learn something. That's all I can promise. Go get your weapon, Cadet." Fyr ran off to do as he was told, that smile still on his boyish face.

Finally, there was just one cadet left. She had her coarse black curls tied back in a bun and she carried herself like a wolf about to charge its prey. Her glare was piercing. "Cadet Larenne Blackwarren, Sir," she said when addressed. "And I want to know, Sir: what does it feel like to know that good men died because of something you did?"

I could almost feel the collective air getting sucked out of the room. Of course, I knew this was coming at some point, and I suppose it wasn't a surprise it came from the King's own daughter. Well, one of them, anyhow. Queen Mariana had managed to produce four children in the relatively short time Kelvaar had been on the throne, each named for celestial bodies. Larenne was the eldest, but the Queen didn't stop having star-children until her first boy. Now, young Prince Edin – named after the Winter Warrior constellation, of course – got most of the attention while the girls were left to do whatever it was princesses did all day. The Academy was an unusual option, to be sure, but princesses tended to get whatever they asked for, even if it was going into a place that hadn't seen another woman since Victoria Arenar, the famous general from the Zondrean Civil War over three hundred years ago.

No doubt, this particular princess also paid close attention to what happened in the Council room of late. I had to deal with her and not worry about whose lineage she came from, or risk losing the respect of the entire class. So, ignoring the various shocked and inquisitive looks of the other cadets, I glared right back at Larenne. My words came from a place I didn't even know I had in me. "You'll know soon enough, cadet," I said. "Let me explain something to you – to all of you. When you leave this place and have a command of your own, you will need to make decisions. Sometimes, they'll be easy; sometimes not. Sometimes those decisions will violate your sense of honor, and there will be no right answer. If you learn nothing else in your time here, understand this: anytime you pick up a weapon in the name of the King, realize that you may be forced to make a decision that will haunt you for the rest of your life. The only thing this Academy can do is teach you is how to fight for what you believe is best, and live to tell about it. That's it. If you want something else from your education, I suggest you go learn how to cut stone or herd cows." No one moved. I don't even think they were breathing.

"Are there any more questions?" Again, not a blink. "Then Cadet Blackwarren, I trust you can find your favored weapon?" She did so without another word, coming back to the line with a basic longsword. If she could have safely spat at me as she did so, she would have.

I paired them up based on weapon and put them through a quick spar. Half of what I saw was lackluster, uninspired, and indeed, just as Janus had warned. The other half was a bit the opposite, far too much energy without enough skill to put it to good use. In any real battle, all of these cadets would be dead within minutes. I stopped them with a whistle.

"All right, that's enough." All movement stopped, eight sets of big, curious eyes staring at me. I paced across the room a couple of times. I thought about the way Janus had taught us, and about the way my father had taught me when I was young. Neither had been gentle, and not always even fair, but I could never accuse them of being dishonest. There was little choice but to follow their lead. "Miller, give me that blade." He did, with a questioning look. "This is too heavy for you. Go get a proper one."

"But, Sir, I…"

"Go get a proper longsword off the rack." Why the slim lad seemed so insistent was beyond me; the huge sword he was trying to wield was heavier than the blocks making up the city walls. I had half a mind to make him take a shortsword instead, but settled for the regular longsword. The big thing I handed off to another cadet, a stocky farm boy for whom it seemed perfect.

I turned next to Fyr. "All right, Shal-Vesper – go get a longsword, and bring one back for me." He obeyed happily, and the weapon he brought back was unbalanced and in sorry shape, but good enough for what we were doing. I tested it with a quick swing.

"Let me show you all something. Take your stance and come at me, slow." With some hesitation, Fyr did as he was ordered and crouched into a good, wide-legged stance, left shoulder toward me. He moved in with a slow, wide-out swing that, even if he'd been moving at full speed, would have been easily blocked, so I did just that, deflecting his blade and dodging over just enough to grab his swordarm with my left hand. "Do you see what happened there?"

"Too wide?" someone piped up.

"Much too wide. Now I have the chance to disarm him, or worse. What should he do now?"

Silence, just a bunch of eyes staring at me. Then, Fyr said, "I could just push you?"

"You could, unless I've got a better base and I'm stronger than you." In our little matchup, this was surely the case. I had half a foot and about fifty pounds on him, and he was not one of the smaller men in the class. "Try it."

If it had been anyone else, I would have worried about hurting him. But not Fyr – he lived for moments like this. He pushed with that swordarm, trying to knock me back, and instead of giving in, I pulled him with me, using just enough force to put him on the ground. He popped back up with a grin, as if nothing happened. "Ha, good one," he said, smoothing out the silver falcon on the front of his uniform.

"Did you all see that? He pushed, but I used his momentum against him. Always look for moments like that. Don't just worry about your own next attack; react to what's happening in front of you."

"Show us again," someone said. Someone else snickered. I was willing to ignore it.

"No, you'll show me. Get back with your partners."

The room filled with the sounds of battle – the ring of steel on steel, various grunts, the occasional curse. The simple stone and lack of furnishings in the training hall made it all echo tenfold, and it seemed even louder now than it did when I was where they were. I found that I couldn't hold my attention on any one of the pairs for very long, my mind wandering to memories of the Academy... and memories of real battles. It hadn't quite occurred to me that serving here as an Instructor would be a constant reminder of things I'd rather forget. That lingering pain at the center of my brow flared as I realized that none of these kids yet knew what it was like to impale someone on one of those blades – or be on the other end. They couldn't comprehend having to clean blood and gore off of those nice black and silver tabards. For them, this was all a show, a demonstration of prowess in order to attain a better station. They could not have been more wrong.

As the smell of sweat grew heavier in the air, I tried to focus on smaller details, and this helped. Rather than see a whole cadet, I saw a stance not quite wide enough, a wild swing, an opening a mile wide. And when I saw those things, I corrected them, barking out criticisms like commands and watching to see if they'd be fixed the next time I passed by. This seemed to be working well until I saw someone drop to the ground.

"I said, stop!" came an angry growl, followed by another, much higher pitched one. *Oh, for Catherine's sake…*

Larenne had Davies Miller struggling to get up from where she'd apparently knocked him back and off his footing. But rather than allow the opponent to stand – as the rules of sparring they'd learned on their *first day* of Academy more than a year ago dictated – she kept right on attacking. Her sword swooped down at full force, looking to make contact it was not supposed to make. She had enough momentum and strength that I couldn't quite keep it from grazing me across the forehead as I swooped in to wrest the weapon away from her. Even blunted, those swords were heavy, and I felt fresh fire erupt above my left eye. When I touched that spot, my fingertips came back wet and crimson.

All sounds, all movement in that room ceased. "Ooh, you are in so much trouble," I heard Fyr say behind me.

I looked down at Miller climbing back to his feet, and Larenne glaring at me while nursing the hand I had just twisted and pried open to disarm her. It took everything in my power to not send her flying across the room. "You two, stay here," I said through clenched teeth. "Everyone else, go outside and wait for me to get you." Absolute silence. "I won't say it again." Lots of movement, cadets literally fleeing out of the room.

Before I even turned to ask what was going on, Miller started explaining with more animation than I thought any member of his family capable of using. "She does this all the time. No one wants to spar with her. She's always hitting too hard, hitting below the belt…"

Blackwarren was incredulous. "I do not! Block better!"

"We have rules, you know, you crazy bitch."

"All right, that's enough!" I tossed down the girl's practice blade, where it fell with a loud *clang*. This was absolutely the last thing I needed, and I felt my temper rising with my developing headache. "What happened here?"

"He tripped."

"She charged me."

"You shouldn't have missed that block. You always miss – you're terrible."

"I am not! You go after people like you're trying to kill them."

"Aren't we learning how to protect ourselves? Isn't that what this is all about? Learn to block. I tried to show you how to do it right."

With a deep breath, I put up a hand to silence them. "Stop. Both of you. There are rules for sparring – I expect you to follow them. I also expect you to have enough respect for your fellow cadet to let him get up from a fall. Someday, you might need him to save your life in a real battle. You don't have to like each other, but you do have to respect each other."

"This is a *competition*," said Larenne with an unflattering grimace. Miller stared at the floor.

"And you think after the competition's over, you'll all forget about four entire years spent in this place? When it's time to go to war, do you think he's going to be your shield if it comes to that? If I *ever* see you attack a man when he's down again, you won't just be spending the next year scrubbing chamber pots. You will be back in the Palace under your father's wing. Permanently. Do you understand me?" If her stare could wield a blade, I would have suffered a lot more than a scratch on the forehead. "Miller, go outside and wait with the others. Your new partner is Stenar." Dutifully, Miller saluted and rushed out of there, but there was still the problem of Her Highness.

She stood defiant. "Sir, I asked you a serious question earlier."

"And I gave you a serious answer."

"Do you know Calvin Cross? I'll bet you don't. He was my steward's brother, and do you know his ashes are on some hill somewhere because of you?"

I was closer than my rational mind would admit to finding a whip. But no, that wasn't the way to solve this, and it was only likely to get me a ticket to another trial. My hands unclenched with great effort as I tried to find words. "Yes, I did know Calvin. He was a good soldier, a brother-in-arms. He used to tell stories around the campfire on off nights. And I'm sorry he's dead – trust me, I'd put myself where he is if I could. I can't. When the day comes, you'll know what that feels like.

The problem is, at the rate you're going, no one will want to fight long enough at your side to call you sister."

A long pause. I don't think I said what she was expecting me to say. A more callous reaction, maybe, to justify her anger? "Am I in trouble?"

I considered her. Oh yes, she was in trouble. Just the mere idea of attacking when a man was down put this terrible, uneasy feeling in the pit of my stomach. It made me think of all of those days interrogating prisoners and, well... I just couldn't bear it. Though on some level, I could empathize with her, too. Let's just say that she was not the first cadet to be disciplined for hitting too hard. "Let me tell you something, Blackwarren. Listen carefully: you will never be considered an equal here. They don't care that you're the King's daughter, because that doesn't matter here. They got over that on the first day. You can be nice to them. You can try to be better than them. Hell, you can *be* better than all of them, but you will never be their equal. This is not going to get any easier. Next year, command squads start. Fitness trials. Field exams. No one's going to give you any quarter – the odds will be against you at all times."

Again, she took a long time to respond, but in that time her brash exterior had faded somewhat. She understood. "It's different for you. You're still a man; you just look different. Do you know what I have to go through just to take a shower around here?"

"It doesn't change the facts. If you want their respect, you won't get it. You'll get close, but not if you make an enemy out of everyone you meet. Do you have any friends, someone to talk to?" She shook her head. "I didn't think so. Make one."

"No one wants anything to do with me. Or they want to... you know, make a pass at me."

*What did she expect?* This was not a place for women – it never had been. "So, tell me this: what are you doing here? Why do you want to be here?"

"I want to graduate. I can't inherit the throne, so I'd rather serve it instead. Maybe... maybe I can become an officer when my brother takes the throne."

"Well, if that's what you want, stop attacking your fellow cadets." She sniffed and looked away. "I'm giving you three weeks chopping wood."

"I already have three weeks in the kitchen."

"Why? Who gave you that?"

"Instructor Quensbury. I ignored an order in his class."

I didn't know if I could override another Instructor's authority, but Quensbury was a prick, anyhow. And besides, the kitchen was just simple drudgery – I spent a lot of time in the wood mill when I was a cadet, and even though it was hard work, it built upper body strength like nothing ever could. She didn't know it, but I was doing her a favor. "Well, now you'll report to the mill instead. Any questions before I made it four?"

"No... Sir." She looked up and her gaze met mine. "I'm sorry about hitting you, Sir."

"Don't let it happen again. Now go outside. You'll spar with Shal-Vesper from now on." At least I could generally trust Fyr to follow the rules, and he could keep pace with her much better than the Miller boy.

Before I went out to join them and pick up the class where we left off, I took a deep breath, tried to focus. I had to admit, I was surprised at myself. I had handled that moment as well as any Instructor I'd ever seen – or at least, I thought I did. But despite all of this attempting to be official and competent and wise, was any of it genuine? I could act the part, sure, but that's all I could do, act. On a whim, I picked up one of those dropped practice blades and swung with all of my might into the wall – a great ringing filled the room as the blade split clean in two. It didn't change anything, but it sure felt good.

On my way out of the building, I found Larenne in the hallway, her head in her hands. "Why aren't you outside, Cadet?" I asked her as I approached.

When she looked up, I could see the tears rolling down her cheeks, despite her attempt to quickly wipe them away. "I... no reason, Sir."

"For Catherine's sake. Never let them see you cry. Ever. Trust me on this one. I expect you out there in two minutes." She joined the class in the courtyard – eyes dry and fierce – within one.

# CHAPTER SIX

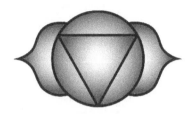

## An Open Mind
*45 Spring's Dawn, 1271*
*Andella Weaver*

Peaceday festival was just five days away – I could hardly believe it was almost here. And with it came that same girlish excitement I always got. Silly, I know, but I loved the songs and the food and the way everyone was so much nicer to each other, if just for that one day. On the first day of Spring's Green, the Book of Catherine says that the world begins to grow anew after its long sleep, and in turn, the hearts of men should do the same. Peaceday Festival is the time when we cast off the burdens of the past, and reaffirm our life's purpose for the coming year.

If only it were that easy.

No, instead of helping priestesses make preparations as I usually did this year, I hovered over a cluster of milky-white crystals, trying to focus so much my brain felt like it would burst right out.

"One more time, please?"

Just one more time. Sure, I could try. I just had to concentrate, and…

Nothing. A big fat nothing. Not even a spark.

"Oh dear. Well, this won't do at all, will it? Do try to remember it should be effortless – perhaps you're trying too hard, yes?"

*Effortless*. Magic was supposed to be second nature, something that came without even having to think, like breathing. You were supposed to be able to call upon it any time you needed it, and not work so hard that it might falter. I learned this from the very woman sitting in front of me, over four years ago. And I worked and I worked at it, and it *had* been effortless, until now. Now, it was like starting over from the beginning.

With a sigh, I tried to evoke something – yet again, just to bring some feeling to the surface – and when I brought my hands together, fingers almost touching, I could feel a faint pulsing between them. I concentrated a little harder, and it seemed to make the pulse stronger. Was there a little light in there? I peeked in between my palms, and did see *something*, but it wasn't much. No amount of further concentration seemed to help, and I eventually sighed and shook my head. "I'm sorry, Archmage. I don't know what's wrong with me. I know it's in there, somewhere, but... it won't come out. I don't know how else to describe it."

I admit, I was glad she was willing to break her research and let me study with her in her laboratory. It was a good arrangement – I would walk with Tristan in the morning, and then we'd part ways as he went over to the Military side of the Academy, and I went to the Magic side. Archmage Tiara even remembered me by name, even though I was surely never her most gifted or prominent student. But, if I knew anything about her, I knew that she loved mysteries. There was nothing of a magical nature in existence that she believed could not be understood with proper analysis.

"Oh dear," Archmage Tiara said. "Hold still. Let me check your readings again." I did as instructed, staring straight ahead as she held up one of her many arcane measuring devices to my face. It was said that the reason magic can be seen in the eyes is became that is the "weak point" in the body, a window to look into one's energy. So, most of these devices required getting very close to, or sometimes even touching, the eyeball, in order to work. I tried very hard not to flinch as two rather sharp pieces of metal hovered closer and closer until she finally pulled the attunimeter – her own invention, as I understood – away.

Then she turned to the massive piles of notes, figures, charts, old books, and Catherine-knew-what-else on the large table in her laboratory. As she fussed over them, tossing things this way and that, dust kicked up into the mid-morning sunlight streaming in through the large windows behind her. Archmage Tiara herself looked normal enough at first glance, dressed in simple dark green robes, somewhere around fifty, with little bits of gray running through otherwise long and vibrant brunette hair that she twisted around her fingers idly as she worked. But if you looked into her eyes, beautiful swirling green of the Earth, there was something more there, a deep understanding of the forces of nature. The fact that she could not figure out which force of nature I currently belonged to had become her personal challenge, it seemed.

"Your friend, Lord Vestarton – he has no troubles like you?"

I shook my head. It wasn't really a question, and she already knew the answer. She'd analyzed him, too, for as long as he would allow it. Oddly, the one who had no prior magical training seemed to be able to use his powers anytime he wanted, even sometimes when he didn't. I supposed that might be considered normal, since those rare men who could use magic seemed to be so much more advanced, but still… Archmage Tiara berated him for not going to the Magic Academy four years ago when he first knew about his gift, but otherwise had agreed to put off researching his powers further, as long as she could still work with me.

"Interesting," she said. "He must let me study him more – he and that other friend of yours, the tall fellow? I'd like to see what the Box says about him." Everyone called that odd, ancient thing that was supposed to evoke magical powers out of a person the Box, because it had no better name. No one really knew how it worked, either, but if you went in there and had some ability, you saw some strange lights, your eyes changed to a funny color, and you came out ready to start using your new magic. When I went in the other day, it was just like my first day registering at the Academy – I saw some lights, felt something stir in me, somewhere, but that was it. Anticlimactic, to say the least. Tiara had been nonplussed by the lack of an interesting reaction, and still was.

"I don't know that he's wild about that idea, but I'll ask him again." She seemed satisfied with that and made some notations on a scrap of paper. When she was done, I asked, "Archmage, I don't understand why I can't use Fire anymore. I'd like to, you know? But it won't come out."

"It's not known that one can carry multiple elements at one time. I've heard rumors, but no one has ever recorded anything substantive. So, my dear, I think we'll to focus on this new thing, this Life magic, as you call it. *Lebenkern*?"

"Right, from that book I showed you."

"Indeed, the one about the so-called prophecy? Oh dear. Do you really believe in all of that?"

I paused. Did I believe it? Every day seemed to bring with it a new interpretation. "I'm not sure, but there was so much evidence."

"Yes, yes, you told me, and your research methodology is sound, I'll admit. I rather do have a hard time believing in things like prophecies without solid facts. Prophecies come from esoteric ideas like gods, which of course, there's even less solid evidence for them. Hm... I just had a thought. There's a book in the Library that I think we need. I have an idea for a theory. Come with me." Green robes whirled around her as she strode out the door, me trailing behind like a first-year cadet.

The Great Library of the Magic Academy was an amazing place. I fell in love with it the moment I ever set foot in there, over four years ago. The smell of parchment and leather binding and ancient mysteries permeated the air, with row upon row of books on almost every subject imaginable. It might take days to find the right materials there, even with the help of the Academy scribes who tried too hard to keep things neat and orderly. Without the scribes... well, one might as well be looking for a coin at the bottom of the sea.

This morning, Scribe Silvana was on duty, and the dapper old woman nodded as I followed Archmage Tiara to the far end of the Library, into the depths where only Academy scholars were allowed. There were books back there most people wouldn't even dream of: Lavançaise incantation books, the writings of the first pilgrims to the fabled "font of magic" at Quiétude, first editions from M'Gistryn's most well-known magic scholars, even "speculative" books with ideas about magic that might or might not exist. Magic like mine.

"Hmm, now where did that go?" Tiara said. "It didn't have a title, but I think it had a red cover. No, black. It was on this shelf."

I stared up at the shelf she pointed to, and I searched. And searched. And searched. "You'll know it when you see it, dear," she reassured me, several times. Still not much luck. I thumbed through *The Nature of Reality*, read a random page from *Alchemical Notions of Magic*, and flipped the pages on three volumes of *Why Magic Exists*. I scanned the first chapter of *Creation and the Elements*, and then the second chapter of *Gods and Elemental Magic*. Nothing jumped out at me. Some of it was written so long ago that the writing was faded, laced with old terms that made little sense.

After a while – an hour, maybe – I did hit upon something that caught my eye:

> *Magic is that which turns the world-wheel. The elements make up the land, the seas, the sky, the sun, the very fabric of time and our very being. We are what magic shapes. The spark of it all lies in each soul, dormant until it be released.*

Those words had to have been written centuries ago. No one ever seemed to talk about life and light and time as elements, but here it was, written in fading script by an author lost to history. "Is this it?" I asked in a hushed whisper.

"Hm?" The Archmage took the book and scanned a few pages on her own. "No, no, but this is interesting. Yes. Hold onto that. Actually..." She pushed the book back into my hands and climbed the nearest stepstool, her thin frame causing it to teeter the higher she reached. "Hmm, you know, this might be it." As she reached up, I heard a cat squeal, then a racket as things began to fall from a high shelf, far above where we were looking.

The cat landed on its feet, but the book just plopped to the floor with an empty thud. "Yes, that's it!" the Archmage said, triumphant as she came down from the stool. The book that guarded both great secrets and slumbering felines was a weatherbeaten, unassuming old thing that looked more like a journal than a tome of any importance. Some writing on the cover – red, after all – seemed worn away, but what I could make out looked like a word in a foreign language. Lavançaise, maybe? Of course, I didn't take Lavançaise when I was studying at the Academy – I had no idea what it said.

"You'll find this interesting. You do know who Drasch Sturmburg is, yes?"

Everyone who knew any history knew that. "The first king of Eisland."

"Correct. Do you know what the legends about him say?" I didn't. "You see, Drasch Sturmberg was known to be a great warrior, but he did not bleed. Some of the legends say he had a sword made of lightning, and everywhere he went, he struck fear in the hearts of men. That's how he united the tribes up there, I suppose. They also said he would regularly visit the Great River. You know of that, yes?"

"Not really, ma'am," I told her, feeling sheepish, "but I think there were some passages about a river in what I read from *Lebenkern*."

"Of course there were. The Great River is where the Eislandisch believe souls go when things die. They travel the current until they're called into the world, an endless cycle of birth and rebirth – no getting off the carriage, as they say. It's not like the Katalahnis who think that after so many lives, you can ascend to some sort of Paradise. Rather a dull way to look at the afterlife, I suppose. Anyhow, look here." She flipped a few pages, lapsing into mumbles as she read to herself. I remembered her doing that quite often during class lectures. "This bit is why this book got my attention in the first place. It's the only place where I've seen anyone talk about Drasch *and* his assistants. He's really such an interesting figure by himself. But, he had stewards, guards, friends, whatever they were – the word the Lavançaise use here is *tuteur*. See here? There were apparently seven of them, all mages, though only one is named. They call him *Oeil d'Éclair,* a great giant of a man who never speaks. That means 'Lightning Eye,' of course. And why else would we have someone who can't bleed and can't be beaten in combat, followed around by a man with a name like that, then if he was using some of these interesting magics you and Lord Vestarton have, yes?"

"You don't think...?"

"That your friend of the half-blood is the next king of Eisland? Oh dear, *no*. I'm not the one who believes in prophecies in old books, remember?" Her amused smirk made me feel very small all of the sudden. "My theory is that this magic has always been around us, for centuries, and we just don't realize it. It's been lost somehow. Doesn't your book on *Lebenkern* say as much?"

I nodded. Stories about the Kaeren had always talked about it being "sealed" somehow, to keep people away from its dangerous power. "Do you think this is all linked to the legend of Kaeren?"

"There's no evidence that such a thing exists," Tiara said flatly. "In fact, it can't, if you believe... wait, what do you have there, my dear?" I showed the cover of the other book I'd found, and the Archmage tilted her head in that way she had when she was concentrating very hard. "Hm, yes, Hariage – thought I recognized that one. Lavançaise sage, spent a lot of time in Eisland and Katalahnad. Always downplayed around here, of course. He believed the Eislandisch 'Great River' was a real place, made of magic rather than blood. Since souls are constantly, ah, we'll say recycled, then they are inherently made of magic. Therefore, we are all capable of magic, in one form or another. The only way to seal magic under such a theory is to stop people from living and breathing. And since that's unlikely to happen, I'd say we've simply forgotten."

"A new age." I took a deep breath. "The prophecy talked about the coming of a new age. If everyone could use magic, that would certainly be one, don't you think?"

"Indeed. And a terrifying one at that. Can you imagine?"

A world filled with people who could use magic? Sure, people could use their powers to do things like keep houses warm and make sure remote villages had water and all the rest, but... those same people could also burn those villages and turn rivers to mud and all sorts of things. She was right – it was a bit terrifying.

"You read through these for a while, yes? Take good notes. You can't take these books out of the Library, I'm afraid, but no one will bother you back here."

"Okay... but I can't read the Lavançaise in this one." I held up the tattered, red-covered book.

"Hm? Oh, there's some Zondrean in the second half you can read. We just need to know more. So, go forth and research. I must be going back to the laboratory – this is quite exciting!" She flitted off with a spring in her step, much like the time our second-year class made the discovery that Air magic, properly focused, could transport a kitten safely across a room within one tick of a water clock. The fact that Miri the cat was now so good at finding hiding places in remote parts of the Library was no accident, after all.

**

Another hour later, the books set aside before me – twelve, all told – had become little more than a blur of strange words. Ideas stopped making sense. I'd caught myself several times wandering off, just staring, unthinking. What was I even looking for? I looked back at some of my notes, but they seemed even less understandable than the books. With a sigh, I set everything aside and decided it was time to take a walk. A nice, long walk.

Outside, the early midday air was hazy and heavy with impending rain. I even felt my dress and the red cloak over it begin sticking to my skin, like it was summer already. So much humidity at this time of year usually meant that the Rains next month would bring colder winds with them – farmers all over Zondrea were no doubt cursing the gods. Despite the warmth, I pulled the hood of the cloak over my head just a little tighter, not so much to avoid a raindrop, but to avoid people looking at me just a little too closely. Alexander used the dark mage spectacles, and that was fine for him, but not me. I thought they were ridiculous, especially here at the Magic Academy, of all places. Everyone *knew* you were a mage if you were hanging around this place.

In the courtyard, there were a few groups of girls making their way to or from wherever it was they were headed next, giggling to each other. Across the way, there were a couple of mages in green Earth robes talking together, then a bigger group of three red-robed Fire and two white-clad Air mages. I didn't recognize anyone – not that I thought I would – and there were no men among them. It was uncommon to ever see them, save for one of the Masters. Men just didn't usually have the talent for magic, and when they did, it was so special that the Academy kept them busy in practice rather than let them go out and have any fun. So, when I saw not just one but two men walking toward me, I was rather surprised.

I didn't see who they were at first, just two ordinary-looking men in nice clothes. Could have been anyone. One leaned on a cane, with the other walking close at his side. They didn't seem to say much until the one with the cane took a bad step and down he went – even his companion wasn't able to catch him in time. As the fallen man cursed at the other one, I rushed over to help, and why not?

Why not indeed. As I knelt to help the man to his feet, I saw Water-blue eyes in a stern, thin face. My blood ran colder than the icy magic in his veins – the same magic that almost killed a lot of people back in Doverton. The same magic that, in a way, brought me here in the first place. It might have set an entire prophecy into motion... if one believed in those sorts of things.

How could I know that, and still be willing to help him? Guess it wasn't up to me. That strange power burst out, small tendrils of violet light leaving my hands and wrapping themselves around his arms, his chest. It came forth with no thought, more effortless than my Fire had ever come after four years of study and practice. I wasn't even in control of it; it just *happened*. He was hurt, after all, and hurt people needed healing – my body seemed to know this even though my brain said to do something else... like find something to protect myself.

The dullness over his eyes lifted, the Water magic in them whirling slowly. He knew. Maybe he understood it, maybe he didn't, but he knew what had just happened. "Amazing," he said, laboring with each word, though his breath seemed to come easier. "But stop. I don't deserve it."

"I... ah, all right." What else could I say? No, you certainly don't, and you're an awful man with an awful temper? My words caught up in my throat the same way the magic seemed to flicker and die out of its own accord, like it knew he would no longer accept it.

Victor Wyndham finally got to his feet between me, his cane, and his friend helping him. "Ha. You know, you could have been me. But I don't think I could be you, eh?" I did not know what to say to that, either. Not at all. He was right, though – he could have hurt me very badly that day in Doverton. He could have killed me. Stupid me, I tried to challenge him, but I wasn't powerful enough for him to give me more than a second glance. "What brings you back to the Academy, if I may ask?"

"I'm here to study." I had to watch what I said – I didn't want to say anything that would get me in trouble somehow. "Look, I have to be going."

"Wait, one minute if you would." He turned to his companion. "Albert, leave us for a moment?" The man – an older gentleman with graying hair and a very sad sort of look to him – did as asked without question. "My brother and I aren't speaking, but at least I still have a butler," Victor said, directing his attention back to me. I had no idea why he wasn't speaking to his brother – maybe he assumed I knew already. Maybe he also assumed I cared. "I have a question for you... Miss Weaver, am I right?"

I nodded. So that was your question – can I go now? Please say I can go now.

"Miss Weaver, do you know why I'm hobbling across town?" I shook my head. "I've been coming to see Master Tarrestar for his work with herbs. He's... brilliant, to say the least. Of course you know that; you took the herbalism class, I'm sure. But it's strange – I haven't felt this good yet after all of the treatments he's given me in the past several weeks. How do you suppose that is?"

I just stared at him, looking into the swirling, once-fierce blue of his gaze.

"You healed Loringham, didn't you? That's how he recovered like he did?"

Nothing, say nothing. Oh sweet Catherine – where was Tristan or Alexander or Archmage Tiara or a knife or *something* to get me out of this right about now?

"I can see it in your eyes, you know. You used to have Fire. What happened?" He coughed again, this time sputtering up a small amount of blood.

"I don't know. Look..."

"I'm sorry to pry – I won't say anything to anyone, if that's what you're worried about. This is just one scholar of magic to another here."

"I really don't have much to say to you."

"I understand. You know, I won't tell you I'm proud of what I did in Doverton, Miss Weaver. Not in the least. I believed what I was doing was the right thing."

My fear began to churn into something closer to anger. "Look, we really have nothing more to discuss."

"Wait. Please. Like I said, your secret's safe – on my honor." I felt my brow furrow in disbelief. "I have nothing to gain. My father's disowned me; I'm lucky to still have a roof over my head. What I did cost me more than you'd understand, and you know what? It's fine. I can live with it. I can live without being a Captain, too. What I can't live with, though, is this pain, and you just took some of that away. Just now, just like that. With *magic*."

Say nothing, say nothing. Holy Lady in Paradise, what do I do? I stood there stone-faced, arms folded across my chest as if that would somehow protect me or give me strength.

"Look, I've trained my share of mages, Miss Weaver. Soldiers, sure, but mages nonetheless. I know how to spot a mage who doesn't trust herself." From the look on his gaunt, pale face, I thought he might never have been more sincere in his life. Here was the stranger thing – I began to calm down. My thoughts said to walk away, and maybe push him over and take his cane before I did so. But, just like the way my magic had offered help of its own accord, deep in my heart I felt something else, not trust, but a sense of... well, *understanding*, I guess. He might have been an arrogant clod, but he trusted *his* magic. He was confident that it would be there for him anytime he needed it, whether for protection or aid or leverage. So why didn't I feel that way?

"Look, Victor... ah, Mister Wyndham, I appreciate your insight, but..."

"Please, what I'm trying to say is, practice. Study it. Don't be afraid of it." With another harsh cough, Victor offered as low a bow as he could manage. "I must say, I'm feeling a lot better. It's truly a miracle, you know that? I understand why you'd hide it, but don't deny its existence. It's too important."

Important? He might have a point there, but still, I shook my head. "I don't even know *how* to practice. It doesn't come naturally."

"Think back to what Master Aretine says about duality. The elements, the elements within the elements – water and ice, earth and stone, that sort of thing. Find the other side of your art, and maybe you can start to work with it." His thin lips drew into a tight smile. "You might even try cutting yourself and fixing your own wounds. Sounds like an unpleasant way to practice, but I've done worse things to myself over the years."

I couldn't say that the thought never occurred to me. Now, whether I had the stomach to do that sort of thing or not was another story. "I'll keep that in mind," I told him.

Victor bowed again, leaning heavily on the cane as he suppressed another cough. "It was nice to speak with you, Miss Weaver. Enjoy your day."

Are you kidding? I started to walk away – in the *opposite* direction. I had a feeling I'd be unable to concentrate or do anything productive for the rest of the day because of that little encounter. I'd be far too busy thinking about the way the magic in Victor Wyndham's eyes grew just a little brighter when I touched his arm, and the way the power flowed out of me without any strain at all. He was right – I needed practice. *A lot* of practice. And I wasn't even sure I had the courage to figure out where to start.

Before I knew it, I was halfway around the Academy Ring, going the long way through the Magic Academy grounds and passing into the Military side. A great, beautifully carved stone arch announced where I was, but it was really the people that gave it away. No ladies here, that much was certain. In a spot near the colosseum entrance stood a group of men practicing archery, and across the path from there was another class sitting and listening to a lecture. Beyond that, a whole row of them stood at attention in full armor while their instructor chastised them for something. Funny, the language used on this side of the Academy was a lot fouler – no one was trying to cover their feelings with formality and high vocabulary here. It was actually rather refreshing.

Near what I thought was this side's main classroom building, I noticed a small group of cadets engaged in some sort of a fighting routine. They went after each other with swords and shields, but everyone was hesitant, unsure. No one tried very hard. I suppose that was good, because if they did, someone could get hurt. But wasn't that the point of learning to fight like that? I wondered how I would fare if I were one of them, like perhaps that young lady there. Wait – lady? Yes, there was a girl among them, with curly dark hair tied back from her face, and even though she was trying hard to fit in with everyone else, her curves gave her away. I had a feeling she spent a good part of her time fighting those other cadets off, in more ways than one. Why a woman would want to be part of the Military Academy at all was beyond me.

Their instructor barked something at them and everyone froze in place. Wait, this was Tristan's class! There he was, arms folded, walking across the gravel clearing that was their training ground for the day. He looked so large compared to the rest of them, a giant of a blond man walking amongst children. He was even taller than the stately, bearded man in the decorated black jacket standing nearby, observing from his place not that far from where I stood. Wait a minute – that was the General. That man Torven. I froze.

Tristan hadn't noticed the General, or if he had, he didn't seem to care. "Good," he said to his cadets, "but none of you are getting the fundamental concept. Cadet, give me your blade and shield." The nearest one, a stick-thin lad with cropped, reddish hair, handed over his weapons. "All right, watch again."

They stood and watched with rapt attention as he demonstrated a lunging move, leading with the sword but following up with the shield, making to bash an invisible foe and send him reeling. Then, he drew back a step and drove the sword down from overhead in a sweeping arc. He made it look so *easy*, with grace and control, like he'd been born with those things in his hands. I realized I had never really seen him fight before – I actually rather liked it.

"He does have skill, I'll give him that much."

The voice gave me such a start I almost shrieked. Instead, I just stared at General Torven and his tall, regal form, not able to say anything. I took a few steps back, though, to give myself enough room to... what? Run? What would he do to me out here, in public? My rational mind said not to worry, to stand my ground, even though my more emotional self said to do anything but stay and engage this man.

"But," the General continued, heedless of my lack of response, "he doesn't quite have the presence necessary. He's not hard enough on these cadets." He might as well have been talking to one of his officers.

"What do you have against him?" I asked after a moment, since he clearly wasn't going away. Was this the Day of Uncomfortable Conversations? I was starting to regret my desire to get some fresh air.

The man hardly even looked up as he marked something with a stick of charcoal into a little field notebook he carried, just as Tristan completed another demonstration. If I angled my head just right, I could make out something about patience, obedience, and skill written there, aligned into neat rows with lines separating the words. Checkmarks and notations in tiny, careful script occupied each row. "In truth, my only real regret is that he knows more about the Kaeren than I do."

"There's no such thing... Sir."

"Then why are your eyes purple?"

I looked away, to the ground, somewhere else, anywhere else. Good Catherine, he *did* know about my magic. What else did he know? What could I say without sounding guilty?

"Don't mistake me," he said. "I've deemed it unnecessary to current objectives to be concerned about it at present. I am not in need of legendary weapons and whatnot – that is King Kelvaar's fancy, not mine. I have dealt with magic on many occasions, and as interesting as it is, I have no need for it."

This might have been the strangest Uncomfortable Conversation I'd ever had. Now I looked back at him, though I still felt my cheeks growing warm. "So you'll leave us alone?"

The General smirked, a look that still seemed menacing despite his apparent good humor. "Young lady, you assume I have something against you and your... friend?" He made another few marks in the notebook. "On the contrary, there are much more important matters at stake in our fair city. I have no doubt you'll understand that soon yourself. Now, if you'll excuse me." One more tick and a flourishing scrawl, and he stalked off, handed the notebook to Tristan without a word, and continued on his way. All of the cadets stopped their sparring to salute with a hearty, "Sir!" – all except Tristan, who simply frowned at the evaluation of his performance, then tossed it aside.

# CHAPTER SEVEN

## The Party
*46 Spring's Dawn, 1271*
*Alexander Vestarton*

The day had been filled with business – not that I minded handling the affairs of my House most of the time. The money's got to come from somewhere, and ours came from all sorts of ventures, half of which I didn't even know about until my father had passed away. Perhaps I should have known that we had not just one but three mines, plus a farm, a winery, and a shipping deal with imports from Starlandia. But my father and I just never had a chance to talk about all of that. He had, thank the gods, explained to me how business ledgers worked and how to count the money that came in and out, and I had watched him consult with the men who managed things for him. So, when they all started coming down asking for gold to do this and that, I knew exactly how much they could have, how to tell them to fuck off if they didn't think it was enough, and how to make them thank me for it later. It was, all in all, a good day, but then I realized that I couldn't just go get some wine and relax – I had to be at the palace that evening.

Now if only I could remember why. It was someone's birthday or some such nonsense, and Dennis sent me out properly dressed in black silk, an eye-catching white tabard, and as many jewels as a man could feel comfortable wearing.

I looked suitably Lordly, even though most functions like that boiled down to little more than making some small talk, running circles around some of the old men during a dance or two, and then getting piss-drunk. This would be the first time I'd be doing all of this wearing those stupid mage spectacles of course, and there'd be questions... oh, the questions.

I rushed out of the house without even checking with my mother and sister, who decided they'd rather stay home. How they could get out of it that easily was anyone's guess – oh well. The palace wasn't that far off, and I could get there before the sun dipped below the horizon if I walked quickly and didn't run into anyone I knew.

Well... I had one of two.

I could have kept going. I could have ignored him, but I couldn't help myself. There, on Spectacle Road, was a familiarly large, broad-shouldered figure in a dark cloak, sitting at a little table outside a café that served overpriced pastries to people that wanted to enjoy their tea and scones in the shadow of the Palace, but probably had no business being there in the first place. He looked so out of place there amongst the Zondrean nobles and ne'er-do-wells that I just had to stop.

"Hey, I know you," I said, walking up to the table. He glanced up for just a moment before returning his attention to a cup of tea that seemed far too delicate for his big, war-scarred hands.

"Herr Vestarton," said the man they called Brin Jannausch – Tristan's uncle on his mother's side. "*Guten Abend.*"

"What brings you to town, General?"

Now, I had the Eislander's attention; he set down his tea with a smirk on his face. "Brin. And I am no General any longer," he said in good Zondrean, but with a thick accent that blurred the words together in a way that seemed so much less pleasant than when I listened to Tristan's mother. "Please, have a seat. Just for a moment, before you attend to your... party."

"How do you know about that?"

"You look like a thief's dream come true. And I have seen women in grand clothes heading toward the Palace. What else would you be doing but having some sort of party, *ja*?"

I pulled over a chair and sat, its meager frame whining under my weight. How something that flimsy was keeping a man *even bigger than Tristan* upright, I'll never know. "Yeah, and here I am, handicapped," I said, pushing the spectacles further up the bridge of my nose.

"People ask you questions."

"Too many."

"I trust you do not answer."

"No, and I don't have to. But you know what? I'll bet you have better answers than I do." I looked at him expectantly, but there was nothing – not even a hint. Not that I knew what I expected him to say. Whatever he knew about my magic, he wasn't telling. "So what brings you out here? Don't tell me you're just sightseeing."

Now that smirk turned into a full-on grin. "You are on the Council for Lords in this place, *ja*?"

Nodding, I leaned in a little. "I am. Why, you need a favor?"

"You sit with people like Loringham?"

"Yeah. What about it?"

Whatever the joke was, it was private, and it bugged me to no end. Still, the smile persisted; he even half-laughed through his words. "If you do not know, then perhaps I am not the one you should be asking, Shifter."

What the hell was that supposed to mean? Did he just insult me? "I'm sorry, what? And what did you just call me?"

He stared at me, right into my eyes as if he could see straight through the spectacles, into my soul. Sizing me up? Trying to figure out if I was an idiot? I couldn't tell, and I almost started to speak again, but then...

Then it hit me.

"Holy hell, you're the one." My voice was barely above a whisper, but looking at him, thinking about the outline of those men in the shadows, it all started to come together. "I saw you. I saw you in some dark corner of a tavern somewhere... scheming something."

"You are already seeing visions? You must be training." The way he said it made it seem so matter-of-fact, so commonplace, like everyone just starts having visions if they do a bit of training.

"What's that supposed to mean?" Silence. "Yeah, well, you were with John Loringham – I saw it. Doing what, I don't know.

But you know when I saw that? Right after I heard about the murder of High Captain Walrich." This got a slight reaction, a tiny twitch at the corner of the Eislander's lip, but nothing more. "What are you doing here? And who are you – really?"

Brin took a slow sip of tea, directing his blue gaze past me and out into the streets. Some couples walked by in colorful finery marred only by the few raindrops that had started to fall. Luckily, it was no one I knew.

"Seriously," I pressed, "what's going on? Why Walrich? Better question: why Loringham?"

"Talk to him. Perhaps you cannot be trusted, or you would already know."

"Trusted with *what*?" My grip on the pleasant noble veneer was giving way. I could definitely see the family tendency toward frustrating communication habits, but I had never wanted to hit Tristan upside the head as much as I wanted to do so to his uncle. Too bad they were both twice my size and capable of pounding me into the dirt, magic or none.

"Who am I to know? I am just... as they say, hired help."

I could hardly believe what I was hearing. I tried to parse my thoughts out loud in the hopes that he would give me something, even a hint. "So wait, you're telling me Loringham *hired* you to kill Walrich? That makes no sense. Unless... you work for Doverton, don't you?"

"I am saying nothing at all. You and your visions can make your own thoughts on the matter." When I gave a most disheartened sigh, he dropped the smile for a moment. Was that a look of pity? "I work for whoever pays the most."

"So you're just a mercenary, then."

"Money has to come from somewhere in retirement, *ja*?"

"Yeah well, if you were a General, then you should know that there's talk of war brewing over this. Unless that's the point?" I searched his face for an answer, but saw nothing behind that pensive stare and scraggly yellow beard. But, when I opened my mouth to start asking more questions, he put up a hand.

"The point, as you say, is not to start war, but to prevent it. My tasks are not done," he said, then reached into a jacket pocket to pull out a small silvery pendant, which he placed on the table. It was a simple piece, a circular medallion with a relief of a bird taking flight, but the edges were worn down, the details lost to years, maybe decades of wear. "Do me a favor, since you are here. This is to go to my sister. I plan to see her, but not for a few more days."

My brow furrowed. "You could give it to her yourself, then, I'm sure."

"I may forget, and it is from... a different time. She will prefer to see it without me there."

"Whatever." Lately, I'd seen Tristan's mother almost daily in going to visit with Tristan and Jonathan, so I shrugged and grabbed up the pendant.

And instantly, I found myself elsewhere again. Back in that dark place where the world shimmered and had no form. Now I knew what it meant, but I had no less of a feeling of utter dread as I searched around for something to focus on, something that made sense to my addled mind.

It didn't come right away, but after what felt like an eternity, things began to shift, morphing into a city street, but this was nowhere near Zondrell. I couldn't tell where it was, but if I looked past the buildings and the lush gardens that seemed to fill everywhere that wasn't building or cobblestone road, I could see mountains in the far distance, tall, majestic, white-capped ones.

Movement to my right caught my attention. Or maybe it was my left? I had no sense of being in this place, no knowledge of where I stopped and the world started. I was here, there, and everywhere all at once. And while during that Council meeting I felt fear and foreboding, this time as the "scene" began to take form, I felt a sense of uneasy calm, not quite peaceful and yet not terror, either. A guarded feeling, like this world I was looking at could transform in an instant if I didn't pay close attention.

So what did I do? I paid attention, of course, turning toward the source of the motion to see a pair of young people, sitting on the retaining wall that bordered a little stream that seemed to worm its way through the heart of this place, this city I didn't know. The man was tall, a blond Eislandisch fellow wearing chainmail and leathers with a dark blue and violet symbol on the chest, some kind of series of interlocking circles. A sword was slung across his back, but it was bonded with a bright blue ribbon, like city guards tended to do so that people knew they were patrolling to keep the peace, not marching to battle.

His companion was a girl, but definitely not Eislandisch – her hair was too dark, her skin looking paler than it actually was by comparison. And though she was on the tall side, she was lithe and slender where the man was wide-shouldered and bulky. I could hear nothing at all, but they were talking, and smiling, and looking into each other's eyes the way people in love tend to do. People in love... who were they?

I tried to focus, to get a closer view. I had no form, no body in this place where I wasn't supposed to be, a place held somewhere in the fabric of time, but I found if I concentrated, I could move around the way one walks around a sculpture in a gallery. Nothing got disturbed, no one noticed me. They just continued doing whatever it was they were doing. But now, at least, I could see them better, and could see that the man seemed *so* familiar. High cheekbones, strong jaw... Tristan? No, the eyes were clear and blue but there was something different in there, something almost wild. If Tristan had ever had a brother, this guy would have been it.

The girl seemed a little familiar too, but I was sure I didn't know her. As I watched her, she reminded me of Onyx Saçaille, the Doverton King's horribly severe Lavançaise weapon master, but while this girl had a similar long oval face and arched eyebrows, the almond-shaped eyes were different. Very different not so much because they were gentle and pleasant where Onyx was businesslike and callous, but because they were purple. And not just any purple, but luminescent and swirling like... like magic. Life magic, like Andella's.

Then the scene was gone as quickly as it had appeared, and I was back on the gray and tan bricked streets of Zondrell, the greenery replaced by taller buildings, the mountains by a great big wall, encircling the city like a mother's firm embrace. And in my hand lay that little bird pendant, whose meaning I did not know, but I did know that it had at least one other owner besides Gretchen.

"Who was that girl?" I asked, blinking reality back in front of me, the reality of an Eislandisch man who was now no longer quite so young, but still had bright crystalline eyes revealing an unpredictable – and maybe a little unstable – spirit.

Brin took one last sip, then stood up, brushing a stray drop of rain from his nose and brow as he did so. "Keep up your training, Herr Vestarton."

"No, wait," I bade, getting ready to chase him down the street if I had to. "Who was she? Why did she have magic like Andella? *Lebenkern* or whatever the hell it's called? Are there other people out there like us?"

"Magic and war are connected. Just keep this in mind. We both have appointments, I think. But for the favor, I would thank you. *Wiedersehen.*" Then he was gone, just like that, disappearing down the hill and away from the palace gates. He'd wanted me to see what I saw, though, that much was certain – why, I had no idea. All I knew was that I wouldn't be able to stop thinking about it anytime soon as I dropped the bird pendant into a pocket and moved on to the palace ballroom, just in time for the drinks to be served.

**\*\***

"Hey, Alex? You're not listening to me, are you? Was it because I didn't address you as *Lord* Vestarton?" I stopped staring mindlessly into the sea of opulence and arrogance that was the current court gathering long enough to glare at Corrin Shal-Vesper, Cen's oldest son and a longtime friend. He and Tristan and I had taken up a somewhat familiar spot on the far side of the ballroom, somewhat removed from the crowd where we could talk at length and drink all we wanted. I hadn't actually thought Tristan would be there at all; he *hated* events like this. But his parents, it seemed, had made him clean up to drag him along. Looking at him in good silks and jewels, one would never dream of all the hardship he'd seen lately.

"Very funny," I said. "So, you were walking down the street when someone just mugged a little girl?" He was wrong – I had at least halfway heard his latest tale from the Zondrell Watch, where he'd been posted after Academy graduation. At least, I caught the important bits in between watching all the people working so hard to look good in front of the King and his lovely Queen. Apparently, it was Marianna's second cousin's birthday... anything was a good enough excuse for a party these days.

"Yeah," Corr said, excitedly going back to his story, "I was on my way to the South Gate with a couple of men when this thief just pushed some girl down and grabbed the purse right off her belt. Can you believe that shit? Right in front of us."

Next to me, Tristan did his best to sound more interested than I was. "So, what did you do?"

"Took about two seconds to tackle him and haul him off. The girl had fifteen Royals on her – *fifteen*. Unbelievable."

I smiled. "Hey, that'll get you three pints of the worst beer you can stomach in most of the inns around here."

"Well, twenty days in prison is what it got him. Stupid kid."

Out amongst the crowd a dance was called for, and soon, people were starting to pair up as the minstrels played "Ode to a Sunlit Morn." There were flowing dresses and pressed silk jackets bouncing about all over the place. Me, I knocked back the rest of my glass of Dykhaniye Plameni – the best Drakannyan brandy that a thousand Royals a case could buy.

"You're not dancing?" Corr asked.

"Don't feel like it."

"You? Really? Are you feeling all right?"

"Okay, that's the seventeenth time this evening that someone's asked me that, you know." I'd been counting. Nearly everyone who'd come up to bow and pay fake tribute started off with some sentiment like, "Oh, Lord Vestarton, how are you feeling? I heard you weren't *well*." Of course, they said this as they tried to peer through the dark lenses of my spectacles to get a better look at the freak I'd become.

"Sorry, but I mean, look at that – there's Victoria Caro and all of her friends over there. You don't want to go check that out?"

I sighed. Yes, Victoria looked good in her sleeveless green gown with the frilly tapestry-like bits in the back, and the moment I'd tell her so, she'd be glued to my side for the rest of the night. The prospect had the potential to get my mind off of other things. "Next one, maybe. I hate this song."

"Yeah, well I'm not waiting. Serena's with her. You gentlemen enjoy your next drink." As Corrin jaunted off full of liquid courage, Tristan and I just chuckled.

"If he ever gets that girl to do more than just dance with him, I'll give him a thousand Royals," Tristan said.

"Fuck, I'll give him twenty thousand. It'll never happen. Why don't you go out there?" He lowered his chin and looked at me with a bit of a glaring half-smirk that I dubbed the are-you-stupid look. Since it seemed to be reserved pretty much exclusively for me, I took it as a sign of affection. "Come on, don't give me that."

"I'll pass. Besides, it wouldn't be right. You know…"

"Oh right, Andella's not here."

"I should have brought her. She'd like this."

Come to think of it, she probably would. All of the pomp and circumstance, the gilded decorations, the ladies in their spectacular plumage – she'd probably never seen anything like this before. "Well, why didn't you?"

"Too many questions. You know." I did know. Did he think *I* felt all that comfortable here, myself, with all of these people and all of the rumors flying around lately? "Neither of us felt very comfortable. She said she'd rather study."

"You really like her, don't you?" This wasn't some great revelation. Anyone who had ever seen them together for more than five minutes knew there was something there, something real. In classic Loringham style though, he just shrugged and looked down into his empty glass for an answer. "Seriously, what's not to like, right?" I pressed. "You thinking to put a real ring on her sometime soon?"

Again, that noncommittal shrug, but there was a sparkle in his eye, too. "I won't say I haven't thought about it. I don't know… there's just too much to think about right now."

"So what? You worry too much," I said, waving my hand as if to wipe away all the cares of our little world. "We'll figure out a way to explain everything away, or at least make people stop wondering. Don't worry – I've been giving this serious thought."

"I keep thinking maybe we shouldn't have come back here. It would have been easier. Less dangerous."

"Yeah, because constantly looking over your shoulder for Torven and the Army sounds a lot less dangerous. I think I'd rather keep lying to all of these twits around here and tell them that I got too close to a fire or drank the wrong liquor or something." He started to try to counter me some more but I interrupted him. "Seriously – it's fine. We're all fine. Are things a little weird? Yes. But we're getting by. You're fine, and you're not dead or in jail, and you're free to worry over us to your heart's content. You have a beautiful girl that you actually think you'd like to *marry*, and you have a job you love. What else could you want out of life?"

"Love? That's a bit strong."

"What, about the girl or the job?" I smiled and it was returned with the most enthusiastic are-you-stupid-look I'd seen in months.

"Don't be an ass."

"Oh come on, you love ordering around cadets just like Corrin loves shouting at the citizenry all day."

It was the first real smile I'd gotten out of him all night. "It's... it's all right. Even with Corr's brother in the group."

"Has he tested the laws of physics much lately?"

"If he does it's four weeks scrubbing chamber pots. We already had that conversation. He assured me he'd stay out of trouble."

I couldn't even begin to imagine Kid Fyr the Fearless as a good solider and officer, but then again, I never used to think Corrin was a good candidate for Watch Captain. "That group... I'd fucking lose my mind. What about Princess Thinks-She-Can-Fight?"

"She *can* fight. She's better than half those guys."

"Just wait until fitness trials. There's more to worry about than swordsmanship. I just barely passed those hateful things."

"I know. I told her that. We'll just have to wait and see what happens."

"Yeah, about that and so many other things. You know, what you need is another drink, my Brother." As a serving girl wandered by, I replaced our spent drinks with two new ones. I didn't know what they were, but they were a translucent bright red, with a matching flower adorning the rim of the glass. "Cheers."

"Good Catherine in Paradise," he said with a grimace after his first sip. It did taste rather like strawberries dipped in acid.

"I've had worse. Anyhow, so... I had a very interesting afternoon." I leaned in, even though the chances of someone overhearing us over the musicians and all the conversations of some seventy-plus nobles seemed rather slim. I had thought about not saying anything at all, but I just couldn't help myself. Besides, what if he had some answers?

"Do tell."

"Well…" I dug into my pocket and pulled out the little silver bird pendant, dangling it in front of him. "Does this look familiar at all?"

Tristan gazed at it for a moment, but shook his head. The confusion on his face was evident. "No. Should it?"

"I don't know. You'll never guess where I got it."

"No mysteries – spit it out."

Another servant strolled by and dropped off two more drinks – more Plameni. We'd need it. "So, did you know your uncle was in town?"

No change in expression… at least, not right away. The confusion started to melt into a mix of concern and irritation. "Wait, you mean Brin? *That* uncle?"

"The very same. He said this was your mum's necklace and told me to give to her. Weird, huh? Here's the thing, when I took it from him, I had another one of those… you know, those visions."

"Really?" He took the pendant from me then, giving the worn silver medallion a closer examination. I'd told him about the first vision I'd had over dinner the other night, and he had hung on my every word. The idea of peeking into the past seemed to fascinate him, where it terrified me. I was just glad he didn't think I was going mad… yet. "What did you see?"

"Well, I saw him – Brin – as a young man. Might have been our age. There was this dark-haired girl with him, and they were in a city somewhere. Hey, which city has four circles on its livery?"

"Quatremagne."

"Right! I knew I'd seen it before. That must have been where they were. Brin had that symbol on his armor, like he was a town guard or something. But the girl… I don't know who she was."

"Onyx?"

"I thought so at first, but this girl was different. Gentler. Here's the thing: she had eyes like Andella's." I let this sink in for a moment. Tristan downed the rest of the strawberry nightmare and turned to his brandy, looking through it as if its amber depths would give him answers.

"I *knew* he knew more," he said at length. "He said he'd tell me 'when I was ready.' Maybe... we should think about a trip to Quatremagne."

"I don't know, Brother. I just know what I saw. It was probably from twenty or more years ago. That girl could be long gone. But he wanted me to see that, I think – wouldn't say anything, though. I mean, it's not like he sought me out. He was just sitting at some café up the street and I walked up to him."

"Did he say why he was in town? Where was he going?"

"Well, not so much." I leaned in further, lowering my voice to almost a whisper. "So Brin... he did say one thing. Said he was 'hired help.' Then I thought about my first vision – you know, the people in the dark tavern I told you about? I know who they were now."

"Who?'

If I had been more sober, I would not have gone down this path, especially not in the middle of a party where just about everyone who was anyone was here – including Tristan's parents. In fact, they were right over there, on the other side of the ballroom. I could see Tristan's mum with her blond hair pulled up into beautiful curls atop her head, nodding and beaming as she talked with someone. A less-drunk me would have waited, but instead, the words just tumbled right out. "Brin and your father."

Brow furrowed, Tristan glanced up into the crowd, searching for a moment. He was taking this a little better than I thought he might; in fact, he seemed far more confused than shocked. "But they hate each other," he said. "That makes no sense."

"I know. I don't know what to make of it. But you know what I think? Someone – maybe your father – hired Brin to kill the High Captain. I saw that vision when I touched the knife that killed him, right? So... oh fuck. I just thought of something."

"What?"

"He was literally a couple blocks away. Just sitting there having a cup of tea, like he was waiting for something. Waiting for... this party, maybe?"

"Maybe." Tristan stared into his glass, the brandy still untouched. "What do you propose we do?"

Good question. And there was unfortunately only one logical answer. "Nothing. What can we do?"

Tristan looked up into the crowd again, settling on his parents as they laughed and postured with a group of other Very Important People. Perhaps he was thinking the same thing I was – what kinds of grand schemes could his father be capable of, and what could possibly be the reason? Sure, Lords plotted around and against each other all the time. That wasn't new, even though John Loringham hadn't seemed the type to fall for all of the political games. I just knew what I'd seen, and like it or not, this Time Magic didn't seem to lie. It hadn't let me down yet.

"Sort of wish I could see the future, too, you know? At least then we'd know when to stay the fuck at home." I started to say something else, but was cut short by a scream.

First, it was just one shrill yelp from far across the room, and I didn't think too much of it. Then another, and another, each one more insistent than the last. Someone called for guards. Someone else started telling the dancers to move aside. Sobering up fast, Tristan and I started over toward the edge of the crowd, craning our necks to see what we could see.

"Stand aside, it's under control," the palace guards said every time someone piped up asking what happened. Off to the side, another guard consoled two girls in long lacy dresses – one of them had a smear of something dark on her white gloves.

Then I heard the whispers.

"She found him out the courtyard."

"How could someone do that?"

"Awful, just awful."

"His wife is devastated, just look at her."

Whose wife? Oh, wait a minute. One of those lacy girls was not just any girl, but the new wife of Meridus, King Kelvaar's primary advisor. And that stain on her glove wasn't just any stain... it was blood. Tristan and I exchanged a glance full of things we didn't have to say aloud.

I nudged my way further into the small crowd nestled around the doorway into the palace's east courtyard, catching bits of conversation to piece together. Murdered, they said. The King's top advisor, murdered at a dance amongst dozens of people. How could this happen? Who would be next in the face of this unknown assassin? Meridus was such a good man; who would want to kill him?

Perhaps someone who wanted to keep Kelvaar from making decisions, to keep him scared shitless... maybe to keep him from starting up some sort of war. I still couldn't quite put the pieces together. But if it *was* Brin who slit that poor sod's throat, then he was damn good at his work – if you could call it that. The guards seemed completely befuddled as they tried to figure out what happened while reining all of us in.

As I looked around amidst the confusion, I caught a glimpse of someone then, his tall and elegant Eislandisch wife looking fretful as she gripped his arm. When he caught my eye, I pushed the spectacles down just enough to peer over them, and mouthed two words to Lord Jonathan Loringham from across the room.

*I know.*

# PART TWO

Magic is that which turns the world-wheel. The elements make up the land, the seas, the sky, the sun, the very fabric of time and our very being. We are what magic shapes. The spark of it all lies in each soul, dormant until it be released.

But where is this world-wheel? What is its purpose?

I contend as such: Picture a water wheel, as that which moves a mill. Instead of water, the World-Wheel lies at the center of everything, turned by the flow of souls and magic. Every thing must move through the Wheel – it is law, a rule that cannot be broken. It's the men who try to break those rules, or covet them for themselves, who create the troubles of this world.

To know magic is to know oneself, to know that there is a World-Wheel inside each of us. How else do we know to eat and sleep and breathe each day? The magic that we will into being comes from a place deep inside us, and connected far beyond the earth beneath our feet. Only the truly enlightened – for lack of a better word, perhaps – can see that the magic they wield follows the rules of the world and can do nothing but. And only the truly enlightened, I believe, can even begin to comprehend the most mysterious of those rules.

– Roumalde Barrande Hariage, Lavançaise mage-scholar, deemed mad and died in imprisonment in the Charmant Tower, 610

# CHAPTER EIGHT

## The Assassin
*1 Spring's Green, 1272*
*Brin Jannausch*

The first of *Frühlingsblume* – the *Zondern* throw parties on this day, a vast festival in celebration of their goddess of peace. I had never seen it for myself, but the sounds of the music and singing from the streets as the sun rose gave me a chill like I had not felt in years. The first time I heard such songs was during the War, after my first big battle as the *Zondern* picked up their dead. Yes, they sang as they carried them off and set fire to the bodies. I was told they believed the fire purified the souls on their way to the place they called Paradise. To my young brain – just a boy in a war of men – this was the most savage, misguided thing I had ever seen. My opinion of their rituals had not changed much in some twenty-five years.

Worse, it was the day of my birth. Forty-two years now – nothing at all to celebrate.

As they carried on outside, I lay in my rented bed able to think of nothing but old battles won and lost. In the past two weeks, I had seen far more of Zondrell and its people than I ever thought I would – or ever wished to. I knew their streets, their marketplaces, their urchins and cast-offs as well as a native. And I knew the noises of the city, too – the movement of morning workers taking their routes, the rattles of armor as guards changed shifts, the sound of hooves plodding across dirt and stone. The flutes and lyres and insistent praise to their goddess pierced that familiar din with a screech worse than cats in heat.

It got worse. After a cup of *Morgentea* that the idiot *Zondern* serving girl had finally gotten right – two parts tea, one part brandy – it was time to make my way outside to see the commotion firsthand. The musicians had danced down the road, but in their place were groups of white-robed priestesses, singing praises of their goddess to anyone who stopped to hear. And people did. They even joined them in song, and helped the girls pass out little cards with prayers to Catherine written on them.

The entire place had gone mad.

"Have a blessed Peaceday," said one of the little priestess types as I turned the corner toward the Market. She pushed a thin strip of wood into my hands. "Spread the word of Catherine to your brothers and sisters, and know true peace."

Looking down, I realized this was what the card said. I looked back at the woman, thin and middle-aged, careworn and fragile. Even under the dark hood of my cloak, she could see that I was not *Zondern* like the rest of them. "And I look like I have brothers and sisters who would want this message?" I asked.

The priestess frowned ever so slightly as she looked up – way up – at me. "The Great Lady is a mother to us all. Even your people."

I could do nothing but laugh and walk away. For these people to worship a goddess of Peace at all was beyond my understanding. They should be banging on drums and praying for war, like they did in Katalahnad. At least the Katalahni never hid their love of blood and death.

In the Market, the festival continued, with merchants shouting their special Peaceday prices over the music. At least half of the dozens upon dozens of merchants in Zondrell's great bazaar were foreign, but none of them were stupid enough to pass up the best sales opportunity of the year. Many people were not shopping, though, but on their way somewhere. They moved along with glee, singing or chattering on in useless conversation.

"What's your Peaceday resolution this year?" a girl asked another a few paces in front of me.

"I don't know… I want to be better at the lute. But then if I spend too much time practicing, I won't be able to help Father at the shop as often."

"Practice in the shop! I'll bet he'd like the music."

If she was any good, I thought with a wry smile. If she was half as good as the lot of minstrels clogging the streets today, the father would be the luckiest man alive. The girls giggled and turned the corner while I continued on down the road. The sun was still low, barely reaching over the rooftops, which was good. I would have time for another cup of tea before the parade began.

Oh yes, there was a parade, too, or would be soon enough. I overhead people chattering on in the streets about it, wondering about the clothes the King and Queen would wear, what the dancers would do this year, what the King would say in his address… and so on. I just shook my head. Back in Eisland, King Keis Sturmberg made appearances from his balcony and walked through the city with his guards every few days. There were no grand displays to entertain the people – what need was there? Keis Sturmberg would speak to any who addressed him, whenever they wished. To wait for a holiday just to get a glimpse of the man who sat on the throne was ridiculous.

At the edge of the palace district, I took a seat at the quiet café that served the good tea. Best tea in the city, perhaps, but still not better than the tea I could get in Quatremagne. Nearly every day for the ten years I was there, I sat at a place like this one to enjoy that hot liquid that smelled of spice and earth. The little *Zondern* man that ran the place had even stopped charging me, so long as I kept it safe from thieves. And I did – the price was well worth it. If there was nothing else that the *Zondern* had contributed to the world, it was that perfect combination of spices and herbs that could bring warmth to the coldest heart.

The serving girl noted me as I sat at one of the two little outdoor tables. "The usual, sir?" she asked. I nodded, and a steaming cup appeared before me a minute later. "Happy Peaceday, sir."

Happy was not the word I would have used. I nodded again and returned her quick smile before she disappeared into the building again. She and I both knew that I would be there for a while, and I had no worry of interference from her. This, I was guaranteed by my employer. But first, I would enjoy the tea and watch the streams of people heading toward the Palace.

Three cups later, the sun hung fat in the sky, and the first calls of the parade horn sounded. It was time. I left ten Zondrell Royals on the table and went to the back of the building, slipping into the alley shadows, unseen by any except the rats. Several wooden crates lay against the rear wall, just high enough to allow me to climb onto the lower roof, then the upper one, with little strain. The café just happened to be one of the taller buildings in the area, and though it did not quite loom over the houses and shops nearby, it offered a unique vantage point. It also was one of the few buildings with a flat roof, where one could sit and observe everything happening below mostly unnoticed. I imagined the owners of this place did this on occasion themselves, as the empty wine bottles in the corner attested.

In the western corner, near a wooden railing that spanned the length of the building, lay a long, thin strip of leather; inside, a bow and a single arrow with a vicious point and ebony fletching. I ran my hand over them, assessing their quality, but my thoughts had wandered. It had been years since I had used a bow. But looking out over the railing and toward the Palace gates, I could see the place where the King would speak, down to the last flowery decoration. A bow in a competent hand, in as perfect condition as this one, would find the distance. During the war, I had landed shots at twice that, but that was a long time ago. Though the strength and the vision were still there, the skill... all skills degrade with age. I was not fool enough to think otherwise.

The other tasks I had taken on had been much simpler. The officer asleep in his bed offered no struggle. Slitting the throat of a drunk man getting some air in an unguarded courtyard was no great challenge, either. I had slipped into the shadows of the maze of walls surrounding the palace before the first scream pierced the night. But this – this was different. The idea sat like a stone at the pit of my stomach. I even felt my hands shake as I picked up the weapon, feeling the weight of the polished wood in my grasp. A chill flooded into my body that not even three cups of spiced tea could banish.

This job was not worth the two thousand gold owed to me – not in the least. Yet, I was here. And I was a man of my word.

I took my position with that weapon and pondered it as I waited for the moment when I would change the world of all of those people huddled in the streets below.

# CHAPTER NINE

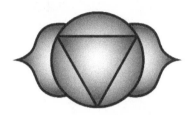

## Prelude
*1 Spring's Green, 1272*
*Tristan Loringham*

I felt the stirring at my side before I even opened my eyes, and I immediately thought the worst – I woke her up. But no, when I looked down, all was well, her head nestled into the crook of my shoulder, still once more. Her auburn hair was so soft against my skin – as was the rest of her – and I thought of how, in spite of everything, I was lucky enough to have her here. Not just here in this moment, but here in Zondrell, here in this lifetime.

*Don't ever forget that.*

I glanced past the curtains veiling my eastern window and realized the sun hadn't quite risen on Peaceday Festival, the first official day of the new year. Only a peek of orange mixed in with the dim gray of the early morning sky. Good thing, because the whole city would be up and active soon, and the festivities would commence. I used to enjoy this holiest of days as a kid, but did I really believe that some astral woman sat in the sky directing our movements and delivering peace unto the people? I was never all that religious, to be honest, but the more I thought about it – and about that moment where I dreamt I stood on the edge of an endless River of blood – the more I was inclined to think otherwise.

*It wasn't a dream.*

Maybe, maybe not. Brin had told me that I had the "look" of a man who had seen the place the Eislandisch believe the dead go to be reborn. And I dreamed about it still sometimes... those were the worst dreams of all. Usually, they ended with me falling into the crimson waters, then waking up in a cold sweat with the most tremendous spear of pain shooting right between my eyebrows.

I never told anyone about those dreams, not Alex, not Andella, not my parents. I never told them how I saw myself walk that River's edge, stepping back at the last moment. Probably best not to bring it up.

She stirred again and her hand came to rest lightly on my chest. Any pain still caught up in my body seemed to dissipate into the warmth of that touch. Maybe it was the magic, or maybe it was just being together... I didn't know. Didn't care, either. I just tried not to move for what felt like a long time, resting in a sort of meditative stillness there.

The sun began to peek just a little more out of the nighttime, and eventually, she stirred once more, blinking as she looked up at me. "Good morning," I said with a weak smile.

"Morning." Her indigo eyes pulsed slightly, their own little lights in the darkness. I had gotten used to it, but it was still... eerie, in a pretty sort of way. "How long have you been up?"

"Not long."

"Okay, good." As she rolled to where she could prop herself up on one shoulder, her delicate features softened into a smile. "So... it's Festival day! Do you have a Peaceday Resolution this year?"

I hadn't made a Peaceday Festival Resolution in a long time. Well, not a different one anyhow. At this time last year, all I cared about was the Academy. The year before that, the Academy. And before that... it seemed like ever since I had been old enough to understand the old Zondrean tradition of setting a personal goal of some kind for the coming year, it had always been the same damned thing. Even now, I was back as part of that same Academy, almost like I never left. But this year, a new resolution may have been in order. "Well... not sure yet. You first."

"This last year's been a little, um, strange, right? So, last year I made the Resolution to do more to help my sister in the church when I got back from the Magic Academy. I held to it for a while at least. Maybe this year... I don't know, either. So much is different."

"Yeah, no kidding."

"I think for now I'll just resolve to stay positive and not worry too much."

"I like that one."

"Thought you might." She began idly tracing lines along my chest, light as a feather, up and down. "You definitely need to be more positive."

Oh, that touch was plenty to keep me very, very positive. It was getting rather difficult to think about much else. "Yeah, well... fair enough. Speaking of Peaceday Festival, after the parade today, would you like to go see the fireworks? I know a place where you can climb the wall and see everything."

"That sounds perfect! The fireworks here are so much better than Doverton's, you wouldn't believe it. But you have to go walk in the parade, right?"

"Right, with the cadets – just when I thought I was done with all that this year. Better than still being a cadet, I suppose. It should be over by midday or so, then the rest of the day will be ours."

"Good." We watched the sky turn from gray to purple-gold until she took a deep breath.

"Hey, so I have a question for you," I said after a few minutes. It sort of just popped out – I didn't even quite know how I was going to follow it up.

"Is it serious?"

"Sort of."

She gave me a confused sideways look. "Life-threatening?"

"No, I don't think so."

"Then, let's save it for later, okay? I mean – it's a holiday. Stay positive, right?" That beautiful smile returned.

You have no idea how relieved I am that you said that. I took a deep breath and smiled back at her. At first, I thought I could say something smart and witty to keep the conversation going, but no words came. Instead, I pulled her into me, kissing her deeply, and she responded in kind. Her warm hands on my back, running through my hair... everything about her was magic, and not the kind you learn about in Academies.

By the time I knew it, the entire sky was rosy and bright gold, and the Peaceday Festival music was in full force. Even through thick panes of glass, we could hear the minstrels and priestesses wishing everyone a happy Peaceday in their full raucous fashion. And it was okay, because whether by blessing of the Lady or something else entirely, it was going to be a happy Peaceday. I was convinced of it.

So I didn't mind that I eventually had to drag myself out of bed, clean up, shave, and get into my dress uniform, complete with partial armor plating, including those hateful metal pauldrons strapped across the shoulders. They were far too constricting for my tastes, but everyone had to be at their perfect, shiniest best in the Peaceday Parade. The little falcons engraved into the steel winked at me in the mirror.

"You look good like that," Andella said. "Very... official."

I wasn't so sure, but I went along with it. "Thanks."

With a smile as bright as the sun outside, she kissed me on the cheek. "Okay, I'm going to go finish getting dressed. Don't leave without saying goodbye, all right?"

"Wouldn't dream of it."

So, I clinked and creaked my way downstairs, where Lissa and Frederick had breakfast out already. And what a spread for Peaceday morning – three types of bread, strawberries, apricots, those odd little fruits that looked like chestnuts that came from Katalahnad, a couple different cuts of meat. As I started making my way around the table, I realized I wasn't the only one in the dining room.

"Looking good, son," said my father with his usual gruffness. He was in his own full regalia, in his long black jacket with the silver trim that he only wore on special occasions – mostly Peacedays and funerals.

"Happy Peaceday," I replied in between strawberries.

"Ready for the parade, I see. Make sure you wear your good weapon, the one I gave you."

"That's all right. My old one's fine."

"No, it's not. It's got scuffs all over it. Wear the good one."

"Actually, I..." I turned to look at my father, ready to explain to him that there were too many bad memories wrapped up in that sword, and I really would rather never see it again. What came out when I met his sharp gaze was a little different. "Right. Of course."

"Very good." He finished the last of his tea and poured another cup, then poured a second one for me. As he pushed it in my direction, his features softened. "So, I trust you have plans for after the parade? With your girl?"

"Yeah, sure. We'll go watch the fireworks."

A rare smile bloomed on my father's face then. "Good. Magic tricks aside, she's quite pleasant. A good choice for you. Spend as much time as you can with that one."

"I plan on it." We drank our tea in silence, but for maybe the first time in my life, that silence we shared was comfortable.

# CHAPTER TEN

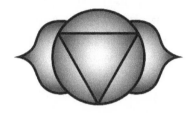

## Men Who Come From Greatness
*1 Spring's Green, 1272*
*Alexander Vestarton*

I t was the first night in weeks that I had gotten up early, on my own, no Dennis to barge down my door at a reasonable hour. I found myself bounding out of bed on Peaceday Festival day, but not because I loved the festivities, fun as they were. No, I could hardly sleep because I was so damned nervous. With so many thoughts about John Loringham and whatever he may or may not have been involved in, by the time Peaceday reared its happy, sunny head, I felt anything but peaceful.

But march in the King's procession, I would, because I had to. I would stand right alongside Loringham and Shal-Vesper and all the rest of the Lords and pretend that everything was just fine. I'd rub shoulders with the King as part of his entourage, leading the parade through the streets of Zondrell with thousands of people watching. And I would do it with a smile on my face because... well, that's what we did.

I dressed for the occasion in the formal long jacket that had once been my father's – black with an intricate silver and gold brocade design across the back. He'd given it to me as a graduation present, knowing, perhaps, that I'd get more use out of it than some new weapon. It would probably be a bad choice for a warm day, but I looked damn good in that coat, and that's all that really mattered, right? I was missing one thing to complete the look, though, one thing that would make me truly look like I belonged amongst the rest of the Council Lords.

My father's sword.

It hung in his study. I hadn't been able to bring myself to go in there since before he'd died. I just couldn't do it – too many memories, too many emotions. In fact, none of us had gone in there for over two months, the door shut tight, locking behind it all of his books, his art and weapons collection, his personal letters and papers. The entire room had become a shrine to his passing. Yet, it was tradition for the Lords to wear their best weapon during the Peaceday Festival parade, and no, the irony of weapons in a celebration of peace was never lost on me. They weren't there to be used, but as symbols of honor and valor and such – the whole parade was one big display of the glory of Zondrell, after all.

I could have taken my own blade, but it seemed wrong, somehow. Besides, what if I might have one of those visions when I touched that sword? What if I might get to see a moment in time where my father was alive and healthy and carefree? Oh, I'd dared to think of that possibility a few times in the past few days, but couldn't bring myself to try it. For some reason, Peaceday made me fixate on the idea enough to be the first to go into that study for weeks.

The handle creaked in my hand; the door squealed at the idea of opening once again. Inside, bits of dust hovered in the sunlight streaming in through the big windows that faced our courtyard. Otherwise, it was just the way I remembered it – everything neatly in its place, not a book or a cushion or a quill out of order. I used to play in here on the floor in front of the desk while Father worked on his ledgers, and there were still little snags in the rug where I had run my toys back and forth over it one too many times. Paintings of my forefathers hung on the far wall, silently looking over the place as they had for many years, including that good portrait of my father as a young solider in silver chainmail, sword and shield at the ready, his nameplate big and bold at the bottom: *Xavier Geraint Cedric Vestarton.*

The one thing that seemed off was a piece of paper resting askew on the desk. It only seemed right to go put it away somewhere, though when I picked it up I realized what it was – a letter, to me, that I should probably have read weeks ago.

My hand trembled as I forced myself to read the flowing script there:

> *Alexander,*
> *Here we are, the time when you're to claim your birthright. I know it's coming sooner than you'd like. I wanted to teach you so much more, but our time is not our own. It's the Lady's, and she's not given me a lot of it.*
>
> *You must trust yourself with this House, this Family. Trust yourself for no other reason than because I trust you to do the very best by the Vestarton name. I always have, and always will. You will take a seat at that Council table and be as powerful as any of the rest of them – don't ever let them tell you otherwise. Cen and Jonathan will look out for you, but you are your own man, and a good man at that. You will carry our Name on your own. I know this in my heart.*
>
> *Go with honor, Lord Alexander Marcus Xavier of Vestarton House, and let nothing stand in your way. You will make our Family proud.*
> *– Your Loving Father*

Not even the gods riding down on chariots of flame could have kept the tears from flowing. I fell to my knees, sobbing till it hurt to swallow. I pounded at the floor with my fist and hoped to Catherine above that my father was not looking down from Paradise right about then.

"Alexander? There you are… Oh, Alex." I felt a warm touch and heard my Mum's voice, but refused to look up. "It's all right. I know, I know."

"This is harder than I thought it would be," I said after a few minutes of sitting there with my mother patting me on the back like I was five years old.

"It's the first holiday without him. It's hard for everyone. It's all right to be upset, dear."

"Yeah." Composing myself just enough, I managed to rise to my feet. Though, when I saw the little wells of tears in my mother's own pretty dark eyes, it hurt. It hurt a lot.

She smiled, and one little droplet let loose down her cheek. "You look so much like him when he was young."

"I don't know about that."

"You do. You really do. So handsome."

As she adjusted the buttons on my coat and fixed my hair, my throat constricted all over again. "He'd be so disappointed in me."

"No! Why would you say that?"

"Look at me." I pointed toward my eyes, my stupid whirling quicksilver eyes with the bizarre magic behind them that I couldn't even use properly when I wanted to. All it seemed to be was a source of torture and annoyance.

Mum shook her head, insistent. "Alex, he was never once disappointed in you. Never."

"He hated magic. And here I am, stuck with magic. It's... it's not what he would have wanted." Hands still shaking, I folded the heavy vellum of my father's letter carefully, so that it fit into my breast pocket. "You know... I guess I can tell you now, it doesn't matter. But I knew. I knew I had some kind of magic for four years – four bloody years, and I hid it from everyone. That's nothing to be proud of. That's called being a coward."

Somehow, I thought this would faze my mother a bit more, but she seemed unconcerned. Maybe it's true what people say – you can't ever truly keep a secret from your mother. "It wouldn't have mattered, Alex. Your father loved you dearly."

"He would have disowned me if I had gone to the Magic Academy."

"Don't ever say something like that," Mum said, shaking her head so hard that the braids in her hair threatened to come undone. "He just wanted to make sure that you would be respected. To him, that meant the military, but we don't get to choose our own paths sometimes. He would have loved you just the same."

It was hard to argue with her, and I didn't have the heart for it. Hell, I'd like to think she was right, but deep down, I wasn't so sure. I supposed I'd never really know. Here's what I did know: Peaceday Festival was going on out there and I was going to be part of it, like it or not. *Stand up straight, Alex – act like a man.* How many times did my father say this to me growing up? Hundreds? Thousands? Time to live it.

I went to the place where my father's gold-etched blade had rested for far too long, reaching for the hilt with anticipation. Maybe the magic would let me "see" something. Please, just a glimpse, that's all I ask… But no, nothing. Just a lump of cold steel. All I could do was wear that slim, elegant weapon in front of the entire city with as much pride as I could summon – damn them, damn the magic, damn it all.

# CHAPTER ELEVEN

## Excitement
*1 Spring's Green, 1272*
*Andella Weaver*

The Vestarton house was a stark contrast to the Loringham house. Where Tristan's family kept a home full of warm wood and textiles, Alexander's was bright, open, and airy, with white marble tiles making up most of the floors, and floor-to-ceiling windows in many of the rooms. Really, it was almost exactly how I'd always imagined wealthy people lived. They even had their own art gallery.

The butler let us in with hardly a word, just as Alex was coming down the grand central staircase. He wore sort of a sad smile, the whites of his eyes a tad red, but something else struck me about him – he seemed more composed than I'd seen him in... well, forever. Maybe it was the fancy clothes. Or maybe it was the fact that he wasn't wearing those dark mage spectacles he usually wore. Now that was odd.

"Lord Vestarton," Tristan offered a deep bow, though there was a wry smile on his face.

Alex shook his head. "Stop that."

"You look good, Brother. Really good." He cocked his head a little. "No spectacles?"

"No. I... No. Not today. Let them stare. Right?" He looked to me then, as if I had an answer to his question.

"Right. I mean, why not?" I asked. "I don't use them."

"Yeah, I know. It's just, well, you know, I don't think Xavier would approve, so... there you are." At the mention of his father's name, he patted the elegant, simplistic gold and black scabbard on his hip. Then I realized then where his bloodshot look came from, as a tiny tear escaped out the corner of one eye. I tried not to notice while he tried not to let another one fall. Tristan put a hand on his friend's shoulder, but was quickly brushed aside.

"I'm fine."

"Yeah, sure. Stop worrying – he's proud. We've talked about this." They exchanged a glance full of something between them, one only they understood.

"Catherine help you if you hold up that parade, boys." Alice Vestarton emerged from down the hall, floating into the foyer in an elegant white dress with pink embroidery. I liked Alex's sister quite a lot, mostly for the fact that she seemed to care little about magic of any kind. She never said a word about it, never even gave me or her brother a sideways glance. It just didn't seem to matter to her, and that suited me fine, even though I had to admit that standing next to her made me feel very, very plain. Believe it or not, it was downright hard to be friends with a girl who seemed so practically perfect in every way.

Alex chuckled. "I'm a lot more concerned about the General than the Lady. But here's the question – are you girls going to actually watch the parade, or just go to the bazaar and shop?"

"Oh, come on, Alex. Cut me some slack. Everyone knows the prices are ridiculous during Peaceday Festival." Alice folded her arms over her chest.

"That's fine with me," I said with a shrug. "I don't have anything I need anyhow."

"Then again, who said you had to need something to go shop in Center Market?"

Alex rolled his eyes, smiling as he did so. "Yeah, just... try not to spend all my money, would you please?"

Alice and Alex both started to talk over each other, but Tristan, in his best no-nonsense tone, would have none of it. "I think we need to go soon, yeah?" Then he turned to me, taking up my hands in his thickly armored ones. The weave of metal and leather bands seemed so cold. "So, we can meet up straight after the King talks, right back here. If you do go to the Market, take this with you." From his belt, he handed me a pouch jingling with coins, which I of course tried to hand back right away. "No, take it. I don't need it to walk in a parade for a few hours. And, ah, you know… be careful."

"You don't trust me at all, do you?" Alice teased. Tristan did his best to smile back at her.

"Just have fun. All right?"

I nodded. "We will. Don't worry. Think positive, remember?"

This time, it still wasn't quite the same smile I'd seen early this morning, but it would have to be good enough. At least it lit up those sky-blue eyes. "Right. I know."

Within a few minutes, the boys said their goodbyes and headed out, leaving me alone with Alice in that massive marble foyer. "So, all the ladies usually watch the parade from our balcony up there," she said, pointing toward the staircase arching up toward a grand windowed terrace. "They'll be here any minute, I'm sure. But you don't want to deal with all that, do you?"

I blinked. What were my alternatives? "So, you do want to go shopping?"

"No, I say we get a spot up front for the King's speech. The parade'll come to us, and we won't have to fight the crowds. Sound good to you?"

"Um, sure. I guess so." Why not?

"Great!" She smiled. "When we were kids, Mum used to take Alex and I over there early so we could see Father standing by the stage. When we got bigger, she started hosting parties on the balcony instead. Honestly, they're a bore. Going to the stage is better. Ready to go?"

"Why wait?" Then we were off, into the bustling streets full of music and celebration and prayer. Some charming young lad offered us a handful of white flowers at the corner, and halfway down the next street, fifty people engaged in a delightful coordinated dance. Even the priestesses handing out prayer cards were joining in. Alice and I, however, steered clear.

"There's so much going on," I said to her. "I mean, in Doverton, there's a lot of people in the streets on Festival day, but nothing like this."

"Zondrell is what, three times bigger than Doverton? Lots of people, lots of celebrating. It's fun, but you know, it gets old after a while. Or maybe I'm getting too old. Who knows? It's supposed to be about the Goddess, right? Like a solemn day of prayer? But really, everyone just makes it an excuse to go out and have fun." She pointed toward an opening in the sea of gathering people, and we picked up our pace just a bit. "So anyway, who cares about the Festival? I want to hear about you. And Tristan."

"What do you mean?"

"What do you mean, what do I mean?" When I didn't reply because I didn't really know what to say, she just giggled. "Seriously. I can tell these things. I've known him his entire life – he's like my other little brother. He adores you."

"Oh, well," I felt my cheeks flush. "I hope you're right."

"Are you kidding me?"

"Well, I mean, I think I how he feels, but... he doesn't seem to do well with feelings. We don't talk like that much."

"Yeah, that's Tristan. He's not good at that stuff, never has been, never will be. But you like him, right? Please say yes."

Well, that seemed a silly thing to ask, but she was quite serious. "I don't think I'd be here if I didn't."

Alice seemed satisfied, happily giving me a quick squeeze of encouragement as we walked along. "Good. Oh, he's such a nice guy," she said. "He deserves a nice girl like you. You're staying around here, then, I hope?"

"Well, yes. I mean, I hadn't planned on going anywhere."

"Don't. Stay here and stay with him. Then find a friend to introduce to my brother, will you?"

Now it was my turn to giggle. "I thought he liked that girl Zizah a lot."

"Yeah, Mum does not like her. Too... Katalahni." I didn't quite know what that meant, but Alice seemed insistent. "No, he needs a nice Zondrean girl – preferably one that he'll actually be loyal to for more than five minutes."

"Oh, he can't be that bad."

"Oh, darling, yes. Yes, he can. Don't kid yourself."

We continued to debate the merits of Alexander's love life for another few blocks until we came to the sprawling royal square, overlooking the entrance to the Zondrell Palace itself. There were some people milling about, but nothing like the thousands that would squeeze their way into this area in a few hours. I followed Alice up to a spot just to the right of the great stage where the King would eventually give his Festival address. We were so close I could smell the flowers adorning nearly every square inch of the thing – every inch that wasn't taken up by statues of the Goddess and falcons in flight, that is. It amazed me that there was enough room for the King and his family when they finally made their way to the stage, leading a massive entourage of soldiers, musicians, dancers, showmen of all kinds. All the noise and the colors and the spectacle... it was almost overwhelming.

As those at the head of the parade began to fan out to take their places before the stage, though, people began to quiet down. Everyone wanted to hear the King, one thin, average-looking man here to inspire thousands. Alice and I exchanged a glance as he began to address the crowd.

# CHAPTER TWELVE

## A Diversion
*1 Spring's Green, 1272*
*Brin Jannausch*

I had to admit, despite seeing how the city had come alive overnight, I was still not prepared for the spectacle of the parade – the colors, the music, the singing, the waves upon wave of dancers. The entire city seemed to join to become one entity, a massive snaking river of people following the King's entourage through the streets. Children delighted as their parents danced alongside white-robed acolytes. Men showered their women with flowers. Musicians struck up chords with anyone who would play alongside them.

Chaos. Drivel. Insanity. Yet, when the square beneath where I sat could hold no more people, that chaos settled into obedience. I had never seen anything like it. Back in Quatremagne, the Zondern quarter boasted more crime and more brawls than the other three quarters combined. During the War, the Zondrell troops seemed to so often strike out and do whatever they wished, whenever they wished. But somehow, after such mass commotion, the unwashed masses of Zondrell had become silent as a church... as if their goddess was watching.

Even raised on a great stage they had constructed for the event, I could not hear the King from my vantage point. His speech came to me in mutterings, but full words sometimes broke through: "... glory... peace... united..." A standard speech from a fey old Dummkopf, but the crowd's attention was held firm in his grasp nonetheless. At times, the people would cheer and delay the next sentence for a time. I had seen more enthusiasm from soldiers told they would likely die in their next battle, but cheer, they did.

There were some, though, who never cheered at all. Out amongst the sea of Zondern, three groups stood before the stage, facing the crowd as little more than stone statues to decorate the King's great stage – the Royal Officers on the right, the Lords in the center, and the Academy men on the left. I knew them by their dress, even though I could make out few distinct shapes among them. The only one I needed to watch was near the right hand of the King. So I watched, and waited.

A black and silver flag waved, just once... my cue.

As I took up the bow and nocked that fated black arrow, I tested the draw – much heavier than expected. Of course, the weapon was brand new, never worn in. It took all my strength to lean into it and pull that string back, and it would take even more to hold it looking for the shot. The old men in the Eislandisch Army had showed me how to aim by feel more than sight... over twenty years ago. A deep breath escaped me as I relaxed the string again.

The price of missing was high. Loringham had been very specific – this was the end of my list, and there would be only one chance. To miss would cost me far more than the gold promised.

"We'll take it from here."

The voice stirred something cold in my blood, and I turned on a man in Royal Guard colors – perfect black with silver threads in the falcon detail on the front – but no armor. He held a tall bow like mine, with a quiver on his belt. When I said nothing to the archer, he frowned. "Do you not speak Zondrean? I said you can leave. Go."

"And what aim will you take?" It was an honest question.

"The General wants professionals on this. Don't worry – I'm sure they'll still pay you."

He moved past me and knelt into a position to scan the area. As I followed his gaze I realized that there were others – a black-clad archer on the west city wall, another two on other

taller buildings in the square. Why so many arrows, and why...
"The General, you say?" I asked.

The Royal archer looked back at me for just a moment, brow furrowed. "Right. General Torven? The man who hired you? Look, you're not needed now, Eislander. Leave the King to us and get out of here."

Oh, I knew who General Torven was. I knew it was his orders I was following, to a point. They'd been... changed a bit. My stomach churned with anxiety, suddenly wanting nothing to do with being up here at all, or even being anywhere near Zondrell. This accursed place with its wretched politics... I could have taken the gold I had in my pocket and left the city to its bitter fate. With any luck, I would have been gone before the riots started and the soldiers ruled the streets. And I would have left if there was no magic here, no Time, no Life... I might curse it to the day I died, and that day might come soon, but it was a fact I could not walk away from.

The Zondern before me had his back turned, focusing on the crowd, on his mark, on everything but what he should have been. Who he might meet at the River's edge, I would never know, and did not care. My hunting knife found the Royal Guard's throat with such speed that he had no time to struggle. The crimson pooled around my boots as I took up his quiver – I would need those arrows.

A stray bit of sweat found its way down my cheek as I leaned heavy into my bow to draw. For a split second, I shut my eyes, then loosed the first arrow directly into the side of the archer on the west wall. A bad vantage point for me, yes, and the arrow did not kill him. The stumble off the wall and onto the ground far below, however, might have.

Another pull, another shot loosed, now on the closer rooftop archer. A further target than the last one, but that just gave the arrow time to find its speed. If the man had been wearing armor, he might not have fallen so fast. My aim, perhaps, was better than I thought – not bad for an "old man."

The far one, though, was another matter. The other building seemed so far, and now, time was so short. At any moment, he would see his fallen comrades, and know that someone did not agree with his orders. I had one chance at the most. As the breeze became barely a whisper, and the sun blazed over the heads of all the obedient festival-goers, I drew the bowstring with all of my might. Whether my arrow would find its mark almost three hundred yards away would be up to luck… or the Peaceday goddess.

# CHAPTER THIRTEEN

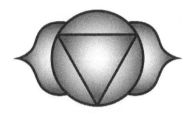

## Suspicion

*1 Spring's Green, 1272*
*Tristan Loringham*

"Why do we have to do this?"

"It's too hot."

"It's a bloody holiday. I wanted to sleep in."

"It's tradition." I glared at my row of cadets as we walked along the parade route, the clamor of music and song everywhere, but mostly coming from directly behind us. After the Academy cadets came the head priestesses from the main temple in the city, their white robes glowing in the sun. Every once in a while, their voices would rise in a great swell and even I would look back, even though we were all supposed to be stoic, perfect soldiers, silent and reverent.

"Why does this tradition have us marching for miles in armor? Don't we do enough of that already?" Fyr Shal-Vesper especially had been unable to keep his mouth shut since we left the north gate an hour ago. I couldn't tell if it was him or the heat or something else, but the familiar headache had returned full-force, like someone driving a sword directly between my eyebrows.

"Be quiet, Cadet. And fix your pauldron. No, on the left." *Stop your bloody whining – and please don't let the other instructors hear you.*

As Fyr tried to figure out which buckle he hadn't buckled, I caught a glimpse of Princess Larenne out of the corner of my eye. At the end of the line, as always, but she was here. She could have donned her finest dress and rode with her father at the head of the procession; instead, she chose to strap on armor and sweat it out with the rest of us. I assumed she had her reasons.

When we finally got to the stage, it felt like hours had gone by. This had to be the warmest Peaceday Festival I could remember; the pungent scent of sweat had begun to mix with the various odors of temple incense, perfume, dirt, and cooking smoke that hung over the entire parade route. Still, we took our places before the stage and stood there obediently baking in the sun while the King began his address.

"This day marks a great occasion for our fair city," King Kelvaar began, straining to project his voice across the entire plaza. The shape of the stage and its curved rear wall helped, but the crowd also knew they had to stay quiet if they wanted to hear anything. "Peaceday is a day of renewal, of change and new growth. We give thanks to the Goddess every day, but this first day of Spring's Green is a special one. On this day, the Lady gave her breath to M'Gistryn and became the breeze, and the fires, and the waters, and the earth under our feet. Her gifts are the glory we all share, and we give thanks for each day in peace and togetherness."

The crowd began to cheer and clap. I noticed a faint smile on Larenne's otherwise stony expression.

Once the cheering died down, the King continued. "And we do this not just as Zondrell's citizens, but as Zondrean people, united in blood with those others who would share our culture, our language, and our beliefs. This day marks an occasion to join hands with the people of Kellen, Starlandia, Riverton, Ten-Towers, Quatremagne, and Doverton, and to that end, soon Zondrell will formally seek to bring back the alliances we once held years ago. We shall bring better trade and more gold to our fair city, to ease your burdens in these difficult economic times."

A little less cheering this time. They knew full well those "difficult times" came from all the extra taxes on just about everything they did. A reminder wasn't quite the best way to win the people over on Peaceday. As Kelvaar went on and on,

I stared out into the crowd, dozens of faces staring back and blurring together into obscurity. Like the faces in the crowd, the words all started to sound the same after a while. There were lots of honeyed words about peace and love and light and all the rest of the shit people say at Peaceday Festival, though the royal family seemed to support it all, nodding and smiling at every grand statement. Even young prince Edin seemed proud and stately, a far cry from the last time I'd seen him at a royal speech – the boy couldn't keep still if his life depended on it.

*By the Lady, my head* hurts. It made the pain of getting stabbed in the shoulder seem like a stubbed toe by comparison. I'd never had a headache so bad in my life, not even in the past few weeks where they were damn near constant. Eventually I couldn't keep up the stoic routine and put a hand to my head, rubbing my temples and forehead in a vain attempt to soothe the pain away. Of course, it didn't work.

"Sir? Are you all right?" Fyr whispered at my side.

"Don't worry about me. Eyes front."

"Are you sure? You don't look so good."

"Eyes front, cadet." If I had to say it a third time, I might have lost my temper. *How bad do I look? And why do I feel like this?*

I had no answers, but when I returned to attention myself, I found it hard to stay there. Whatever the King said might as well have been in Drakannyan. As my gaze wandered, I did notice something strange at the other end of the square – movement, and a fair amount of it. Royal Guardsmen leaning in, speaking to each other in hushed voices. Some of them seemed to be looking up, over the crowd and to the rooftops and the city walls.

Now it was my turn to break our ceremonial silence. "What do you make of that?" I said just loud enough for Fyr and maybe a couple of the others to hear.

Some hesitation to answer. "What's that, Sir?"

"The Guard. Watch them."

Fyr did. So did Davies Miller – I could see him trying to stand up on his tiptoes as gracefully as he could in steel boots. On down the line, others joined him. "What are they looking at, do you think?" he asked.

"Not sure."

"Oh, up there. The roof of that building. There's a man on it." He was right. There was indeed a man on the roof of a two-story shop across the square, though it was hard to see any more than the top of his head. The eyestrain wasn't helping my headache much, either.

"Shut your cadets up, Loringham," growled someone behind me. It could be none other than Instructor Quensbury – I could actually hear the sneer.

I didn't even bother looking back. "The Guard is mobilizing. See for yourself."

"It's not our business."

"You're not the least bit concerned?"

Now I could feel his presence close at my shoulder. "Shut the fuck up, Loringham, and shut your kids up. You're embarrassing the lot of us... again."

*Don't hit him, don't hit him, don't hit him...* It took a lot more than I would readily admit to not turn around and break Quensbury's jaw. Now that would have been embarrassing. Instead I kept my eyes on the man on the rooftop, until he suddenly dropped out of sight. Kneeling? A fall?

"Archers!" Fyr grabbed my arm then, shaking it with some force. "Archers!" he said again.

I followed where he was pointing, toward another rooftop much closer to us. Again, I saw little save for the top of someone's head... someone's *blond* head. There was also a gleam coming off of something he held, something that began to bend back slowly.

*What the hell was that? That couldn't have been...*

"Archers!" I shouted, pointing with Fyr and now several other cadets. "Archers on the rooftops!" From that vantage point, they could easily take out the King and his entire family. Why they hadn't already was beyond me. They had all the time in the world. It wasn't like anyone was moving to protect the King. Dozens of his personal guard were over there, including the General himself, and no one moved an inch. Maybe they knew something I didn't, but everyone around me had already leaped to their own conclusions.

Larenne was the first to act. She broke ranks and bolted toward the stage faster than anyone could stop her. Worse, her weapon was out. I called out after her, but she ignored me and kept on moving, charging past the older cadets to climb up onto stage. Princess though she might have been, she was also my responsibility, so I could think of nothing else to do but chase after her.

"Larenne? What's the meaning of this?" Confused, the King turned to his eldest daughter with glints of anger alight in his sunken dark eyes. Beyond us in the square, the people began to look much the same way, becoming a swirling mass of burgeoning panic. Their voices rose in a swell of unintelligible words.

Before the Princess could do much more than point to the rooftops, five Royal Guards were there to push us back, weapons at the ready. On instinct, I pulled her back toward me, holding her tight by the arm and not letting go despite her insistence I do otherwise.

"I'm sorry, my Lord," I said to the King with an awkward bow, not sure what else to say.

"Indeed, you should be," I heard General Torven say as he stepped onto the stage with us. The ornate black patina on his armor was so polished that it seemed to absorb the sunlight. Now *that* was armor worth wearing – absolutely beautiful. "Can you not control your cadets, Mister Loringham?"

"We spotted archers on the rooftops, Sir."

His steel-colored eyes seemed to bore a hole right through me, then he turned to the King. "I had intended to discuss this with you later, My Lord," he said, "but my men were aware of a potential attack on your life. I had posted archers to monitor the situation. It's been handled and there is no more danger. You are free to continue your speech – all is well." Before turning away, he shot me with that soul-rending look again. "You may return to your posts."

"Yes, Sir." The pain at the center of my brow flared as I led a hesitant Larenne from the stage.

# CHAPTER FOURTEEN

## A Plan Unravels
*1 Spring's Green, 1272*
*Alexander Vestarton*

D id he just say what I thought he said? A general roar of voices and movement and Catherine knew what else had begun to fill the plaza, and maybe I just couldn't hear things right. I mean, I thought I heard Tristan tell the General he saw archers on the rooftops. And then I heard the General say there might have been an attack on the King's life. There was no way I really heard that, though. Couldn't be.

I felt Cen Shal-Vesper lean in from the row behind before I heard him speak. "What's going on? What's Tristan doing up there?"

At my side, Jonathan Loringham barely stirred. I couldn't tell from his wide-eyed blank stare if he was fearful or just angry. "His 'student,' the Princess, just ran up there. I think they said they saw archers."

"Archers? As in more than one?"

Nope, he was definitely livid. He had that same growl in his voice that he had the time Tristan and I broke a statue playing harpball in the house. "More than one."

"And not an arrow in sight."

When no one chose to elaborate, I couldn't help but ask the obvious. "That's a good thing, isn't it? So there's no problem and Kelvaar can get on with his talk?" Though it wasn't like anyone was going to listen to him now. He'd had a pretty loose grip on the people's attention at that point in his ramblings anyhow; the interruption just gave them the opening to break free.

Cen gave me a sideways glance, as if I'd said something very odd. "Did you not speak to him, Jonathan?"

Jonathan didn't move. He just stood there, watching his son drag the princess back away from the stage. Even when Tristan seemed to stumble, an act of very uncharacteristic clumsiness, Lord Loringham did not react. "Speak to me about what?" I asked him. No answer. I turned to look at Cen and his gaunt, pale face gave me no answers either. My heart sped up. "Seriously. Speak to me about what?"

"This isn't the time," Loringham said at last.

Oh, but I knew things. I knew more than he thought I did, at any rate. "It's Brin, isn't it? You hired him? For this?"

Up until this point in the day, Loringham had avoided looking at me, looking into my weird, exposed mage eyes. He didn't understand what he saw there. Hell, neither did I, but today I had decided to stop caring about it so bloody much – it would have been nice for everyone else to follow suit. Now, though, he narrowed his focus on me, unblinking, intense. "I told you, Alex, it's not the time."

"Yeah? Let me tell you something." I reached out then, just to give him a little nudge, a gentle push on his chest for emphasis. But when my finger connected with a big silver button on his coat, whatever I was going to say next escaped my mind, evaporating in a puff of darkness.

Holy fuck. This again.

All of the people melted away except for two, two men in a dark room... no, a courtyard. Little blue flowers arranged in a semicircle caught the moonlight, while two figures stood on a stone patio surrounded by the walls of an impressive home. They could barely bring themselves to face each other. I sensed real hatred there – I don't know how I knew that, but I did.

I knew the place; it was the Loringhams' quaint garden. When, I wasn't sure. Not that long ago, a few weeks, maybe. And the men... I knew them too, but it wasn't who I expected to see. John Loringham, yes, but General Torven? There, of all places? Why? What were they talking about? I wished I could hear in the strange "time vision" place, but as it was, all I saw was an angry General – aggressive, moving his hands about as he spoke – and a passive Loringham who did nothing but shrink back against the General's verbal onslaughts. I had, in fact, never seen Loringham so... meek. Scared. Yes, Lord Jonathan Loringham was visibly frightened of a man he could buy and sell countless times over. Why?

"Alex? Alex?" The sudden rush of sound was so jarring, I almost screamed. The garden washed away as if a high tide had just come in, and I was back in the square, in front of the King's Peaceday stage and thousands of people. "Alex, are you all right?"

"Torven... You..." I didn't know how to construct a sentence out of those thoughts. I looked up at the stage, at the proud falcon-general himself in the gaudy armor of high-ranking officers. He doted over the King but there was some sort of disagreement between them. The longer they deliberated, the louder and more unruly the crowd grew.

"He's double-crossed us."

The words didn't come from Loringham or Cen. They came from just ahead, at the top of the little Lordly triangle formation we stood in... the Head Councilor. Andrew Miller turned his head just slightly toward us. "I hope you're prepared for this," he said.

Holy fucking Catherine-on-a-pike – prepared for *what*? Heat rose in my body, my cheeks went flush, suddenly that wonderful black jacket I wore seemed like nothing more than an uncomfortable burden. Worse, it had little to do with the sun beating down on us.

That was when the Royal Guard started to move, signaling for the city guards and the soldiers to spread out amongst the crowd, to move the citizens back, out of the plaza. But not all of them left the King's side – about ten of them started to surround the Lords, hands on weapons, blank looks on their faces. The heavy plates on their ceremonial silver and black armor reflected the sun in a strange sort of way, to where I could see individual rays of light jumping off of them. They moved so slowly, too, as if caught up in mud.

Magic snarled in my veins, crawling under my skin with the ferocity of a Katalahni sandstorm. I couldn't tell if I was actually using that magic, or if it was using me – regardless, the way the world pulsed around me made my stomach flip and flop in a most disconcerting way. Too bad none of that seemed to affect anyone else, as the members of the Guard continued to watch us, stonefaced, waiting for their General's next command.

"Gentlemen," Torven said, addressing from the stage while the King stayed oddly silent. "The time of bickering and family legacy ends today. Zondrell deserves better. Today, we return to true glory. Today, we cast off the reins of the past."

"What the hell are you talking about?" I shouted back at him. I was the only one. Why weren't the others as outraged over any of this?

"Don't play coy, Lord Vestarton. I know of the plot, and now Lord Kelvaar knows of it as well."

"What plot?" I looked around, searching for answers in the faces of the other Lords. They knew – they *knew!* They all fucking knew and no one had the decency to tell me anything. Now we were all going to prison for it… or worse.

Miller dared to take a step forward, and the Guard in front of him drew his blade. To his credit, the old Head Councilor refused to back down. "General Torven, did you tell His Majesty about your role in this 'plot,' as you call it?"

This got quite the start out of the King. He pulled at the General's arm, saying something I couldn't quite hear over the racket behind us. Now it wasn't just the townspeople – I could hear the Academy kids as well, shouting at us, at the King, at each other, at anyone who would listen. Swords began to leave scabbards. It was only a matter of time before they started the biggest brawl in Zondrell history. And on Peaceday no less… couldn't be more fitting.

I felt the magic swirl around in me so much that it made it difficult to breathe, much less concentrate on what was going on. But I couldn't just… let it out. What would I do with it? It might make things a million times worse, so I just stood there, holding it in. Miller and Torven lobbed insults at one another, neither giving in to whatever the truth of it all was. And at my side, John Loringham looked more pale than I'd ever seen him – more so than in the vision I'd just had. He looked ready to faint on the spot.

"What's happening?" I asked him, fighting through the magic-haze. I didn't even know if my words made sense.

"It's all gone to hell, that's what's happening. I should have known better. He was too smart for me."

"Who? Brin?"

"Torven."

# CHAPTER FIFTEEN

## Chasing Shadows
### *1 Spring's Green, 1272*
### *Andella Weaver*

"They're pointing swords at my brother. Why are they pointing swords at my brother?" Alice's grip on my arm was tight, and there was real fear alight in her dark eyes. "What the hell is going on?"

Everything around us was in chaos. People, sounds, just... everything. We couldn't hear what they were saying up on the stage – really, we couldn't hear much of what anyone was saying because it was all just a jumble of noise. Some of the crowd had started to run off, but others were still, like us, entranced by whatever was going on between the guards and the Lords and the King. General Torven, wearing the most decorative armor I'd ever seen, made remarks up on the stage, while the King seemed to be unable to move, caught there with this strange look on his face. Anything regal about him was all but gone.

"Zondrell must be saved from itself." I heard the General's stern words drift over all the racket, his regal bearing overshadowing anything the King could have done or said. "This city needs better, deserves better. Join me or not, the choice is yours to make. But this day marks the end of the Zondrell that we have known for so long, the Zondrell that cowers in corners and makes deals with its enemies at the expense of its people. Kelvaar V, you now stand trial for your endless taxation and abuse of power."

Then it happened, the unthinkable. The General drew his blade and cut down the King, just like that. It was so fast, almost like a fake fight in a theater production. Yet, somehow, it didn't seem that shocking, not from a man like that. Oh sure, he seemed like a man of great honor, on the surface. People said so often. Yet, if anyone could cut down an unarmed man without a second thought, it was General Torven – I had no doubt about that.

"Oh no," Alice whispered as the King wilted on the stage. Her eyes were wide, disbelieving, starting to tear up.

Around us on the street, what was left of the crowd had started to panic. The city guard had been rounding people up, trying to get them to leave, but Alice and I had ducked out of their sight, standing by the opening to an alley. We still had a good view of the stage and everything going on, but it was... I don't really know how to describe it. Insanity is the only word that comes to mind.

"This is ridiculous," Alice scoffed. "Some Peaceday this is."

Indeed. But I wasn't going to just sit there and watch it happen, or let the guards shuffle us off somewhere. I couldn't. I pointed toward the depths of the alley. "Hey, do you know where this goes?"

She shrugged, confused. "How would I know?"

"Doesn't matter. Come on!" If I could get near the stage somehow, maybe I could help with my magic, because that was the right thing to do. Wasn't it? I might even be able to help the King, though I was pretty sure I wasn't capable of raising the dead. And from the wound he got, well... at any rate, magic was something I could do. Besides, the shadows of an unknown alley seemed much safer than anywhere else at the moment.

We turned left when we got to the wall. How far that path went was anyone's guess, but we were going toward the Palace, I knew that much. From somewhere behind us, we heard a scream so loud and so shrill it could have been made by the Goddess herself. "What... what do you think that was?" Alice asked in a hushed tone.

"I don't know. Don't think about it. Keep moving." But we both knew that we were thinking about it, and the thoughts weren't good.

Further down, we hit a dead end and a looming pile of garbage gathering at the back of some building. Ugh. Best to keep moving but there was little alley left. Two houses over and we'd be back in the daylight. Maybe that would put us where we needed to be? I had no idea. The shouting and the sounds of confusion still drifted through the air here, but they were muffled now. I looked to Alice, but she was already on her way toward the street. I rushed to follow.

"There's Royal Guard everywhere," she said softly, peeking out past the building but taking care not to be too visible. She was right – there were ten or more men clustered by the rear of the stage. Beyond them, I could see all sorts of activity at the edges, but the great curved wall of the stage itself blocked most of the view of whatever was happening in the square.

"Do you think they're all loyal to that man... the General?" I asked.

"If they weren't, they wouldn't be just hanging around. And yes, they're all very loyal to Lord Torven. You see it all the time – they love that man. Oh sweet Catherine, the world's gone mad, hasn't it?"

"Well, we can't just wait here. We have to do something."

She cocked her head, brow furrowed. "Like what? What are you thinking?"

"The King, Tristan and Alex, any of them – I can help. You know... with my magic? I just have to get to them."

"Are you insane?" She grabbed me by the shoulders, staring at me with all of the fierceness of one of those soldiers out there. "Andella, listen to me. They started a bloody civil war right on the other side of that stage. You don't want to go over there. We shouldn't even be here. We should... we should go back to the house. I mean, it'll be safe there, right?"

But I wasn't listening. I had already made up my mind. The problem was, I didn't know the first thing about what to do next. Could I trick the guards somehow? Could I sneak past them? That all seemed rather unlikely – they were on edge, some with their weapons out. They'd probably sooner cut me down than listen to any sort of reason, trickery, or anything in between.

"Wait. Who's that?" My gaze went to where Alice had started to point, and could hardly believe what I saw there.

"That... that can't be," I said. No, I was seeing things. He shouldn't have been here. Didn't we leave him behind in Doverton?

"Wait, do you know him or something?" Maybe he heard her, because he turned his head toward us then, and we scrambled into the safety of the shadows.

"Good, stay there," he said to us as he walked past. "This place will need a Saint."

Of course, I knew the big Eislandisch man with the sword on his back. He didn't even have to come any closer, but as he walked past us, I was struck by how tired he looked. He seemed... lost. Out of place. Searching for something, maybe. He had the same look the first time I saw him a couple of months ago, covered in blood and grime as he literally dropped Tristan on the floor of my sister's church and told us to "fix him."

"I know him from Doverton," I whispered to Alice. She didn't need to know the rest of the story right now, or that the imposing, brutish stranger was related to Tristan. "I don't know what he's doing here, though."

"What did he just say? Something about a Saint? Saint who?" I of course had no answer. "I think your friend is a madman. Look – what's he up to?"

We watched, trying to stay as much out of sight as possible. There was an exchange of words, too far away for us to hear. Something about a job? One of the guardsmen grew annoyed, insulted maybe, and bared steel. The man who called himself Brin Jannausch took a quick glance back in our direction, then pulled the great blade from its strap on his back.

The battle, though, never started.

"Sweet Catherine – it's the Prince," said Alice, watching as a little boy ran with all of his energy past the soldiers and down the street toward us. The armored men hesitated, then some of them started to give chase, pushing past Brin with their armor clinking and clanking the whole way. Would they catch him? Maybe. It was hard to tell but the boy already seemed winded, fear alive in his eyes.

I darted out of the shadows just enough to catch his attention, ignoring Alice's pleas to stay put. "Over here!" I waved. Even though he had no idea who I was, I wasn't a solider, and that was all the encouragement he needed.

As I pulled him gently by his disheveled silver tabard into the alley, he struggled to catch his breath. "I can't let them get me," he said.

Alice and I looked at each other. What she really thought of the whole situation, I had no idea, but she flashed the best and most reassuring smile she could. "They won't, Prince Edin. Come with us."

And we started to run back through the alleys, the sounds of men and clashing swords getting further and further behind us.

# CHAPTER SIXTEEN

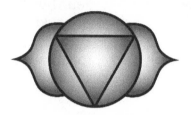

## Light in the Darkness
*1 Spring's Green, 1272*
*Tristan Loringham*

N<sub></sub>o *man is truly pure of heart.* So says the Book of Catherine. Only the Goddess Herself is pure... only the Goddess Herself would break up her own celebration just to dethrone a so-called corrupt King solely for the good of the people.

It didn't matter who launched the first blow in the plaza that day – history would just make up something anyhow. History might even say we should have stood by and supported the General in his quest to "bring glory back to Zondrell." Well, it might have saved some lives if we had. As it was, the square had erupted, various factions of soldiers loyal to the King or the General taking to their blades while the citizens – the very citizens the General was trying to "save" – fled for their lives.

I found myself trapped, pinned back by four Royal Guards that I had no wish to kill, even though they clearly had no qualms about killing me. Behind me, I heard the shouts of Academy cadets rushing off to battle to protect fathers and brothers. And at my side was someone else who had every desire – and maybe every right – to search for openings between those shimmering black armor plates of theirs. Larenne Blackwarren hit with increasing force, her face wet from both tears and sweat. The problem was, that intensity was not matched with skill, and she had never held a blade against a man like this before. If today had never happened, she might not have done so for many years, if ever.

So, I did what I could to protect her from blows she had no chance at blocking while keeping an eye on the Lords, just beyond our opponents. Oh, and trying not to lose my footing from wavering vision and that throbbing headache. It seemed like every time I moved, it got worse. A good strike from one of these Guards might have almost been a welcome escape, but I wasn't willing to go out like that.

I parried a strong blow coming in on my right. The force sent a tingle through my arm, but also knocked my opponent backward and exposed his temple to the butt-end of the beautiful sword my father had bequeathed to me. He fell in a mighty crash of heavy armor.

Now I could better see the Lords clustered together, those with weapons shielding those without – Lord Shilling who was too old to pick up a sword again, and Miller and Wyndham who had never taken one up in the first place. *Alex, Father... hang in there. Please.*

My distraction almost cost me my leg. A Guard swooped in then, but I saw him just a second too late. It was the first time I was ever thankful for my formal armor, as his blow bit into the plate strapped to my right thigh, rather than into flesh and bone. Surprised, I wheeled back, parrying another quick swing with one of my own. This man's face was a mask of rage, stored up perhaps for years. *Was Zondrell really that bad? Was serving King Kelvaar such a distasteful task that these men would draw steel just to be free of him?*

Maybe it was, if it created all this.

I dodged a thrust, followed by a wide swing to the left. With his flank now exposed, it would have been easy to find the soft spot and puncture a lung or a kidney. Instead, I kicked him in that open flank, putting everything I had into it so that he went down. The end of my blade at his throat was enough to keep him there, at least for the moment. A certain part of me, the one that fed so readily off the rush of battle-energy, would have been happy to keep going and drown him in his own blood. And when our eyes met, he knew it, too, wisely deciding to stay on the ground.

Still, it wasn't over. I took a deep breath and left my thoughts behind, charging in too fast for the third Guard to defend, smashing him across the face and grabbing his own weapon with my free hand. Disarmed and disoriented, he had little recourse but to fall back.

I took one glance back at Larenne to make sure she could hold her own against the final man, and she could. She'd be fine – she'd have to be. I needed to be closer to the stage, and I needed to be there now. Torven was nowhere to be seen, but he'd left some of his best men behind, more Royal Guards once sworn to protect the King and the Council. Now, they were mercenaries in gorgeous armor.

When I saw Alex hunched over, clutching at his left side, my breath caught in my throat. *Why? How? Why wasn't I there?* But I couldn't stop moving – I had to get there. Amazing how a hundred feet can seem so much like a hundred miles.

I wasn't fast enough.

As I raced forward, a tall Guard faced off against my father... my father, who I had never seen hold a blade against another outside of our practice sessions when I was young. He had always been graceful, light on his feet, but that was a long time ago. Now he moved with caution, but also with an anger I'd never seen in him before. Anger could fuel strength, but it could also make one careless. Careless enough, perhaps, to miss an otherwise easily blocked swing.

One second faster. One moment closer. Even just one more step. That's all I needed. But I didn't have it. That Guard's blade sliced through the front of my father's long jacket while I watched, helplessly too far away to do anything but stumble forward. I felt like I could feel the pain of that wound inside my own head, an agonizing shock, fit to burst.

Suddenly everything was engulfed in a great flash of light. Blinding, white, like I'd just looked straight into the eye of the Goddess. I shut my eyes but I could still see it, and the pain... by the Lady, that *pain*.

I dropped to my knees. *What just happened?* I could barely think. I heard sounds all around me, none of it making much sense. High-pitched voices, the rumble of people scattering in every direction, and somewhere in the middle of it all, someone at my ear saying, "Sir! Sir!" over and over again. When I gathered the courage to open my eyes, the light was still there, but softer now, hovering like a translucent curtain over my father, Alex, all of the Lords, everything around us. It had a glimmer to it, but if I squinted I could see that the sheen was not consistent, but rather made up of a network that looked like tiny lightning bolts arcing this way and that across its surface. As I took all this in, I realized something else, too – a Guard's sword was somehow *buried* in that curtain of light, stuck there and held fast with no obvious reason, no explanation.

"Sir! Are you all right?" Dazed, I stared up at Larenne Blackwarren, trying to blink away the bright spots in my vision. I had no words. "How... how did you do that?"

*Wait, I did that?* It wasn't possible. I realized that the ground was razed where the light shimmered, like someone had taken a great sword and dragged it across the plaza. There was no way in Catherine's creation that *I* could have done such a thing. That light, that whatever it was...

*The Light. Lichtenkern. Third magic of the prophecy.*

I reached out toward the field of light that may or may not have come out of me. Even though I could feel nothing against my skin, there was *something* there, or rather, it was devoid of matter. It was a barrier of... nothingness. An empty place where nothing could enter or exit. A tear in reality.

*This whole day was a tear in reality.*

"Sir? What happened, Sir?" Now it wasn't Larenne, but a man's voice, and then, hands on my shoulders. Fyr Shal-Vesper helped me to my feet. The going was slow – I felt disoriented, disconnected. "That's some trick you just pulled, Sir."

I finally found my voice. Then I regarded him, his eager round face that usually held a smile now earnest and frightened. Nearby, Larenne looked much the same, pale as if she were sick to her stomach. "It's no trick, it's... Fyr, listen to me. Get Larenne and the others out of here. Go back to the Academy, anyplace that's safe. Can you do that?"

"But what about my father?" Fyr gestured beyond the light wall. "He's over there, too."

"I'll look after him. You get the cadets together, and get them out. That's an order." They didn't need to die here. I couldn't bear the thought if they did. Fyr – perhaps reluctantly – agreed, and sped off, dragging the Princess along with him.

# CHAPTER SEVENTEEN

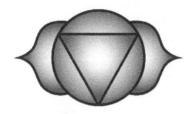

## No Glory
*1 Spring's Green, 1272*
*Alexander Vestarton*

T here was no reason, no sense, no bargaining. General Torven was far too angry – with us, with the King, with everything. Whatever was supposed to have happened didn't, and this was a man who was nothing if not inflexible with his plans. He didn't rant and rave, though; he was measured, cool as ever, but he made it clear under no uncertain terms that the Lords were all idiots and that *he* would put everything "right."

Fuck him. Say what you will about Kelvaar, but he was still the King. No one wants their King to die. Not like this. He didn't even have a chance to defend himself, for the Lady's sake. It was wrong. I didn't care what the "deal" was, who struck it, or at what price.

"You have no right, Torven – call off your men." For his part, Head Councilor Miller *was* ranting and raving. So were all of the other Lords. Me, I couldn't quite find my words. I was too busy trying to make sense of the chaos the Festival plaza had become. Some fucking Peaceday… somewhere, the Goddess was crying her eyes out.

"Gentlemen," I heard Torven say, "if we are not in agreement, then it might be assumed that your allegiance lies elsewhere. For that, I have little patience. You clearly don't understand – I'm doing this city a favor." He really believed that, too – I could see the conviction in his storm-colored eyes. If he lived through today to look in the mirror tomorrow, he'd see a hero, not a murderer.

Yet more ranting, an odd combination of insults and pleas for it all to stop. And Torven would have none of it. He didn't even respond. Instead, he just shook his head and made some kind of flourishing gesture to the soldiers gathered near him. He seemed to fade away as they rushed toward us, drawing weapons.

"Now wait just a minute," I said, my gaze trying to follow the General. "You can't just leave!"

Oh, but he could. It wasn't like I was going to catch him – as soon as I tried I was met with an explosive pain in my side. What the fuck just happened? The svelte, curving blade of a Royal Guard, that's what happened. Right into me like I was nothing. It could have been worse – I could have been cleaved in two. Instead, the asshole just twisted it a bit as he wrenched the blade loose from my flesh. As I struggled to stay on my feet, I felt every tiny movement, each bringing with it new pain unlike any I'd felt before.

Worse, the Guard wasn't going anywhere; in fact, he reared back for another blow, and what was I doing? Hunching over bleeding all over my best coat, of course. Fucking helpless. If I had better control over my magic, maybe... but I felt so *drained* all of the sudden. I tried to concentrate, but it wasn't easy. I imagined what would happen if he just froze there, caught in mid-swing like a commemorative statue. Oh, wouldn't that be something?

The power began to move through me, that feeling of something foreign and snakelike crawling beneath my skin, burrowing new pathways through my body. It stirred and it swelled and it faltered and it spread, and I watched as that sword halted its descent toward my skull. The sun gleamed in a sterile sort of way off its edge, and his eyes looked much more like glass orbs than living organs.

By the gods – I *stopped* a person. Was he dead? Did I just kill a man?

I didn't know. I didn't care to know, and I wouldn't find out. Someone grabbed me from behind then, pulling me out of the way – out of danger? The whole place was dangerous. In the time it took for me to figure out what was happening, five Guards had taken aim from different sides, with Shal-Vesper and Silversmith and Loringham standing against them. Five on three – not great odds. Maybe I could make it four, if I could just… if I could just fucking *concentrate*.

That's when I saw Lord Loringham fall backward, a massive gash across his chest. The strength went out of my limbs.

Two seconds later, the world blew up.

I could actually hear the magic come into being, coming down from an unseen place in the heavens like a bolt of lightning and spreading out into a massive bulwark that bathed everything in the purest of light. It didn't do it gently, either – the whole ground shook as it hit, gutting the street, shattering bricks like they were made of tinder. Perhaps the Goddess had had quite enough of us and our arrogance.

But this wasn't just a light. This was light with substance, with texture. Blinding though it was, I couldn't bring myself to shut my eyes. I had to know what it was made of, how it got there. The translucent wall that had sprouted before me pulsed at my touch, particles of light and electricity moving out of the way but not retreating, holding fast together like tiny living bricks.

On the other side, I could make out one of the Guards, quite shocked as he tried in vain to pull his weapon out of the light-wall. How was it held there? Where did all this come from in the first place? And whatever did happen to the man I'd "stopped?"

There were more important things to worry about.

Trying to shrug off the pain, I moved to kneel by John Loringham, who had not moved much though he struggled to sit up, clutching at the front of his jacket as the blood began to seep through and pool around his fingers. He coughed, trying to form words that would not come. "Stop," I told him. "Just lay back. Don't move."

"I should have…"

"I said stop – you're hurt." Hurt bad, too, but I wasn't going to say that part. His wound made mine look like a paper cut.

"You both are. Holy hell." I looked up and saw a rather welcome sight then, a big, tall, Eislandisch-looking gent in his best armor – now scraped and dented up, just a little. Tristan almost fell to the ground before us, all the color drained from his face, but the weirdest part was his eyes. As we looked at each other, I saw little streaks of white against the blue of his irises, a bit like clouds wafting in on a summer's day. It was so impossible, so *bizarre*. Well, no more bizarre, I supposed, than time magic or healing magic or whatever else was out there. Why *not* the ability to conjure up big walls of light?

"Brother, you..." I started, but he cut me off.

"We need to get you out of here." Tristan was trying so hard to keep what was left of his composure. His expression was set in stone, though his hands shook as he tried to assess the extent of his father's injury.

The pain in my side began to feel a lot like guilt. "Brother, it's my fault. I should have been there." I didn't know what else to say – I let the words just fall.

But Tristan just shook his head. "It's not important. Just try to keep pressure on that wound for a minute."

Blood had now darkened a large part of my jacket, and I could feel my clothes wet against my skin where the Guard had struck me. Since there was no sense in arguing, I did as he said, holding my left side with my right hand to try to put a little pressure there. It made the whole experience decidedly more unpleasant, pain shooting out in all directions from the source. The world crackled and wavered around me.

The other Lords were now coming to our aid, and perhaps to his credit, Cen looked ready to turn that blade he held so fiercely on the next person who tried to challenge any of us. Otherwise, there was all kinds of doting and hang-wringing going on, but through it all, Tristan remained focused. He tore strips from his father's once-perfect jacket to dress his wound, moving fast but with a certain level of detached calm. He then did the same thing with me, all the while looking back and forth between what he was doing and to the rest of the plaza.

"The mage detachment is here," he said, almost too soft to hear. Or maybe I just couldn't hear over the thundering of my heartbeat and the roar of the square. "We've got to go."

The last thing I remember clearly is looking through the wall that shouldn't have been a wall and seeing the man I'd "stopped" there, still as motionless as marble. Then I met with the luminescent white streaks in Tristan's eyes one more time before it all faded to incoherent darkness.

# CHAPTER EIGHTEEN

## Union
*1 Spring's Green, 1272*
*Brin Jannausch*

I felt it before I saw it, like that moment just before a storm's first lightning strike. The rush of energy, an empty feeling in the air as the world holds its breath.

The Light.

I had seen it before, years ago, but the people around me had not. The Zondrell Royal Guard began to flee; the townspeople still left wandering the area followed. No one was sure what to think of the way Light spawned not from the hands of some god, but from a man. Strange it would come from that particular one, but I knew. Not even looking, I knew. Call it Prophecy, Fate, talent... blind luck? I once heard it called an "awakening" – that might be most fitting.

None of those rushing past me even looked in my direction, and maybe to my surprise, my blade was still clean. I had been ready to cut down the ones pursuing the boy Prince, but no fight was necessary. The Light had turned the Royal Guard's attention away from me and to their own safety. Cowards, all of them. Nonetheless, I remained on edge, wishing the mage-girl and the boy hadn't darted into the alleys, but I trusted I would find them again. As I started to move in that direction, I heard armored footsteps close behind me.

"You," I heard a stern, familiar voice say. "Eislander."

My hand tightened around the hilt of Beschützer, itching in anticipation. Oh, what I wouldn't give... But no. Not yet. I turned on Jamison Torven in all his finely etched platemail, his silver and his jewels, standing there unscathed while the rest of his city burned. Quite literally, in fact, at this point – mage reinforcements had started to descend on the square. The swell of their magic joined the energy of the Light, thickening the very air.

"I should have your head for what you've done." Torven was most displeased, but I would not give in to his wolf-like sneer.

"Escaping from the scene you created, General?" I asked. The question caught him off guard.

"No, *you* created this. You were paid to do a job. It was quite simple."

"You sent others. They failed."

Torven's storm-colored eyes narrowed. "Do you take me for a fool? I ought to kill you where you stand." His hand went to his blade then, sitting in its sheath while the blood of a King still oozed from the opening. And he was not alone – others were around, a small group of loyalists hovering near him. Too many, and most of them in full armor. I had nothing but the blade on my back, and I found myself hesitant to draw. We stood there staring at each other, the sounds of mass confusion settling over us like a pall.

One of the soldiers said something in the General's ear. Then another started to move on, and after taking a moment to spit on my boot, Torven followed. "Your gold is forfeit, Eislander," he said as he and his contingent hurried on down the road.

Your *life* should be forfeit, I thought. Though that's not what I said to his back. Instead, I told him, "So this is how one General treats another. I will remember that." If his men were not with him, coaxing him on as they were, he might have stopped. I saw the hesitation in his step. Not that I expected him to know me by sight, not twenty-five years later. Still, at the last battle of the war, it was I who threw the *Zondern* high commander into the Drachensprung gorge, putting Herr Torven in charge of Zondrell's troops. That day, he surrendered as the Light filled that gorge with its thundering death – not a week later, the treaty was signed and the war ended.

By the River, those were strange times. A fleeting thought made me wonder what Torven remembered about that battle, what he thought he saw when the Light descended upon his men. I will never say I understood it; many men would even say what I remembered was the ramblings of a lunatic. Even those running from it now would never truly believe what they saw.

A part of me wished Torven would turn around and ask. Was it the same Light as before? It was just a small part, though, because such reminiscence would no doubt come at the tip of a blade. I had no wish to take on those ten men at once, not when I had other concerns – three of them, to be exact. So I let my would-be quarry disappear into the streets of Zondrell, going to the palace he thought was now his.

First things first: the Saint. Where did she run off to? I told her not to go far, but it was no certainty that she would listen. I supposed it was fortunate she was near at all – the situation could have been much worse. I tracked back to where I'd left her, in the alleyway just up ahead, then followed along to the east, away from the doomed festival plaza. This was the only logical way to go, and soon I found what I was looking for.

The two women and the little boy had stopped at a crossway, trying to decide which way to go. When they heard me, they jumped in terror. I held out empty hands and shook my head.

"What are you doing here?" the red-headed healer asked, violet eyes wide and piercing, much the way *hers* used to be. It took a second look to be sure I was not seeing a different Saint, from a different time in my life. They looked so alike in that moment. Emotion rushed through me, and try as I might to push those thoughts away, they came in like a tidal wave… or like Light pouring forth from Drachensprung Gorge.

I tried to shake the thoughts loose as I regarded the others. The older girl looked a bit like Herr Vestarton with her dark hair and light bronze skin – pretty, even for a *Zondern*. She clutched the boy's hand, while the child himself just blinked at me. He seemed, as they say in Eislandisch, *unter Schock,* his face gone blank, dark eyes vacant. I did not blame him – I would be the same way at his age if I had just watched someone slaughter my father in the coldest of blood.

"I told you, this place needs a Saint."

"What does that mean?"

"It means there are men here who need healing. But you knew that already."

Now her face softened, honey-colored brow wrinkling. She started toward me. "Is it . . ?" The words stuck in her throat.

"Did you not feel the magic? I can only guess. Come. See for yourself."

The girl, Andella, looked back at her companions, then again at me. "What about the boy? Do you even know who this is?"

"I do. He should be careful if he values his throne."

This was all it took to put the child in tears. Ready for that throne, he was not. The dark-haired girl put her hands on his shoulders, tried to comfort him to little avail. "And what do you propose we do, eh?" she said, turning on me. "We're not leaving him here, and you're not taking my friend to who-knows-where alone. I don't know who the hell you think you are."

This one was definitely related to the Shifter... that's what we used to call the Time mage, so long ago. Herr Vestarton was our Shifter now, though, and this woman clearly shared his look and temperament. I took a step closer and leveled my gaze at the fiery *Zondern* woman. "Vestarton, *ja?*" She cocked her head. "Your relation is up the street. Maybe hurt, hard to say. Come or not, but your friend is needed."

The two women exchanged glances. Then Andella knelt by the boy prince to speak to him on his level. "Prince Edin, can you make it if you come with us? You'll be safe, I promise you."

The boy wiped his pale cheek and nodded. Where else might he go on his own, after all? As young as he was, he still knew the value of safety in numbers.

"Are you sure about this?" the Vestarton girl asked.

"I told you, I know him... we have to go back."

The Vestarton girl nodded with a wistful escape of air, took the boy's hand again, and they followed me back through the alleys, out into the now nearly deserted street, toward the stage. The closer we got, the louder it got – fighting, shouting, running. The stench of sweat and gore and battle grew worse, too, hanging in the air like a nagging cough that refuses to go away.

The Light had faded. It no longer bathed the whole plaza in its glow, becoming a sheer glimmer, stretching halfway across the street. Twisted stone lay in its wake. On the other side of the stage wall, I had to admit I was relieved to see that the fading was a natural occurrence, and not because its caster was on the brink of death. Others around him, it seemed, were not so lucky.

Andella almost lost her footing running to them. The Vestarton girl was close behind, pulling along the boy king with tears in her eyes. The plaza around them was littered with trash, lost items, and bodies, dozens of dead and wounded. Even one was standing, paused by Time magic in mid-battle and now quite, quite still. Perhaps it all could have been worse, or perhaps they had just taken the fighting to other streets. At any rate, it was a scene that made my blood harden in my veins.

Torven was right about one thing. I *had* created this, all of it. But what choice did I have? Following through with what Loringham had paid me to do would have ended the same way. Those soldiers were ultimately loyal to the General, not to the King. Damn these *Hurensohn* people and their politics. Damn my stupidity for thinking I could do the right thing – I should have known by now that "right" did not exist, not here.

I stood apart from them, watching them find each other, searching for meaning amongst the loss. Andella was at once admonished and praised for being here, in a place she was not supposed to be and yet, was needed so badly. Half a Council of old rich men stood about, confused and angry; the fat one fought over custody of the boy with the Vestarton girl while the others watched in disbelief as the violet glow began to envelop Andella. She seemed to have limited control over it, as her light faltered and started, a soft but troubled brilliance that sparked at times, seeking to fulfill its purpose and aid those in need. It was, in a word, beautiful... just as it always had been.

The magic began to build and reach its tendrils out to the nearby wounded. Nearby, Herr Vestarton writhed in and out of consciousness while my sister's husband laid still on the ground, blood-splattered, torn and held together by makeshift bandages. It was to him that I went, but not without my most formal bow to his son first.

"Lightbringer."

Young Tristan's eyes were wild and they reminded me... no, not like before. The Light in Tristan was streaks of brilliance against the blue, not those careful concentric circles. These were the spokes of a wheel, lines of stars coming from the darkness at the center. As he stared at me, trying to find words that would not come, I realized that he was as much *unter Schock* as the little boy prince. Well, given the situation, I could empathize. I turned from him before he decided to draw his blade or do something else equally daft, though – I could sense it coming. It was the sort of thing men like him did when all else seemed lost.

I knelt at his father's side. "Johann," I said. I found it difficult to look him in dark eyes that were fading, yet still open and aware.

"What happened?" he breathed through the pain. "This... wasn't supposed to be."

"Torven did not trust you. He posted his own archers." I chuckled in spite of myself – as much as I hated to admit, it was a brilliant move.

"You should have... taken the shot on him when you could."

"Either way, the outcome would be the same. I told you the loyal ones would draw steel for him. And they did."

Loringham's head dropped back a bit, gazing toward the sky. "You're... probably right, but it was our best chance."

"Our only chance," said a man at my back. I turned to glare at a gaunt-faced, spindly man – another of these Lords of Zondrell. "Now it's all fucked up."

"You did get what you wanted in the end, *ja*? A dead King?" At this, the man and a few others within earshot scoffed and postured.

"No, for Catherine's sake, man. We wanted one that would act in the best interest of Zondrell, that's all."

"So, someone... pliable." I snorted and turned from them, eying the little boy prince for a moment. I wondered if he understood that these men might not be his friends for very long.

Before the conversation went further, the Saint was there, joining me by Johann's side. She had tears in her eyes, not as much from sorrow but from the magic flowing out of her. It was not, as I understood, an "easy" magic to wield – there was surely pain, and much of it. Would she have the strength to bring healing to all of the wounded here? I rather doubted it, but this girl was one who would try.

And try she did. Her cheeks grew flush with the strain but indigo light filled the holes in Loringham's chest. It snaked around his body and embraced him, then moved on, seeking more blood to staunch, more wounds to quell. The magic floated along almost on its own, an elegant ribbon of blue-purple that was not quick, but its movement was purposeful, guided by this slip of an auburn-haired girl. I watched the violet whirl within her eyes once more until she collapsed, saved from bruising herself on the hard ground by the quick arms of her man.

I might as well have been looking in a mirror from twenty-five years ago, and the thought sent the coldest of chills through my being.

# PART THREE

"Awaken," said the Gold Dragon in a booming tone. "Arise and come at me once again."

But the noble Sayaf could not. He ached and he bled and he wheezed, but the Gold Dragon had never touched him.

"Why, Gold Dragon? Why can I not best you in combat?" he asked.

"I am not here to be bested, good Sir. I am here to serve you."

But the noble Sayaf would have none of that. He reared back, sword in hand, then fell on the spot.

As his soul broke free of its mortal shell, he smiled. "Finally, I see," said he. "And I am awake!"

-Unknown Katalahni author, 542 (approximate)

# CHAPTER NINETEEN

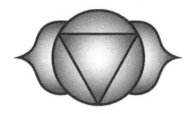

## Awakening
*3 Spring's Green, 1272*
*Andella Weaver*

I had the strangest dream – so vivid, more than any dream I'd ever had. I was walking through a forest and came upon a sheer rocky wall, a cliff that went all the way up, up into the sky. Clouds covered the top, and I couldn't see where it ended. It just kept going up, maybe for miles. It was nothing like the rolling mountains of Doverton, pockmarked by rocks and valleys within valleys but not really all that tall. This mountain was enormous, its rocks forming sharp edges like razors. Or swords... wait, on a little outcropping just above my head I could see a row of real swords, driven blade-first into the stone. I climbed up to investigate.

It wasn't just one row. When I got there, I realized there were dozens of them on this ledge, aligned in perfect straight lines, north to south. Each one was a little different from the next – a thin Lavançaise-style sword here, a wider Zondrean broadsword there, and so on. Some had decorations, some were plain, but all had one thing in common – they were covered in blood. The blood of their enemies. Enemies who won, in the end.

"Do you hear?" a woman's voice said, making me jump. I didn't realize I wasn't alone. The owner of that voice was kneeling at the far end of the sword-rows, dressed in a simple white dress with a brown cape draped over small shoulders. Its hood obscured her face.

"I don't know," I said, not sure what I was supposed to listen for.

"The wind. It sings with the blades."

I listened, and after a while, I could hear it, too, a high-pitched tinkling sound, whistling as it weaved its way through the rows. "What is it?" I asked the girl.

"It carries them to their next place." Her voice had the twisting lilt of a Lavançaise.

"Next place?"

"Wherever you believe it to be. Paradise for these ones... *oui*?"

"I... guess? Who were they?"

"Soldiers of Zondrell. I feel bad – I could not help." Now she looked up, and I could see slivers of white-lavender light peeking out from under the hood. "That is wrong, *oui*?"

"Wrong to want to help?"

"I work for the yellow-haired Eislandisch, over there." As she pointed somewhere to the right, I saw nothing but roiling mist. "Zondrell is the enemy, but I feel bad. Do you think these men wanted to die?"

I shook my head. "Does anyone?"

"The ones I cannot help, they go so fast. They charge toward death. I think... maybe some men do want to die. Maybe they have nothing else to live for."

"But everyone has *something* to live for, don't they?"

"Who is to say, Mademoiselle? Not I." Quickly, she rose from her spot and started to walk toward me, though her face was still shrouded by that cloak. I so wanted to see what was underneath. "When you find out, you will tell me?"

She started to walk away then, turning toward the mist and whatever lay underneath. It didn't even occur to me right away that her feet hardly seemed to touch the ground. "Wait!" I called after her. "Who are you?"

"You do not know *une Sainte* when you see one? They must not have mirrors in Zondrell." Awkward girlish giggles followed her out of sight, and I was left with the weapons of these unnamed soldiers, wondering what in Catherine's name an "*une Sainte*" was.

**

I might have had other dreams after that. I don't remember them. Eventually, my eyes blinked open to a dim room lit by some small candles on a desk off to the right, a large mahogany desk with elegant carvings on the front and two neat stacks of books on it. Slumped over it was a not-so-neat head of yellow-gold hair.

"Oh... Ouch." My back and neck felt so stiff, even though the bed was as nice as money could buy, fluffy and soft and clad in good linens. It was dark outside the window, so maybe I'd been asleep for a few hours. Well, I didn't even remember how I got here, but it was good to be back in the quiet confines of the Loringham estate.

As soon as I swung my legs over the side of the bed, Tristan was up, alert in his chair. The realization that I was awake seemed to come over him the way molasses pours from a jar. Once it finally hit him, he leaped up and wrapped me up in his big, strong arms.

"Well, it's nice to see you too," I said into his silken shirt. We parted then, and I looked up into eyes that weren't amused or even happy. They were very, very tired, but relieved... and they had the strangest luminescent lines in them, too, little brush-strokes of pure white spoiling his otherwise clear blue irises. I didn't remember seeing that before. Well, I didn't remember much of anything from earlier. "What's wrong with your eyes?"

He shook his head, ignoring my question. "I thought you might not..." he started, then trailed off. "Are you okay? Let me get you some water or something."

As he started to get up, searching in a bit of a panic, I pulled on his sleeve. "Hey, um, it's okay. I feel fine, I guess. Why, how long have I been asleep?"

"About two days, two and a half. I just, um... we've been worried."

Two days? Yeah, I'd be worried too. And suddenly, I was. "You're kidding, right?" Of course he wasn't – he was as serious as a sword through the chest.

"I wish I was. Are you sure you feel okay?"

"Um, I guess so. You don't need to dote over me, if that's what you mean." My smile wasn't returned, but it didn't last anyway. I tried to recall what happened before I fell asleep for two days, and it came in little flashes, just here and there. I remembered feeling the magic, so much energy moving through me, definitely effortless but there was a burning sensation there too, unlike anything I'd ever felt with Fire magic. But I didn't have much control over it, and so it was just flowing, going everywhere and anywhere. I also remembered seeing blood all over those nice clothes that the Lords had on – Alex, Lord Loringham, some of the others I didn't know. I wanted to help them. I think I did. "So, does that mean everyone else is…?"

"Alex stayed here overnight, went home yesterday. He'll be fine."

"Your father?"

Tristan looked away, off to a dark, empty corner of the bedroom. "He's still asleep. He, um… hasn't stirred much."

"Oh." I didn't know what else to say to that. "Wait, what about the boy? There was a little boy there, I remember – oh, the Prince!" Yes, the Prince, how could I forget? The poor child. My mind's eye leapt to a picture of the fright in his sweet little face.

"I guess he's safe with Lord Miller, but it's pretty bad out there."

"What do you mean?"

He gestured toward the front window that faced out to the street, and I went to it, eager to know. What I saw was a very different sight from Festival morning. It was nearly night, but red moon Sarabande hung low and brilliant already, helping to light the way even though all the street torches weren't lit yet. Not that it mattered – there was hardly anyone out there anyway. Usually, Gods' Avenue was teeming with people going this way and that, lots of nobles in fancy clothing, the occasional carriage or horse-mounted rider, that sort of thing. This evening, though, the only people down there were grim-faced soldiers, moving along at a sharp clip. Some wore the traditional black and silver livery of Zondrell with the big falcon on the front, but a few were just in plain black, many of those with no armor at all, just a sword or a spear in hand. Oh yes, they were all armed, and they were all at the ready. Ready for what? I wasn't sure I wanted the answer.

"No one's allowed out after dusk," Tristan said in a low voice. "It's too dangerous, at any rate. We've all paid to have those mercenaries guarding our street, but there's a lot of fighting around town."

"Fighting?" I couldn't imagine people just hauling off and hitting each other all over the city like that. It was... barbaric.

"There's factions – the ones who supported the King, the ones who didn't, the ones somewhere in the middle."

"But the Prince is now the King, right?"

"They don't know that. Torven's on the throne right now. Don't expect he'll give it up easily."

Torven. The General. That man in the dark ornamental armor. I remembered his face, full of determination... almost valorous in a way, despite an unmistakable streak of cruelty. I wondered how all of this even happened in the first place, and why. Well, I'm sure it wasn't the first time the throne of Zondrell or anywhere else was contested like this. I had read many historical accounts of just such events, but that was all in the past, some in the far, far past. It didn't happen today. We were civilized folk, after all, weren't we?

Looking again into his eyes, another flash of a memory struck me. A flash of a flash, if you could call it that. I remembered a glow that wasn't any magic I'd ever seen settling across the square, a sort of bright radiance that hovered in the air. "So, can I ask you something else? About your eyes?"

He uttered a mirthless chuckle and looked down at the stone floor. "Yesterday, while I was watching after you and Father, I read your book, on *Lebenkern*. Most of it, anyhow. It's not the easiest read. And the answer is, I don't know. It tells this story about an old man and some other men who protect him from all sorts of things that happen along a journey to Lavancée from Eisland. Turns out the old man is a king, and the others heal his wounds, turn his enemies to statues, and shield him with bolts from the heavens. When they get to Lavancée, the king holes himself up in a mountain somewhere to meditate, and his friends' magic fades. End of an era, or something like that."

"I got some of that, when I tried to translate it, but it has that prophecy in it..."

"That part was what the king said before he closed himself off to the world." He looked back up at me, and I swear those streaks of white in his eyes flared for a second. "Look, I don't claim to understand any of this. I know what happened to me – it was exactly like it said in that book, a shield from a bolt of lightning. And I think I could do it again, if I tried. Not sure about that, but it's the sort of thing that could... help people? *You* can help people. Alex can help people. We might be the only ones in the world who can do what we can do."

Those words had weight, real weight. I had thought all of these things before, of course – it was at once both terrifying and amazing. "Maybe," I said. "Archmage Tiara thinks that maybe everyone can use magic, but we just don't all know it yet. Speaking of which... what about the Academies? Are they safe?"

"More or less. The Military cadets are guarding the mages. No one gets in or out of the complex right now. Probably better that way." He came up to me and caressed my hair and cheek, gently. "Don't worry about it right now. We can try to go over there later."

He was trying so hard to be calm and reassuring, but I could tell it wasn't easy. That hand trembled as he drew it away, and his lips were drawn tight into what couldn't quite pass as a smile. "Right. Sure," I said, getting ready to say something else until a soft knock followed by the door opening wider behind us interrupted my thought.

"I thought I heard you. This is good to see." Tristan's mother, Gretchen, was the pinnacle of grace, even with eyes rimmed red and skin even more pale than usual. As she smiled at me, a tiny tear escaped the corner of one eye.

"I feel a lot better," I said. "How is Lord Loringham?"

At this, her angular face darkened. "He is... quiet," she replied in that rolling Eislandisch accent.

I needed no further push. I started toward the door – the Lord and Lady slept just down at the end of the hall. "Let me go help. I can try again with the magic."

"You're not up to that, are you?" said Tristan, folding his arms across his chest. "I mean, I don't want you to strain yourself." No, he didn't, but I could also read him a bit better than he might have given me credit for. He would have liked nothing more than to see his father wake from his long sleep tonight, too.

Maybe I was overconfident, but I felt good. Strong. Almost normal. And now I thought I understood the "secret" of my newfound magic – as long as someone needed it, the magic would be there. When they didn't, it lay dormant. I wasn't sure if I would ever be able to just summon it on command, but when there were wounds to mend, it was at the ready, as bright a spark as my old Fire magic, flowing so freely I didn't even have to think about it. I... well, I guess I could live with that.

I followed Tristan and his mother to where Lord Loringham slept, now calm and breathing deeply, but I could tell there had been times of unrest, too. The bedsheets – lavish, silken, and brightly colored like everything else in the vast master bedchamber – lay askew over most of his body, save part of his chest and shoulder peeking out on one side. As I sat on the bedside chair that was still warm from where Lady Gretchen had been keeping her vigil, I could smell the poultices under his bandages. A rich, earthy smell, a little minty, and it so reminded me of caring for Tristan, back in Doverton. They didn't really look so much alike though, Tristan and his father, but looking closely, past the salt and pepper beard and the slight weathering in his bronze skin, it was there. Their eyes were the exact same shape, more almond than round, and even though the nose and cheekbones were definitely not the same, the fullness and shape of the lips were identical. It made me wonder what Tristan would look like with a beard, which was an awfully silly thing to think when I should have been trying to work on my magic.

Well, what was there to work on? It just "happened," didn't it? So I waited. I watched Lord Loringham's chest rise and fall with his breath. I started to wring my hands together, as if somehow that would help speed things up. Was he not hurt enough? Maybe if I touched him... I reached out and put my hand by his heart, so gentle, almost hovering there. And in that tiny space between my hand and the sheets, I felt something grow warm. A tiny bit of purplish light peeked out, but I resisted the urge to pick it up and look, to see it in its full glory. Even when it got so warm that it was almost unbearably hot, I held it there, hoping that energy was doing its work.

Then it was done. Over, just like that. I didn't will it to stop – the magic just decided it was finished for now. It left behind a chill like a winter wind had just swept through the room, and I drew my arms across my chest for warmth.

"Is he...?" Lady Loringham had stood there in the doorway watching me the whole time, wide-eyed.

"I guess he's better than he was before," I said, not sure what else to say. He was still unconscious, though his breathing seemed steadier, less forced. "You could take a look at his wounds, I suppose."

Tristan shook his head, putting his hand on his mother's arm before she took off to start unraveling bandages. "Give it some time. Let him rest. We've done all we can do right now."

"Right, all we can do." I didn't know if that was true. I wanted to keep going – why couldn't I? Then again, I was so tired, and cold. Maybe if I waited and tried again, it would be enough to bring Lord Loringham back to consciousness. Yes, that's exactly what I would do... right after a nap.

# CHAPTER TWENTY

## Questions

*3 Spring's Green, 1272*
*Tristan Loringham*

I tried to go back to sleep, but I just couldn't – too much to think about. That first night, I hadn't slept much at all, and the second I only found respite in total exhaustion. I had spent a good part of that day sparring with my practice dummy in the courtyard, trying to get my mind off of everything. So much worry, so many questions… I had grown accustomed to that, but this was a whole new level of anxiety. My mother kept looking at me for answers I didn't have, Andella and my father were both in a coma – at least Alex had woken up and was as "all right" as he was going to be for the time being.

Now, nearly three days later, my father was still not awake, despite Andella's best efforts. My mother, miserable and frightened yet as stubborn as any Eislander, refused to go to sleep, to let me take over her vigil at his side for a while. She damn near shoved us out of the bedroom once the healing magic had done all it was going to do.

"Go rest," she bade. "You need your rest."

"So do you, Mum. Really, let me…"

"Go. Rest."

*Damn it, just listen to me, please?* But that was the last I was going to hear on the subject, so I sighed and nodded.

For her part, Andella was in agreement, and seemed to have no trouble going back to bed. I even laid down with her for a while, staring up at the ceiling counting divots in the stone as she drifted off. She was still weak, much more than she let on, and using more of that magic probably didn't help. I knew that and still, I let it happen. *You don't own her, jackass. She can make her own decisions.* I guess I knew that, too.

By the time I could see the late-time moon peeking into the black sky, I couldn't take it anymore. I could only listen to the random sounds of the night – the little bumps and thumps – for so long. Ever so quiet, I made my way downstairs, thinking maybe a stiff drink might force my eyes shut.

*My crazy eyes.* Even in the dim torchlight of the downstairs hall, I could see myself in the mirror there, and I couldn't help but stop. Alex sometimes called himself a freak... I was starting to see what he meant. Not that I cared so much about what people might say. Dozens saw me, saw what I was suddenly capable of – it sure wasn't a secret anymore. But the way it touched my eyes, I couldn't quite understand. I had never had any magical talent before, or even any interest in it, so maybe that was why it didn't seem "complete," just a few brushstrokes of white over what was always there. They seemed to come out of the pupil, a set of spokes like in a wheel. Toward the top, there were many lines, maybe ten or twelve, but as they circled around toward the bottom, they grew more sparse. They sparkled, too, but didn't whirl and pulse like I'd seen in other mages. If someone asked me to use that magic right then, I wouldn't have had a clue. Maybe it was fear of doing something wrong, but during the past two days I had thought about how to summon that force within. Nothing came, nothing stirred. I felt as normal as normal could be, all those familiar dull aches and pains still lodged in my muscles. Everything was just as it had been, except for those eyes with their weird streaks of light.

Good Lady Catherine, I *definitely* needed a drink. Though when I entered my father's study, where the best stuff was kept, I found the decanter on the center table empty, and one of the bottles of brandy in the cabinet missing. I might have found this odd if I didn't see the reason right away, leaning back in my father's good chair and staring out the nearby window. While he wore good clothes – a clean brown tunic and simple pants to match – he also sported a ratty yellow beard with the tiniest bit of white mixed in.

"What are you doing here?" I asked in Eislandisch, thinking I'd get a better response with his native language.

My mother's brother slowly reached for his drink. A hundred Royals a bottle, and the man was just drinking straight from it like it was common swill. "Your mother insisted I stay, since there is no leaving this city now," he replied, words a bit more slurred than usual. He spoke Zondrean, though – odd, but it was his choice, I supposed. "Do me a favor, *ja?*"

"What's that?"

"Make sure your father gets that." He gestured toward a hefty bag of coins on the desk as he set the bottle back next to it. There had to be several thousand Royals in there, and a quick check confirmed it.

"That's... a lot of coin."

"I am giving him his money back. You can count, if you must."

"Not necessary," I said, shaking my head. Not that I trusted him – I just didn't care that much. My interest was much more in what that money represented. "What did he pay you for?"

"Your father tells you nothing of his business?"

"No, not really." *And maybe he'd never have the chance.* I tried to push that distressing thought out of my mind.

"Well, it matters little now. The whole thing, as you would say, is gone to hell." Brin chuckled, but there was a shadow over his rough, angular features.

"Alex said that my father and the others were double-crossed."

More chuckling, breaking into a full, hearty laugh. "They were doing this themselves. What did they expect? Your Lord Torven is no idiot." When I looked at him, puzzled, he took some pity on me and continued. "My target was Torven. The Councilmen and the General already had an arrangement to target the King. Who double-crossed who? Had they simply gone through with what Torven wanted, things might be different. Or, maybe worse. Hard to say. Either way, the city loses." He lapsed into silence, taking another drink.

"I just don't understand why they did this in the first place. Why now?" I said, filling that awkward hole in the conversation.

"Not for me to know what you *Zondern* plot and plan. I am just hired help. Why not sit and have a drink with me, Lightbringer? Or do you prefer Golddrachen?"

"Tristan is fine."

His smirk turned into a wide grin for a moment, showing a glimpse of his upper teeth. "Then get us another bottle, Tristan, and have a seat."

*What was there to lose except more sleep?* I took another Dykhaniye Plameni out of the far cabinet and took the chair on the other side of the desk, the one that my father's employees and associates sat in when they came to do business. It felt more than a little strange to be there. When Brin failed to say anything for a few minutes, though, impatience took over. "Are you just going to drink down my father's whole collection then?"

The big man glanced at me with piercing clear blue eyes, then at the half-empty bottle in his hand. After taking a long pull, he offered it to me from across the desk. "Have a drink."

I hesitated, but that brandy was clearly not going to finish itself off. So, I gave it some help, the liquid going down smooth, but with a fire from the deepest pits of the planet. Another sip, and I could barely feel my lips.

"The Drakannyans do know their liquor," Brin said. "Do you know the first time I had this? It was a long time ago. In the War. You see... well, perhaps I should start in a different place."

"Start what? Is this a story with a moral?" *Or a point, for that matter?* I hoped so, and that's the only reason why I stayed and listened to him. He knew about the magic, about a lot of things – I knew he did, but he wasn't about to just spit it out, unfortunately. It occurred to me that there might be pain in those memories, which could explain the drinking. It could explain a lot.

"A moral? I leave that to the listener. But *ja,* a story you will get." Brin paused as he looked toward the window again. Half a dozen armed mercenaries strolled past, mostly quiet, but I could see a couple of them engaged in conversation. Catherine only knew what they could be discussing at this hour. "Reminds me of Kostbar. The city was occupied for months, you know. A whole winter. The *Zondern* will tell you that the cold and the snow drove them out – but we all know they like to bend the truth to their own means. No offense, of course."

"None taken." We both took another drink. Soon we'd need to open that second bottle.

"I was about fifteen when they came. They put us all to work. We fed them, we clothed them, we made their weapons and their armor. They turned us into traitors against our own people." Another pause to watch the armored men outside. "Do you know what I did? I chopped wood for their fires. Not a fun job, but it kept me busy. I only tried to take the axe to one of them once – they put irons on my legs after that."

"What about my mother? What did she do?"

"She made food, like many of the women if they were not sewing or sweeping. Or doing other things, at the will of the *Zondern*."

"You don't need to elaborate."

He looked down at the floor for a minute before continuing. "Do you know something about being a boy of fifteen tied to a tree stump all day? People tend to not pay much attention to you. And I heard them talk all the time. I would listen to what they said and try to make sense of it. Eislandisch and *Zondern* – the language is not so different. They say we all came from the same mothers in the beginning. After a few weeks, I knew some words. Another week, and I knew more. By the time of the snows, I could make a sentence. Imagine the look on their faces when they heard me tell them where they could stuff their axe, their irons, and their wood."

Now I felt a smile creep onto my own face. It didn't take a stretch of the imagination to see Brin as a scrappy young lad, happily telling every Zondrell soldier who would listen to him to go fuck himself. "They could have killed you for that."

"Could have, but I was... valuable. Or so said a certain Captain. I could learn, which meant I could be taught, and there was need of messages to be run around between different parts of the city. So they would send me to the streets, running until I knew every corner and every alley like my own bedroom."

"Alone?"

"Oh no. People who can learn also cannot be trusted – even the most *dummkopf Zondern* knows that. They would pass me off from one to the next across town, back and forth every day.

I was told I would have no family if I chose not to cooperate, and I believed them. Besides, their messages were interesting. Important. I knew where the officers stayed, and what they did with their day. I knew when things were to be delivered, and whether they had to worry about Eislandisch troops outside the walls getting to them first. Of course, they never thought a boy would understand any of those things." That wild spark in his eyes caught the light with his grin. "Our saviors came from the capital and landed the killing blow, but words pushed the *Zondern* out of Kostbar in the end, not weapons. That day, the Hauptmann leading those troops asked me how old I was. I told him I was eighteen, and he believed me. I left with his army the next morning."

"Just like that? What about...?"

"My sister? She was already gone, with her *Zondern* suitor. Our mother let her go, because she was in 'love,' you see. So, there was nothing much left for me in Kostbar."

How sad. But he didn't see that way, I could tell. I wondered if he ever had. When I closed my eyes, I could almost see Kostbar, blood staining freshly fallen snow as two armies vied for the city's future. And among the proud, light-haired Eislandisch stood a boy, tall enough to pass for a little older than his real age, taking his great big two-handed sword to the enemy.

"You saw a lot of battle, then. More than three years," I said. I only knew that because my parents met in 1245, and the war was over the year after I was born, in 1249. The way I'd heard it, my father's tour had ended just after Kostbar, when he got to go home to have a proper wedding. Alex's father came home with him, but was sent back to the battlefield the next winter. He finally returned about a month after the treaty signing with a bad limp that never quite healed. One of my earliest memories was hearing the story about how he'd taken on ten enemy soldiers at once and survived. I never knew if it was all true or not, but it made for a good way to entertain excitable little boys like Alex and me.

"Most of that time is not that interesting. I learned how to kill, and how not to get killed. You know how that is – the same for any soldier, anywhere. It was only the last few seasons when things changed." He finished off our first bottle, but not without a silent toast to someone, or something, off in the aether. "Do you get the headaches much?"

The change of subject caught me off guard. "I… yeah. Well, not so much the past day or two, but on Peaceday, right before… well, you know… I had a splitting one. Right here." I touched the center of my brow.

"Funny how some things are the same."

"Wait, you're not saying…" Well, I wasn't sure I knew what he was saying, and I was afraid to guess.

"That I am like you?" Now his smile was big again and his laugh so boisterous I thought he might wake the whole house up. "Not in my wildest dream. No, I knew someone who had the headaches, though. Listen, Tristan, if I keep going, you will learn, but you will also have more questions, and no answers. Do you want to hear this?"

Of course I did. "I'm ready," I told him. "Tell me what you know."

# CHAPTER TWENTY-ONE

## Fate's Path

*13 Dämmerungherbst (Autumn Twilight), 1247*
*Twenty-five years ago*
*Brinnürjn Jannausch*

The mornings were the same, most days, when out in the field. And I rarely left the field since the day I joined the army. I found I liked the routine – get up with the sun, patrol the perimeter, go have some *Morgentea* by the fire, then pick up and march. Some days, if we were close to a lake or a river, we got to take a bath – that was a treat. We never held camp for very long, as it was too easy for the enemy to figure out how to pin us down that way.

On the other hand, the *Zondern* would hold camp for weeks and months at a time, putting up outposts and makeshift villages in places they thought were strategic. At first, I thought this incredibly stupid. Why would they want to just be there, right out in the open like that? We could surround them, take our time to plan our assaults, put archers in the trees and the hills. Then we lost a battle, and I understood what Hauptmann Tausch meant by the word "entrenchment." That's what they did, fortified themselves in those camps and made us come and drag them out – the task was often harder than it sounded.

I transferred units... oh, about seven times, maybe eight. I liked Tausch, and wherever he went, I wanted to go, too. We trusted each other. He knew that when it was time to go to battle, I would go with no complaint. I would hold the front line. I would make sure no one got to him or his kommandants, and I would hunt down the enemy with no holding back.

For his part, Tausch could always be trusted to do right by his men. He never made us go a day without rest and food. He never ordered us to do something he was unwilling to do himself. He was a good swordsman, too – I learned a great deal in that first year just by watching him. Eventually, I learned enough that he wanted me to be one of his kommandants. You see, the Eislandisch army trains men on battlefields, not in schools. Officers keep the rest of the men protected, looking out for sneak attacks and doing whatever they could to protect the integrity of the unit. No one needed to go school for that.

So there I was, an officer in the army and two weeks shy of seventeen. It was funny every time I thought about it. I even got double the pay for all the danger that officers tended to face, which I took three quarters of and sealed up in an envelope. Each month, when we met up with the couriers, I sent that money back to Kostbar, to my mother. No note, just the money. I had little to spend it on out in the field anyhow. My fifteen gold a month kept clothes on my back and my blade sharp, and that was all I really needed.

I fought for Tausch for another year and a half. He still had no idea that I had two seasons until my eighteenth birthday, rather than my twenty-first, and I still found it all quite humorous. The trees had turned their bright gold and red when we joined a larger unit southeast of Kaiserlich, by Leuchtender See, the lake near the center of Eisland that seemed to glow with a silvery-yellow light at night. I had never seen it in person before, of course, just heard about it. That first night, I might have stared at it for a good hour and a half. It constantly amazed me how much there was to see outside the safe walls of my native Kostbar. No one knew why the lake glowed the way it did, though some said it was probably some creatures or fungus that grew there.

Some of the men had just pulled a good haul of fish from that very lake and were frying it up when Tausch approached me, our third evening posted there. He looked sullen, not himself.

"Jannausch," he said, coming over to where I sat with a group of other kommandants and soldiers. "Need to talk with you."

I gestured to an empty spot to my right. "Sit with us, Hauptmann. This man Aayden here says that he has a bottle of juniper berry wine to share with us."

"You, in private."

This was not like Tausch. He was cheerful, jovial, if a bit impatient at times, and not a man of many words. But, he never kept secrets. When he got an order, we got the same order. So, for him to want to speak to me in private was very strange indeed, but I complied. He was still my commanding officer. When we had moved to a place away from the crowds, I turned to him. "What is it, Sir?"

"I have a letter here." From under his leather breastplate he pulled a folded-up piece of paper, held closed with an intricate wax seal. "It's from Keis Sturmberg himself."

"What?" Keis Sturmberg, the high King of all of Eisland, did not send letters to just anyone. I had never met him, but I was fairly certain that he had better things to do than send letters to a single Hauptmann in his massive army.

"Here, read it." He handed it over, and I lifted the wax star-shaped seal. It opened with ease since it had already been broken once. The script there was as purposeful as its writer, neat and careful.

> *Hauptmann Eckhard Tausch,*
> *Your service to the Eislandisch army is commendable, and I am therefore honored to serve you with this request. The Kommandant in your service, Brinnürjn Jannausch, is required at Südensonnentor. Please ensure that he arrives before 17 Dämmerungherbst. I trust that you will be able to comply.*
> *Keis Sturmberg, High King of Eisland*

"You should be able to get there before the seventeenth, if you leave by morning," Tausch said when he thought I'd had finished reading. I had, but I was reading it again. And again.

"Why me? How would he even know my name?"

"Well…" Tausch trailed off, in the way that he sometimes did when looking for the right things to say. "I did send a commendation request about you to Königstadt. That was last spring, though."

"Commendation?"

"For what you did in the Battle of Falke Fällt. You should be in charge of your own unit, Jannausch. You don't need me holding you back."

My brow furrowed. "Holding you back from what?"

"From being a great warrior. You have a gift, boy, and it should belong to a more important unit. Schreiber's unit, maybe." There were seven Generals in the Eislandisch Army: Nülzin, Feuermark, Leidersonne, Läsgod, Risi, Sitenn, and Schreiber, the one that sent Tausch his orders. Generals were hand-picked by Keis Sturmberg himself, and they had to be good, strong, dependable men – or women – who could both fight and lead others to the fray. They had to be willing to make sacrifices, and hold their soldiers accountable. To me, Tausch served this description as much as anyone I knew, and yet, no one was making him a General.

"What about you?" I asked after a few minutes, trying to wrap my head around the idea of fighting for someone else.

"What about me?"

"You're a great warrior. You should go to Südensonnentor, too."

Raising an eyebrow, Tausch shook his head. "No. They're assembling something big down there; they need better men than me. What you did in Falke Fällt… I've not seen much else like it. How many *Zondern* did you send to the River that day?"

Of course he knew that I would have the answer to that. I had a collection, a pile of those little silver tags that the *Zondern* wore around their necks to tell who they were. After more than two years of combat, I had collected dozens of names, even though the act of taking those names never bothered me that much. Gore washed clean. Taking those names was my contribution to the cause, to rid Eisland of these vermin *Zondern*. They would find out just how unimportant, how *misguided* they were when they met the River's Edge. Besides, this was my life, the life I had chosen the minute I walked out of Kostbar for the last time.

"Thirty-seven," I said to Tausch, picturing the tags I had collected from that battle. It was the most I had ever taken in a single day. Without those men dead, including two of their countless dozens of do-nothing officers, we might not have marched out of the Falls. They might have taken our bodies all the way out to the sea instead, or we might have been living as slaves somewhere. But I was not about to take sole credit for our victory. "I saw a weakness in their defense. I was just trying to keep them from gaining an advantage."

"No one had as many kills as you that day. No one, not even the archers. I say, let their High General start to fear you, instead of just their lowly 'sar-gents,' 'loo-tenants' and 'kap-tans.'" I had to smile at Tausch's interpretation of how to pronounce some of their many inconsequential titles.

"So you think I should go and leave you all here, if I am so valuable?"

"I do hate to let you go." A tight-lipped frown came across his grizzled features. "But you have a brighter future down at Südensonnentor. Keis Sturmberg himself says so."

That he did – I had it in writing.

That was the last time I saw Tausch, after I left Leuchtender See the next morning. About two months later, I heard that their unit was ambushed by a traveling *Zondern* army. The lake made for bad cover – they had defended it and won, but not without many casualties. I assumed Tausch was among them, and perhaps I would have been, too. Fate had a strange way of doing its work.

# CHAPTER TWENTY-TWO

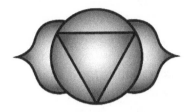

## Shifter
*16 Dämmerungherbst, 1247*
*Brinnürjn Jannausch*

On my own, I could move fast, and stay in the shadows of the trees. I had a map to tell me the way to go, which was good because I had little idea of where I actually was. Everything looked the same, just trees as far as the eye could see, great pines that shot up to the sky, punctuated only by the occasional rock formation. For two days I sought out the biggest of those rocks to make my camps by, as they would provide good cover in case the enemy was about. I never slept longer than a few hours at a time, though – my nerves were worse than I would have admitted to anyone out loud.

I only saw one enemy patrol, not far from what I thought was my destination. Twenty men, most of them in the typical plate with the black and silver livery – standard soldiers. The clinks and clanks of their armor would have awoken spirits out of the River, but even if they were still, they would never hear me. One of the first things I'd learned in the Army was how to move quietly. I melted into the forest, watching them, listening to their banter as they marched. The more I followed them, the more my hatred grew. Here they were, trespassing in my lands, and daring to laugh about it?

Twenty men. One of me. But I was the one who had once taken thirty-seven men to the River in an afternoon... and I was seventeen. Like most boys my age, my judgment had yet to fully catch up to me.

I crept in, moving only when they moved, pausing with the lulls in their metallic orchestra. They stayed on the road, of course, which meant I would have to leave the safety of the trees, but no matter. I had my father's sword, Beschützer, to protect me. I pulled it from its safe-strap on my back and drew it slow, with no sound, and it went into the throat of man at the back of the line, causing little more than a gurgle and a spray of blood. So far, the battle was mine.

I'd caught their attention, though. The next few wheeled around, grabbing at belts for their simple longswords. One raised a shield to bear. I attacked him first, hoping to knock him off balance and put him down fast – shield-bearers were almost more annoying than archers. A sweep to his knees was enough to force a stumble, not quite enough to push him over but enough to make him lower that shield. Blood spilled out of his neck like water flowing down the mountainside.

"*Ehre für Eisland!*" came my standard war cry as I spun around and felt my blade sink in between the chest plates of another soldier. From the side, I saw a flash, and a longsword skittered off the leather on my back as I dodged away. It was a dance of instincts, knowing when to move and when to strike, and it came easily for me. Even when someone's blade did find flesh, I barely felt it. Indeed, I reveled in it – it was all battle-thrill to me.

Dash. Slash. Block. Impale. By the time I knew it, six of them were dead. The next few seemed more hesitant than the last, but that just gave me more of an advantage. I leapt into them, Beschützer leading the way, crashing through the closest one's meager attempt to block. He fell backward into the man behind him, giving me another clean opening. That armor was only as good as the seams between the plates, and I knew every single one.

A clang followed by a loud "swoosh" by my left ear gave me little time to review my handiwork. I ducked low and stepped back, anticipating where he would strike next. This one was smarter than most – a blow I thought would come from the top darted in from the side instead. His blade bit through the leather and into my shoulder with a tearing sound and plenty of fire. More fire to fuel my rage.

I bore down and put the whole of my body into the man, knocking him several feet back, where he tripped and crumpled to the ground. His groan of pain, cut short by a sword through the windpipe, was nothing short of satisfying.

"Fucking hell, this one's mad," I heard one of them say to another.

"Leave my country, and you can live another day," I replied, using their native language like another weapon. It always did disturb them when they heard one of us "stupid brutes" speaking their tongue.

They were down to twelve, and me, I was hardly winded. I was quite ready to introduce them all to the River personally, but as I said, I was a boy – a headstrong boy with more fight in him than sense. I never thought to check and see if they had any wizards with them.

Something hit me square in the chest with tremendous force, and I found my vision spinning backward until I saw nothing but pines and clouds. The wind left my lungs. I gasped and clutched at my chest with one hand. Then something else struck me in the head, something unseen but with enough strength to make those clouds up above whirl and flash.

I heard armored boots approach, and grabbed for my blade. I could get up, I could focus, I just needed to get my bearings. I rolled to the side, leaning on Beschützer to help me to my feet, but one of those boots in my stomach put me right back where I was. I growled and tried again, this time keeping my sword free for use in my right hand while I clawed my way to something like upright with my left.

They underestimated me. I knew they did. With a battle cry dying on my lips, I lunged at the nearest wall of black and silver. When Beschützer hit something soft, I felt the spray of warmth across my face and it felt good. So very good.

But that feeling would not last. An invisible hand forced me face-first into the rocks and dirt then, and would not relent. Damnable Air magic – the worst kind as far as I was concerned. I could hear them laugh as they came up to me, readying blades, relishing in what would be their victory.

I came to a hard realization in that moment. I would die here, face-down on a road in the middle of nowhere, hundreds of miles from home. No one would know. No one would care. I could only hope to get revenge when I was summoned back from the River someday. I remember hot tears blotting out my vision. I remember struggling for breath.

Then the force holding me down was gone. I heard a voice, a strange voice in the distance, and laughing. But this was not the laughs of the *Zondern* – this was someone different. As I struggled to pick my head up, I realized how quiet everything had gotten.

They were still there. Eleven standing there, one with a blade risen high into the air overhead, but it did not come down. He was frozen, somehow become a statue of flesh and bone. No movement, not in his eyes, no air escaping his lungs in puffs of smoke against the chill air. And they were all like this, as if caught by an artist's brush.

"Ha, you are lucky one," said a man's voice with a very strange accent. I looked around, searching for its source, when someone moved amongst the *Zondern* statues. I gasped for breath and tried once more to stand. "No, no, you do that slow. I help you." Then there were hands on me, pulling me up from under the arms. I snarled in pain – now that the battle-thrill had faded from my blood, I was left with misery.

He got me to my knees and I put an arm up, warning him not to keep going. "Just... I need a minute," I said through clenched teeth. At least now I could get a good look at this stranger.

He was not tall but not short, stocky but not fat, with reddish dark hair and pale skin on boyish cheeks, marked with freckles. His thin almond-shaped eyes slanted down at the corners, but what was most interesting about them was the color. Silver, almost white, and I would swear they were glowing. More magic? Had to be. I reached for my weapon, laying discarded a few feet away.

"Whoa, whoa!" He waved empty hands over his head. "We are friends here, *da*? Friends!"

"Who are you?" I asked, not taking my eye from my blade. My voice sounded weak, cracking like an old man's.

"Me? I am Vremya!" His smile went from ear to ear. "You, you are man they send from the lake. Kommandant Jannausch?"

I nodded, not willing to offer much more information.

"*Da!* They said to watch for you."

"They? They who?"

"The Blondmen. You know, your people? You know, friend, you should not travel by yourself. Very dangerous."

I looked past him at the carnage I – we – had wrought. I still could not understand how men could be frozen with no ice magic. Who *was* this strange foreign person? "They had a mage with them."

"Yeah, he's done now. They're all done. And you? You can stand up?"

I was unsteady as hell, but yes, I could. I accepted as little aid as possible as I did so, coming face to face with the *Zondern* who would have put his sword through my skull. I had seen dead men with their eyes open, of course, but this was different. This was far worse, somehow. I thought to touch the skin of his cheek, to feel if it was truly alive or dead, but hesitated.

"No worries, friend," Vremya said at my back. When I turned to him I must have had the most concerned look on my face, because he reached up and patted me on the back. "He's done, like I say. No more threat."

"How?"

"It's... ah, magic. Vremya magic!" Something about this made him laugh aloud, inexplicably, for several minutes. "My little joke," he said when his chortling subsided. "Real name: Tokarov Nikita Vadimovich. Is long name, *da*? So Vremya is easy for people. It means 'time' in my language. So, is funny, you see?"

I did not. I was still wrapping my mind around the idea of magic that could end a man so... abruptly. That, and I needed to do something about my injured shoulder. With a small amount of help from Vremya, I wrapped it with a spare bandage from my pack. It wasn't much, but it would hold until I could see an herbalist.

"Some of you Blondmen call this magic 'shifting,'" Vremya continued. "Don't know why. But you can call it that too. Anyway, you no worry about them. We should go, *da*?"

"Go where?" I asked, blinking at him.

"To the place where the army is. South... Sunny... Something?"

"Südensonnentor?"

"*Da! Da!* That's what you call it. Come on, we should not stay here. They find their men like this, they get testy, them Zondrean."

I collected myself and put Beschützer back into its sheath, then back on the safe-strap across my back. As we moved down the road, I kept looking back at the frozen patrol. Even when they were well out of sight, I still looked over my shoulder every once in a while. Meanwhile, my companion hummed an unrecognizable tune, just loud enough for me to hear. "Vremya," I said after a while, "where do you come from to speak like you do?"

"Drakannya!" The strange little mage – shifter? – puffed up his chest, standing straight and proud. "Zolotoy Bireg. Nice place. You know it?"

I did not. I only knew Drakannya as a strange and distant land south of Lavancée – I could pick it out on a map. Women coveted the gems and gold that came from there, and I knew that the people had a reputation for being loud. This part fit Vremya well enough. "Drakannya is very far away," I said.

"*Da.* You not joke about that. I am long way from home. Your weather here, is not very good. Too cold."

"So what are you doing here?"

His laughter was sort of a half-snort, half-chuckle. "Work! Money! Why else do people come to this place? Eisland is very rich country."

To me, rich meant that people walked around dressed in fur and jewels and drank wine all day, which did not describe my experience of Eisland in the slightest. "What do you mean?"

"Them Zondrean, they want your gold, your diamonds, your silver, all that stuff. Lots of it in the mountains, and not that many people to guard it. Easy picking. Or so they think, *da*?" He smiled knowingly.

I spat a wad of blood-tinted phlegm on the ground. "They don't deserve to live," I said under my breath.

"'Every man gets what he gets.' Drakannyan saying. You, you got luck. You got me! But I seen you fight, too – you're good. No wonder they want you."

I still had no idea who "they" were, or what they wanted with me. All I knew was that I hurt all over, and I was certain I had a rib out of place. We continued on in relative silence for another hour or so until we came to the crest of an embankment overlooking a vast green glade, nestled deep into a crevice overlooking a much wider valley. A river flowed in from high in the mountains, ending in a pool there, surrounded by campfires, with people milling about alongside them. It was not quite dark yet, but the fires lit the place in a cheery sort of glow.

Südensonnentor. It was a gateway, a wide opening in the mountains that made passage into Eisland easy for Zondrell and its allies. It was through here that the *Zondern* sent in many of their men, stationing them at the city-state of Kellen to the south. Why we did not just go and march on Kellen, I had no idea, but it was not exactly close to the border. They had outposts that were, though. So far, Eisland had not pressed beyond the border into Zondrea at all save for Doverton, that small city-state in the west that was already half-Eislandisch anyhow. They welcomed us with open arms, no fighting required – I had been there, too, more than a year ago now.

How many miles had I marched since then? I had lost count, but looking on the map, it had to have been hundreds upon hundreds. And my body, at that moment, felt those miles, every one. I made it into the campsite with Vremya just as darkness had descended, and promptly fell asleep.

# CHAPTER TWENTY-THREE

## Saint

*17 Dämmerungherbst, 1247*
*Brinnürjn Jannausch*

I woke when the sun had just barely scratched the sky, sending tendrils of yellow, red, and purple over our mountainous cocoon. Rotermond, the moon the *Zondern* called "Sarabande" for some reason, still blazed overhead while Blauermond – "Larenne" – was just a sliver over the rocks to the east. Though there were many troops here, a hush had fallen over most of the camp, a hush so deep and still that I just sat and enjoyed it for a moment, letting the cold air fill my lungs.

Lungs, air... I could breathe so easily now. I felt at my ribs and there was no sting, no ache. How could that be? One night's rest could make a man feel better, perhaps, but it did not heal broken ribs. I began to pull off my tattered armor and undershirt, revealing nothing but pink skin. Some scars graced my chest and back, of course, scars I would have with me always, but the wound on my shoulder from yesterday was just another one of those, a fine white line. What was this? Some sort of dream? If so, then it was very real; I even slapped myself across the cheek to see if I would wake up. All it got me was a faint burning sensation.

"*Os de Chantal*," said a gentle voice behind me – a woman's voice, very unusual. Unlike the broken foreign cadence of that Vremya character, these words were smooth and lilting, almost songlike.

I spun around with a start to look upon a most striking creature, standing near my bedroll with dark robes wrapped around her for warmth. She was tall, though not as tall as most Eislandisch women, with thick black curls hanging about her face. Not a *Zondern* face, though. Despite the hair color, she was much prettier than any *Zondern* woman I had seen, with sharper features, more like an Eislander. Maybe she was some kind of Halben – a half-breed. But that voice, that language she used sounded nothing like Eislandisch or *Zondern* or anything else I had heard before. Her slightly dimpled cheeks were tanned bronze from spending too much time in the harsh northern sun, making her eyes stand out that much more.

Those eyes... I was as helpless as a rabbit in a trap. Up until this time in my life, I spent little time worrying about women. Oh yes, I had my childhood flirtations, but then the War started, the *Zondern* came, and I joined the Army. Women were often the furthest things from my mind, unless they were ready to carry a sword or spear to the front lines. But this woman was a different story. This woman had indigo-purple luminescent eyes that pulsed with their own special energy, and seemed so deep that if I looked long enough, I might fall right in. I could only hope for so much.

She smiled, accentuating her dimples. "*Comment allez vous, Monsieur? Mais no, pardon – Kommandant, oui?*"

I had no idea what she said. Frankly I didn't care. She could have talked to me all day in gibberish and I would have listened. Though I did understand the word "Kommandant." I shook my head with a shrug.

"*Non? Ah, non mots! Voici!*" She paused with a finger to her lips for a moment. "I have no Eislandisch," she said in words that were barely recognizable.

"Do... do you know *Zondern*?" It was worth a try.

She clapped, that smile back in full force. "Yes! You know that?" Her *Zondern* had a thick accent, but it was no better than mine.

"I know enough."

"*Bien sûr!* Then I can ask you: you are all right?"

"I guess so. I was hurt, before. Last night. Then I woke up, and I'm not so hurt now."

"*Oui*, I helped you. You fell asleep so fast you missed it." The way she said it, she sounded so pleased with herself.

"Missed what?" I asked, not quite sure I wanted the answer. If she had magic – and surely she did – I had never heard of magic that healed. If it was anything like Vremya's magic that froze people dead, I was unsure I wanted to know more about it.

Again, that finger to her lips. "If you are not so lucky, you may see it yet. You know, you should move around. The muscles need to work, and stretch. Come, I will help you."

Reaching out for her hand sent all kinds of thoughts into my mind, the myriad thoughts of the typical seventeen year-old boy. Now standing and closer to her, I could see her even better. Those eyes! I could not stop staring into them – they seemed to go on forever. It took a while to realize that such staring was not exactly polite.

With a smile, she brushed a curl away from her face and looked off toward the lake. "Over there, they make the food. You should have some to have more strength. I think Monsieur le Roi is there, too. He wanted to see you last night, but you were asleep! No good for conversation."

"Who is... Messer le Hua?"

Now her whole hand went to her mouth, sealing in tinkling laughter at my very poor attempt to repeat her strange words. "You call him something else, I think."

We did. We called him Keis Sturmberg.

I had never seen the man with my own eyes, but the circlet around his brow with the seven-pointed blue stargem set in it was all I needed to see. The King of all of Eisland himself was right here, right now, sitting by the fire just like any other soldier. This man was not just important, he was legendary, and he was in front of me – in the flesh! I dropped to one knee in the scrubby grass and bowed my head. It occurred to me then that I should have put on a fresh shirt instead of the sweaty and bloodstained old one from the day before.

"Kommandant Jannausch," he said, his voice deep, just a tad hoarse.

"Herr Keis Sturmberg, I... ah..." My words failed me. Tausch had said this was to be a big battle, but to have the

King here? I could not fathom what sort of commendation he'd written to get me summoned to Keis Sturmberg's side.

"Stand up, son. No need for all that. In fact, take a walk with me." He paused, said something in a foreign tongue to the mage girl, then stood and started off. Hesitant, I followed, keeping a pace behind, out of respect. Or something. Anyway, it seemed like the right thing to do.

"I expect that sort of thing from my servants, but not from my soldiers," the King said over his shoulder. I picked up my pace and dared to look straight at him, into sullen yet haunting eyes the color of a winter storm. His shoulder-length blond hair was thin but neatly groomed, as was his beard with small colored gemstones woven into it – the sign of a highborn Eislandisch man. He wore no jacket, his arms exposed to reveal a twisting mass of tattoos, though they were different than the kind many soldiers bore. His were colorful, intricate, pictures of everything from swords and spears to a series of seven interlocking reptilian creatures, things like something from a legend chasing each other in a perpetual circle. "That's a bit better. Hauptmann Tausch spoke very highly of you, you know."

"I... am honored to be here, Sir," I replied. As we walked by, a group of men starting their morning fires waved at us. Keis Sturmberg nodded back his greeting.

"You know, Brinnürjn Jannausch of Kostbar, I took the liberty of looking up your birth record – unusual name you have there. Family name?"

"No, my Lord. My parents were just fond of old ways of speaking."

"Indeed. So, how it is that one so young could be so accomplished, I wonder?"

My eyes went wide. I stared straight at him, almost unable to hear myself over the thundering of my heart. "My Lord, I only live to serve Eisland and drive the *Zondern* out."

"In that, I understand you are quite effective." He paused, one corner of his mouth rising in a sly smile. "I know what you're thinking, Kommandant. You can relax. Though if you were my son, I'd have you lashed to a post."

"My Lord, I only wanted to..."

"Fight. Yes, I know. It's what we all want. Almost as much as we want to keep our sons and daughters safe. I hope you at least send letters home."

"I send my pay to my mother every month, my Lord." I left out the fact that she very likely had no idea where I was, or if she would ever see me again. I had said nothing to her before I left with Tausch's army.

"Very good. Well, you are here now, and your reputation precedes you. Vremya told me you defended yourself against an enemy patrol yesterday."

Straightening, I lifted my chin. "I took down nine of their men, my Lord. Herr Vremya took down the rest."

"Well done. One less patrol to worry about. So what did you think of Herr Vremya?"

Good question. "I, um... have not seen magic like that. He seemed very powerful."

"Oh, he is. Most of the men here have not seen his work yet – it might disturb them. What you saw is indeed very unusual."

Unusual was not quite the word I would have used, but I pressed further. "That girl, too, the one with the purple eyes? I think she healed my wounds, overnight."

"She did. Didn't even need a bandage. Some of the men around this camp who have experienced her work say she is a Saint. I let them think this, but she's a rather ordinary Lavançaise girl from Quatremagne. Her name is Jade." That smile widened just a bit. "Tell me something, Kommandant – do you know the stories about dragons?"

"Dragons? No, my Lord." What was a dragon? Somehow, this was not how I thought a conversation with the King of all Eisland would go.

"Maybe I will have my other mage here tell you one sometime. She is Katalahni – they started all those legends, you know. But, the moral is that there are seven dragons, each one representing a certain type of magic: Fire, Water, and so on. One cannot exist without the other. An interesting allegory of sorts."

"So, all of your mages are foreigners?" It just slipped out. I knew it was rude as soon as I said it, but why would the King keep so many foreigners around him in the first place? Were there *Zondern* running around here, too?

"Just three. My Generals will tell you that these are my 'special' mages, and they are that. But I don't lay claim to them. I was just lucky to have found them and brought them here." We came to a stop before a rocky outcropping, where a blue banner bearing the seven-pointed star of Eisland fluttered in the breeze. "Do you know why I asked for you to come here, Kommandant?"

Not at all – I just shook my head. I was still trying to figure it out.

"Because I was looking for good men – the best men – to lead in what might be our most critical battle. I had a good feeling about you after I heard of your victory at Falke Fällt. Such a good feeling in fact, that recently I had a dream of you. My advisors think I'm seeing things, hearing voices, partaking in too much wine in the evenings, that sort of thing. I assure you, that's not the case. Dreams led me to Vremya, Jade, and Safaa. Dreams led me here, to Südensonnentor. Dreams led me to bring you to this battle. And we shall see how all of it comes together."

As a boy, I dreamed of playing by the water, of the occasional monster, of what it was like to be an adult. After I joined the Army, I had different sorts of dreams, most of them a tangled mass of brutality. They never bothered me – I never woke in a cold sweat, nightmares gripping my heart the way they did to some of my comrades. But I most certainly never had a dream that I thought would lead me somewhere, or left me hidden messages to decode. Rather than see this as a sign of madness, though, I wondered if Keis Sturmberg had dreams like that because he was important. Perhaps such dreams were specific to Kings. Though, if that were the case... "Did you have dreams before the *Zondern* invaded our lands?" I asked.

"I wish that I did, son. I wish that I did." The sly smile faded, just a little, as if the King were in deep thought. "These things I tell you because I feel you have a right to know, and we may not have this chance to speak later. For now, come, you need to learn more about the battle ahead."

And so we went back into the heart of the camp, where more soldiers had awakened to face the day, including a cluster of men wearing copper officers' bands at their throats. As Keis Sturmberg and I approached, I noticed a figure among them in dark-painted armor of small metal plates over leather. Some sort of sheer veil covered the person's head and face, wrapping around the neck like a scarf with the ends hanging down the back.

This person was the first to greet the King, stepping forward with a bow. From its slender form, I assumed it had to be a woman, and when she started to speak, it was confirmed. This one with a different kind of accent all together, guttural and very precise – the Katalahni who knew about dragons, I assumed. "The day finds you well, Sir?" she asked.

"Yes, Safaa, it's a good day," Keis Sturmberg said. "This is the new Kommandant I told you about, Herr Jannausch."

It felt strange to receive a bow from a woman such as this, when I couldn't even see her face, but I returned it in kind. "*Guten Morgen.*"

"Pleased to meet you. I assume by your rank that you have fought much?"

"I've been in the Army for almost three years."

Up close in the brightening light of dawn, I could see just a little through the filmy scarf around her head. Her skin appeared dark, black like coal, forming the outline of a thin face from beneath the tan-colored cloth. But even more interesting were the eyes peering out of a thin slit in that veil – I could hardly believe what I saw there. Instead of one color, I saw bands, circles of interchanging brown and white, surrounding her pupils. The white parts danced like the distant sparks of a storm.

I must have stared too long, as she put her hands on her hips and raised her chin. I could feel those eyes inspecting me, and a small "hm" escaped her throat. "I know what are looking at, Kommandant, and before you ask, I am simply awake. That is all." She must have taken my dumbfounded look as acceptance, as she moved on with no further explanation. "It is good that you have experience. Then when we talk of tactics, you should understand."

Tactics… well, I hoped so. To be honest, I thought it silly to plan out a battle so carefully when it would just become a mass of chaos on the field. At Falke Fällt, the plans Tausch and the others had drawn up fell apart within an hour – many of our men died because they knew the plan and nothing else. They failed to improvise. Me, I just charged ahead, seeking out the smallest enemy groups I could, taking them on one by one until the path lay clear before me. Maybe it was pure luck that one of those groups held their top captain, but when he was a bleeding corpse at my feet, suddenly the *Zondern* had no plan, either. It took little for us to gain back the advantage.

The plan for this battle was more complex, but it was all in the positioning. Some men on the ground to rush the *Zondern* outpost on the other end of the valley. Some sweeping in from each side. Some on ridges and overlooks, including the archers. We would squeeze them within their own walls – more of a hunt than a battle. If everything went as they said, our victory would be assured within the day, maybe two, and the enemy would suffer a tremendous blow. It might even keep them from sending in new troops permanently.

**

The planning discussions went on for hours, well into the afternoon. Every officer, from General Schreiber himself on down to Kommandants like me, knew their place and their duties, but by the time Blauermond was back in the sky, I was unable to think straight anymore. So much to remember, so much to take in. Too much, in my opinion... humble as it was.

As the officers parted ways for the evening, I found the purple-eyed girl – Jade – sitting by a campfire, a few soldiers around her. Standing in line, actually. One sat next to her, talking in a hushed tone, and two more appeared to be waiting their turn. Interested, I took my place behind them. What were they waiting here for?

Healing, of course, and maybe some confession so they could free their souls before they made their trip down the River. Each man in turn prattled away at her about things that bothered them while she evoked some kind of light, forming purplish ribbons that dove in to wrap themselves around wounds, seeking out pain like ice sharks circling prey off the coast. It was at once fascinating and frightening to watch. Suddenly I was glad I was unconscious when this must have happened to me.

After some time, the sky became speckled with jeweled stars, and it was my "turn." The solider ahead of me stalked off with little more than a nod in my direction, and I took his place. Jade smiled at me, eyes sparkling in the firelight, though her pretty face showed signs of fatigue.

"Oh, you too, hm?" she asked, in Zondrean.

In truth, I just wanted to sit by her. "That was your magic? Does it make you tired?"

Jade shrugged. "It does, but I am doing good for these people. I speak no Eislandisch, and yet they talk to me. I would be happy to know what they said."

"They are telling you their sins."

"Oh." A shadow darker than the circles under her eyes passed over her features. "My people do not have this idea. I know what sin is, but why would they tell me?"

"You tell someone else, a holy person, what you did wrong in your life, so that when you die, your soul floats in the River instead of sinking to the bottom."

"*Oui*, they do think I am this holy person. Saint, they call me. It's strange. My people have one goddess; she sees all and knows all, and she gives us magic. If everyone who had magic was a Saint, well, there would be a lot of holy Lavançaise people. But your people feel better when they say these sins. Maybe it is a good thing." She paused, then brightened again, cocking her head as she regarded me. "So you have these things, these sins, that you want to say to me?"

I was not raised in the most religious household. Oh, I believed in the River, that our souls went there to be reborn, but that was about the crux of it. Most Eislandisch I knew were this way. Some did believe that gentle souls that ran orphanages and apothecaries and such were Saints, and went to them to ease the suffering of their minds and hearts. These were the ones who didn't seem to understand that all life was suffering – the River was the place where you got to cast it off. Or so I liked to think. So when faced with this idea of confessing something, I was unsure what to say. "Well..." I started, trailing off.

"You can say it in your language, if that helps."

No need. The words came forth almost of their own accord – in Zondrean. "I am a liar, I abandoned my family, and I do not feel bad when I kill *Zondern*. In fact, I like it. Every battle makes me feel... alive."

For a time, Jade was silent. I stared into the fire, avoiding her gaze and thinking that I probably shouldn't have said all that. But it did feel good, in a strange sort of way. Eventually she reached over and put a small hand on mine. Her touch was electric. "It's all right," she said in a small voice. "I understand."

No, she didn't, not really, but that was all right, too. There was no need for her to understand. Just being nearby was enough.

# CHAPTER TWENTY-FOUR

## Lightbringer
*17 Dämmerungherbst, 1247*
*Brinnürjn Jannausch*

W e set out early the next morning, to make the journey out of the valley and up into the foothills, where we would attempt to position ourselves above and surrounding the big *Zondern* outpost just beyond the border. It was the size of a town, and even had makeshift walls constructed from stone and wood. The closer we edged to it, the bigger it seemed, but we were five thousand strong – according to the scouts, the outpost only held about three thousand. The advantage was ours.

I was part of the west assault unit, standing with five hundred other men, led by a Hauptmann named Korisch. They were broken up into divisions of fifty, each group listening to a Kommandant like me, but together we would stand as one, in the shape of a wedge with spearmen leading the charge. Nearly all of them, including the men under me, were veterans, war-grizzled not unlike myself, though I was not fool enough to think I knew better than those who had served Eisland for many years before the war ever began.

"They'll see us up here," snarled one man to another behind me.

"They may, but they won't care," said another. I was on his side – though we had the furthest to move before we got to our position, and the fighting would start well before we got there, I had to believe that they would be far more concerned with the thousand men trying to bash through their front gate than with those still climbing down from the rocks.

Horns sounded from the outpost. Our men were in position; the battle was joined. I heard the other Kommandants shouting at their men to move faster, and I mimicked them. Time was no longer on our side.

*Zondern* were already waiting for us when we got closer to the west end of the outpost – archers and mounted cavalry, the worst of them all. In many places, the rocky lands were not good for horses and Eislandisch rarely used them for war. But the *Zondern* would push their faithful beasts, force them to go places they should not go. This land was soft and flat and horses could move well enough, giving the enemy height and speed that we lacked.

We did have archers, though, behind us on the ridge. Volley after volley of arrows sailed past our heads, seeking *Zondern* targets, human or animal. It never failed to fascinate me how an arrow loosed from a few hundred yards could sink so deep into a man, past armor, through flesh and bone. One fell from one of our blue-feathered arrows right in front of me as I rushed in, Beschützer leading the charge. It was now or never.

I swung with all my might, screaming battle cries and cursing every enemy as my sword bit into them. They were everywhere, but so were we. It was a twisted mass of bodies, all trying desperately to walk out of there alive – and I loved it. I loved the thrill of it, the way the fire surged through my veins. Oh, that those nice tabards they wore would have been white instead of black, so we could see them turn to crimson in the light of day. I sent seventeen men to the River in the span of half an hour, sometimes grabbing their names from their necks before they even hit the ground.

The horsemen, though, were another matter, and there were still plenty of them. My unit fought on the left side of the wedge formation, near the center, at first encountering only regular soldiers. It took a while for the cavalry to notice us carving through their ranks, but once they did, things changed.

"Defensive stances," I yelled at my men, but they knew what to do. No one needed a boy to tell them to form up, bunching together so that their spears and swords and axes would keep the riders at bay. It worked, too – after a few initial losses, the cavalry began to turn, some riders even dismounting to take out their swords and fight like men instead.

Not all of them did this, though. Some hung back, waiting, watching. Regrouping. They were going to charge again, as soon as we were spread out and confident.

"Fall back!" I commanded, but my men were overconfident and high on their own battle-thrill. As far as they were concerned, the fight was theirs for the taking. But they were wrong. "Get back in position – defensive stances!" I yelled this over and over again, getting only about half of them to listen.

The others met with the thunder of hooves, with arrows and spears coming far too fast. Maybe they thought that *Zondern* were too stupid or too self-righteous for such tactics, but I knew better. They were above nothing. They brought magic to almost every battle and would sooner torture an enemy than let him die with his honor intact.

As the horsemen charged into our formation, I dove low and swung high, my blade seeking a limb, or at least to knock one to the ground. I got the latter, casting a rider free from his saddle with a shriek of surprise. As the horse ran off, I took no time in severing the man's head from his body.

More arrows sang through the air from both sides, finding targets wherever they could. Sometimes, an enemy arrow seemed to hover in midflight, pausing, suddenly reduced to a picture in a painting. It gave our own archers a chance to step aside, find their own targets, and make every draw count. As I watched an Eislandisch arrow rip clean through the chest of a light-armored cavalryman, I felt something heavy push me backward with such force that I could not catch myself. The earth came straight out from under me, but there was no pain. Even when I saw the heavy, black-fletched arrow buried in my own stomach, I felt nothing – nothing but a chill as warmth flowed out of that spot.

*Not today, not today*, I said to myself. Even though my arms suddenly felt weak, like I had only been in the Army for one day instead of hundreds, I kept hold of my blade. *Not today, not today*. When an armored *Zondern* dove at my supine form, instead of the easy kill he sought, he got that blade under his ribcage and into his heart. When he fell on me, pushing that arrow in ever deeper, I thought only of how much better I felt with his blood staining my armor.

"Fall back!" I heard someone screaming in Eislandisch – our Hauptmann. What now? Yet, he continued shouting his orders, and I heard troops pulling away, with *Zondern* chasing after them. That was when I heard the roar of flames.

Magic. They had magic here? Our scouts had said nothing – at least, not to me. That mattered little in the face of this wall of Fire streaming down on us, trying to destroy everything in its path. The heat of the sun filled my lungs, stole the breath from them, but it singed only the dead man on top of me. I was alive, if perhaps just for the moment.

Another gout, another roar overhead, like the sound of some huge angry bear coming to feed on our corpses. The problem with magic was that it was so hard to fight unless you had some of your own, and all I had was my father's heavy sword, the kind that required two hands so I never carried a shield. A shield... my fallen enemy had one. It rested to the side, still attached to its owner. If I could roll free, I could use it as some protection against another onslaught. Maybe. It was worth a chance, and better than dying.

*Not today.*

With all my strength, I heaved the dead man and his eighty extra pounds of platemail off of me. The pain set in then, filling my body with agony I had not thought possible. Random wounds were one thing – cuts and bruises, even fractured ribs were normal, even expected in bigger battles like this one. I had suffered my share. But I had not yet had the pleasure of being shot with an arrow. The feeling of my insides twisting around the foreign thing in my gut brought fresh waves of pain with every movement I made.

Still, I moved. I forced myself to my knees, to grab up the shield, to heft the thing in my left hand and hold the sword in my right, ready to chop at anything that got in my way. I started to walk, then run, gaining back strength with each step. Screaming battle cries at the top of my scorched lungs seemed to help.

"By the River!" I heard someone say at my side – one of the Eislandisch veterans. "Thought you were gone for sure. You can yet fight?"

I looked at him, a spearman with a light frame and long yellow hair that spilled in wiry, frazzled waves around his shoulders. "The magic..." I started to say, my voice hoarse and sounding like a stranger's.

"Arrows got them, I think. Might not be the last."

"What about the other units?" I wished I could see beyond the outpost walls, but I could hear the battle all around, echoing off rock and wood, a constant thunder of noise.

"Not sure. Archers are still on the ridge. Hauptmann Korisch hasn't said to retreat, just fall back and regroup. Can you make it, boy?"

I would give myself no choice. My borrowed shield blocked a stray arrow as I followed him away from the wall, where the formation of Eislandisch grew more defined. A smaller wedge now, but a wedge again, nonetheless. We would go in for another run.

"You, stay back, find cover," another Kommandant said to me as I lurched toward a position. "I'll take your command."

"No, I can fight," I told him. I might have to drop that heavy shield to do it, but I had no intention of giving in now.

"No. You stay back."

"You don't command me." My words were fierce, my growl fiercer, but my body... less so. I could barely fight off strong hands on me, pulling me back, away from the others.

I turned around to look at the Hauptmann himself, a tall, barrel-chested man that had shared his bread with me just yesterday. That had felt like ages ago now. "Live to fight another day, Kommandant," he said in my ear. That was an order, and I had little choice but to obey. My knees buckled under me as the rest of them began to charge in once again.

Their cries became one shrill call for vengeance, the only thing I heard for that one short moment. As they clashed with the remainder of the *Zondern* troops, they cleaved through the front lines the way an axe chops through a log. The cut was clean and precise and tore a gaping hole in defenses with so few horses or spearmen left. From a distance, it was truly a beautiful thing to behold; it made my pain lift, if for that one moment.

Alone now, I crawled back as ordered, toward the ridge and our archers. Every step was a chore, and I was slow, easy bait for enemy archers and stray infantrymen. Oh, but I was ready for them, dragging along my shield and my sword... and my honor. At a swell of rocks, I stopped to break off the arrow shaft lodged in my torso, knowing not to pull the whole thing out or risk taking half my organs with it. The pain was still tremendous.

I kept going, then stopped again, not because I hurt, but because now I could see the front face of the outpost, where we had sent in our thousand men. At least a few hundred more had joined the fray now, filling in the gaps where others had fallen. How things were going was hard to determine – from my vantage point, I saw more leather armor than platemail, and heard our Eislandisch war cries rising above all else. There was a certain cadence to it, music that only a soldier could appreciate. It made me want to be down there with them.

Then again, I might not have to go far to find more enemies to take down. Approaching up the hill was a small unit of *Zondern*, maybe just a few dozen men surrounding one in lacquered plate with gold and silver swirls etched into its surface – an elite soldier, probably an officer. How they got through the fray below, I had no idea, but there was no way I was letting them leave my sight.

Yes, I knew I was wounded. I knew I was in pain. But the desire to see these men dead outweighed good judgment. I fixated on that garish armor and raised my weapon, howling like a wolf. My will and my strength rose with my voice – I would show them their mistake in invading my lands.

Surprise gave me the advantage I needed to cleave through three of them, and bash down a fourth with that shield. It mattered little that more would flow in from behind, because I was moving too fast, too wild. They tried to protect their gilded leader, a futile effort that only strengthened my resolve. Even a glancing blow to my hip and another at my back did nothing but make me angrier. I wanted that *Zondern* dead and none of them were going to stop me. He wasn't even a big man, and that armor, lovely as it was, was like paper in the face of Beschützer. I used my shield to knock him off balance, then my sword became a spear, thrusting with malice over and over. Sprays of warm blood that tasted of sweet copper hit my face.

The others around me grew tense, uncertain what to do without their officer to tell them. A few looked back at the battle raging at the walls, and so did I. Things seemed to be changing, with now many fewer Eislandisch standing, many more men in plate joining the battle. As my hand tightened around the hilt of Beschützer, my eyes narrowed.

Then the men started to flee from me, toward a small detachment of Eislandisch troops just a little further down the hill. No, they sought that detachment, swords raised in some sort of celebration. What did they think they were going to do?

They were marching toward glory. And glory meant a chance at taking down Keis Sturmberg himself.

The King had his honor guard with him, along with a dark-skinned woman in darker armor. Had they seen the encroaching *Zondern*? No, they were looking toward the battle, and Safaa seemed to be hurt, bent over with her head in her hands. Distracted as they were, they would be set upon in minutes.

Jolts of pain shot through my body as I took up my weapon once more, but I had no choice. I cried for the *Zondern* to die the most painful of deaths as I rushed them from behind. There were many of them and only one of me – I could take a few, maybe even distract them enough to make them want to stay and fight here. I had little to lose.

Beschützer flashed as I brought it down onto one man's skull, flinging aside his corpse with the shield while I dove in at another. We both crashed to the ground in a heap, the soldier grabbing for my throat with his steel-plated fingers. The only way to break his grasp was to let go of the shield, so I could put all my weight into shattering his nose with my elbow. He growled, but refused to relent. My air came in shorter and sharper gasps as I hit him again, and again. A fourth time was enough to ravage his senses, and the last thing he saw was the hilt of my sword heading straight for his bloodied face.

I rolled away and got to my feet, every nerve aflame. I moved slower now, I knew I did, and could do nothing about it. I had to keep going. I had to get down that hill and slow down this assault before they reached the King.

I engaged two *Zondern* running shoulder to shoulder, hoping to be able to cut through both of them. I only got one on the first pass, the other whirling around on sure, light feet to dodge my incoming swing. His quick, small blade carved the air with precision, darting in and out around my much wider but slower strikes. Every time he got in too close, I moved back, not willing to give him the opening he sought.

But he did get his opening, of a different sort. My distraction with him allowed his comrades to slip further away, and over his shoulder I could see them start to engage the King's honor guard. *Hurensohn* scum. Enraged, I waited for the quick man to launch into what would have been a deft thrust, then grabbed for his wrist, pulling him straight into a waiting Beschützer. I had to kick his impaled twitching body to free him from Beschützer's blade.

The slope grew steeper and I stumbled down the last few steps into the skirmish below. No matter, as my sword led the way, rending a hole in a soldier from behind just as he was about to land a blow on an honor guardsman. Then to my right, I saw a flash, and instinctively moved to strike. The force of my blow pushed a man back just as his weapon would have connected with the Katalahni mage's heart. I glanced at Safaa only for a moment before moving in on the enemy, parrying his counter. Though not unskilled, he was too eager, too willing to try again with a similar strike. I sent him to the River without looking back.

Safaa wore no veil now, and her long black hair was pulled back from her face to reveal wide, bright eyes set in a thin, dark face with a prominent nose and full lips. Sparks danced in between the dark rings in those eyes – so very strange. "Thank you," she said, bending to pick up the long, thin blade she must have dropped while fighting the *Zondern*. Then her gaze narrowed as it settled on me. "You are hurt, Kommandant."

I was, and I cared little. Battle kept me going. The taste of *Zondern* blood kept me going. There would be time to wallow in my misery later. I started to take to the fight yet again, but the Katalahni held up a hand. When it came down, the most terrific peal of thunder put me on my knees. The land around us brightened as if the sun had fallen out of the sky and engulfed the land.

By the River, what the hell *was* that? I could not see – everything was light, bright and white and searing. Around me, all I could hear was shouts of alarm and fear.

I felt hands on my arm then, pulling me gently forward. "I... apologize," I heard Safaa say in my ear. Her voice sounded strained, as if she were in pain. "I could wait no longer."

"Wait?" I asked, still unable to open my eyes.

"To put up this shield. Are you not glad you are inside?"

Shield? What was she talking about? I dared to open my eyes, just to chance a look, but the light was softer now, less intense than before. I could squint, just a few spots hovering in my vision as I realized that this light hung like a veil around us – around me, Safaa, Keis Sturmberg, all of his honor guard. And on the other side, I saw the vague outlines of *Zondern*, rushing this way and that, running for their lives.

"Safaa, we need you," I heard the King say. "You can do this?"

The Katalahni put one hand to her forehead, rubbing at it for a moment, but she nodded. "Yes, my Lord," she said, turning toward the battle at the outpost walls. From here, the two armies looked like one massive beast, writhing and swirling in an arcane rhythm.

Then it exploded in white light. I stood transfixed as bolts of lightning shot down from the heavens into the ranks of the *Zondern* army below. Every strike made the very earth under my feet tremble, blasting all in its path. It was like the greatest storm the land had ever seen had been centered directly over that *Zondern* outpost, and when it was over, the place was a burning husk. The walls cracked and shattered, the people within dead or dying.

Through it all, our men watched it from behind the safety of their own wall, a wall of light as high as the foothills themselves. Near me, Safaa started to sink to the ground and I reached for her, giving her the last of my strength so she could steady herself.

"It is done." Her voice came in wisps of breath, and blood trickled from her nose. Nearby, honor guardsmen and the King began to cheer. Blue banners began to wave up on the ridge, and down at the foot of the hills.

Victory was ours. I could rest.

The last thing I remember before I collapsed was a wide purple-white streamer of light winding its way through the air, searching for where it was needed most. As I let the darkness take me, I thought of the Lavançaise "Saint" and how tired she would be caring for all of those wounded men. So many of them, and one of her. Maybe she was a warrior in her own right, as powerful as one who could fight against hordes of enemies, or one who could make time do as he wished... or one whose lightning could cast judgment upon the land.

# CHAPTER TWENTY-FIVE

## Old and New

*4 Spring's Green, 1272*
*The present day*
*Andella Weaver*

"You loved her, didn't you?" I gave them a start, Tristan and Brin both turning on me in surprise. "When I woke up and couldn't go back to sleep, I heard voices downstairs, and... I couldn't help but listen."

"How long have you been there?" Tristan asked, voice just a tad slurred, and not so much from lack of sleep. There were two empty liquor bottles on the desk between them, and they'd just opened a third. A part of me wanted to partake myself – seemed like the right thing to do on a night like this – but that brandy was like drinking molten metal. Give me a nice glass of wine or some sweet firemint any day, but that stuff? It was enough to knock someone straight into next week – well, someone without Eislandisch blood in them, at any rate.

"Since before the battle," Brin answered before I could, then turned to me looking far sharper than he should have for the amount of brandy they'd consumed. His expression was pensive, caught in a quick daydream. "To answer your question, I never said I stopped."

"What happened to her?" I asked. Suddenly, I *needed* to know, but this question got little more than a stone-faced glare. Something happened... oh, please don't tell me this Jade is dead, I thought. I'm not sure I could have handled that.

"A story for another time."

"She's alive, though?"

At this, he nodded, then took a big drink from the new bottle. "*Ja,*" he said, "she is alive."

"But if you loved her..." I caught myself. Why pry? It wasn't my business. Though, I could only imagine what could have happened to bring that kind of reluctance and pain to a toughened old soldier like Brin. I decided it was wise to change the subject. "Wait, Archmage Tiara told me about the legend of Drasch Sturmberg. I think maybe it's talking about him in my book on *Lebenkern*, too. He had mages who attended him just like what you told us about Keis Sturmberg. Some of them had strange powers."

"As I have said, I give more questions than answers. I just tell of what I have seen."

I walked across the room and put a hand on Tristan's shoulder. He felt solid, tense, and didn't react to my touch. "Maybe we should go to Eisland," I said to him. "I mean, Brin knows the King, right? He can vouch for us." At this, he looked up at me briefly with red-tinged, sparkling eyes – despite the liquor, his gaze was as sober as I'd ever seen him.

He directed his reply to Brin. "I can do what Safaa did, what you said happened at Südensonnentor." It wasn't a question, more of a... revelation – not a happy one.

"She saved many lives," Brin said, matter-of-fact.

"She took a lot more."

"It was because of her that we were victorious."

"I've studied history, I've read about that battle. No one ever mentions that it ended with magic like that. Why?"

That was a good question. I wanted the answer to that one myself. How was it that if all this magic existed, it still seemed so arcane and rare and extraordinary? But Brin just shook his head, a faint smile on his weatherbeaten face. "When you tell people that you were saved from death by some miracle magic, what do they say to you? I will tell you – they call you mad. They call you a liar. The best legends are the ones no one believes are true, *ja*? Besides, Keis Sturmberg is no fool. He protects what is his very well."

"Well," I said, "I think we should go there and talk to him. That is... later, I guess." Through the window behind Brin, I could see more of those soldiers walking around, holding torches as they patrolled in the depth of night. I wondered if I could get back to the Academy to talk to Archmage Tiara. Oh, and I'd have to bring Tristan with me – the very thought of being able to do research on this "Light" of his would surely make her giddy.

Tristan followed my gaze, then reached for the brandy and knocked back a gulp before resting his head back in his chair, looking up at nothing in particular. "Yeah, much later."

I could have asked a million more questions that Brin probably wasn't going to answer. Did he see the magic again? What was Jade like? Where was she now? Was she the girl from my dream? Well, she must have been. A Lavançaise girl with dark hair, calling herself a "Saint"... it was her. It had to be. Maybe I could have visions, like Alex had? I sighed. Brin was right – I felt like I knew even less than I did before, and I *so* wanted to understand.

Wait. Jade was Lavançaise. And hadn't Onyx Saçaille been so very concerned about the prophecy and that book in my sister's church in Doverton? Something clicked in my brain and I blurted out the newest question that sprang to my mind. "Is your Jade related to Madame Saçaille somehow?"

Brin's smile got so wide it split his square-jawed face. "Like I say, that is another story, for another time."

Ah-ha! I wanted to keep going, to keep asking until I understood... well, *more*, but a shout from the hallway interrupted my thoughts. It wasn't in Zondrean, and it was a woman's hurried, almost shrieking voice. Lady Gretchen! Tristan was out of his chair and gone in seconds, but as I raced to catch up, Brin put up a hand.

"Heed her. She only wants her son."

"But, I..." I tried to protest, but Brin shook his head slowly.

"Heed her. The time when you are needed will come. The time for family is now."

"What's happening?" But I knew what was happening, didn't I? Or a dreadful dark corner of my mind did. Maybe I was overthinking it. Maybe Lord Loringham was waking up and he just wanted to see Tristan. Could I have misheard the urgency in her voice as dread when it was really excitement?

"Time tells these things. Not I."

"Shouldn't we go up there, though? What did she say? She sounded upset."

"I told you – not yet."

"Yes, but..."

"But nothing. Wait for the right time." Gesturing for me to sit, Brin swallowed down more of that fiery gold liquor, his smile long gone. I hesitated, still watching the open door to the hall, but decided to go ahead and take Tristan's seat. It was still very warm, and smelled vaguely like soap, leather, and spiced drink. "Tell me something," Brin asked, "do you train your magic at your Academy?"

"Me?" The question threw me off – of course that was probably the intent. "I try to, but it's not like practicing other kinds of magic. I think maybe... I think someone has to be hurt first, don't they? I wish I was stronger. I could have helped Lord Loringham more, and Alex, the other day."

"You did as much as could be expected. The result is no longer in your hands. Do you think that one girl was able to heal the wounds of five thousand men? Magic is still mortal."

This gave me some pause. "I'm sure she was more powerful than me. How did Jade train?"

"Jade was in a war. She did not have to seek training."

"But the war ended. Then what did she do?"

"She stopped. She swore off magic when we..." He trailed off, and I could tell he was caught up in reminiscence.

I couldn't help it. I *had* to ask, had to pry just a little further. I leaned back, pulling my knees to my chest with my simple yellow house dress floating down, just covering my bare legs. "Did you marry her? Where is she now? I'd love to meet her."

Another drink. And another. The bottle was almost empty now. He regarded me with those fierce, wild blue eyes for so long that I started to feel uncomfortable. He looked like he was either going to answer me, or reach out and snap my neck. Finally – thankfully – he did speak, relaxing back into his cushy leather chair. "Back then, she was very curious, like you. You would get along well, I think. But if I told you where she was, I would break a promise. The fact that I am here, and not with her, means that I already broke too many promises. So you see, I have reached my limit."

"I understand," I said, even though I really didn't.

His arms folded across his massive chest. "The reason I asked you if you trained was because I want to know if Herr Vestarton trains too."

Not sure where this was going, I shrugged. "Sometimes. Not that much. Archmage Tiara is very interested in his abilities, though. I think he's getting very powerful."

Brin went quiet. What was he thinking about now? Something to do with Alex? I wanted to ask, but the question sputtered on my lips. I had a hard time with the silence, though, and felt the need to fill it with *something*. I came up with a better question. "So, do you think my idea to go to Eisland is a good one?"

"*Ja*. You should meet Keis Sturmberg. He has better answers for you, I think, but only if he will grant you an audience."

"Oh. You mean we could get all the way there and he might not even talk to us? Then what?" Königstadt was a long way away, several hundred miles at least. I shuddered at the thought of making such a journey only to come back empty-handed.

"A wise man told me once that to get anywhere, you can only take one step at a time."

One step at a time. Not bad advice, but it didn't exactly put me at ease, either. There was just so much to know, so much to do. I clutched my knees tightly to my chest as we sat there, Brin turning back to the window, me staring at the floor. I strained to listen to what might be going on upstairs, but couldn't hear much. Finally, a voice cut through the stillness – Tristan's. I had never run up a flight of stairs so fast in my life.

# CHAPTER TWENTY-SIX

## Surrender of Pride
*4 Spring's Green, 1272*
*Alexander Vestarton*

W orking numbers in ledgers was very relaxing. I know, a strange thing to say, but I had to admit, I actually found it somewhat enjoyable. The tedium, the predictability of doing the same formula over and over provided a sense of calm that didn't come from too many other places anymore.

*(You know you killed a man, with that magic of yours.)*

Ten cases of wine from fifty, multiply by the price for 4250 Royals. Send that ten to some noble in Kellen for 7000. Profit. Next line, more of the same, this time five to a restaurant in Riverton. Take taxes on that one, too many. Raise the price, still profit. Next line... and so on. Then I'd have to tackle the ledger for the silver mine, a little more complicated but not beyond my capabilities. Who needed accountants when you could do the work yourself for free?

Most accountants worked when the sun was up, though, and normally I would too, but I had been sleeping all day. Literally. I woke well after the rest of the house had gone to bed, very awake with nothing else to do except ledgers.

*(And think about how you killed a man. You stopped time for him. Just like that, by a thought.)*

Shaking my head as if that would free those little nagging thoughts that kept prying into my business affairs, it occurred to me: I didn't even know whether we'd be able to do business outside the city anymore. Would there be many ledgers to catch up on soon? Would Torven just starve all the Lords out until we came to him on hands and knees, begging to be part of his new, "evolved" kingdom? Come to think of it, I'd do exactly that if I were him. Well, that is, if I were a self-righteous prick with a taste for blood.

*(Maybe you are. Where's the spot on the ledger where you're going to send money to that man's family? You know, the one you...)*

"Stop it," I said aloud in the darkness. The force in my tone almost made me jump. "It was self-defense. What's done is done." That was the truth of it – it wasn't like I'd tried to murder that Royal Guard in cold blood. On the contrary, that's exactly what he was trying to do to me. I sighed and stuffed the nagging thoughts down into a dark hole somewhere. There were so many other things to worry about nowadays that such thoughts almost seemed self-indulgent.

I had, however, successfully avoided most of the political talk and schemes and whatnot for the past couple of days on account of being wounded, and that was fine by me. Honestly, a sword in the gut was the favorable alternative. Turns out that sword had gone in deep enough to nick some organs and my hip bone on the left side, something that would have been much more serious had it not been for Andella. Thanks to her – and some good herbs from Zizah – getting around was now a mild inconvenience, rather than a distant memory. Still, I had a "pass" as the other Lords tried to figure their way out of the mess they had no small hand in creating. Though, what kinds of strategy they thought they could talk through with an eight year-old crown prince, I could not imagine. Hadn't the kid suffered enough?

The candle I worked by started to flicker, so I found a new one in my desk and lit it. Better. Now, back to the...

"My Lord?"

I looked up at Dennis, standing in the doorframe looking almost as pale as the white robe he wore. "Sorry, didn't mean to wake you, old chap," I said, stirring in my seat just a little.

"My Lord," Dennis said again, clearing his throat.

"It's fine, Dennis. Really. I just woke up and couldn't get back to sleep. You know how it is."

But Dennis was still so pale, so quiet. He tried a third time. "My Lord, Sir Frederick from House Loringham just came to the door." A deep breath. This was so unlike the grandfatherly, rather outspoken butler I'd known for all of my twenty-three years. "Lord Loringham has passed, m'Lord," he finally said, words coming out slow and deliberate.

Lord Loringham has passed.

*(Good job. You probably got him killed, too, you know.)*

That couldn't be. I was sure I didn't hear right. His wounds were bad, but... No, I heard right. That cold and distant look on Dennis' face told me as much.

"Can you get my coat, Dennis?" I asked, using the desk to help me stand up.

"It's waiting for you downstairs, m'Lord. Are you well enough?"

"It's three hours till dawn and my best friend's father just died." I went to his side, my gait still more of a hobble than a proper walk. "I'm as well as I'll ever be."

My mother and sister were already downstairs, getting ready to go. Alice had tears in her eyes as she fumbled with some plates of food, while my mother kept telling her to hand them to her. I took one of them from her grasp, a tray of pastries, to end the debate.

"I just don't believe this," she said, voice hollow.

"Yeah." The thing was, I did believe it.

*(It's all your fault. You were there. You could have done more.)*

It all happened so fast – what could I have done? What good was this ridiculous magic I was supposed to have, anyway? How was I even supposed to face Tristan now?

*(You better hope he doesn't blame you. Idiot. Coward.)*

Questions and inane self-abusing thoughts swirled around in my head over and over as we went across the street, ignoring the mercenary patrols who looked at us sideways. Frederick was already at the front door, ushering in the Shal-Vespers – the whole damn crew. Cen's wife, Dona, had a basket of something tucked under arm, and Corrin, Fyr, and their little sister Elena were all close behind. No one was dressed well. No one's hair was combed, no faces washed.

They had all been roused right out of bed like we had, at one of those rare times when appearances were no longer important.

Corr brightened a little at my approach. "Alex, good to see you up and about."

"Bad fucking night for it," I said to him, unconcerned about how my language might have offended the ladies present.

Corr's father clapped my shoulder, a tight-lipped grimace on his thin face as we entered the Loringham's house. It seemed strange to me – he'd done the exact same thing, with that same expression, when my father had died. A chill rocked me as I realized how similar all of this was to a couple months ago. The women with their food and their tears, the men with their somber looks all trying to stay strong.

I *hated* this part.

The quiet house burst into activity. My mother and Dona immediately sought out Lady Gretchen, while Cen kept his children in check. Frederick brought out some tea. Gretchen's brother was there too, his blue eyes calm and vacant – first time I'd ever seen that. And here I thought he would either be gone, or taking some satisfaction from this whole affair. Brin acknowledged me, but said nothing, clearly more interested in keeping tabs on his sister.

I finally found Andella sitting on the stairs leading up to the second floor, knees folded into her as if she was trying to get as small as possible. A few tears escaped down pink cheeks when she saw me.

"Alex," she started, but didn't have anything else to finish the sentence. She didn't need to. As I lumbered my way over to her, she got up and put her arms around me, burying her auburn head in my shoulder. There wasn't much else to do except hold her trembling, thin form, and let her cry. The longer we stood there like that, the more it felt just slightly wrong. Sometimes, I had to remind myself that she was not – under any circumstances – any more than a friend. "I couldn't help him," I heard her say through the sobs. "I tried and I just couldn't."

"You did all you could do," I said, knowing full well this was not much consolation. Our roles in this exchange could have been easily reversed.

"I feel so bad. Tristan... I think he hates me."

*(Not a chance of that. But* you *on the other hand – he knows you're a coward.)*

No. That was a stupid thing to think, wasn't it? What if things were the other way around, and that was my father in the plaza that day? Things happened so fast, but the first people I would blame wouldn't be my friends.

*(So stop torturing yourself, idiot. Do the right thing here.)*

With a start, I pulled away, looking into her oddly violet eyes. They were so dim, the light in them hardly moving at all. "Don't say that. That would never happen. Just – hey, look at me. You did your best. Doesn't matter what we are, we're still just people. There's only so much we can do. Whatever happens after that is up to the Lady. Right?" Right? The wisdom of my own words echoed back at me. I wanted very much to believe everything I just said, though it still felt forced, too hopeful.

"I guess." Andella wiped the back of her hand across one side of her face.

"Is he upstairs?"

She nodded. "He told me to come down here, so I did."

"Don't worry, okay? He doesn't hate you. He just doesn't want you to see him upset. Trust me." Trying to convey as much reassurance as I could, I gave her one more squeeze before continuing up. I knew I was right, but she hadn't spent twenty-something years being his best friend – she didn't really understand. The thing was, Tristan just... didn't fare well in these sorts of situations. His typical emotional response involved breaking things, more often than not. No woman as sweet as she needed to witness any of that.

At the end of the hallway of bedrooms upstairs, I could hear my mother and Dona and Gretchen talking and crying together. Most the talking came from my mother of course, putting the best face on the situation like only she could. Even when her own husband died, she had been the picture of optimism, keeping most of her grief to herself, behind closed doors.

And standing there, leaning in the doorframe of that room, was Tristan – the Lord of House Loringham.

As I approached, with a bit of caution, he turned. I noticed the front of his half-buttoned shirt sported streaks of drying blood. He looked through me rather than at me, his mind somewhere far away. "Internal bleeding. His heart. He couldn't hold it in anymore, all the blood," he said, glancing down at his shirt. "Alex?"

"Yeah, Brother?" My voice sounded so hoarse and odd.

"I don't know what to feel right now."

"I know. It's normal."

He sank to the floor then, sitting there cross-legged in the hallway. It seemed as reasonable a thing to do as any, so I joined him, and put a hand on his arm, just below where he had that tattoo of a gold dragon. We sat that way for a good long time until he spoke again. "Did your father say anything to you, when he died?"

"Not much. He was sort of delusional at the end."

Another long pause. Resting his elbows on his knees, his eyes cast downward as he stroked his temples. Behind us, I could hear the women continuing their soft mourning. "He told me... he told me I was a good man, and he was proud. He told me he wished he'd been a better father. And that was it." He sniffed and his whole body seemed to convulse with the effort. A tear or two dripped into his lap.

"Brother, I'm sorry." It was all I could think to say.

His hands began to clench into fists. "He didn't believe that. When was he ever proud of me? He always used to speak for me because he thought he had to. "

"Brother..."

"And do you know that's the first thing I thought about? Why? I shouldn't be thinking about the bad things, and here I am. I can't stop. There were times when I..."

I cut him off. "Don't say it, Brother. You know it's not true." I knew what he was going to say, because I had those thoughts, too – I still do, in the darkest and quietest moments. That nagging feeling that my father was never really proud of me, that he didn't want me taking over his House... that he hated me. Granted, my father and I had a much closer relationship than the Loringhams had, and it was easy to not allow those feelings to become my reality.

"But I'm not a good man. I can't... do this. It's my fault. If I had been just one second faster..."

*(Here we go. You know what to do.)*

"Brother, if I was one second faster, we wouldn't be here. If Andella was one tiny bit more powerful, we wouldn't be here.

Or maybe we would – we don't know. We can all blame ourselves till Catherine walks the fucking streets, but you know something? You're just going to make yourself miserable. It's no one's fault. If you want to blame anyone, blame Torven."

He continued his downward stare, fighting the grip of sorrow. If he were anyone else, I would have told him to just let it come and be done with it, but this was Tristan Loringham we were talking about. He did not accept suggestions under these circumstances. There was one thing I could offer, though, as we sat there amongst the weird din of voices mixed with grief and periods of crushing silence.

"Look, Brother," I told him, "don't worry about anything. The arrangements, all that, it's taken care of. Everything will be done right. Just leave it to me." He looked up, getting ready to protest. "A couple months ago, this is what your father did for me... and for his friend. It's the very least I can do." In the back of my mind, I had a flash of being so miserably drunk I could barely stand, while Jonathan assured me that all would be well, that the funeral was already arranged. No need to worry, Alex, everything will be all right. I remembered crying on his shoulder for a good half an hour.

The odd white streaks in Tristan's eyes flared, like a breeze hit the wick of a just-burned-out candle. "You don't need to do this."

"Yeah, I do." I meant that. I moved to stand, putting my hand on his shoulder partly to support him, and partly to support me. "I'm going to go pay my respects, all right? You take your time. Do whatever you need to do. I'm not going anywhere, neither is Cen. Whatever you need, we'll handle it." Because you're one of *us* now, I thought grimly. Catherine-on-a-pike, what an awful time to become a Lord.

As I stepped away toward the bedroom, he said something almost too soft to hear. "Alex – thank you." But I needed no thanks. This wasn't about me.

Three ladies of the most powerful houses in Zondrell looked up at my approach, all of them red-eyed and puffy-cheeked. Again, I was reminded of a similar scene at my own house, not so long ago. Except that time, Lady Gretchen was doing the consoling, and she did it in her own way – stoic, gentle, but always selfless. She had stayed at our house for a full week to make sure my mother had everything she needed, and to help keep unwanted guests with their fake sympathies away.

When Gretchen saw me, a whole new flood of tears sprang into her azure eyes. "Oh Alexander," she said in that lovely accent of hers. "Tristan is well?"

I went to her and hugged her like she was my own mother, letting her hold on for as long as she wanted. "No worries, m'Lady. I've got it covered."

"You are such a good friend."

"It's all I can do."

When she pulled away, her pale face was still wet, but no more tears were left. Even in grief, she seemed elegant, graceful, her long blond hair tied back with a simple black ribbon. "Johann always said you were a good boy. He liked that you took care of Tristan the way you do."

I smiled in spite of myself. "Mostly, it's been the other way around, but I do what I can."

"You are a good boy," she said again, with more conviction in her tone. She reached out and ruffled my terribly unkempt hair. "He loved you. We love you."

Behind her on the bed lay the man himself, covered with a blanket. The beautifully appointed room, with all its rich fabrics and textures of blue and white and purple seemed insignificant in the face of this one satin sheet. I went to the bed and knelt beside it, thinking to pray though not sure what to pray for. Having rarely paid close attention in church over the years, I was never good at that sort of thing.

Jonathan Loringham was a gruff man who was hard to get to know, and harder to come to trust others. He barely even seemed to trust his own family. Yet, he was as good-hearted and loyal as anyone I'd ever met. My father had trusted him with his life, called him a man of utmost integrity. Had he made some mistakes along the way as a Lord? Perhaps, though perhaps not. He worked to make Zondrell a better place for everyone, not just those of us living on the Gods' Avenue. His votes, his arguments always reflected that. And what his wife said must have been true, because he protected me from the most... devious of those efforts. I could accept that. I still didn't like it, and still felt anger rising in my throat when I thought about how awry this secret plot to take down Torven had gone, but I could accept it.

How different might things be right now if they'd succeeded? Hard to know. There might still be blood flowing through the streets for a while, but without Torven, King Kelvaar would have been far more open to the Council's wisdom, and one could only assume he'd start making smarter and less costly decisions. On the other hand, Torven knew how to keep the coffers full and the taxes low, but that could mean sending huge numbers of boys to war. Zondrell would go back to being the martial state it was so many years ago.

We got the latter option. It wasn't what Jonathan wanted, and he had to give his life for it. He died defending me, his allies, and what he believed in. It should never have come to that.

"Thank you, my Lord," I whispered. "I'll do my best to see the right thing done. I swear to it."

# CHAPTER TWENTY-SEVEN

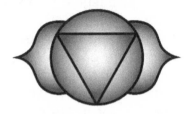

## Peace on M'Gistryn, as in Paradise
*7 Spring's Green, 1272*
*Tristan Loringham*

In the days after my father's death, I signed untold thousands of legal documents. I got all the advice I could stomach from a dozen different people. I stood around looking dutifully clean and pressed while various friends and family hovered around me, on guard to intercept any well-wishers I didn't want to talk to. I had to admit, I was thankful for all of them – even Brin, who took to the task of consoling his sister as if there had never been a twenty-five year rift between them. In the state I was in myself, I was of little use to my mother.

I slept a lot, too, and in between long, self-pitying naps, I sat in long, self-pitying thought. *Why did this have to happen? Why couldn't I have stopped it? What did it really mean to be a Lord, especially with the throne under dispute? Was I ready for any of this? How could Father just leave me?*

No answers were going to come by sitting there and stewing over them. I realized this during the funeral, as I stared into the flames of his pyre. I hardly even paid attention to the Pyrelight who danced to the flames, responding to the prayers that the circle of priestesses in white called out in a systematic chant. Andella had lamented hourly that she wished she could have performed the rites herself – her original calling in life – so finding the right person to do them was the best she could offer. I had no doubt that she felt this woman from the Magic Academy was quite qualified to help guide souls to Paradise. The fact was, I was glad that Andella did not have to expend her magical energies for such a sad, pointless task. When I had faced death, there was no beautiful goddess in some lush Paradise waiting for me. Whatever awaited my father in the *next*, he would find his way. Of this I was certain – Jonathan Colwyl Michael Loringham approached nothing, not even death, without pride and purpose.

When it was time to give the eulogy, I read a short speech I had scrawled on a piece of paper a few hours prior. I told the people gathered – a good number, despite the conflicts outside and armed guards everywhere – how much I respected my father, how much I learned from his guidance. He had taught me the sword, how to conduct myself with nobility and honor.

He was also a hard man to love, and judged my actions harshly. He'd even raised his hand to me on occasion, before I grew bigger than he was. At different times in my life, I was convinced that he hated me. Taking a few days to think on it made me see things a little differently, though. If I took a second to stop focusing on the bad memories, I could also remember how his chest swelled with pride when they pinned that High Honor medal on my chest, and how he brought in the best doctors anytime I so much as scraped a knee. I could remember many long bouts of sword practice in the courtyard, first him letting me win, and later, me letting him win. And just the other day, he'd had that twinkle in his eye talking about Andella. He'd stopped just short of telling me to propose immediately lest she get away somehow.

I didn't tell the congregation all that, of course. I kept it short, sweet, to the point. The past mattered now just about as much as who lit that pyre, and I vowed then to cast those bad memories straight into the flames. *I don't need them anymore – take them and let me be free of them.* But I didn't cry like my mother and her friends and so many others there. I had grown... numb. The time of worrying about how to feel was over. The emotions could stop having their way with me, leaving behind a merciful sense of emptiness. Even my omnipresent magical headache had ceased.

Oddly, in that moment, it was the best I'd felt in days.

Retrieving the ashes was the final step, the priestesses collecting them into an urn and delivering it to the family so the final wishes of the dead could be fulfilled. I didn't actually know what my father had wanted, but I assumed my mother did and would act accordingly. As I stood up by the altar, waiting for the priestesses, I could watch the people as they talked amongst each other, hugged, cried, and prayed. *So many people – I don't even know half of them.* Many "friends" come out during funerals like these, opportunists with open palms trying to figure out what they can get from the next one in line. No matter what they said about my father marrying "that Eislandisch villager," or what they said about him having a half-breed son, they still appreciated our House's station. My father's business associates didn't know what to make of me, and to be honest, I didn't know what to make them yet, either. I had kept them firmly at arm's length so far. Family and friends were another matter. There were people out there that I hadn't seen since I was a child, but they had all offered to help me with "whatever I needed." If I could remember any of their names, I might even consider that someday.

Then there were the other Lords – all of them, even Wyndham and his family. Well, everyone except Victor. No, wait, Victor was there, just not sitting with them. He sat at the end of one of the pews, close to the west wall, near the Silversmiths but not really with them. His mage eyes stood out amongst the faces in the crowd, winking little blue lights. *Oh great, can they all see my magic, too?* Of course, the rumors were no doubt out of control, as so many had witnessed some amazing miracle with magical lightning in Peaceday plaza. Yet, no one said a word to me directly, or to Alex or anyone else that would let it get back to me. Alex himself wore his dark spectacles today, though he claimed it was about not wanting people to see him teary-eyed to anyone who asked. And Andella? She stuck close to me and my mother, and didn't say much to all these strangers.

Then there was a group standing at the back of the temple, a handful of men in the traditional white and gold of the Goddess to signify mourning, but with black soldiers' cloaks on their backs. From where I stood, I couldn't make out their faces. *Old Army acquaintances, probably. Why didn't they sit down?*

The ashes were set in front of me, held with reverence by an older woman, one of the head priestesses. Her face was kind and gentle, careworn around the eyes and mouth. "My Lord? It is done."

"Thank you," I said, taking the gold urn from her by its two ornamental handles. It was not as heavy as I would have expected. An entire man, his life and his body, in one tiny pile of ash. *Maybe the soul weighs more than we realize.*

"Catherine guide you and your family. Peace be with you." She patted me on the arm and withdrew, along with her colleagues, while the assembly got up and started toward us.

*This... this is the worst part.* Everyone wanted to shake my hand, to hug my mother, to express their respects in some way or another, and they'd do it in a long, seemingly unending line. But Alex was there, too, and Cen Shal-Vesper, and they headed off some of the least desirable guests with small talk and fake pleasantries before sending them on their way. Their teamwork seemed well-practiced by now.

Every once in a while, they'd look to me for approval before letting someone come see my mother or me. I got such a glance when Victor approached, but I nodded. He wasn't my favorite person in the world, by far, but we had a certain... understanding. And today, while he still leaned on the cane, he seemed to hardly need it. His breathing came easily and he looked far less frail than I'd seen him in weeks.

"Retirement's not all they say it is," he said as he came to stand before me. "I'm sorry for your loss."

"Thanks, Victor. I appreciate you being here." That was a stretch, but it was the proper thing to say.

He paused, looking for words, but really what he was looking for was what to make of my eyes. I wasn't stupid. I cocked my head at him and cleared my throat.

"Yes, you heard correctly, and no, I don't know anything else," I told him curtly. With so many people around, I really didn't want to have a conversation about magic right then.

Victor's sharp features seemed softer in the dim torchglow of the temple. "I understand. It's just, as a scholar, I find the whole thing... fascinating."

"I'll bet you do."

His vivid blue eyes narrowed. "Though, next time you have the opportunity to save my father from the brink, I suggest you think better of it." Now he leaned in, his voice nearly a whisper. "He's not to be trusted."

*You think I'm blind? I trust him almost as little as I trust you.* "Thanks for your insight."

"I might be disowned, but I still hear things. If you want to chat sometime, let me know." Victor bowed, coughed out a thank-you, and continued on his way.

Alex's eyes narrowed as he turned to me in between well-wishers. "You're *not* going to chat with him."

"I might, if it's worthwhile."

He rolled his eyes with a huff, then put on his best false smile for some pretty girls from a minor house somewhere. I didn't know them, and they didn't make it any further through the line. Things continued like that for another hour or so, until the temple had grown much quieter, and only a few people were left – the men in the back, the men in the black soldiers' cloaks.

Oh dear Catherine, that was General Torven. I rested my hand on the hilt of my sword, and yes, I wore a weapon into the church. It was ceremonially appropriate for the funeral of an officer, and besides, one always carried a sword around these days. This was thanks to the man who had come to stand before us, bowing in deep respect.

"You've got a lot of nerve," Alex said with his hands folded across his chest, tight as if to keep from reaching out and strangling the General with his bare hands.

Torven looked right past him, to me. "I just want to offer my sympathies. Your father was a good man. I was so sorry to hear of his passing."

*How dare he? Who the fuck does he think he is?* My weapon was out and pointed at his heart before I could think about what I was doing. Gasps rang out amongst the priestesses behind us, and I think my mother said something about putting it away. I did not.

"Lord Loringham," he said, suppressing any emotions at all, "if we could speak in private for a moment?"

*What could he possibly want?* "I'd rather not."

"If you'll just give me one moment of your time? I'll be quick."

I tried to look through the storm-colored eyes, through the perfectly trimmed beard and the expression of a man who fancied himself a King, to see him as he really was. A part of me wanted to understand him, to understand why he did what he did. So I lowered my blade – just a little – and pointed toward the far corner with it. "No further," I said, gesturing for him to lead the way. Everyone else stayed behind, his personal guard uncomfortable under death-glares from Alex and Cen.

When we got to our corner, I continued to hold my blade on the General. "I want you to know," he started, "that I never betrayed your father. On the contrary, he betrayed me."

I couldn't really deny that. That was more or less what Brin had told me. "So that gives you permission to do what you did?"

"I've been trying to make this city a better place for years. I even wanted you to be a part of that. You would make a fine General in my Army. You have many... gifts."

My hand tightened around the hilt of my weapon. "You tried me for treason and kicked me out of your Army. Don't give me that."

"Do you consider yourself as much a patriot as your reports might indicate, Lord Loringham?" The way he said "patriot" made my skin crawl, so many accusations locked behind one simple word. When I failed to answer, he pressed on. "Indeed, as I expected. No matter, what's done is done. Then again, it depends on your definition of the word, doesn't it? Some might say your father was a great patriot, I among them. Others might say otherwise. I do know that he cared a great deal for you. He wanted you unharmed, and was willing to put his beliefs on the line for it."

"I'm sure you threatened him."

"I wouldn't say that, but... well, I can't say I'm proud of how I've handled many things in the past few months. Sometimes choices are more forced than we would like, even if one is the General. For instance, you think I sent you into the mountains on that horrid mission? That was all Kelvaar's idea. He read the histories far too much, looking for glory and riches and things he could use against the other city-states. Oddly, he sent you there looking for something that didn't exist, and you came back with treasure after all."

"Get to the point," I growled. I really wanted to run him through, but he was clearly wearing armor under his gold-trimmed white tunic, and who knew how many men he had waiting outside? His men inside also hovered within an arm's length of my mother and my girl. *How fast could I get across that temple? How many could I take on at once?* He had me quite literally cornered, and if he noticed how my eyes darted around the room, he knew it, too. The General continued.

"You know, no one talks much about the War of the Northlands these days, but I saw some pretty amazing things in Eisland. Things that people say was just a trick of the mind, like the dreams you get when you've lost too much blood – you know the type. One time, I even saw lightning come out of a clear blue sky. Then I saw it again the other day. Interesting, eh?"

"Your point?" *Make it fast – you're losing time here.* I knew what he was trying to do, and it wasn't going to work. He could go tell everyone in the city that I had some sort of special magic, and I wouldn't care one bit. Not now, not when I could use it to protect those very same people from the likes of him.

"The point, Lord Loringham, is that you have gifts. Gifts that can help make Zondrell a better place. Isn't that what we all want, if we claim ourselves to be patriots?"

"I don't make deals like my father did. So if that's what you're looking for, turn around and walk away now."

Torven frowned, considering me. Then he asked, "Have you been outside recently? I mean, truly outside, away from this well-protected street of yours? My men are doing the best they can, and I know the city guards are doing the best that they can, too. But it's a real problem, trying to get everyone to agree on what the law is anymore – a much bigger problem than I anticipated. I can't say that the men I believe answer to me still do. In fact, I'd daresay that most answer to another master."

I snorted derisively. "What, you thought everyone would just bow down to *you*?" He had always carried an air of superiority around him, one that many people confused with honor, with the discipline of a supreme soldier and leader. This, however, was a most unmistakable new level of arrogance.

"No," he said, looking to the floor for a moment. "I admit, I wasn't quite prepared for the way events unfolded on Peaceday. I was... disappointed, and unwilling to let a good opportunity go to waste. You have no idea how long these plans have been in place. There's no way to move now but forward – I'm sure you can agree?" He waited for me to say something, but came up short. "I wish to have a meeting with the Lords to discuss the current situation, and find a solution, but they have so far refused my invitations. Being... new, I thought perhaps you would be willing to give the matter further consideration."

The thing was, he seemed so *earnest*. Was he delusional? Did he actually think we would all just lay down arms and hold hands under whatever banner he had dreamed up? Yet, if it would end the conversation faster... "I'll consider it, but nothing absolves you of what you've done. I hope you realize that."

"I do. Thank you for your time, Lord Loringham." With a glance toward the altar, then up into the intricate stained-glass dome of the ceiling, he started away toward the door. His men followed close behind.

"What was that about?" Cen and Alex asked almost at the same time, rushing up to me.

I sheathed my weapon. "He wants to have a peaceful discussion."

"No, he doesn't," said Cen. "He's already met with Miller twice and it was nothing but posturing and shouting. We're lucky to even have the curfew in place."

"That's what he said; that's all I know." As I glanced at Alex, I realized I didn't have to say anything else, about Torven's understanding of things he saw as "gifts." Of course he wanted to use our magic somehow. He'd be a fool if he didn't, and that man was no fool. Alex just shook his head, a mirthless smile on his lips.

*Peace... patriotism... what were any of us fighting for anymore?*

# CHAPTER TWENTY-EIGHT

## Surprise Gifts

*7 Spring's Green, 1272*
*Alexander Vestarton*

"You do your job well." The deep voice with the heavy Eislandisch accent caught me off guard as we walked in procession back toward our homes. I was moving slow, limping along even though the pain in my side wasn't really that bad. One more round of healing from Andella had done much good – I'd have a fantastically hideous scar forever, but I wasn't prancing around shirtless much these days anyhow.

"What, being a bodyguard?" I smiled. I suppose I had taken to the role quite well, I thought, and Catherine knew Tristan needed one. He wasn't like me – my best friend did not soothe himself with alcohol, or any other choice substances. He was quite content to just sit there and wallow in misery, and yet was too polite to send away all the people who wanted a piece of him. When one is drunk, those same people tend to steer clear, because their niceties disguised as requests won't be remembered the next day. Self-preservation in these kinds of situations really was key.

"You talk fast," Brin said, taking a few extra steps to keep pace with me.

"People just don't know they're offended when you're charming about it. Try it sometime."

"Indeed." A wry smile hit his features, then was gone. "So tell me, Herr Vestarton, are you still training?"

I slowed, and he did the same. I wasn't sure what he was getting at. "Haven't been to the Academy lately. Some things have come up, in case you hadn't noticed."

"Indeed," he said again. "I noticed you have not done what I asked."

"What do you mean? Oh, that necklace, right? Yeah... that wasn't Gretchen's, was it? That was someone else's." Of course, he knew I had already picked up on that, hadn't he?

"Perhaps."

"You were testing me. Why?" He said nothing, so I pressed further. "What do you care?"

Brin stopped walking, so I stopped – luckily, there was no one directly behind us. We moved over to the side of the road, now less than a block from our homes. This was good, because the guards were relaxed enough now to keep going and give us our space. Not that I *wanted* to stand here and have a conversation with Tristan's morose and sometimes downright perplexing uncle. A week ago, this man was executing orders of assassination around town; before that, he was doing the same things in Doverton, and almost killed his own nephew – on purpose. Now this week, he was dressed up, beard neatly trimmed to a flax-colored chinstrap, and helping the sister he hadn't seen in gods-knew-how-long around the house. It was downright disconcerting.

"Show me. Show me what you can do," he said. Yes, he was definitely insane. Did he really want to talk about this *now*?

"What do you mean? You know already."

"You see things that happened before, *ja*?"

"Sometimes. I can't force it to happen. Trust me, I've tried."

"You 'see' through touch."

"That seems to be the way of it. Tristan said you know others who can... do what we do. So what else do you know? Wait on second thought, I don't want to know. Not right now – I'm not in the mood." And I really wasn't. After losing my father not a couple months ago, the last thing I'd wanted to do was watch another funeral. It helped to have a purpose, and it helped to not be the one on display, but I still felt like garbage. Torven, of all people, showing up with his idiotic talk of peace did not help. It all made me want to crawl into a bottle somewhere, and do it sooner rather than later.

From some hidden place on his person Brin produced a small blade, a knife like the kind hunters used to skin animals, with one sharp edge and one serrated. A simple weapon, not really meant for killing, but somehow I had a feeling this one had seen its share of that. Even though he offered the item to me handle-first, I admit, I flinched. "I had a thought," he said, continuing to hold the thing out for me.

"Really, I'm not in the mood, Brin," I said with a dismissive wave. On the street up ahead, the procession had broken up, with a few people lingering but everyone else going back to their homes. A number of them would be back later on, bringing sweets and food and wine over to Tristan and his mother. And yes, we all knew that they would have plenty of those things already. That wasn't the point – the point was to stuff each other silly to forget about the pain of loss for a while. This was, by far, the best part of any funeral, if there was such a thing as a "best part."

"I have no guarantees. Humor me, *ja*? It might be worth your while."

Humor him. Okay fine, what the fuck? I reached for the dagger and felt... nothing. Nothing at all.

I blinked at him. "What's *supposed* to happen?"

But Brin didn't say anything, just watched me. And didn't he seem different? Well, yeah he did – he was a kid. The beard was gone, the clothes were little more than rags, and he had that bright gleam of youth. Still tall, still intimidating, but more because of his energy than because of a well-honed physique. This was a boy who could run all day, with no inhibitions, though he was old enough to know the weight of responsibility.

That responsibility was in his hands, a woodcutter's axe just big enough for him to lift. Gods' Avenue melted into velveteen nothingness, and in its place was another street, a square somewhere, but it couldn't have been anywhere near Zondrell. In fact, it didn't look like any Zondrean city – the buildings were too low, spaced too far apart, and shaped oddly with steep, peaked roofs. Maybe that was to keep the snow from piling up. Fat white crystals floated down around young Brin as he grabbed up a wooden log, set it up on a short tree stump, and drove the axe down into it with all his might. It split clean in two.

There were others doing the same thing, men of different ages but all very Eislandisch in their look and stature, all chopping wood in the snow. None of them appeared to be shackled to their stumps, though – just Brin. Every once in a while, he glared down at the iron on his right leg, sometimes attempting to adjust it or itch underneath.

Two men strolled through the site then, moving toward Brin. These two were not blond and blue-eyed, though, but dark-eyed Zondreans with short-shorn brown-black hair. They both wore the black and silver falcon tabards of the Zondrell army, and they both displayed armbands and medals signifying high rank. Captains, I believe they were. One smiled and laughed at some joke he might have told, while the other quietly acknowledged that it may or may not have been funny.

Brin looked up at their approach, pausing with a heavy log in his hands. He looked ready to throw his burden right at them, but instead, he said something to them. The two officers looked at each other, then back at the Eislandisch boy before them.

"What did you just say?" one of them asked.

Wait, did I just hear him speak? I had never heard anything in these visions before. And I recognized that voice, lighthearted and smooth, rarely angry. The face, too, now that it was closer, was very familiar. In fact, watching the officer with the handsome, boyish face and the slightly rumpled uniform was just like looking in a mirror.

That was my father. Captain Xavier Vestarton! Oh, that he could see me! Of course he couldn't. This wasn't real, it just a memory, a play-act of sorts.

The other officer put his hands on his hips. "Say that again," he said to young Brin, more forceful, more intimidating. I knew this voice, too, didn't I? A strong tone, proud, sure of himself, just like his bearing. Just a slight almond shape of the eyes, angular face – a good Zondrean face, really, though not as striking as Xavier's.

Yes, this was Captain Jonathan Loringham, standing in front of me as a young man, barely older than I was now. His hand was on his sword as he spoke to Brin again, and I noticed that he had a bandage around his arm, poking out under his sleeve. "Say what you just said again."

"You should be cut. Like this wood," young Brin said, in Zondrean, even though his speech needed a lot of work. He was nowhere near the bilingual adult I knew. This kid could barely form the words properly.

"Didn't you try that already?" Xavier said with a chuckle.

Jonathan turned on him. "It's not funny."

"It *is* funny that you weren't on your guard."

Brin set his log, and took up his axe to cut it. Both Zondreans took a step back. "I try again, *Zondern*. Sometime."

"So you can understand us? And you can speak like us?" My father seemed interested, even impressed as Brin brought the axe down in a fine display of youthful strength.

"This one is dangerous," Jonathan said.

"Yeah, and useful. Think about it."

Jonathan considered, but seemed far less excited about the whole situation. His dark eyes narrowed, brow furrowed in a way that was so familiar I wished I could have said something to him. Did he have any idea that his son would grow up to flash people with that same withering look that confirmed their stupidity? Of course not, and I had no sense of being able to move, much less laugh at how funny that seemed.

The best part? Xavier knew what that look meant. I guess I never noticed them do this to each other when I was growing up. "Come on, don't look at me like that. A good messenger boy would be worth his weight in gold around here. We need more runners."

"He tried to kill me!"

"Stop flirting with his sister."

Brin snorted as he unleashed another bit of vengeance on a log. "*Ja*. Stop."

With a deep breath, Loringham dared to get within range of that axe. "Tell you what, boy," he said, speaking slowly and evenly. "We'll let you off that chain, but you have to do what we say. Do anything else, and bad things might happen. Things Captain Vestarton and I won't be able to control. You'll go straight to High Captain Moss, and so will your family. Do you understand me?"

He didn't mean that. I knew he didn't mean that, anyway, but Brin did not. The color draining from his face said everything, and he nodded. "I will do this. You stop... my sister."

"We'll talk." With half a smile on his face, he fished out a key and moved to remove that shackle on the boy's ankle. Xavier took the axe away from him and held his hands behind his back first – probably wise. The officers then bade Brin to follow them, walking away from the stump. I couldn't follow, though. I was held fast, wherever I was. I wanted to follow. I wanted to see them more, see them as young soldiers, laughing with one another, being... regular men, not Lords, not important figures in a hierarchy of nobility.

The one thing I did see as they moved off into the distance – off of my little vision-stage – was Brin reaching toward Loringham's belt. Deft, with practiced art, he pulled away a small knife. It disappeared into a pocket on his ragged trousers, and then the scene was gone, too – all black, melting away.

When the familiar sight of Gods' Avenue was back, I realized my cheeks were wet, and that very same knife from young Captain Loringham's belt was in my hand. "You stole this from him. From Jonathan," I said, wiping my face with the back of my hand.

The smile on Brin's face said a lot. It said he knew what I had seen, that I had seen what he *wanted* me to see. How did he know? "I considered giving it back to him. Give it to his son now, I... cannot."

"Why? Why not just tell him all that?"

"Better you. Better you could see it for yourself."

He started to walk away, leaving me with an odd sense of realization. That was a gift, what he just did – a great gift, at that. But also, it was something else. "So your friend, the one who was like me," I called after him, "he could do all of this?"

The big man paused, but did not look back. "He could. Maybe more. He practiced, searched for ways to look into Time. Just be careful. It needs control to be most useful."

"What does that mean?"

"It means it can drive you mad." With that, he continued on his way, leaving me alone on Gods' Avenue. Mad, eh? I could see how too much of these sorts of visions could drive one to the edge, but this last one, this was different. This was special. It eased something deep in my soul just to see my father and

Jonathan like that, to hear their voices. No one else would ever hear those voices again. If only I could pass along that gift somehow, but I didn't think I could. All I could do was find the right time to give Tristan that knife, his father's knife that had taken a long, crazy journey to get back here to Zondrell.

I clutched the weapon close to my side as I hurried home to change.

# CHAPTER TWENTY-NINE

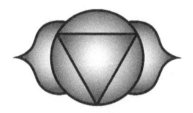

## The Spark
*7 Spring's Green, 1272*
*Tristan Loringham*

I t was time to go home. We would host a feast this evening, in honor of the dead and in celebration of my... ascension, I suppose it could be called. It was my House now. I had a study full of deeds and writs and ledgers to prove it.

This thought struck me rather hard as we left our escort of city guards – led by Guard Captain Corrin Shal-Vesper in his best armor, of course – and walked through the front door. *My House.* It had been taken so easily from my father. He fought it to the end, but there *was* an end. Unexpected, just like his ascension had been. I was a boy when my grandfather passed at age fifty-two, and after an argument with his younger brother that had cut an entire branch of our family tree off from Zondrell high society, my father became a Lord. I understood the significance of that word only slightly better now than I did when I was five.

*My House.* Suddenly, I felt an almost palpable bolt of energy. *Inspiration? Yes, now's the time.*

"I'm going to go take a walk," I told my mother and Andella as they started through the front door. The other families had gone off to change clothes and produce suitable gifts to bring back with them.

"Now? Where will you go?" Mum asked, suspicious eyes watching the soldiers depart. A hand went to the blue diamond pendant she wore, one of the last gifts my father ever gave to her, a long teardrop cut nearly the length of her thumb.

"Just down the street. Not far."

"You cannot be gone long. Dinner will be ready soon."

Andella raised her finger in the air. "I'll go with you."

"No, you stay here," I said, shaking my head. "It's safer."

"So you admit it's not safe?" This got unpleasant looks from both women.

"I'll be fine." Underneath my black longcoat with the Zondrell silver falcon embroidered across the back was the jewel-studded blade my father had given me. I patted it against my hip, its solid weight more comforting than an embrace. "Like I said, I'm not going far."

I kissed them both on the cheek. They tried to protest further, but I was already headed down the street, ignoring the looks from a cluster of mercenaries as I passed them. The sun was still up, but would set below the artificial horizon of the city walls soon enough. I had enough time to get to Center Market before the curfew, if I walked fast. So, that's where I headed.

Not many were around – in fact, streets that once bustled with life were almost empty. As I turned down Filigree Lane toward Center Avenue, I noticed several shops with broken windows, debris scattered and valuables long gone. Further down, an overturned carriage stood over the rotting corpses of two men. Neither appeared armed, although thieves might have made off with any weaponry. *By the Lady, it's like a storm tore through this city.* The temple stood at the west end of Gods' Avenue, and that street had thousands of Lords' gold protecting it. Everywhere else was clearly far less fortunate.

Next block, more of the same. A dead woman with her head bashed in. Three unidentifiable city guards, weapons and armor stripped. A house still smoldering, burned to the ground. It brought a lump to my throat as real as the one I'd just fought through for the past five hours. For better or for worse, Zondrell was my homeland, a majestic, modern city. At least, it *was*. I was almost glad my father was spared from seeing it like this. All his ideals, all his plans... reduced to rubble.

When I reached Center Market, ten armed men, mostly city guard, flanked the entrance. Another ten stood at each of the four entrances to the great square, which still teemed with life. I heard it had been declared more or less neutral ground, giving people a place to go during the day and merchants a chance to continue earning some business, since no one new was allowed into the city. I wondered if the merchants had to pay for their protection the way we nobles had.

I only wanted to visit one stall, and I headed for it without delay. A smile as warm as Katalahni sands and painted red as spilled blood greeted me. "Oh, *Sayidi Tanin*! I hear about your news. I am so very sorry for you." Zizah hurried to pour some rich, spicy tea into a cup for me. "You take this – makes you feel good."

When I looked at her, I couldn't help but think of Brin's stories of the mage Safaa. This Katalahni had dark skin, too, though more like oiled bronze and not coal, and there was that glimmer in her eyes. I knew she had some magic, but she hid her nature by puffing on *tsohbac* sticks. Alex might have known what kind of magic she carried, as they were... close, but if so, it was their little secret. Well, one of a few secrets. I did see the attraction – she was quite striking, in her way, with jewelry on every available bit of her, gleaming in just the right way against that dark skin.

It was the jewelry I had come to see, though the tea wasn't bad either. It tasted of cinnamon, clove, and something else I couldn't quite place, and went down smooth. "It's very good," I told her.

"You need strong herbs to help you through times like these, yes? I give you some." She dipped under the counter of her stall, then pulled out a small paper packet, folded at the top. "Put a pinch of this in hot water anytime you feel stress."

I reached inside my jacket for some coins. "How much?"

"Oh, *Tanin*, no, no!" She moved her hands about in the air as if to shoo me away. "I could not take your money for this. It is my gift to you." That's when she noticed something that made her words catch in her throat. She leaned in close, almost pulling herself over the counter to get a good luck at me... into my eyes.

"You hear a lot of things, I know," I said to her. "You didn't hear about what happened on Peaceday?"

A smile brightened her face. "I did, *Tanin*, but I did not believe. That magic, it is like the stories."

"Which stories are those?"

"You let my sister put a gold dragon on your arm and you do not know of the stories?"

Indeed, one of her sisters ran the best tattoo operation in the city, a shop called Three Sisters Curios and Artistry not far off. While Zizah ran the Center market stall displaying her jewels and silks and the like, the other two Katalahni girls tended their store. *That shop – were they hiding from looters like so many others?* "Your sisters are all right with everything going on right now?"

"We have hired men to keep us safe. So many are willing to lend their swords, many men with no more law or lord to keep them. But do not change the subject, *Sayidi.*"

"Of course not," I said with a quick smile. "No, I don't really know the stories you speak of. I mean, I know the one about the gold dragon that can't be killed. I think everyone knows that one."

"There are many others, about many dragons. You should look for those stories – they would interest you. They would interest *Habibi* Alexander, too, I think." When I looked at her, expecting something more, she just poured me some more tea.

"Do these stories tell more about... what we can do?"

"Our holy men, the *Rusul,* know of these things. I am just a merchant, *Sayidi.* Maybe you should plan a trip to Katalahnad one day. Seek the *Rusul* and ask them."

A book in old Eislandisch about the magic. Brin recalling his time with three mages from three different lands. Now stories from Katalahnad about dragons. *How come every culture knows about these strange magics except the Zondreans?* Perplexing, indeed, but I wasn't here to talk about magic; in fact, it had been the last thing on my mind most of the day. No one had said anything to me, or to Alex or Andella, even with all of those different nobles around paying their respects. And perhaps it was exactly that – respect – that made them keep their comments confined to whispers in corners.

"Maybe I'll do that someday. Right now, I can't. I have a favor to ask instead. Can you show me some of your best jewelry?"

Zizah's red lips curled into a smile. "If everyone asked me such easy favors, I would have a very simple life, *Sayidi.*"

Happily, she reached down under the counter again, and pulled out a large glass box, its opening locked with a sturdy padlock that thudded on the wooden counter as she set the box down. I peered through the slight cloudiness of the glass, watching her finger as she pointed to different items in turn. "I have these pieces that are my most fine. Only good to sell to ones like you, with gold in their pockets. I have this bracelet that just came to me from Drakannya. And... oh, I have this necklace with diamond and ruby. Very nice, yes? Hmm, and there is this silver pin for your coat, *Sayidi*. Yes, that would be very nice on you, I think."

"It's not for me. I'm looking for something else." *By the gods, just say what you want to say.* "For a woman. To, um..."

I didn't have to say it aloud. Zizah was on to me. "*Sayidi!* Yes, yes, I have just the thing." She continued to smile as she pulled a key from her bodice and unlocked the box. It opened with a creak. "There, I think that is it. Yes, this one. A proper thing for such an occasion."

With delicate hands, she held out an exquisite ring and bracelet, linked together with a network of fine interlocking chains, silver and gold weaved together in an intricate pattern. The ring and bracelet had matching patterns of swirls etched into them that outlined a series of different gems – ruby, sapphire, diamond, emerald, and amethyst.

It was as beautiful a betrothal band as I could ask for.

"*Ya, Sayidi*, it is nice, yes?" she asked as I took the attached items, inspecting them carefully. "You think of many things on a day like this. Of the future. Of things you must protect, yes?"

"There's a lot that needs protection lately."

"Sometimes, death makes us think of life. I think you do a good thing, *Sayidi*. A wise thing."

I swallowed hard. "Only if she says yes."

"She will, I have no doubt. I have seen you together, and she cares much for you. No woman would say no to this piece anyhow, *Sayidi*. Drakannyan gold, Katalahni silver, made by a great artist in the desert. I buy many things from him, but this is the best one I have had in a long time."

"How much?" I didn't need the sales pitch.

"For you, I give to you for... half price. Three thousand."

She wanted me to haggle with her – that was their way. But I didn't have the heart for it, nor was I lacking in funds, so I pulled out three thousand-Royal coins from my inside jacket pocket. It might have been more than she had made all day, or all week, based on the way she stuffed those coins into her bodice.

"The sun sets soon. You should go. I wish you much fortune, *Sayidi*."

Realizing she was right, I put away the betrothal band and my bag of whatever herbs she bade me to take, hurrying on my way with a bow. As I traced my steps back toward home, the headache seemed to pulse along in rhythm with my racing thoughts. I might not even have the courage to go through with it. She might very well decline. She's known me for what, a month? Maybe a few weeks more? And people would talk – oh, how they would talk. Not that they didn't already. They were talking right now, whispering about Loringham's poor half-breed boy, left alone to care for an estate. Not ready for it, not ready at all.

*Stop worrying. You're a Lord now, for Catherine's sake. Be a man.* That's what Father would have said.

As I turned back onto Filigree, three men in the silvered platemail of the Royal Guard approached from the opposite direction. I moved over to avoid them, but they followed my lead. I crossed the street again, and they followed, intent on a collision course. As I got closer, one of them held up his arm.

"The curfew is in effect," he shouted.

I looked up at a sky that had just started to turn pink and ashen. "I'm almost home," I said, not slowing down.

"No one is allowed on the streets after dark."

"Well aware, soldier. It's not dark yet, though." I edged to the left to pass between two of them, when the one who spoke caught me by the shoulder. His heavy gauntlet pressed hard, right into the place where I'd been injured and was still a little tender. "Can I help you, soldier?" I asked him through gritted teeth.

"It doesn't seem you *are* aware. Lord Torven has declared that no civilians can be out after dark. And yet, here you are."

*Lord* Torven. My stomach dropped just thinking of him. "Well, if you'd kindly remove your hand and get out of my way, soldier, I'd already be home."

But the man did not loosen his grip. "Lord Torven extends his sympathies for your loss," he said. He didn't have far to meet my gaze – he was quite tall, a broad-chested fellow with a fresh scar on his cheek, making him all the more imposing in his royal plate.

*Who does this asshole think he is?* "I don't require any sympathy from your lord. You can tell him I said that." Applying some force, I pushed him away, hoping he'd let go of me and that would be that. He did let go, but not without a few choice curses hurled in my direction.

"Fucking half-breed scum," he said at my back. "You think you're important now? The Lords are ancient history." The other two with him started to laugh. They thought they could laugh loud enough to mask the sound of swords leaving their scabbards.

I felt something deep within then, something electric – a spark, for lack of a better word. My entire body tensed as that energy pulsed through me, lighting up muscles, heating blood. This wasn't like the usual surge of adrenaline I felt in battle, though. That feeling I knew all too well. This was different, subtle, yet more intense at the same time. *Powerful.*

I turned on them, drawing my weapon as I did so. The big one was already in a full charge, blade extended, but I was ready. I easily sidestepped his approach. The two others drew with a shout and moved to close in, attempting to flank me on either side. This wasn't a bad idea – they wore full armor, while I had none. They could easily overwhelm me... if they were fast enough.

The one at my left lunged in, blade seeking purchase where I could not parry him. I jumped back to avoid him, then twisted to meet the second one head-on before his swing could find flesh. Instead, the strike hit my blade, the echo hollow across that empty street.

With a curse, the big Royal Guard came at me again, from behind, along with his friend in the front. As I moved to block with my sword, I reached out to grab with my left hand for an arm, a throat, something, and did get hold of a breastplate. It came with a price, though. Heat washed over my forearm as a sword sliced through my sleeve and into flesh, but I refused to let go and pulled the smaller of the two attackers off his balance. He crashed to his hands and knees before me.

I hesitated. I could have driven my weapon through his neck and severed his spine, but did he deserve to die? *No. His "lord" does, though.* Still, I felt that spark, that electric intensity. It goaded me to action. It begged me to fight, to use that gods-given talent for what it was born to do. *No, I can't. I won't.*

Perhaps I should have. The pause in my step allowed the big man and his other friend to team up for another strike, one coming in low while the other came in high. Swings from two ends – can't dodge both. Can't block both. Either way, I would get worse than a cut on the arm.

The spark knew what to do, even if I did not.

In a perfect circle around me, half a dozen bolts of white lightning arced down from the cloudless twilight. Stone and gravel flew in all directions and the ground quaked from the force. They left behind little more than an odd sense of relief and the screams of men. The one on his knees had taken the brunt of it – he had collapsed into a heap of metal on the ground, unmoving. Behind me, the other smaller man had been knocked back at least ten feet, lying spread out on his back.

The bigger man writhed on the ground a few feet away in the opposite direction. He cursed in between gasps for breath, hands searching for the weapon that had dropped and skittered away. When I went up to him, all movement stopped.

I leveled my blade at his throat. "You. You go tell Torven to enjoy his castle while it lasts," I said, my voice even and solemn and coming from somewhere otherworldly. "We're coming for him."

# CHAPTER THIRTY

## Chances

*7 Spring's Green, 1272*
*Andella Weaver*

The house teemed with life – servants cooking and preparing the table, friends and extended family gathered around in different corners for discussion, everything now relaxed after the long funeral procession and ceremony. It was as if everyone had breathed a collective sigh, ready to talk now about something other than death. Now was the time to remember happier things – to remember life – and to be thankful.

This was actually a teaching from the Book of Catherine, but most of the people gathered here didn't seem like they wanted to talk about religion. They'd clearly had their fill of it already and were talking about everything from fashion to family goings-on, and occasionally gossip about the state of politics in Zondrell these days. If my sister were here, she could tell them all kinds of wisdom from the Book, things that would help them, and...

I paused. I wondered if Seraphine was doing all right, there in the roadside temple by herself. Maybe Madame Saçaille was watching out for her, stopping in now and then to chastise her or talk philosophy the way she used to do. Our parents were of course long gone, my father taken by that plague back when I was just a little, tiny girl, and my mother from the red fever the year before I left for the Academy. I still missed them when I thought of it, every now and then. I thought of them today while sitting in that funeral, trying to remember how it felt when it first happened. My father, I barely remembered, but Mother... it was so sad. My heart felt like it would just burst. I cried and cried, while Seraphine had worked so hard to be the wise older sister. She was good at that sort of thing.

I tried to be like her today, strong and dependable, and it had worked for the most part. It was easier than I thought it might have been, though not because I didn't think Lord Jonathan was a lovely man. He was, in a gruff sort of way – generous, dedicated, thoughtful. And I had done everything I could to help him. I used every ounce of power I had to try to heal him... it wasn't enough.

Perhaps the Lady's Fate had a purpose for him, something none of us could understand. I did believe in Fate, believed that Her will guided us all, and after much prayer and tears thinking on it, I realized that Alex was right. I had done everything I could. I had poured every bit of power I had into him, but it wasn't... meant to be. Then later, as Lord Loringham's pyre burned and I watched, pretending I could be the Pyrelight dancing through the rites again, I did feel that he was going to Paradise at peace. It was hard to admit, I must be honest. A part of me wanted to cling to this idea that I had failed somehow. I did fail. But yet, Tristan didn't seem to think that, his mother didn't think that, no one did. They all continued to embrace me as one of their own, as a part of their lives. I didn't get kicked out or chastised or who-knows-what could have happened for not being able to save this man, a father, a husband, a pillar of the social structure of Zondrell.

It was now up to his son to take his place – I hoped Tristan was up to the task.

So far, things looked grim indeed, since he'd wandered out for a walk over an hour ago. Where was he? While everyone else talked and laughed and commiserated, I hovered in view of the foyer, checking every so often to see if Tristan had walked in.

"So, when did he take this walk?" Alex asked, coming up to me with a glass of wine in each hand and offering me the lighter-colored one. It would have been rude to refuse, even though I preferred sweeter red wines myself.

I shook my head and a stray bit of hair fell out of the tenuous, braided pile tied with ribbons atop my head. "About an hour ago. Maybe longer."

"Does he realize it's not safe out there?" Here, Alex had no spectacles on again, though he'd worn them through the whole funeral. Unfamiliar company from all corners of the nobility had been there, and while they would gossip and speculate, none of them needed to know anything for certain. The people in the dining room now? They knew everything – about him, about me, about Tristan – and yet, no one seemed to treat us any differently. That was how to spot true friends, I supposed.

"He went with his sword. But..." I hesitated. I didn't want him to get upset – he did that well enough on his own.

"And it's been over an hour? Mother of Sarabande." His eyes were whirling patterns of quicksilver. He gulped down his wine and headed for the door, so I followed.

"You're not going to go look for him?"

"Do you have a better idea?"

I didn't, unfortunately. "But how are you feeling?" I asked him. I had summoned some power to heal him more yesterday, but it still seemed like it wasn't enough. He still strained every time he sat down or stood up.

Alex poked at the side where that sword had struck him, wincing. "I've had better days, but that's not important right now." Wasting no more time, I followed him outside into the cool evening.

It was so quiet, an eerie artificial calm over the whole city. It was much darker than normal, too, since most of the tall torches lining all the main roads weren't lit. I wondered if that meant the people who went around lighting them at dusk – mostly Fire mages hired by the King – were out of a job. Or maybe something happened to them... I didn't want to think about that.

As we moved down Gods' Avenue, toward the temple standing in shadows and silhouettes, I stuck close to Alex's side. A cluster of mercenary guards saw us, but said nothing when they realized it was their boss.

"Maybe you should ask them?" I said, almost whispering. It would have felt wrong to say something too loud and shatter the heavy silence.

"Not necessary," Alex replied. "Follow me." With a sigh, he picked up his pace, and I followed suit.

At the corner, a flash and the booming sound of thunder stopped us in our tracks. It wasn't supposed to rain tonight, was it? I looked up into a clear evening sky lit with purples and blues, but Alex was looking straight ahead, down the next street. He cursed.

"Did you see that?"

"What was it?"

"Lightning." He cursed again and started to move, faster than I thought he could, the tails of his pristine corded silver jacket dangling behind him.

I had to hurry to keep up, which was not easy to do in a dress. "Lightning? How can that be? It's a beautiful night."

"You didn't see it – from the other day – did you?"

"See what?"

"The Light magic."

No, I hadn't. Tristan had told me about it, a little, but I never saw it with my own eyes. A part of me really wanted to witness how spectacular something that could end a battle of thousands of people like Brin had described could be. The idea was scary at the same time, though.

By the time we got to the next block, a figure approached, purposeful yet quick. I tensed. I almost grabbed Alex's arm until I realized that large person in the dark jacket was none other than Tristan. Alex cursed, doubly so, as we raced up to him.

"What are you doing out here?" Alex sounded like an angry parent, his words falling in between heavy gasps. All this running about was not likely good for his recovery.

Tristan tried to shrug it off. "Trying to get home, what does it look like?"

"You had us worried," I started, "and... oh, what happened?" He held his left forearm with his right in an odd sort of way, squeezing as he held it against his body. He was hurt – hurt! What was wrong with him coming out here like this? I mean, just looking around could tell anyone that the streets of Zondrell were different than they once were. There were hacked out doors and broken windows and wrecked carriages... and not a few shapeless, unmoving lumps in the shadows that were probably bodies. Good Catherine in Paradise, how horrible. This was the sort of thing that happened in far-off places with no law and order, where men killed each other for sport. It did not happen in Zondrell.

"There was a disagreement on when the curfew starts. It starts now – come on." We went back to Gods' Avenue where it was relatively safe as quickly as we could. All the while, I kept my eye on that arm.

"What did you do?" I asked once we could slow our pace a bit.

"I went to Center Market."

"No, after that," Alex said, adding a derisive insult for good measure. "Just now. I saw lightning."

"I told you, there was a disagreement, with the Royal Guard. It's fine – it's handled."

"Royal Guard? Are you kidding me? They picked a fight with you?"

"They knew who I was. A good target."

"Unbelievable. Just unbelievable. Did Torven not just talk to you about peace?"

"And he's proven so trustworthy lately." He chuckled in spite of himself, and after a moment, so did Alex.

"Did they... did anyone get away from that? What you did with the lightning?"

Tristan's lips drew into a line. "I think so. They attacked – I just wanted out of there. I didn't even mean to do that. Look, let's worry about this tomorrow, all right? Don't say anything to Cen."

Alex seemed inclined to agree, nodding, but I could tell he was still tense. "Fine, yeah," he said. "Hope you've got another cask of that Starlandia Valley Red for dinner. I think we'll need it."

"There's two. No worries, my friend."

We were almost to the house now, which was good – I really wanted to get back indoors. The night had begun to cover everything like a sick, dark pall. "You're still hurt," I said to Tristan, looking up at the way the light and shadows played on his square and clean-shaved features.

"It's not serious."

"I'll be the judge of that." I was an "expert" in these sorts of things now, after all, wasn't I? Not really, but I did want to see if I could take care of it. "Why suffer if you don't have to?"

At the front door, Tristan relented. He nodded for Alex to continue inside, which he did with a sideways sort of glance. What was that all about?

"Fine, here you go," he said, holding out his arm for inspection. The sleeve of his jacket had been cut clean through, and two halves of cloth fluttered open as he released his grip on them. Underneath was a cut from wrist to elbow, a dark, straight line outlined in bloodstained flesh. If that had been on the other side, where the big veins were? I shivered at the thought.

"This is not just a cut. Look at this. Doesn't it hurt?" He didn't answer, but he also didn't resist as I took up his arm, cradling it with one hand as I inspected with the other. Without even trying, without even thinking about it, a violet glow lit under that hand, and I felt that searing warmth that was now becoming familiar – a sensation both painful and relaxing all at once. When I pulled away, there was nothing but remnants of blood, the skin stitched right back to the way it should be.

"It used to hurt. It stopped now," he said, a hint of a smile forming. "You're amazing."

"Not really." I tried to look him in the eye, but just couldn't. He forced me to do so, though, with a gentle nudge of my chin.

Was he smiling? Yes, a faint one, but he was. None of this was funny – what was he thinking? "You are, really. That was a miracle, what you just did."

"A tiny one. Hey, what were you thinking going out there by yourself, and starting a fight?"

"I didn't start anything. Look, don't worry about it."

"Don't worry? You know, you're acting very strangely."

He took a deep breath. "I'm sorry. Can you do something for me? Just... in a few minutes, we're going to go in for dinner. I'm going to have to say some things, to everyone. I'm going to ask you a question, and when I do, I want you to promise to me that you'll answer honestly. Okay?"

"What? Okay... I guess?" He really was acting very odd. Losing someone close to you will do that I suppose, but this was a different Tristan Loringham than the sullen one from the past couple of days that slept a lot and said almost nothing to anyone. This one was alert, looking at me with a piercing gaze, those streaks of Light in his eyes like little falling stars. This Tristan had purpose, and he seemed more... Lordly. There was no other word for it.

"Just promise. Oh, and cover for me for a minute while I go change?" He kissed me on the cheek in that way I was beginning to realize was his method of reassuring me, even – and especially – when I didn't want to be reassured. It would have been charming if it wasn't so blasted annoying.

**\*\***

"I'd like to thank you all for being here." Tristan stood at the head of the long mahogany table, now dressed in a crisp gray tunic with long sleeves and a decorative green hem that just covered his belt. He wasn't as fashionably dressed as some of the other men there, like Lord Shal-Vesper in his ruffled cuffs and swirling black embroidery or Alex in his high collared shirt with the front open down to his heart, but then again, I couldn't imagine Tristan in ruffles.

"You act like we have somewhere better to be, my Brother," Alex said, raising his glass and inviting everyone to join in a toast. "To Jonathan. And to House Loringham." Many cheers went up around the table, which quieted after everyone had sipped from their glass of wine or brandy or whatever they had. They looked expectantly back to Tristan, who seemed to be fighting so hard to find the right words. Everything he said was very careful, deliberate, as if he'd rehearsed it all but now had a case of stage fright. No matter – no one cared, no one judged.

"My Father loved all of you. I know he would be happy to know you were all here, and that you've been taking such good care of my mother and me. You... don't know how much that means to us." He paused, taking another sip of his wine – Starlandia Valley Red – then turned to the man seated by his mother, who sat directly across from me. "I know it's not easy for you to be here, to have spent these past few days with us," he said to his uncle. "But I want to thank you for your help,

Brin. You've been there for my mother when I was not, and I'm in your debt."

As the big Eislander folded his arms and nodded to Tristan, saying nothing, I noticed a peek of some sort of tattooed artwork hiding under the split in his collar. Honestly, I too was amazed Brin was sitting with all of these Zondreans. I could see the discomfort in the lines at the corners of his eyes, the tension in his jaw. On the other hand, he had barely left his sister's side since the night Lord Jonathan passed. To the casual onlooker, it seemed like he did it grudgingly, but I wasn't so sure. A man like that did not shave and put on good silks unless he meant it.

Tristan nodded back a silent salute, then turned back to the whole group. "I, um, realize I haven't been the easiest to talk to in the past few days. I've taken a lot of time to think, maybe too much. I know I'm prone to that – my father used to tell me that a lot, growing up. And while I'd like to think that he was proud of me, I know he wasn't. Not always." Across the table, Lady Gretchen sighed and reached for her son's arm. "No, it's okay. Like I said, I've been thinking a lot. It used to bother me – sometimes we would even fight. But... I realize that he was trying to prepare me for this." He held up the hand not in a deathgrip by his mother, the one that wore a large gold signet ring with the "L" for House Loringham carved on it.

Then for a few minutes, he seemed to forget what he wanted to say next. The pause started getting uncomfortable, and glasses clinked as people took their drinks. No one spoke, though, not even Alex. I tried to read some of their faces, to pick up on what they might be thinking. Alex looked curious, while Lady Gretchen seemed sad, almost wistful. Lord Cen's expression was stoic even though his posture was alert and tense.

Finally, Tristan took a long, deep breath. "I'm not prepared for this," he said, his tone one of finality. "Just like the Academy doesn't prepare you for a real battlefield, there's no amount of schooling my father could have given me. He did the best he could with what he had, and for that, I'll always be thankful. I learned a lot from him in twenty-two years; I just wish I had understood all those lessons a little earlier. I will do everything in my power to do what's right for this House, for my family, for Zondrell. Alex, Cen, I promise you that I will be the ally that my father was to you."

"There's no doubt of that, son," said Lord Cen, gaunt features softening.

"I appreciate that, but I know I'm not the same man my father was. Nor can I say I'll always emulate him. I'm my own man – I intend to stay that way."

Seated next to me, Alex smiled, a big wide grin. He raised his glass again. "Please do, Brother." There was another toast, but Tristan didn't sit down. He had something else to say and again, it seemed to come slowly, as if his mind were working out all of the possibilities and nuances first. He reached into a pants pocket and pulled out something, fist closing around it so no one could see what it was. That's when he turned to me.

Well, he didn't so much as turn, but actually knelt down on one knee before me. For once, I wasn't looking up at him, his towering stature made suddenly humble. The way the light danced along the white streaks in his eyes reminded me of new snow glistening in the sun. I had no idea what I looked like, but I was pretty sure my mouth had fallen open. What was he doing? No, he could not be doing what I thought he was. Why would he…?

He reached for my hand and put something made of metal in there – I could feel a latticework of chains – but he didn't let go just yet. His hands were warm as they closed over mine. "Tristan, what…?"

He cut me off, eyes intense, searching as he plodded through careful words. "Andella, I know we haven't known each for very long, but it feels like… we've been on a long journey together. I owe you a great deal – I owe you my life. Nothing I can give can repay that, but even so… I guess I'd like to start. I'd like you to share this House with me."

I started to say something, then stopped. I looked around. I saw Alex, that wide smile still on his face – he knew this would happen! Well, of course he did, they were best friends, after all. Lady Gretchen also smiled, approving, even encouraging me with her eyes. Oh dear Catherine in Paradise.

Before I could find words, Tristan found a few more. "Remember what I told you. Be honest." He pulled away then, leaving me with the chained thing, so delicate with a network of gold and silver that connected a bejeweled ring to a matching bracelet. Five different colors winked at me, sparkling in the light of the chandelier above my head. Breathtaking, just... breathtaking. This was what men gave to women when they asked them to marry them.

Oh dear Lady... he was asking me to marry him!

I had never thought much about getting married. My experience with men was fairly limited, really – I spent most of my teenage years helping out at the church, and when I went to the Academy, my interests were in my studies, and my magic, and putting it toward becoming a Pyrelight. Most men, believe it or not, aren't interested in girls who want to spend their time at funerals. I mean, there was Stephen the aspiring Air mage, but that didn't last long enough to consider marriage. I wouldn't have said yes to him even if he had – his lazy, carefree nature was nothing short of annoying.

Tristan, on the other hand, was not annoying. Moody sometimes, sure, and his communication needed some work, but he was stalwart and good-hearted, the kind of man my father would have liked to have met, no doubt. And yes, he had money. Quite a lot of it. Many women would consider themselves lucky to find a life with even half the luxury he could offer. I had known girls at the Academy who would have sold their soul twice over for such an opportunity, even if they had no feelings at all for the man in question.

By the Lady, was I even breathing? No, I was stupidly staring at the jewels in my hand unable to speak, while a room full of people sat on the edge of their seats. Somewhere, I heard whispers. Behind me, Alex shifted in his chair. I could only imagine the look on his face.

I blinked many times in succession as I finally looked to meet Tristan's gaze. Stars danced along his streaks of Light but otherwise, his expression gave away almost nothing.

"I... yes." I almost breathed that word. Yes. Did I really just say that? "But I don't know how to be a Lady."

The twitch at one corner of his lips turned in one of those sideways smiles I liked so much. Hadn't seen that in days. "I don't know how to be a Lord. So, it's perfect."

It felt strange to do so in front of all of those people, but I felt compelled to lean in and kiss him then. Oh yes, a real kiss, full on the lips in front his mother and the Lady above and a whole table full of nobility. I'm not sure how appropriate it was, but I didn't care, and neither did Tristan. The glee in it, the abandon in such a simple act, the cheers from the onlookers... it was good. Happy. Catherine knew we needed some happiness in our lives for a change.

**

Later, after a lovely dinner where people shared stories and memories around the table, with more food than I think I'd ever seen in one place at one time, just two of us were left at the table. Tristan poured a fair amount of the wine from the last bottle of the evening into my glass first, then emptied the rest into his own.

"You know," he said, "I didn't think you'd say yes."

"I've hardly known you more than a couple of months."

"I know." The wine swirled in his glass as he held it, staring into its depths with an absent sort of look.

"And you know, I almost did say no." I bit my bottom lip as I waited for a response. It just popped out – maybe I shouldn't have said that.

But, he was smiling. "I know."

"Oh. Really?"

"You think people are going to say you're doing it for the money."

"Well they are, aren't they?"

"Why do you care?" he asked, then took along sip from his glass. I did the same, and the warmth of the vibrant red liquid seemed to make my skin light up.

"I know how people are, at least around here. But I mean, I don't want you to think that, because it's not true."

The half-smile was back. "Even if I did, what's mine is yours. All this is... nice to have, I suppose, but money's just not that important when it comes down to it."

"Yeah." I looked down at my left hand, where metal gleamed and gemstones glittered against the torchlight around us. It fit well, too – the ring had slid right onto my finger, and while the bracelet was loose, it was comfortable. And goodness, how gorgeous! The gold and silver weave of the chain felt a little odd resting against the back of my hand as it was, but it was light and the way it contrasted with my skin made it seem like it had been made just for me. I couldn't believe he bought something like this without even thinking I'd accept it.

"Fate brought us here," he said after a few minutes. "Might as well make the most of it, right? It's not like we have to have the wedding now. Maybe in a few months. Next year even."

Now I couldn't help but smile myself, watching the starlight in his eyes dance and wink. It was fascinating, so different from other magic. I couldn't help but think that I wanted Archmage Tiara to see this, and soon, but instead of bringing up such thoughts, I paid attention to his manner instead. "You're in an awfully good mood, you know. Are you sure you're all right? This is not normal for you."

He leaned back, his gaze moving off into the distance somewhere. "I've had a lot of time to think. I feel like... I can see more clearly." He shook his head.

"What do you mean?"

"I... think I've found my Path, you know?"

No, I didn't. I didn't know what that felt like, not yet. I wished I did, but I felt I was further from my Path than I'd ever been. Not because of him, of course – that felt good, right. I wanted to be with him, but everything else felt like it was caught in a storm, blowing every which way. I didn't know which end was up. The Book of Catherine says that those who have the power to make change in the world do so not out of pride, nor out of certainty. There is nothing assured other than the fact that the Lady provides a Path for each of us. The Book says we choose to understand that Path, choose to accept it. I wanted to understand, didn't I? So why couldn't I feel comfortable with my magic? Why couldn't I make it do what it was supposed to do? Why couldn't I help people who needed me?

There were no answers in Tristan's gaze, nor in the bottom of my wineglass.

# PART FOUR

G rand beasts bask in the mountains beyond the desert, great enough to be mountains themselves.

Red, flame of the sun,
Bright, healer and destroyer,
Where it all begins.
Blue, the water's flow,
Without it, there is nothing,
Parched ruination.
White makes the breeze blow,
Seeds born aloft to the land,
The earth grows greener.
Green, land under our feet,
Trees, plants, stones, all that we know,
Nourishing all life.
Silver, flow of time,
Unrelenting forever,
Gone, sun never rises.
Indigo, life breathes,
Without, blood runs cold, lifeless,
No light in our eyes.
And Gold, pure and true,
Casting away all shadows,
Lighting, purging all.

Their code is law, their rules perfect, intertwined, and beyond knowledge. Oh, humans approached, they did, tried to know what they could not.

But the dragons pitied the humans, in their way. One day, they each broke a scale from their backs and buried them in the sand, glittering beastly things that sank to the core of the earth itself, and spread their power through the world.

– A myth of the birth of magic,
attributed to Katalahni scholar Azim al Suqur, 351

# CHAPTER THIRTY-ONE

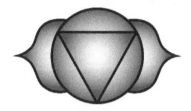

# Belief

*9 Spring's Green, 1272*
*Brin Jannausch*

One thing – perhaps the only thing – that I liked about the lands beyond Eisland was the rain. We did have storms in the summer, thunder-filled monstrosities bringing cold rain mixed with ice that pelted and tore apart everything in its wake. Those storms were the exact opposite of what I found in Zondrell, this gentle springtime rain that ebbed and flowed with the winds, cooling like the mist from a waterfall. The Zondern thought me quite odd for taking off my shirt and going out into the courtyard to enjoy it. Even my sister, who had become as much like them as she could without changing her hair color, gave me a strange look.

"There are better ways to take a bath," Gretchen said to me as I passed through the dining room and opened the double-doors that led outside.

"That may be," I replied, "but where else could I train and bathe at the same time?" This made her laugh, an unusual thing for her of late.

Her giggles echoed in my mind as I strode into the courtyard, where I could see her still sitting there through the massive windows with her breakfast, a book, and a cup of tea. It seemed a regular place for her, a spot where she could watch anyone using the training rack at the center of her well-tended garden. The blue frost-tips were in full bloom here – little reminders of Eisland – and the large weapon rack and chained man made from blocks of wood looked out of place among them. Instead of using their courtyard as a place to entertain guests or do whatever Zondrell nobles did to while away their days, the Loringham men used this spot to practice their art.

I pulled a dulled blade from the rack, one much smaller than my own Beschützer. Something about it reminded me of Johann – simple, but refined, maybe too much for its own good. This was a weapon many common men would be thankful to have sharp and at the ready. Instead, it sat out here, blunt, its only prey a man that never bled. Wasted, much like the life of the man who had owned it.

I tested the blade with a firm hit against the long block serving as the dummy's torso. It swung on its chains, giving just a little and making a satisfying cracking sound. I hit it again, harder to make the chains creak under the strain. Then again, and again, the grooves I sliced into the wood melding with all of the ones that had come before until they joined a familiar sort of pattern. I found myself going through stances and forms that I had not used in years with that light weapon. My angles were sharp, my movements quick, even in bare feet and wet leathers that had begun to cling to my legs. The rain splashed against my face, flowed down my back... and it felt good.

But it did nothing to wash my thoughts away. The River was not ready for Johann – I felt this in my bones, and yet, he was gone. If I had wanted to watch my sister weep, I would have killed the man myself years ago. Yet, she had followed him all the way here, to this alien place full of alien people and soft rains and bright greenery; this was love. I knew this. Even as a boy, I knew this, though I detested it. And now he had to go and die, and Gretchen's tears fell. It seemed... unfair.

Shaking water out of my hair, I took up the blade once more, but hesitated. "Ladies prefer to stay inside during rain, ja?" I asked the presence I felt behind me.

"Might as well get used to it," Tristan's betrothed Saint said from under her little umbrella. "It'll be this way all month."

"*Wunderbar*," I replied.

"You like the rain?"

"It is warm here. Rain makes it more… tolerable."

"If you say so." From the way she huddled in her cloak, I assumed she did not agree. Yet, she did not leave.

"Do you need something of me?" I asked.

The auburn-haired girl shook her head, then pawed at the stone underneath with one idle boot. "Not really. Tristan's gone out to some kind of business meeting with Alex and Lord Cen, so I thought I'd come see what you were doing out here. Don't you know you can get sick if you're out in the rain too long?"

I laughed. *Dummkopf Zondern* and their silly ideas. "Where I come from, cold is all there is. Never got sick – not from that."

"Oh."

"Besides, training is better in cold. Gives you strength." Training was not better with an audience, however. After a few more strikes at the dummy, I paused to regard her. By the River, those purple eyes… too much like Jade.

"So, I was wondering if maybe you could think about possibly, um, showing me how to do that? What you just did there?" She stumbled over every inch of her words, and it brought the smile back to my face.

"You think you need training?"

"I think I need to be able to defend myself." A pause, and a deep, frustrated breath. "I lost my Fire. What if something happens, you know? Something else? I mean, I asked Tristan about it, a long time ago, but things have been so busy, and now… I don't know. I just feel like I need to do something."

The wisdom in this was not lost on me, though she was so small, so meek. Andella Weaver was not the kind of girl who could bear a sword against an enemy. Some could, and some could not – such was the way of things. Men were no different. "Nothing will happen to you under the care of your man, I am sure."

"Oh I know, but… I mean, we can't be together every minute of every day." She went to the sword rack, looking up at the array of weapons of all sizes – mostly swords, the favored weapon of the *Zondern*, but there were at least three spears, an axe, and some staves. A canopy sheltered them, somewhat, but she started getting wet the minute she put the umbrella down to reach for a sword with a broad, traditional blade.

"That is heavy for you," I told her. Yet, she continued to struggle with it as she pulled the thing off its hooks. It slipped from her small, wet fingers, but I caught it before it tumbled to the stone, taking it from her and replacing it with my smaller one. "Use this one if you insist on this."

"Okay," she said, grasping it firm by the hilt in exactly the wrong way. By the River...

I found myself correcting her like I had done to new recruits decades ago. "Your thumb should point out, like this. Hmm... *sehr gut*. Now, stop pointing it at me, and point it at the thing you wish to kill. *Sehr gut*. Put your feet wider. Put your shoulder – no, this one – toward your enemy."

"Like this?" She did not look comfortable. Her stance was unnatural, her balance tenuous, and she rested her elbow against her hip to keep the blade up off the ground. Even after more direction, she seemed like a small child playing with toys she should not. Yet, she seemed eager, so I gave her the cue.

"Swing."

She lashed out at the training dummy, missed, and promptly fell. But I was there to keep her from the hard stone beneath our feet, grabbing her tiny form from the left to avoid the wild arc of that blade – of course, I made sure not to harm that new jewelry of hers as I did so. "Damn it," she spat as she got her feet back under her.

With a flourish, the Saint tossed her cloak aside, and her simple women's tunic and breeches instantly spotted with raindrops. No matter – now she was serious. She got back into her battle stance and tried again. Still a miss, but she was upright.

"*Sehr gut*. Hit the target this time, ja?"

Another swing, all her force in the blow. It connected, but no grunt of pain came from that wooden man. It came from her. "Good Catherine in Paradise! That hurts!" Her face twisted into a grimace as she looked to me, rubbing her shoulder.

"Wooden men are unforgiving. Real men, just about as much."

"I can feel it up and down my whole arm." The tip of her weapon scraped wet stone as she let it drop to the ground.

Time to end this. I set the sword aside then gave her small shoulder a quick squeeze, looking for signs of damage. Yes, the girl could heal, but this was no reason to let her try to hurt herself. "You will be sore, but it will pass. I think the blade is not your calling."

At first, I thought she would protest, but such words failed her. Instead, she reached for my arm, a gentle gesture that suddenly became something much different – something painful, an unexpected burning that flowed through her touch. It wrapped itself around my arm and squeezed like a serpent, searching for ways into the deeper cores of my body.

We recoiled from each other, the pain subsiding as soon as I broke away. "Oh my... I'm so sorry! What just happened?" She squinted against the raindrops as she held her hands to her chest.

"If I knew, I would say." But I didn't know, and neither did she, though a thought occurred to me as we looked at each other. "What else does your magic seek besides wounds, I wonder?"

The mage-girl's eyes widened, flashing dark purple brilliance against the gray of the day. There was true horror there. "What do you mean? I didn't do anything. At least, I didn't try. By Catherine, are you saying that this magic can hurt people, too?"

"I say nothing, because I know nothing. What I know is that you were hurt, and I was not. Then, I was the one who felt pain."

"That's crazy. How could that be?"

"You say yourself you know little of your power, *ja*?"

"I don't know anything," she sighed. "I mean, could Jade do that, what I guess I just did?"

"I do not know. I took care to ensure that she never needed her own services."

"It felt just like the regular healing magic, sort of, but didn't really... burn as much. I didn't try; it just sort of came out." Andella's brow furrowed, and her reddish hair began to cling to her face and neck. "It's life magic, right? So life means healing and... the opposite? Good Lady, how can I... I can't control this. I don't even know where to start." She started for her cloak, dropping it several times in her nerve-wracked haste before she could clutch it around her slim shoulders.

"You focus much on what you cannot do," I said to her.

She froze in place. "How can I not? I mean, honestly, I have this gift, and still, what can I do? I just feel so... scared all the time. Worried. Nervous. I don't want to hurt anyone – I just want to help them. I can't even do that right. I'm sorry I hurt you like that. I really didn't know what I was doing."

"Do you see these?" I pointed to the art along most of my left side, a sinewy, colorful pattern of lines and shapes and figures tattooed into my skin from heart to hip. "Under here are scars – many, many scars. They are always there. They will never go away. Do you have any idea how many times Jade healed me? Hundreds of times. But she could not erase my scars. To this day, every morning when I wake, I feel pain in them, some days so much I cannot think. She could not make that pain go away, even with all that magic. You are not a god – you are one person, young, still learning the path to follow."

"'Accept the path you walk and Peace reigns in your heart.' That's what the Book of Catherine says." Her voice came from a very distant place.

"Good advice."

"Yeah." She frowned and pushed wet hair out of her eyes. "You know, I had a dream about Jade, before you even told me about her. I mean, I didn't know it was her, but I saw this Lavançaise girl, in the mountains somewhere. There had been some sort of a battle, and she said she was sad because she couldn't help everyone."

"She hated the fighting." An image of her arguing with armored men twice her size over who to heal flashed in my mind. So many wounded, too many to save them all, and yet, she always tried.

"Why did you leave her?"

"You assume it is I who left."

"I... oh, I'm sorry. Can I ask what happened?"

A simple "no" seemed unlikely to end the conversation, but I did not fully oblige. "You say you are scared. So was Jade, about many things. Her fear told her to seek a safety I could not provide."

"Madame Saçaille said that the world isn't ready for people like us. I think she was right," she said, voice full of reminiscent sorrow.

"If you believe something to be true, then it is. All Eislandisch know this – most *Zondern*, Lavançaise, they do not. You think truth is only what is in front of you." I knelt to retrieve the practice sword, returning to my position before the wooden man. A few more rounds with him would do me some good yet, and the rain still had years of old memories to try to wash clean.

"Thank you, Master Brin," I heard her whisper at my back as I went in for a heavy lunge. Laughter guided me back to my stance.

"Master of what? Killing wooden men?"

Cool rain grazed rosy cheeks as she stood staring into the sky, a slight smile on her lips and her thoughts in another place, far from this courtyard, far from the realm of swords and blood. In that moment, I hoped that someday she would speak with Jade – they would have much in common. I also knew exactly what prompted the boy to ask her to spend her life with him. "Master is what we called most of the instructors at the Magic Academy. Besides, you're not my uncle just yet," she said. "But anyhow, thank you."

To this, I turned back to her and offered a proper Eislandisch salute, sword to chest, pointed downward. Water dripped off my brow and nose as I bowed my head. "*Die Ehre ist ganz meinerseits*," I told her. "The honor is mine, Fräulein."

# CHAPTER THIRTY-TWO

## Pain and Suffering
*9 Spring's Green*
*Andella Weaver*

Y ou focus much on what you cannot do.
Those words from Master Brin stuck with me, echoed in my head over and over as I made my way back inside. My clothes were wet, my hair a disaster – I probably looked more like a street urchin than some kind of proper lady. Well, whatever I was, I wasn't who I thought I was an hour ago. Who was I kidding? I *never* knew who I was.

Because he was right. I was scared – of the future, of myself. I had this *power*, this amazing power that only a few people in the whole world might have ever known. This was the kind of thing that Academy mages were supposed to yearn for, something worthy of an entire lifetime of study and research. I had it running through my very veins, and yet I treated it like some kind of burden.

"So... is everything okay?"

I looked up from the beautiful wooden floor of the dining room, where water had begun to pool around my boots. Several pairs of eyes stared back at me, and I felt my cheeks go very warm despite the damp chill in the air. "Um, yes?" was the only thing I could squeak out.

"Okay," Tristan said, coming up to me and taking my cloak from my shoulders. He set it aside for Frederick or Lissa, then reached out and brushed back a bit of hair from where it stuck on my forehead. "Well, just because my uncle's insane doesn't mean you have to follow suit, all right?"

From the table, Lord Shal-Vesper laughed. "That man does strike quite an impressive figure out there, though, doesn't he?" And indeed, Brin did, his tattooed and muscular form moving with ease through a series of fancy sword techniques. Not even winded, he continued to strike mercilessly at the training dummy, unaware that a whole group of people were now staring at him through the window.

"I had to ask him something, and we got to talking." I looked up at Tristan and still felt the heat of sheer embarrassment on my face. It didn't help that the amused twinkle in his eyes had very little to do with magic. "Sorry, I'm getting everything all wet."

"It's okay," he told me, gentle fingers sliding down my cheek, under my chin. "Why don't you go clean up and change?"

"Right, but there's something I have to tell you. I just figured something out, and…"

"Can it wait?" Behind him, I saw Alex and Cen and that older Lord – Shilling? – seated at the dining table. And yes, they all looked like they were waiting for me to hurry up and get out of there. Even Alex seemed rather pensive, dour, not quite his usual chipper self. I felt my heart sink into my stomach.

"Um, sure," I said, biting my lower lip, then took my cue to go clean myself up… not without giving Tristan a kiss on the cheek, of course. Whether this was inappropriate or not in light of the company, I had to admit, I didn't really care. It seemed like the sort of thing one did when they needed support, and even if he didn't need it, I sure did.

Good Catherine, was I shaking? I put one foot in front of the other but I felt so weak, so light, like I hadn't eaten in a long time. Nonetheless, I made it upstairs and to my room, finding a simple silver-gray dress to throw on and scooping up my hair into a bun.

I paused to stare into the mirror, expecting the slightly-too-thin, slightly-too-short girl staring back with weirdly luminescent, indigo eyes. But that's not who was there. The person I saw in the mirror was a woman, still not that tall, but graceful in a way, her clothes hugging curves in the right places, hanging free in others. On her left hand hung a delicate, beautiful chained betrothal ring in the traditional style – this *woman* was getting married soon, and she seemed confident about it, ready for the next stage in her life. And those eyes... they *were* pretty, weren't they? The lightness of the lavender streaks was so delicate, and the indigo undertones so strong, vibrant, yet compassionate. Fire-orange didn't even quite suit her.

I turned away from the woman in the mirror, still with questions dancing in my mind much the way the magic danced in my eyes. What now? There was so much yet to know, so much yet to research and understand. Good Lady in Paradise, I was more than just a healer, and I still had no idea what it all meant! Could I just take the life right out of someone at will? The idea both fascinated and horrified me. It *should* have just been the latter, but at the same time... well, I had to admit, it was interesting. When it happened, it was like this tremendous warmth flowing into me, not the kind of warmth when you sit too close to the fire, but a beautiful gentle flow of energy radiating from within. I guessed it was the exact same thing others felt when I healed them, and in turn, I got that similar yet achy, burning sensation as the energy left my body. Maybe healing wasn't so much some sort of mysterious magic, but a... transfer of energy from one person to another? Duality of the elements, just like Victor Wyndham had said.

Wait, the book! What did the book have to say? I went to my nighttable where that old book, *Lebenkern*, the book of Life magic, sat patiently shrouding its secrets in foreign words and allegories. Tristan had translated most of it now, his notes there with the book written in his deliberate script with its long lines and perfectly spaced letters. I had already looked through them once, delighting more in the fact that I finally understood the text more than anything. It read like a story, about a man without a name who goes on a long journey, meets all kinds of people, does all kinds of things along the way. There were mysteries wrapped up in every passage, with multiple meanings everywhere. The "new age" spoken of in the bit I thought was a prophecy never seemed to arrive, though, at least not in the story. By the end, the man was old, and spent his last days traveling in the mountains, alone under a sunlit sky. His friends? Well, they seemed to be gone, but not before performing some sort of ritual. They focused crystals, it seemed, over... their souls? Their bodies? Literally? That part seemed very unclear and there were a lot of scratched-out words on Tristan's notes here. Maybe there were actual crystals, maybe not.

The mention of *Lebenkern* came up all over though, in fits and starts at times, but always in the context of helping others. It never talked about the taking of life, only giving it. At different times when the man was hurt, he found comfort in the form of a magical light held by one of the three friends who protected him. Was it a true story? Did these people really exist? I didn't know, but it did remind me just a little of Jade, Brin's "Saint."

I scanned the notes, pausing briefly at the spots where Tristan had circled a word or scrawled something extra in the margins. What he wrote didn't always make a lot of sense, and sometimes it was even in Eislandisch, using different words, which didn't really help. Still, no mention of the nature of life energy, nothing useful that I didn't already know. Maybe Archmage Tiara was right – it was just a story, no revelation, no prophecy handed down from some spirit somewhere. I had no doubt that the person who wrote it knew something much more about these magics, but the specifics seemed lost to history now.

Archmage Tiara's answer to this problem would be in research, of course, but I was doing that, wasn't I? Reading this book? Reading all the books I'd read already? Except, that was just one kind of research.

I suddenly had an idea.

On the desk was a dagger used to open letters, a small thing with a rather sharp edge. I picked it up and it felt heavy and cold in my hand. What if I... oh, that idea sounded so simple. It was a good idea, an idea that Archmage Tiara would endorse heartily. Sure, I could make the pain go away, but there'd still be... well, pain. And blood! But how else would I ever practice?

My stomach twisted in on itself as I held the blade against my left palm, the edge tickling the skin. All I had to do was close my hand around it and pull with the other, right?

Deep breath. You can do this, Andie. Don't be a weakling. People suffer far more for far less all the time. Practice is important. You'll never know if you don't try.

The letter opener bit into flesh and I almost let out a gasp – it hurt even more than expected. A thin line of fire smoldered in my palm, wetness leaked out down my wrist, but I couldn't break my concentration. Not yet. It took a lot of effort to move that pain into my right hand, to pull it right out like one might tug on a rope. It wasn't as easy as it sounded – that "rope" felt like it was attached to a lead weight. I thought about what it was like to let the magic out and seek things to heal, about that warmth and the way the ribbon of energy curled around wounds. I tried to picture it, tried to feel the same feelings, and before I knew it, it was happening. It was happening! A gentle purplish glow lit in my right hand, and the cut on the left got smaller and smaller and smaller. Then, pain, sharp and eye-watering, burning that exact same cut into my right hand. It appeared there from nothing, but the blood trickling out was no trick. It was real, and it really hurt.

My fingers closed around the new wound as I inspected the other hand, where only trace bits of crimson remained. The cut there was long forgotten. "I can't believe I did that," I said to no one. And I was true, I really couldn't. But I kept at it, practicing, moving the energy back the other way, from right hand back to left. Could I send just a little, and have cuts on both hands? I could! I could start and stop it at will, pulling on that ribbon of lifeblood in all kinds of different ways. Just a little, quite a lot, until finally I was able to keep the cut from reappearing on the opposite hand. It was just healed, closed and final, leaving streaks and drops of blood all over me.

Amazing, absolutely amazing. This was a real discovery. I thought to go tell Tristan and Alex, since this was really more important than their drinking with their friends, when I heard a sharp voice waft up from the dining room. Until then, I had paid the Lords and their muffled low voices little heed, but the pitch had now risen. Who was that? Was that Alex?

"...not a chance. Let's just... I won't sign..." I couldn't make out all the words, but he sounded tense, insistent. Then, a string of words that were unmistakable as curses – yes, definitely Alex.

"...making a big assumption." This sounded like Tristan, and there was more after that, but his deep voice got lost so easily.

"...your father would have..." This was Cen, his humble, no-nonsense tone rising up through the floorboards.

"I am *not* my father. Don't assume I'll just do whatever he would." Oh, this was Tristan again, and he was *not* happy – his words were crystal clear.

Now Lord Cen's voice had risen. "This is about the future, boys, do you not see that?"

"'Boys'? Whose house do you think you're in?"

Oh my. I had no idea what the argument was about, but it seemed to be escalating. Concerned and not a little curious, I padded out to the hallway and leaned over the banister, gazing down to the floor below. The dining room was too far down the hall to see what was going on from here, but the voices were more distinct now.

"I'm not agreeing to this."

"Look, there's two of you – you're outvoted on this. I don't understand the problem."

"You don't? Are you kidding me? Come on, Cen, you're just giving in."

The conversation went on, punctuated by choice curses and awkward pauses. If I knew what they were arguing about, that might have helped – something about the General? The Prince? Whatever it was, it didn't sound like Alex and Tristan were interested in bargaining.

"This is not uncommon," Lady Gretchen's cool, heavy accent lilted near my ear, startling me so much I gripped the wooden railing hard to steady myself.

"What are they fighting about?" I asked.

"It seems they talk of peace, or a lack of it?"

"Right, I heard that too. Why wouldn't they want peace?"

The older woman with her long blond braid cascading down her back just shook her head. "The right kind of peace has a price, I think. My husband and my son are... very different people. Very different ideas."

I wasn't sure what that meant, but from the way her lips curled ever so slightly, I had a feeling she had her own opinions on politics as well. "They sound really mad."

Downstairs, another flare of conversation, some loud retort from Alexander punctuated by curses. So really, this was normal? Weren't they all supposed to be friends? Well, I guess I had a different interpretation of friendly debate.

"Listen to me," said Lord Cen in a much calmer reply. "This is the only solution that makes sense. Both sides will be satisfied, and all of this rioting can stop."

"It makes sense if you're Torven," Alex snorted. "You're rewarding him for what he did. How does that make any sense?"

"Didn't you read the document? It clearly states…"

Tristan cut the older man off. "You're trying to solve this with politics. Torven's a soldier. He doesn't think like that. Torven spoke to me at my father's funeral. He asked for a peaceful meeting; not a few hours later, I was attacked by Royal Guards. Whether they acted on his authority or on their own, I don't know, but a politician wouldn't slaughter Lords in the streets. Real assassins are much better as political tools, wouldn't you agree?"

Lord Cen was not pleased. "What's your point, Tristan?" he barked.

"Point is, that man thinks we're all cowards. The Council tried to double-cross him and have him killed, and he outmaneuvered you. Now, one thing I know he's not doing right now is sitting up there in the palace trying to figure out how he can capitulate to you and play along in some game."

That *was* a good point, wasn't it? It must have been, because the voices softened a bit and went back to a level where we couldn't hear them as well. I turned to Lady Gretchen. "Did you ever interrupt them when they were like this?"

She looked at me as if I were from another world. "That is… not done, dear. Do not worry, it will be over soon."

The voices erupted again. Now they were incomprehensible, four men all talking over each other at once. And people said women had a way of sounding like wild animals when shrieking their way through an argument. I wanted to go downstairs. I wanted to tell all of them to just stop and listen to themselves for a minute, but that probably wouldn't have been very ladylike. Then again, I wasn't officially a Lady yet, was I?

"You can take that piece of paper and shove it where..."

That was it. I started down the steps, with Lady Gretchen hissing after me. She didn't follow, though – perhaps I was doing something she might have liked to have done someday herself, but could never quite bring herself to break whatever code kept the women upstairs and out of the men's business.

"Um, excuse me?" I said as I entered the dining room. Tristan was pacing on one side of the room, while Alex was seated with his arms clasped over his head, chest puffed up for all it was worth. The older men sat across from him, with an empty bottle of wine between them and sour expressions on their faces. No one looked in my direction, so I cleared my throat and spoke again. "Excuse me? Gentlemen? I couldn't help but overhear you. Well, everyone in the house overheard, and, well, you see..."

Now I had their attention, all eyes settling uncomfortably on me once again. But now, I wasn't a wet mess. I was a poised woman with a very sincere request that they come to a peaceful resolution and remember that they were all friends here. This was what I wanted to say, anyhow, but most of those words got caught up and mangled in my throat. Still, I continued on, focusing my attention on Shal-Vesper and Shilling and their surprised but kind faces. Somehow, this helped. "You see, there's much bigger concerns right now that require Lord Loringham's and Lord Vestarton's attention at the moment, and it sounds like you all need to take a break from your meeting to, ah... relax. I'm sure the servants would be happy to get you something to eat while you wait?"

Shal-Vesper rose from his seat and stretched his back. "Indeed, perhaps that's wise."

"Oh, please, sit and we'll have Frederick bring you something. Tristan? Alexander? Can I speak with you out in the hall?"

I couldn't really tell if they were unhappy with me or still seething from their argument, but they actually did as I asked without a word. After a tense moment, Alex finally turned to me with a sly grin on his face. "That's brilliant, what you just did there. Did you guys talk about this ahead of time?"

"What?" I asked, taken aback. "No... I just overheard you all yelling and I thought you needed a break."

"Well, it was well timed. I think your fiancé was about to hit old Cen with a lightning bolt or something."

Tristan took a deep breath, staring and Alex then me in turn with that strange sort of starlight dancing in his eyes. "No, I wasn't."

"So that little extra something in the air was just my imagination. Sure, whatever." Alex's smile widened considerably. "Let me tell you, though, Brother, I don't think you should lose your temper indoors. It seems like a bad idea."

"Well, stop putting me in positions where I might." While not nearly as amused about the situation, he did chuckle and shake his head as he turned to me. "So, yeah, that was brilliant. A little... forward, but well-timed."

My eyes darted back toward the stairs at the end of the hall. "I think your mother is mad at me. But I really did have something important to tell you, and it couldn't wait anymore."

Tristan started to say something, but instead noticed dried blood on the hands I found myself wringing together in front of me. "What did you do?" he asked, taking my hands in his.

"I found out I can do something else with my magic. We have to go to the Academy and talk to Archmage Tiara. Today. There's a duality to my healing... you know, like there's duality to the other elements?" From the way his brow furrowed, he didn't know that. Of course he didn't – why would he? "Every element has two sides, in some way," I explained. "Fire consumes, and yet it also warms us. Air can be gentle or it can be wild and angry. Water can be liquid or it can be ice. You know what I mean?"

"So what, like light and dark?"

"Or past and future." Alex leaned casually against the wall in such a way that he could keep the dining room in sight while still focusing on us.

"Maybe. I know I can give and take life. I cut myself, then absorb that to heal it and make the cut happen somewhere else. I can do it with others, too. I found it totally by accident, but I can practice it now, and train. Isn't it exciting?" It didn't seem nearly as exciting to the two of them, so I offered to demonstrate. "If you get a knife, I can..."

Face sour and pale, Tristan shook his head. "A knife? No, no, I don't know that I like that kind of practice," he said. "I mean, that hurts, doesn't it?"

"Well yeah, but it's not so bad. It could be worse."

Alex snorted. "It's macabre."

"Not very ladylike, either, is it? Well, that's too bad." I couldn't help but smile, looking down into my open palm one more time. I had control over this magic now. I *understood* it. This was huge. "Can we go to the Magic Academy? Right now? It's not far and it's still fairly early."

Tristan shook his head. "There's a three-block barricade in front of the Academy entrance, Andella. They're sheltering people in there, and protecting all the weapons and such. You can't get near it."

"But we *have* to talk to her. Don't you want to know more about your own magic?"

"I do." Tristan and I both looked at Alex in surprise. "No, really," he said. "We can talk our way through that barricade. It's a better use of our time than haggling over idiotic politics."

He must have had a point, because Tristan nodded in agreement after a minute or so. "True, but that wasn't haggling."

"What was it? What happened?" I dared to ask.

The men, though, didn't hesitate to explain further, although they did lower their voices even more to be absolutely certain no one in the next room could overhear. "The other Lords want to put the Prince on the throne with Torven as regent. That way everyone's 'happy.'" Tristan's last word was almost forced out through his teeth in bitter sarcasm.

"It's ludicrous," Alex added, dropping a few added curses to his speech as well.

"Not to mention insulting."

"Yeah, you watch – the city will burn straight to the ground." After a big gulp from his drink, Alex raised a finger in the air with something like a revelation. "Look, I like this Magic Academy idea. Besides, this way, Cen's less likely to follow me home and try to talk more 'sense' into me."

"He'll try me first," said Tristan.

"He's already given up on you, Brother. I think you made your feelings quite clear on the matter." Indeed, I agreed with him – a good bit of the worst shouting was Tristan's voice, not Alex's.

"And you didn't?"

"Trust me. It's just better to stay out of the house."

They sent off the guests with a whole spread of good food and a bottle of wine each, with the promise to talk further some other time, and then we were on our way. I could hardly contain my excitement, not just at my little "victory," of course, but also because we were on our way to get more answers. We were so close now! I imagined Archmage Tiara herself had this same anxious feeling when on the verge of a new discovery – I would find out soon enough.

# CHAPTER THIRTY-THREE

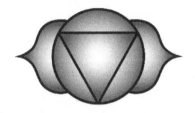

## An Eislandisch Saying
*9 Spring's Green, 1272*
*Tristan Loringham*

O ur street might have been well-guarded, but it was nothing compared to the fortress that had become the Academy complex. Rough barricades had been constructed blocks ahead of the grand archway protecting its entrance, with both armored men and robe-clad mages stalking the whole area. I hadn't come here since Peaceday – what was the point? Operations had been suspended, and while some cadets and Instructors had returned simply because their quarters were there, they had become part of the guarding forces. While the Academies were relatively untouched by the insanity of the city around them, they had become a popular place for people to seek refuge. But, letting just anyone in was not a good way to maintain their safety – hence, guards and barricades. The place seemed better protected than the Palace.

The walk there had been under a slight peek of midday sunshine in a bleak but now dry sky, and we chose to go it alone, no soldiers in tow. I did go armed, though, my weapon's comforting weight at my hip. As soon as we stepped foot near the perimeter, at least six people raised blades, and on instinct, I almost went for mine. Almost.

One lowered his as he recognized us, though. "Instructor! Come to check on us, eh?"

I shook my head. "Actually, well... What are you *doing* here, Fyr?"

"It's my shift," Fyr Shal-Vesper said with a slight puff of his plated chest. "I'm not going to just sit back and relax at home. No, Sir. I've got a duty to stand by my post, Sir."

"Too bad no one's going to give you and your brother medals for all of this duty and honor you're performing," Alex sniffed.

But Fyr could have cared less about medals anymore. He, like his brother Corrin, were doing their part to make the city just a bit safer. *A bit more like it was supposed to be.* Where many people with means were holed up in their homes, men like Corr and Fyr braved the streets and defended whatever they could. It made me want to stop all this silly Lordship and magic nonsense and join them instead. "Don't need all that, Sir," Fyr said. "Anyway, what are you doing up here?"

"We're visiting the Magic Academy," I told him, which meant, of course, that he wasn't who we should be talking to. The little white-robed woman near him looked up from a set of papers in her hands when she heard the word "magic."

"Do you have an appointment?" she asked, white glimmering Air magic racing across her pupils. Though short in stature, this woman of indeterminate age made up for it with a proud, officious demeanor.

"We're here to see Archmage Tiara."

"She's expecting you?"

Andella took a step forward then and offered the mage a slight bow of respect. "Well, it's sort of important, and I know she'd want to see us. I'm studying with her, and..."

"Do you have an *appointment*?" The woman's countenance matched the cold granite archway before us. If she recognized me or Alex, she gave no indication, and even if she had, I doubted she would have cared. She was perfect for her job, I'd give her that.

We had just one weapon in our arsenal against someone like this, and he needed no prompting. Alex stepped forward, leaning in uncomfortably close to her. The mage raised an eyebrow but did not move. "Look, Miss... ah, what's your name, darling?" A bold move, calling this one "darling," but she did not attempt to cast him aloft over the sea cliffs – yet.

"Karissa. Warlock Karissa."

Alex flashed his best smile at Warlock Karissa. "Karissa? I love that name! That's my cousin's name. Warlock Karissa, tell me something – are you from Zondrell?"

"Yes."

"Great, then maybe you know what this is?" He held up his right hand so that she could see the stylized V for Vestarton set into the diamonds in his ring.

"I know who you are, Lord Vestarton. Others of your... station *do* know how to make appointments. We must keep very strict limits on these things nowadays. Wouldn't want the rabble in this gods-forsaken city getting in and mucking everything up, now would we? Of course not." With another withering glance at us, she returned to her papers.

"Rabble? Are you telling me..."

"Well, here's the thing," I swept in before Alex had a chance to finish his sentence and lose his charming façade. "We sent word here to the Archmage yesterday, didn't we, Andella?" She nodded. "Right, one of my men should have brought a letter here a few hours before sunset."

"Letters, Sir, are not appointments," said the Warlock, flipping through the papers in her hand. One of them was indeed the letter I wrote, scrawled on a piece of parchment at Andella's behest to tell the Archmage we had something of great import to discuss. "Archmage Tiara hasn't had time to read this letter."

"That's likely because you haven't given it to her."

Karissa raised an eyebrow at me, and her glare could cut steel. "If you haven't noticed, Lord Loringham, things are not running at their normal capacity lately."

"Look, neither of us have time for this. The Archmage requires our presence. Go and ask her yourself."

"I don't run errands for those of your ilk."

*Okay, now I'm getting mad.* I took a deep breath, trying very hard not to do something I'd regret. Nearby, I could tell Alex was doing the same thing, and Andella just looked unsure of herself and the whole damned thing. Alex recovered the fastest, though, and that perfect smile bloomed on his face once again.

"I think perhaps we have a different definition of the word, 'appointment.' So, tell me something, madam Warlock," he beamed, "what does guard duty at the gates of the Academy pay these days, if I may ask?"

Three hundred-Royals later, we were walking up to the Archmage's laboratory in the Magic Academy Great Hall.

**\*\***

I had never seen Tiara's laboratory myself, even though I'd walked past it a few times with Andella after the lunch bells had rung. For a few weeks at least, we enjoyed something of a normal Academy life, Instructor and scholar, walking the grounds, training, learning. If I had known what was going to happen, though, I doubt I would have ever have let her leave the Academy at all. She would have been safer there. Of course, she would have fought that the whole way, wouldn't she?

As for the Archmage herself, I had met her only once, a quick meeting in the hallway. Then, she had dismissed me as neither interesting nor important, but now... well, now things were a bit different. Now she had rumors and an interesting case to research. The somewhat haughty woman with green blazing in her eyes stood on tiptoes, uncomfortably close, examining me and those strange streaks in my irises with intensity. She applied an item that looked a bit like a sextant up to my face for a moment, then turned and made some notes on a piece of paper.

"This is fascinating," she said, more to herself than to any of us. "Yes, most fascinating. I've heard of this phenomenon, of course, but have yet to see it. It's like the magic's peeking through, although there's never been any report that mages afflicted with this condition are less powerful." *Afflicted?* It sounded like she thought I had a disease. Maybe I did. "How do you feel, Mister Loringham?" she continued after some more inspection through the device.

"Fairly certain that's *Lord* Loringham," Alex said off to the side. A hint of a smile touched the corner of the Archmage's lips.

The Archmage's bright swirling green eyes never moved from me, though she cocked her head as if considering Alex's suggestion. "Thank you for the reminder, *Mister* Vestarton, I'll take that correction under advisement."

"Look, I feel fine," I told her.

"Normal?"

"I suppose. I get headaches, right here." I pointed at the center of my brow, where the dull ache throbbed even now. "It's not so bad now, but sometimes it feels like my brain wants to pop out of my head."

"Ah!" She made another notation. "Well, rest assured, that rarely happens. And this headache comes on at certain times?"

A glance at Andella and Alex in turn made me feel almost embarrassed; I didn't know why, it just did. Maybe it's because I knew that I almost sent a bolt of lightning through my own dining room about an hour ago. Alex wasn't wrong – I was *very* close. Yelling at Cen, getting embroiled in the politics, listening to him chastise me like I was a boy half my age... I was mad. Worse than that. And I very nearly let that magic out. It *wanted* out, badly – it took everything I had, but once I had it under control, the swell of energy calmed to something more manageable. "Well, it's sort of always there. It gets bad when I get... upset."

Now the sextant-thing was in my face again, turned a different way, then another way again. *Measuring me?* The Archmage squinted and smirked as she held the device at different angles, getting closer and closer to my eyes. "Anxiety, anger, that sort of thing? Stop blinking, please."

I took a deep breath. "Right."

"Indeed, that's how it usually happens. Untrained mages have a bit of stress and all of the sudden they're tearing up the countryside. You know, I heard there were some very interesting things going on with some sort of lightning in the plaza the other day. Everyone here was buzzing about it – well, they buzz about everything lately. So that was you that did all that. Very, very interesting. And you can do this at will?"

"I... I don't know. I guess so. I haven't really tried."

"Well, we'll have to change that, won't we? You went to the Military Academy, didn't you? Did they not put you in the Box downstairs?"

"They did. I didn't see anything."

"Yes, of course you didn't, because you don't seem to be much of a good liar." She shot a knowing glance at Alex, then turned back to me. "We'll need you to get in there for another reading, yes? Yes, that's what we'll do to start. Do you know no one might have seen this kind of magic in thousands of years?"

Of course, that wasn't true, unless my uncle was a better liar than Alex or anyone else this side of the Sea of Stars. No, I didn't believe that for a moment – his story had been too detailed, too intricate. Why it was so rare, or so hard to believe, I still wasn't quite sure. *And why did it have to happen to us?* By the gods, if I knew the answer to that...

The sextant-thing was removed from my face and now thrust into Alex's. "First, I need readings on you two. Hold still, yes? There you are, Mister Vestarton. Oh my, you've been practicing."

Alex made a low sound at the back of his throat. "A bit, yes."

"And?"

"And I... I guess I can see things. Things that happened in the past. Sometimes."

"Oh! Just like the stories on Drasch Sturmberg and his mages. That is fantastic, just *fantastic*! I don't suppose you think you've seen anything from the future?"

Another low sound, this one more like amusement. "If I could do that, madam, I'd be in a much better mood about the whole thing. Or I'd go fucking off myself." The sextant-thing bore down on him, but to his credit, he didn't move and didn't blink. Obviously, he'd been subjected to this odd device before. I watched as the Archmage took various measurements, moving levers and dials and noting groups of numbers on her paper. *What the hell is that thing? Is it somehow magical?* I almost asked, but kept my mouth shut.

Then, the sextant was turned on Andella, who erupted in a torrent of animated explanation. She could have cared less about the device, looking right through it as she told the Archmage about her discovery. The "push and pull of life," she called it. To me, it seemed bizarre, and I didn't like to think about her "practicing" through hurting herself. Something about thinking of a loved one cutting themselves like that... it turned my stomach in a way that the sight of blood usually never did.

"Andella, dear, this is marvelous. Perhaps we'll turn you into a real battlemage yet, hm?" At this, Andella screwed up her nose in distaste. "Oh, if you could get your Fire back, just think of how potent you would be. You'd best keep that one to yourself, too, I think, yes?" The Archmage kept measuring for a few more minutes, humming an off-key rendition of "Midlight Parade" as she did so.

"Very good," she said at last, tossing the sextant-thing off to the side. "These readings are helpful – I'm so glad you all arrived. I've been just itching to do some better research. Can't very well do much else around here lately. Do you know how badly I could use some more nebula salts? All this shutting down the city business is quite disappointing. You boys can't do anything about that, can you?"

"Um, we're working on it," Alex told her, and that was all that needed to be said on the matter. For Catherine's sake, I didn't even want to *think* about all that right then, and I don't think he did, either.

"Keep working on it. That General and his men are preventing important scholarship. Why they don't see that is beyond me. Well, at any rate... the Box, shall we?"

I did not relish the idea of getting into the Box again. I didn't like it the first time, even though it was only for a minute or two. Crawling into a tiny, cramped space with no light at all was not quite my idea of a good time. Doing all this in front of onlookers made it that much worse. "The Box is downstairs," I said after a moment. "Won't everyone walking by see what we're doing?"

The Archmage shook her head with a chuckle. "Oh dear, that's just a replica, something they made a few hundred years ago based on the real one. It performs its functions, I suppose, but the readings are always off and I highly doubt it's accurate. I've never liked that one. The real one is across the hall here."

"Wait, there's more than one of those monstrosities?" Alex's eyes widened in disbelief.

"Yes, of course," Tiara said, matter-of-fact. "How else to understand some ancient and important source of power like that 'monstrosity,' as you so affectionately call it, then by trying to make another one? Funny thing is, they still don't quite know how it works."

"And you put people in there anyway?"

"Well, we know the obsidian intensifies magic powers inside the body, and the direction of the stone's grain is very important."

"And?" From the look on his face, I could tell Alex was growing more and more appalled by the minute.

"And there's a bit more to it than that but it's all very technical, Mister Vestarton. Suffice it to say that neither Box has yet to cause anyone any lasting damage. It's quite safe, I assure you. You know, I'd like to get you in there as well – we need better readings on your powers, but we'll do that later." This idea clearly didn't sit well with Alex, who grimaced but held his tongue. Besides, Archmage Tiara was already heading past the dusty piles of notes and books and Catherine knew what else into the hallway. We followed before she had to encourage us.

"Like she said, it's safe," Andella said, patting me on the arm. I must have been a lot more tense than I realized. "I went in and everything was fine – not that much different from the first time I was in there, years ago. You might see some colorful lights or something."

The obsidian thing was there, a giant brick of blackness in the middle of a much smaller room than the laboratory. Wide enough for the four of us to enter, yes, but *just* wide enough, and with its clutter of books and papers laying around, we couldn't do much else but stand there. The Earth mage started to dig through the papers, distracted by some thought as she hummed to herself. Alex and I exchanged a look, and I could feel the apprehension coming off of him in waves. Andella, on the other hand, seemed excited.

Me, I was less so, but what the hell? *Let's get this over with.* "So, I should just... look for lights?" I asked as I stepped up closer to the Box. It actually seemed to emanate something, radiating the same faint energy that I felt sometimes when sitting with Andella and being very, very still.

"Any reaction at all. The instrumentation should give me some indication, though. Just pay attention, yes? Try not to fall asleep or something." She gestured toward a small table text to the Box, half covered by scrolls and writing instruments.

Whatever those metal implements sticking out past the scrolls were, I had no idea. It looked more like scraps getting ready to go into a blacksmith's fire to me. "All right, in you go, my boy. Don't worry, it's unlikely to be uncomfortable."

*Don't worry, indeed.* I stepped in and she shut the door behind me, sealing out all light in an instant. Total blackness enveloped me, dark so thick it had texture, like seawater. The only thing I heard was my own heartbeat, growing just a little louder in my chest. Colored lights were nowhere to be seen. *Maybe it's not magic after all. Or this thing, whatever it is, doesn't work.*

*Wait, what's that?*

Off to my left – at least, I thought it was my left – I noticed something shimmer. I turned and reached out, expecting to brush my hand against the stone wall of the tomblike Box, but instead I felt something soft, almost silken, yet organic.

A flower. *What is a flower doing here?* Well, of course it wasn't really there – I had to be dreaming. Or hallucinating. Yet I could feel its petals brush against my fingertips, and I could see its delicate reddish hue, standing out somehow despite the darkness. As I inspected it, I noticed another beyond it, then another, and another, until suddenly a whole field of them spread out before me, miles and miles of little flowers with no end in sight.

No end, except for the place where they met the banks of the River.

I knew this place. I had been here before, but then… things were different. I *felt* it was different. I was in control here. I could come and go as I wished. Nothing urged me to go up to those rushing crimson waters – I moved toward them of my own accord. I stepped lightly at first, then more confident, the flowers springing right back up as I trod over them. A gentle silvery light followed my path, not the bright abnormal sun I had seen before in this place, but a light that flowed with my movements, illuminating just what I needed to see. And I *needed* to see that River.

*Spazieren der Flussrand – walk the River's Edge.* It's how the Eislandisch wish each other good fortune, but I didn't feel any luckier. In fact, I felt nothing at all, good or bad. I felt… emptied. At peace. There was nothing to fear here, nothing to worry about, because I was here of my own volition. I could leave at any time, but this stroll down the banks of the Great River of Blood seemed oddly calming. It shouldn't have. I could look down into the water and see how it rushed past, faster than the blink of eye, carrying thousands of corpses in its dark currents – spirits, I supposed, not corpses in the traditional sense. These were the souls on their way to wherever it was they were headed next, a place unknowable. Before, the sight had been so terrifying, but now, I didn't know how I felt about it. Acceptance was the only word that came to mind, an understanding that this was the way of things.

*He's here.* People, animals, all sorts of creatures flew along with that current, but somewhere in those waters was the soul of my father. I imagined more than knew this, as I could see nothing distinct amongst the blinding flurry of strange beings. Nor could I feel anything, no special presence, no familiar entity watching each step I took. *No judging glares, either.* I almost laughed in spite of myself.

I don't know how long I walked. It could have been minutes, it could have been days – time had no meaning in this place. I did eventually find myself walking up an incline, a gentle hill that got steeper and steeper as I continued. The terrain never changed, though the water seemed to move slower the higher I climbed. *Shouldn't it be moving faster up here?* Something stood out over the rushing sound of the River up here, a faint whisper, hoarse and deep.

I stopped to listen, but it sounded like nonsense. Just my imagination, perhaps. *Then again, maybe this whole thing is from a very overactive imagination.* Yet it felt so real. I was *here*, like I'd been before. The circumstances were different, and I didn't know how I got here, but I was here nonetheless, a casual wanderer through the shadows of death.

"You were always different." The whispers became words, forming around me with no body to attach to them. The tone was familiar, but it couldn't be...

"Father?" I couldn't hear myself in this strange place, so I wasn't sure if I actually said it or just thought it.

"Always so different. You've almost reached the top."

Behind me, there was nothing but the path I had walked; before me, the slope continued upward. To my right, the blood waters flowed without end, and to the left was nothingness. But nowhere was there a source of that voice... and I suddenly, desperately wanted to see it for myself. "Father? Are you here?"

"Don't linger, boy. Your path is behind you."

"Why? What do you mean?"

"I knew... I knew. Always so different, and now you need to go back."

It made so little sense. *Go back now? But I've come so far.* I shook my head and kept walking. The hill had to end at some point, didn't it? The River had to have a source – all rivers started somewhere.

As I climbed, the whispers faded. If I did go back, would I hear them again – hear *him* again? Could I talk to him, see him? Yet something told me to keep going. Looking for my father in this River would not help me. Nothing would help me, except for finding the pinnacle, the source of it all. So I continued on, never feeling tired even though I must have walked for miles by now.

The land eventually flattened, and the land before me became a sea of darkness. *Eternity – this was what eternity looked like.* The water, or blood, or whatever it was, was perfectly calm here, not even a ripple marring its surface. How such a still, perfect pool created the roaring rapids of the River, I wasn't sure, but this was the Source – I was sure of it.

And it was *beautiful.*

I stood in awe for what might have been a very long time. But time... it was just a tool, a way to make sense of one aspect of reality. This was a place beyond those kinds of rudimentary constructs, a place where time and life were in a constant state of flux. A minute could be an hour. An old man could be reborn a babe in an instant. And up above the eternal pool there shone one light, a single bright beam, casting its glow over everything below.

It was not perfect and still like the water, however. Within that light, something stirred, swirling notes of shadow in red, blue, green, white, silver, purple, and gold. They were distinct yet not, separate but together, moving with and around one another. I wanted to get closer, to understand those indistinct forms, but...

*You need to go back.*

But I wasn't done yet. What was hiding deep within that light? The forms were so vast, so serpentine and writhing, almost beastlike, things of legends and stories told to children at bedtime.

*You need to go back.*

No! Not until I saw it. I couldn't leave just yet. I had to see, to know what was hiding there... to understand the Source, not just of the River, but of *everything* – magic, life, nature. The core of existence?

*You need to go back.*

The light winked out of existence then, shapes collapsing in on each other, the pool and the River and everything plunging back into darkness and the cool dampness of the Box. The door slid open.

"Oh dear," the Archmage's voice wafted in through the assault of light on my vision. The world outside the Box drove spears of sensation right into my skull, and as I half-fell out of there, I almost lost my breakfast. Strong hands held me upright, and I heard a lot of concerned talking, though the words seemed to have little meaning. It took a good five minutes before I could make sense of any of it – it didn't help that they were all talking over each other.

"Brother? Hey, talk to me, Brother."

"What happened? Are you okay?"

"Goodness, do you have any concept of the *readings* I saw just now? What did you see?"

My senses began to normalize. The throbbing headache began to subside into the dull pulsing I was used to. The violent light began to soften and mold into colors and shapes – bright mage eyes of different colors swirling like mad, set in concerned faces. I fixated on the purple ones until the world stopped spinning and I could clearly make out Andella's soft features and the wisps of red hair that hovered around her cheeks.

"I..." I started, not sure how to continue. "I saw... everything."

Everyone seemed confused, including Andella, but that sympathetic expression never left her. I became aware of her gentle, reassuring touch against my cheek. "What do you mean?"

"The River. I was at the River again."

The excitement in Archmage Tiara's voice cut through the room like a thunderclap. "You mean *The River*, from

Eislandisch religion? *Again*, you say?" I nodded. "Oh dear. Tell me you're not an alcoholic or some such. I don't have room to accommodate hallucinations in this type of research."

"What? No, of course not. I was just... there. Like before, when I almost died. But this time was different. I was more in control, like I could come and go as I pleased. I followed the riverbank up a hill – felt like I'd walked for ages. Then I was finally at the top and there was this pool there, an ocean, still as glass. It was the Source."

"The Source?"

"Of the River. I'm sure of it. The light there didn't look like the sun, like it did when I was down below. It looked like a single bright beam coming from somewhere. It had shapes in it that sort of... danced around. I don't know what they were – I can't really describe it."

I doubt I could have said anything that would have made her happier. The Earth mage positively beamed, any concern for my well-being replaced with the excitement of discovery. "This is so *interesting!* Oh, this goes right along with Hariage's theory. I just *knew* that wasn't complete hogwash. Ha! Well, I suppose we can't prove it all wrong just yet. Tell me more. Was the River truly made of blood like the Eislandisch say, with corpses in there and the like?"

A glance at Andella and Alex made me hesitate – I had never told them about the River before. For a time, I thought it was just a dream, but I've had dreams of it since then, plenty of them. None of them felt like that first time when I stood at the edge and considered jumping in. Every time, I knew I was dreaming, but when I was there, really *there...* it was so different.

"So," I started, slowly, "I don't know what happens when we die, okay? I'm not saying anything like that, but that day in Doverton... there was no Great Lady waiting on a cloud somewhere to take me to Paradise. That's what I know."

"You didn't die, Brother," Alex said, his voice quiet, tense.

"You guys pulled me back." I let it lie there. I would never know the real truth of that first visit to the River, and quite frankly, didn't want to know.

"This is quite monumental indeed," Tiara interrupted as she started writing down something on some scrap parchment. "Do you realize that visions like these haven't been recorded for centuries? Not legitimate ones, at any rate. Oh, the High Sorcerer will have a fit over this... which is precisely why we won't tell him yet, of course. Tell me more, all the details, yes? We'll need to record this." She looked up. "In the meantime, Mister Vestarton, step in there for a moment, will you?"

"But we have to go."

"Excuse me?" The Archmage scowled, the lines in her face deepening slightly. "That idiotic curfew isn't over for several hours and we have *much* to discuss here."

"No, you don't understand – we have to go." I looked to Alex, then Andella, searching their eyes. Didn't they know it too? Feel it, somehow? I thought maybe they did.

*You need to go back.* I heard it echo in the back of my mind.

# CHAPTER THIRTY-FOUR

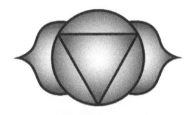

## Redemption
*10 Spring's Green, 1272*
*Alexander Vestarton*

Gods, I hated the Rains. They usually began about a week after the first Peaceday of the new year, a month of gloom and drizzle accentuated by the occasional storm sweeping in off the coast. They also brought with them cool, wet air that seemed to seep right into the bones, and combined with the pain in my side and the way my magic always twisted and writhed under my skin, it made for a most unpleasant sensation.

Running about all over town did not help matters – neither did the bizarre nature of our current conversation. I looked to Andella, who seemed just as fascinated as the old woman, and then back to Tristan. My best friend, my Brother, a man I'd known all my life... a man who was getting *married* soon. It still hadn't quite sunk in, even though we'd talked about it before. A couple of times, actually. He really, *really* liked that girl, and who could blame him? She was sweet, cute, intelligent, maybe a little odd, but hell, who among us wasn't these days? Besides, we were all locked up together in our little "new magic club," and membership seemed pretty exclusive at the moment.

And my best friend was also a man who knew what it was to die. I had a hard time wrapping my mind around that, but he was as serious as he ever was. No tricks, no jokes, no flights of fancy or hallucinations. He really *believed* he had seen this so-called River of Blood.

Now he was prodding us to go. "I heard him say we had to go back," he said, soft and deadly calm.

"Him?"

"A voice. My father's voice."

Oh, good Catherine in Paradise... or wait. Maybe there was no such Lady now, after all? Whatever. "You heard your father say something to you? From where? This... River?"

"I guess so. Look, I know, it sounds crazy."

"That's a strong word." Batshit insane was even stronger. Not an unreasonable assessment, though.

"I know I was there, and I know what I heard. You don't feel that? A need to go back home right now?"

Well, now that he mentioned it... "So, what if I told you I did? A little. Don't know why, just a hunch."

He turned to Andella, but she seemed less convinced. "I... I think I need to stay here. There's a lot of research yet to do, and I have so many questions." She looked to the Archmage, who seemed more than happy to have someone with such "fascinating readings" follow her around the laboratory. Then, she looked back at Tristan and her smile seemed sad, apologetic. "I can stay here for the night and come back in the morning. I should be okay. Or you can come get me. I just feel like I need to keep working here. We're right on the edge of something really important."

"On the edge? Oh dear, we're in the middle of it," Tiara said with a laugh. "It's quite exciting, isn't it? I knew you were cut out for good solid research after all, dear."

Tristan hesitated, and I knew what he was going to say. He had no interest in leaving his girl behind, in a place he had no control over. We all knew this, but Andella seemed quite stuck on the idea. She wasn't budging. Rather than let them start some kind of a fight, I took Tristan by the elbow. "When we go out, we'll tell Fyr to keep a close watch on this building. There's no way anyone's getting in here anyhow, but just in case, you know?"

This wasn't what Tristan wanted to hear, I knew that, but he relented a lot faster than I thought he would. Maybe his mind was still addled by his trip into the Box. "All right," he said. "We'll be back as soon as we can, first thing tomorrow. I think... maybe it's nothing, but still, we need to go back home. Can't stay here right now. I wish I could explain."

"You don't have to. Go. It'll be fine." She reached out for him and kissed him lightly on the cheek in the comforting way that only a good woman can.

"Wait, one moment before you go, would you?" Archmage Tiara flitted across the hall into her laboratory, a whirl of green robes, and came back a moment later with a clear-white crystal, a little smaller than a man's fist. It was a miniature version of one of those focusing crystals she'd made me stare at those few times I'd come here to practice. I didn't quite understand the whole crystal thing, but it did seem to make the power flow easier somehow, and that sensation under my skin never felt quite as horrid when I was staring into one of those stupid crystals. "Take this with you," she said, holding it out for Tristan, "and later on tonight, hold it up to the place where you get those headaches. I've been working on attunement recently, and I have a theory. Tell me what happens first thing in the morning, yes?"

"What about me? Can I use it?" I asked, reaching for the crystal before Tristan could. For some reason, I didn't want him to touch it. Something about the word "attunement" didn't sit well. I didn't know why, and it was stupid to reach for the thing, because sometimes when I touched things, I had those visions.

Like now. I was falling into the blackness. I should have been ready for it, though I wasn't really surprised. Crystals, like anything else, had a history, had been around, had seen things. This one had seen a lot of things, perhaps, being from the Magic Academy.

What I saw was a place. A laboratory, but a different one from the disaster that was Tiara's. This was a clean, perfectly kept room, with books in alphabetical order all lined up on shelves without a speck of dust on them. The tables were tidy, the instruments polished and set in neat little rows – perfect, in every way.

The sole inhabitant of this laboratory was a man, a tall, thin fellow in blue. His back was turned and I couldn't see his face, but I had the impression that he was young, perhaps just an apprentice. He mucked about with some bits of metal that looked like a set of metallic tubes. Something stirred, and the door opened to reveal some grand mage in good silk robes, royal blue trimmed in silver. When the apprentice turned, he almost dropped his tubes, but that's when I saw his face.

Victor Wyndham? Why the fuck did I need to see *this* vision? He had nothing to do with anything as far as I was concerned. The very last thing I cared about was his time studying magic.

The grand mage handed him something. Strangely, I couldn't hear them – another one of those silent visions. Not that I cared about what they talked about... or did I? No, I did. I wanted to know why I was here with this vision, after all, and not looking at any number of a thousand other visions that little crystal could have shown me. Why the fuck should I care about anything Victor Wyndham ever did?

Maybe... because he was powerful. The grand mage used that same wedge-shaped instrument that Tiara used on us a while ago, something to do with measuring the magic through the eyes. He looked astounded at his readings, and Victor, of course, looked pleased with himself. He pointed to the focusing crystal behind him, a great giant thing standing on a pedestal, and said something. What did he say? Whatever it was, the grand mage seemed pleased, gesturing toward the crystal with a great flourish. Victor did the same, but when he did, magic leapt from his hands, water flowing over the crystal. It ran through all the cracks and crevices and the shards, then hardened there, becoming ice, and the entire rock – as wide as the table and as high as a man's arm – cracked apart into a million pieces.

The little piece I held in my hand was one of them. The world came back into focus as I stood there staring into its depths. Its... energy, or whatever it was, tugged at my own magic from the inside, almost like it could change the course of my bloodstream.

"Mister Vestarton?" the Archmage asked, staring into my eyes at such close range I could smell the sage and orange oil she wore.

"Sorry, just one of those visions again, of the past," I told her, dropping the crystal into my inside jacket pocket. It felt warm, even through the fabric.

"Really? What did you see just now?"

"How you got that crystal. It was broken from a larger one by Victor Wyndham."

"That it was." She sounded genuinely surprised. "That dolt, he and that arrogant Master Lebonne. Anyhow, start recording these visions if you can, please? We'll need to study that, too. So much to do. First things first, I need to read Hariage again, I think. Andella, come with me? And remember, gentlemen, I want a report in the morning?" And with that, we were dismissed.

Tristan and I made our way back outside, into renewed mud and another Rains-drizzle in full swing. My boots splashed through puddles as we walked, mostly in silence, back through the barricades and through the half-empty, despairing streets of northwest Zondrell. "So, do you know why we need to go back so fast?" I asked, finding myself working hard to keep up with Tristan's long strides. It wouldn't have been so bad if my side hadn't stung every time I took a step... and if Tristan had an answer to my question. But he didn't.

We rounded the next corner and noticed a few Royal Guards loitering about on the opposite side of the road. "Assholes," I muttered under my breath, but did my best not to make eye contact. Tristan did the same.

Not half a block up, though, was another group of five of them, moving toward us with purpose, as if they were actually doing something productive. In today's Zondrell, that could be almost anything, and almost none of it could be good. The Royal Guard, as a group, was quite perplexing. Most of them were so far up General Torven's backside, it was frightening. Yet, I'd heard about Royal Guards fighting in the streets in the name of the Throne, and about others who had cast off their armor entirely and had sold out as mercenaries. As such, I wasn't quite ready to assume they were all mindless lapdogs.

"Lords," one of them acknowledged us before we had a chance to react. I wanted to move to the other side of the street or something, but Tristan seemed less inclined. In fact, his sword arm was twitching, and that was not a good thing. I had no interest in getting into a fight here.

"Well met, gentlemen," I muttered, trying to find a friendly smile. I don't think I succeeded.

"Are you headed..." another one said as we came within arm's length of one another. He paused, regarding us with squinty eyes, while the rest of them clinked along in unison, parting to let us pass between them.

The first man, a taller Guard with a scar over his right eye, stopped and nudged his friend with one elbow, cutting him off. "Good day to you, Lords," he said to us. "Heading home?"

"Curfew's almost up," Tristan snapped at him, so much so that the man took extra step back. "Well aware. Thank you."

"Indeed. Stay safe out there, Sir."

If he had been in a different kind of mood or had a drink or two in him, Tristan might have replied with a stern, "Fuck you." Instead, he let his cold expression do his talking for him. As for me, I thought it prudent to offer something a little more cheerful... or at least, sarcastic in the most friendly way possible.

"You boys going back to the Palace, then? Give the General our deepest regards."

The two men looked at each other, then continued on their way without another word. Well now, that was a bit odd, wasn't it? I put the Royal Guard from my mind, though they didn't stay gone for very long. As we neared the next corner, we heard a shout, a brief flurry of activity and some metal scraping on metal. "Hey, wait," I said to Tristan, voice low, but he was already stopped and looking toward the source of the noise.

The two groups of Royal Guards were arguing. Blades were out. What were they shouting about? I couldn't quite tell as their voices bounced off the faces of buildings and became nothing but unintelligible noise.

"I thought they were all on the same side," Tristan said. His hand was on the hilt of his own weapon.

"Yeah, I don't know about that. What are you going to do? Go rush in and help? Don't be an idiot."

"Who's to say they won't turn around and come back this way?"

"They look a bit too busy for that, Brother. Let's just get out of here."

Yet it was hard to look away. Here were nine soldiers, trained in combat, chosen specifically for their discipline and dedication to serve the King himself, killing each other in the streets like a bunch of beggars arguing over who would get the last scrap of cast-off food. If I wasn't seeing it with my own eyes, I'm not sure I would have believed it. Within minutes, one was bleeding out on the ground – which side was which, it was hard to tell. All I saw was a mass of silver and steel.

"Why?" I said, not expecting an answer. I got one, regardless.

"Something's not right. Did the ones we talked to seem off to you?"

"What do you mean? They all seem off. Look at them."

"No, I mean, like they were hiding something."

"Maybe. We'll never know, now."

"I don't know. Let's just go." We turned away from the bloodshed, but it took almost an entire next block to escape the sounds of battle. Far, far too long for my taste.

Back on our block, everything was more or less just as it was supposed to be. Soldiers trampled through puddles along the road, and paid us little mind other than a curt nod as we approached our homes. Otherwise, no one else was out, not even a servant sent on some errand. The entire city had grown to become a strange place, a place I didn't know. I hated it.

"No emergencies here," I noted under my breath, then cleared my throat. "Look, I'm tired. Walking around like that is a little much for me. See you for dinner?" Tristan nodded, going off to get further entrenched in his own thoughts for a while. Me, I just wanted to go lay down and think about anything *but* magic for a while.

**

I said little to my sister or my mother when I came in. Instead, I just sat back in the overstuffed chair by the sitting room fireplace, staring up at the ceiling. What I thought I'd find up there was anyone's guess – it sure wasn't enlightenment. Speaking of which, what did that Archmage say? Hold that crystal up to your head or something? Well, not my head.

Tristan, she wanted to give it to Tristan, but I wanted to hold onto it. And I forgot to give it to him. Well, that could wait, and no time like the present to figure out what the big deal was about this "attunement" business.

I pulled the stone – still a little warm – out of my pocket, and held it up to my brow. Why not?

Nothing. Sort of an odd feeling, maybe, like I'd been through a glass of wine already. In fact, my cup was untouched, sitting next to me on the table. Except... wait. Did I pour a glass already? Well, I might have, but that wasn't my glass. Our glasses didn't have winged patterns on them, they were just plain, with a gold rim around the bottom edge. I didn't know where this garish winged thing came from.

Holy hell, this wasn't my house. I looked around, realizing that the bookshelves were in all the wrong places, the fireplace was the wrong shade of granite, and the rugs were black fur, not white. Why wasn't anything the way it ought to be? What was happening? Was this the Academy again? I had a hard time believing there was any place in the Academy that was this well-appointed. That place was made up of scholars, not nobles. The sitting room I was in was lavish, with paintings on the walls, sculptures on the shelves, nothing but the best – just like my sitting room. Except it wasn't mine.

I turned and noticed a cane propped up against the back of the chair. Not mine again, of course, but a familiar cane, a simple one with a worn rounded top. And the person that came in from the doorway wasn't my brother, either, because I didn't have one.

Peter Wyndham. This was the Wyndhams' house, and that was Peter standing there and I was sitting in the place where Victor was sitting and... oh, this was all too odd. It wasn't like the other visions. I wasn't just a casual observer here. I *was* Victor, moving the way he would move – slow. I found myself rising to my feet nonetheless, pushing against the chair for balance, but avoiding the cane. I needed to stop using it, didn't I? I'd get reliant on it, after all. And what did Peter want, anyhow? I was tired, and irritated after yet another argument with my father. He wanted me out, and I refused to leave. Peter needed my protection, even if no one else saw it that way, not even Peter himself. At least he was talking to me now.

As soon as I started to say something to the expectant Peter Wyndham, the world changed forms again. I was sitting, again, just as I always had been, and that crystal fell away from my fingers with a tiny dull thud as it landed on the floor. My floor, in my sitting room, in my house.

I blinked. What the fuck just happened? Was that vision, or whatever it was, all happening right now, in real time? I looked down at the crystal, thinking to pick it up and try again, but another part of me decided against it – probably the part that felt like vomiting. The weakness in my limbs, and sour taste in my stomach, none of it could be explained by anything but that vision. Worse, I had the compulsion to... what? Go to Wyndham's house? Talk to Victor and Peter myself? Why in Catherine's name would I want to do that?

And yet, I did. I did want to talk to them. I *needed* to talk to them. Despite the pain and the woozy feeling, I pulled myself to my feet and headed out. I didn't even tell anyone where I was going. It was still early afternoon, and they only lived two doors down. By the time I was done, it'd be almost dinnertime. I had just enough time to go figure out what the fuck I needed to talk to Victor Wyndham about so bloody badly.

The Wyndham maid greeted me at the door with fake pleasantry – she was just about as charming as the people she worked for. "The Lord of the house is not here at the moment, Lord Vestarton," she said to me.

"That's fine. I'm here to see Victor and Peter."

"The Young Master and his brother?" She said "brother" as if it was some kind of curse. "I will see if they are accepting visitors." The fact that she left me to stand outside in the rain was a *bit* shocking, but I only offered her the most tight-lipped of curt smiles when she returned. The door opened further and I was ushered in without ceremony.

"Well, to what do we owe *this* honor, Lord Vestarton?" Victor said, coughing and hacking his way into the Wyndham's grand entry hall. Now, I'm no expert on home décor, but the Wyndham home was downright gaudy. Gold trim everywhere, all kinds of paintings and artwork, a life-sized statue of Percival Wyndham's grandfather in the center of the room... it was all a little much for my taste. I squinted at the statue for a moment before turning back to Victor's hawkish visage and piercing blue stare.

What was I going to say, exactly? I had a feeling that, "Hey, I had this magic-induced vision of you," was not the best conversation starter. Instead, I came up with something that sounded a bit more normal. "You know, Victor, it occurred to me that we haven't spoken much since... that day. I heard about your troubles here at home and wanted to offer my condolences." Good Lady in Paradise, those words made my blood go cold. Did I just say that?

Victor snorted, and I realized that he wasn't on his cane anymore. While he still looked haggard, and really did cough a lot, he wasn't struggling to move and breathe as he had been during the trial. Good for him, I supposed – I wouldn't have thought him strong enough to recover from a stab wound and a collapsed lung, but here he was, making progress. "Thanks, I suppose? Aren't you supposed to be at the Palace right now?"

"The Palace?" I looked at him, dumbfounded.

"My father left about an hour ago. Supposedly a big meeting there or some such."

From the shadows at the back of the room, Peter emerged, round face sallow and dark eyes sunken. He looked like he hadn't slept well in a while. "It's a Lords' meeting, with the General," he said, quiet.

"First I'm hearing of it," I told him. "Did your father say anything else?"

"He doesn't talk to us. He just shouts. I'm not allowed to know." With that, Peter continued on to wherever it was he was going, wandering off like a disembodied and lost spirit.

"I have to watch him," Victor said, keeping an eye on his brother until he disappeared behind a door. "He tried to kill himself the other day, you know."

"What?" That wasn't the brash bastard that I knew. Peter Wyndham was a lot of things, but a suicidal coward wasn't one of them.

"Yeah, this whole thing with Doverton and the trial... well, it's my fault. And Father really does do nothing but yell. Peter's taken it rather hard. But why am I telling you all this, anyhow?"

"I'm sorry." I couldn't think of anything else to say. Suicide was not an act of honor in Zondrean culture – it was anything but. Even at their lowest, most people would never even consider it. And despite how I felt about the Wyndham family, Victor and Peter included, I felt genuinely bad.

"Don't be. Like I said, it's my fault. You know it as well as anyone. But hey, I wanted to ask you something, Vestarton."

"What's that?"

Victor leaned in, looking right into my eyes. I knew what he was looking for, and after a second, I turned my gaze to the floor. "The magic you have," he said, "you used it against me that day. It wasn't like anything I've ever seen. Can you heal people, too?"

"Heal people?" It wasn't much a secret now, was it? All of the Lords saw what Andella could do, and they saw what Tristan and I could do, too. So instead of denial, I just shrugged and told him the honest truth of it. "No, I can only do what I do – things with time. I have to admit, I don't know that much yet."

"It's impressive. Everything I've heard about it is... more than impressive. Did Loringham really stumble on some sort of secret up there near Doverton?"

I shook my head. "No, no secrets, no legendary weapons, nothing like that. It just happened. I can't describe it. If I could, I'd tell you." Because at this point, what did it matter?

"Well, if you ever feel like studying with someone, let me know. I'd like to get back to research. Figure that's what I'll do when things go back to normal, go work at the Magic Academy. If the Military side will have Tristan, I guess the Magic side might take me, right?"

"I'm sure." Would they have him there as some sort of researcher or instructor? He was quite accomplished as a mage, even if he was something of a prick. "Look, speaking of Tristan, I have to go. It sounds like we're late for a meeting."

"Who knows what they're meeting about? Hopefully you're not too late."

"Right. Thanks, Victor." With that, I raced out of there as fast as I could, heading straight for Tristan's house.

# CHAPTER THIRTY-FIVE

## Facing Fears
*10 Spring's Green, 1272*
*Andella Weaver*

I slid into the Box for the fourth time in the past hour, since the readings weren't "quite right" the other times. Alexander would have been horrified at the thought, but I simply let the darkness envelop me. It wasn't so bad – in fact, I liked the lights when they appeared. Each time, I noticed they grew a little brighter, a little more vibrant, and the colors changed more frequently. A week ago or so ago when I stepped into the Box, the lights were mostly white and blue, but now there was the yellow of a daffodil, the orange of a tiger lily, the purple of a crocus, and so much green! I'd never seen so many different shades of green. Red, too, the most brilliant vermillion, like a perfect rose. I had no idea why the colors were so intense, but by my final time in the Box, they were so crisp they almost had texture, like I could reach out and feel them.

"The colors are truly amazing now," I said as I stepped out to see Archmage Tiara writing notations on every scrap of paper she could fine.

"More intense than the last time?" she asked.

"Oh yes, much more. Why does that happen?"

"That all depends on how you think the Box operates. The basic theory is that the construction of the Box heightens power, brings it to the surface."

"Is that what you think?"

"I have a suspicion that it's a little more complicated than all that. Otherwise your friend would not have gone off to the River like he claims."

"You don't believe him?"

"My dear, I don't believe anything until I can prove it for myself. But, I certainly would like to hear more about it. A better question – do *you* believe it?"

"I do." Because I knew, didn't I? I knew something happened to him that was more than just passing out from an injury that day in Doverton. I could never pinpoint what it was, but that same moment that I healed him then, I felt *something*. A jolt, a... pressure. A sense of being in multiple places at the same time. I'd never felt it again, but it wasn't the magic. At first, I thought that's exactly what it was, but no, it was more than that. I could only hope he'd talk to me about it someday, but the way he was with that sort of thing, it didn't seem likely. Finally, another thought occurred to me. "Archmage, have you ever done the experiment on yourself? Gone in and out of the Box, I mean?"

She cocked her head to the side as if I'd said something very odd. And maybe I had. "Oh dear, well now that you mention it, I can't say I've done that in a long time. I ought to try it again, yes? Can't very well take notes when it's dark, though. That's the problem. And you don't know how to work the instruments, so... we'll try that some other time. For now, what I want you to do is take a crystal and try it out." She darted across the hall to the laboratory, and I followed eagerly. After a few minutes of searching, she came up with another small crystal, like the kind she'd handed Alex. An "attuned" crystal – I wasn't sure what that meant exactly, but it was clearly one of her many pet projects.

"You said hold it to your forehead?"

"Books on the nature of magic from people like Hariage say we have energy points in our bodies where magic is at its strongest. The brow is one of the more important points, but there are others in your hands, at the center of your breastbone and along your spine, that sort of thing. There's whole diagrams in... oh, now where did that go?" She rifled through a stack of papers for a moment, then scowled. "At any rate, most of my colleagues here do not believe in such things. However, I've had good results with these crystals so far. Just hold it there, right at the center, and tell me what you feel."

Energy centers? Attunement? None of this was taught in my Academy classes, but we were also trained to keep an open mind to the possibilities of this world, so I didn't consider the potential consequences. I just did exactly as she asked, pressing the hard stone against my forehead, right in the center where Tristan said he got his awful headaches. Immediately, I felt a woozy feeling come over me, tipsy like I'd had too much wine. In fact, I stumbled to lean back against the nearest table – I thought I might pass out. With a start, I pulled the focusing crystal away again, and immediately, the world stopped its sickening spin.

Strangely enough, though, my hands were glowing with blue-purple light. A ribbon of energy leapt from them and snaked over to Archmage Tiara, wrapping itself around her until it vanished into nothing. It was like the crystal pulled the magic right out of me. I stood there staring into my hands, confused but feeling this wonderful surge in my body. I felt... alive. No, that wasn't quite right. It was more like that feeling after a really good stretch, when the body feels empowered and open and just plain good.

"Well, isn't that something," the Archmage said, flexing her fingers about in all sorts of funny ways. "Do you know how long it's been since my hands felt this flexible? I could write for days at this rate. My dear child, *that* is your healing magic?"

"I guess so. The crystal sort of pulled it out of me."

"That's what it's supposed to do. It works like a charm, doesn't it? How do you feel otherwise?"

"A little strange, better now. The crystal made me feel funny, almost like I was drunk."

"Indeed. It gets easier. Do it again, dear, try to hold it longer? I'll take some readings." She moved to gather her instrumentation when a soft knock made us both look up. Visitors did not usually come up to the laboratories unless they were accompanied by a researcher, and the researchers never knocked. However, this person was alone, and most definitely not a mage of any kind.

The girl with the curly black hair had a sword at her waist and wore the black and silver of a Military Academy cadet. She bowed formally as she stepped through the doorway, and I realized I knew her. Well, I had never spoken to her, but she was the girl from Tristan's class, and apparently one of the King's daughters. Alex called her Princess Thinks-She-Can-Fight, though her confident demeanor suggested that she could fight just fine.

"My apologies, Archmage," she said, stiff and formal, "but I was told Instructor... er, Lord Loringham was here?"

"You missed him. He went home about an hour or so ago," I said, jumping in before Archmage Tiara said something rude – she had that look on her face. As it was, she went over to the bookshelf and began poring over it, searching for just the right tome.

"Oh. I was hoping to talk to him."

"Is there something wrong? Weren't... er, aren't you one of his students?"

"Yes, ma'am. You are his betrothed?" She eyed my hand with the linked ring and chain dangling upon it, and a hint of a smile graced her features. "I heard about that. Congratulations. Do you know if he's coming back?"

"Tomorrow. Why?"

The girl let out an exasperated breath. "Do you happen to know anything about my brother?"

"Your brother... the Prince? Prince Edin?"

"Right. Have you seen him lately? He was staying at Lord Miller's house, and I just heard that they've carted him up to the Palace for something. I don't like it. I want to know what's going on. Is Loringham there, then?"

"I don't think so. They said they were going home... ah, he and Alex... Lord Vestarton." All these titles – I didn't quite know how to refer to them in the presence of royalty.

"Right. They said nothing about the Palace, then?"

"No. I suppose you could probably get to the house well within the hour – it's not that far."

"I'm not wasting time with that. Thank you, Miss... ah?"

"Weaver. Andella Weaver. What are you planning to do?"

"I need to get to the Palace. Luckily, I know a few good ways to get in." She started to turn and run off, but something about the Princess and her words intrigued me. What if Tristan and Alex *did* go to the Palace, and what if something dangerous *was* happening there? I didn't think I could just stay around here doing research with all that in the back of my mind.

"Wait, Princess?" I called, and she hesitated, eyeing me over her shoulder with intense dark eyes. The idea of a princess usually conjured up images of pretty girls in prettier dresses and jewels, but this young woman was very far from that. Not that she was unattractive, but nothing much about her screamed "princess," either. She looked like she'd sooner join a band of mercenaries than shake people's hands at fancy parties. "I, um, I'd like to go with you. I mean, if something's wrong, I could help."

"You're a mage?" she asked, and I nodded. "Stay close, then, Miss Weaver."

Archmage Tiara wasn't that pleased with the idea of me heading out when dusk was approaching fast, but I left her without much say in the matter. The Princess had little patience, after all, and had no trouble leaving without me. So, we found ourselves leaving the barricades at the entrance to the Academy grounds behind, just as the sky had begun to turn from blue-gray to dark slate.

"There's some backstreets this way," she said, leading me down a narrow alley and into the twisting streets of a small neighborhood. We hardly saw a soul along our path, no patrols, no wanderers, no thieves, no one. I had never imagined the streets of Zondrell could ever be *this* quiet, especially now. We walked past broken windows, barred doors, burned-out husks of ruined buildings, but everything was still, the whole city, silenced. It was so unsettling I felt my heart begin to beat faster, my arms and fingers tingling with pent-up anxiety.

"So you're a mage, then," the Princess said in a low voice, breaking the silence and giving me quite the start. I tried to hide my nerves as best I could. "You're not the one people are talking about? From the Plaza on Peaceday?"

"I guess that depends on what you mean," I replied, sheepish.

"The one that healed all those wounded people, the Lords and such? Sorry I missed that. It sounded pretty incredible."

"I... guess it is. But yes, I can heal."

"I've never heard of a mage doing something like that. Then again, I've never heard of a mage summoning shields made of lightning, either." She shrugged. "Did you go to the Academy for that?"

"No, it just sort of happened that way. I did go to the Academy, but I was trained as a Fire mage."

"Fire's helpful. If something happens tonight, you can use Fire?"

I frowned, even though she was walking faster than me and couldn't even see my expression. "Well, not really. Not anymore."

Admittedly, I was glad I couldn't see her expression right then, either, because the tone of her voice said it all. "Stay close to me then."

"Do you think we're going into battle here?"

"I have no idea. All I know is that I don't like what they're doing to my brother. If they try to give him up to Torven or something, I'll have their heads."

"Earlier today, Tristan and Alexander told me the other Lords wanted to put the Prince on the throne and make Torven a regent." Should I have told her that? Maybe not, because she sped up her pace, and her hand went to her sword as if she would draw it at any moment. I quickly added, "They were against it. There was a big argument."

The Princess spoke some very un-Princess-like words. "They have no right. He's eight. He doesn't know what's going on, but I know for damn sure that he doesn't want to cozy up to that lying prick Torven. I'm not going to let them to do that to my little brother."

We continued on in silence for a while, darting this way and that through the side streets, avoiding any building that had lights shining in the windows. She was a smart one, this Princess, and cautious, but she was also very, very angry. When we finally emerged from the neighborhood and onto a wider street, I realized we were near the docks. The smell of sea air grew stronger and the rhythmic sound of the waves crashing against the cliffs gave me pause. It seemed so loud when everything else was so deathly quiet.

"Princess?" I asked, voice soft.

"Larenne," she corrected me.

"Larenne, can I ask you why the General did… what he did? Do you have any idea?"

"He wanted my father's throne, pure and simple. I just never thought he was like that. He was a great man, Miss Weaver. People respected him – I respected him. My brother adored him, and hell, my father did, too. I don't know why he did it, and frankly, I don't care. But he's not getting what he wants without a fight."

"I hope it doesn't come to that."

She turned and started at me then with those haunting eyes, like the eyes of a predator glittering in the darkness. "Jamison Torven has proven himself a coward, and if I have anything to say about it, he'll die like one. It might not be today, but it will happen – I swear on my name as a Blackwarren."

# CHAPTER THIRTY-SIX

## Boys and Men
*10 Spring's Green, 1272*
*Tristan Loringham*

"Catherine-on-a-pike, man, I haven't done this in years."

My uncle had told us how to get into the Palace undetected, but his technique was not as easy as it sounded. Then again, I supposed if it were easy, then thieves would be breaking in night and day. Alex and I were no thieves, yet there we were, climbing the outer wall of the city so that we could drop down on the other side of the palace gates, into courtyards that once routinely held revelers and courtesans at this time of day.

We were not quite as light as we had been as kids, and helping him up that last push to the top of the wall made me rethink the whole thing. Oh, we made it, but even still relatively skinny and short, he was a hell of a lot heavier than he had been at ten. Back then, we would get up on the surrounding walls of the city all the time, though in a different and much safer part of town. Here, the ocean was literally right on the other side, maybe a hundred feet down the cliff. *One bad step is all it takes.*

"Fuck. Don't look down," Alex said between labored breaths.

"Eyes forward, mouth shut," I replied.

"You're not scared shitless right about now? What the fuck are we doing up here? We're insane, aren't we?"

"We used to say that in our patrols all the time, up in the borderlands. Eyes forward, mouth shut – supposed to help you focus. So, focus." I didn't tell him that I had always hated that phrase, just like I hated those patrols.

It took a while, or it seemed to – the sky was the color of granite by the time we reached the courtyard. The entire time, we hadn't seen a soul on the ground below, no servants, no guards, no one. The courtyard itself lay dark, the torches out, the Queen's prized topiary starting to bloom into misshapen masses. It was so strange, like the Palace had been abandoned. We knew that wasn't the case, though. No, there was a party going on, and we were missing it, according to Alex. I just hoped he was right, because I was in no mood to do all this just for a cheap thrill.

"I'll go first," I said, moving to the place where Brin said to jump down. There was a little gazebo in one corner of this courtyard, with a sturdy roof strong enough to hold a man. The misting Rains made everything slicker than I would have liked, but nonetheless, I knelt, gripped the edge of the wall as best as I could, and lowered myself down, one foot at a time. The drop to the roof was only about six feet – a slight shock to the system, but not nearly as bad as twenty or more. Problem was, the roof of that gazebo was less flat than it appeared, and I immediately started to slip backward. Fast reflexes and four years of running laps around the Academy Ring kept me from an unceremonious crash to the ground.

Alex allowed himself to breathe again. "Fuck me. Brother, are you okay?"

"Yeah. Just be ready when you drop. This thing is at an angle."

I thought I heard his low growl of consternation as he turned and got into position as I had. "You just held onto the edge? I can't get a good grip on this."

"You only need it for a second, just long enough to soften the fall." He growled again, looking over his shoulder. "Don't look down."

"Fuck you." But he didn't look again as he set his hands and started to lower down. His rough boots sent tiny rocks skittering down, some striking the gazebo with a dull thud. His drop was perhaps a bit too soon for his liking, but he landed squarely and didn't slide much. Of course, I was there to stop him if he had.

The drop down to the ground was a little harder, though the rain-soaked earth helped cushion the blow. That, and tucking into a roll on the way down. We both knew that trick from the Academy, though it probably wasn't the best thing to do a week after getting a sword in the gut. Alex grunted as he hit the ground, and I had to help him to his feet, moving slowly, carefully. To his credit, he shrugged it off a minute or so later. We had things to do, after all.

"Let's never do that again," Alex said through gritted teeth.

"Agreed."

As Brin promised, the doors to the courtyards did not have locks. *Seems like a real oversight, but what the hell? Works in our favor now.* So, we slipped into the east ballroom where not so long ago, we sat and watched pretty girls dance while enjoying a drink. Now it was quiet, empty, the pristine surface of the dance floor gleaming even in the low light. I wondered if this place would ever see another party again.

"Where would they be?" I asked, looking to Alex as if he were some kind of oracle that held all the answers. I knew that was silly, and his frown said as much.

"Council Room? Maybe?"

"Which is where from here?"

He thought for a moment, then eventually pointed toward the north. "This way. I think." He knew better than I, so I took his word for it as we threw our wet and soiled cloaks off to the side and hurried down one of the long corridors. At least here, the torches were lit, but there were still few signs of life. It was so quiet I could almost hear our hearts beating. *Something is so wrong about all of this, except...*

*Wait.* "Do you hear that?"

"Yeah, the Council Room is up there, I think. See, what did I tell you?" The closer we got, the louder the voices became. Familiar voices – Cen, Shilling, Wyndham, Silversmith, and of course Miller, their fearless leader. A band of old men plotting Catherine-knew-what behind closed doors. Then a stronger voice rose over the rest of them, still very, very familiar.

Jamison Torven.

Alex and I looked at each other. "What do you want to do?" I asked him, whispering.

His eyes narrowed and that gleam of quicksilver in them was almost unnerving. "We go in there like we own the place."

So we did. We slicked back our hair, straightened our jackets, and puffed up our chests. We were Lords – we belonged in there. *Didn't we?* Well, even if I wasn't fully convinced, Alex could carry enough confidence for both us.

The heavy door creaked open and in we went, through the back entrance behind where the King would normally sit. I expected to find Torven resting there, resplendent in his formal armor the way I pictured this scene in my mind, but instead he stood next to the throne, dressed in silks and that sharp black jacket he often wore, covered in medals from dozens of victories won over the years. He wasn't even armed – at least, not with anything in plain sight. The dark-haired general whirled around as we entered the room, then immediately softened his stance.

"Sorry we're late," Alex said in his most brash, overconfident tone. "Our messenger must have picked up a case of the rattles or something."

We ignored the slack-jawed stares of the Lords and of Torven as we took our respective seats at the grand round Council table. Every single one of them seemed speechless. Then I noticed the most speechless of them all, perched on the gilded throne, looking as pale and expressionless as the day his father was killed. The Prince's little feet didn't even touch the ground, and the ornate chair seemed to swallow him up whole.

Finally, Miller found his voice again. "Then how exactly did you gentlemen find your way here? Your risk to come join us is notable." His tone oozed fake civility.

I adjusted my belt just to let everyone know there was a sword on it. "A little bird told us," I said, and Alex flashed me an approving grin.

Percival Wyndham snorted in his characteristic jackass manner. *I can't wait for you to find out your boy was the little bird in question, you old prick.* "Well, your votes don't count anyway," he growled. "What's the point? Go home, boys."

Bristling, Alex leaned in toward the aging Lord. "You know, Wyndham, everyone has something they don't like. Something that just... rubs them the wrong way. You know what I hate? I hate being called a *boy* when I'm in charge of more money than your House can possibly dream of. It just really pisses me off, you know?" He turned to me. "Don't you feel that way?"

Even seated, I towered over everyone in this room. Sitting here with them, on their level, as an equal, truly gave me a new sense of perspective. It felt like years had gone by since I stood before them pleading for my life. Now, things were different – now, I was one of them, but I could be even more than that, if I chose. I folded my arms across my chest and set my jaw, thinking for a moment before answering. "You know, come to think of it, I agree," I said. "I'm fairly certain that the proper and respectful term of address is 'Lord.' Am I right, Lord Miller?"

The fat man nodded, but it was reluctant. "Lord Loringham, that you are. But you have made your case against this vote very clear to this body, and it was rejected. There is therefore no reason for you to be present here."

"I beg to differ. I've read the Code, and it clearly states that all votes must be carried out with all seven Lords present."

Another Wyndham snort. "Well, I think we can all agree the Code doesn't mean a whole lot these days."

"That's not my fault, now is it?" I caught a glance at Torven then, who shifted in his stance a bit.

"Besides, if the Code isn't worth much, then why bother with voting at all?" Alex asked. "Just do whatever the fuck you want, whenever you want. Wouldn't that be easier? Seems to be the way things go around here of late." Silversmith looked down at the floor. Wyndham rolled his eyes skyward, and Miller cleared his throat. Cen sighed and shook his head, while Shilling just sat back, watching it all like it was a stage play. "I mean, holy hell, if we're going to pretend that we're civilized all of the sudden, has anyone even asked our young King here what he thinks about all this? What do you want, King Edin?"

The boy might as well have been frozen in place. His eyes were wide with fear, big, round dark pits in his small visage. At being addressed, his head darted to the General at his side, then back to the Lords again. "I, um," he started, voice shaking, "I want..."

Miller interjected before Edin could finish his thought. "The Prince – King – is the one who asked for this to happen, Lord Vestarton. After consultation with him, I agreed, and here we are."

"I want to put the city back," Edin said then, voice more confident though still not the least bit kingly. "And stop the fighting. Call off all the men."

Alex raised an eyebrow, the magic in his eyes starting to pulse and whirl even more than normal. "Better tell that to your new regent there, my Lord."

Torven took a step forward, but I couldn't read the expression on his face. In fact, I couldn't even figure out why he was being so meek. When he finally spoke, I began to understand. "Many members of the Royal Guard answer better to gold than to their General these days. Or were you not aware of the fact that half the Army is being funded by your colleagues, Lord Vestarton?"

"I... was not." The realization set into Alex's face as I'm sure it was doing on mine. It washed over me, a cold, empty feeling. For Alex, it must have been a bit warmer because his cheeks went flush.

*I couldn't have heard that right.* But I did – there was no question. "You paid them," I said, hoarse and quiet as I looked to a table full of Lords in various degrees of sheepishness. I didn't even know where to direct all the shock and anger roiling in my blood. I wondered if it was their men who attacked me on the street after my father's funeral, not Torven's. How easy it would have been to get rid of the new Lord with no heirs... it sure would have filled their coffers that much more. This level of clandestine evil was no doubt expensive. "You *paid* to ruin the city. Why?"

It was Miller who finally answered me. "Settle down, Loringham. Yes, we've paid the Guard, the ones who will listen. Trust me, if we didn't intervene, things would be much worse."

"Good people are dying in the streets. You have no right..."

"Without our men, things would be utter and complete chaos. We have secured nearly every neighborhood by now."

I could feel sweat on my brow now, and a piercing headache coming right along with it. "Secured? Have you been outside?"

"Now, now, Lord Loringham, even you must agree that the people need protection." Miller tried to stay calm, even, sure of himself, but as I listened I could hear the way his voice quivered, something trying to sabotage his confidence from just under the surface. "The General here hasn't seemed to think this necessary, but I can assure you, I've been out, and the troops loyal to us serve a valuable role in protecting people from... themselves. It can't be helped that the General's own men refuse to see things in a different way."

It took a great deal of control to keep my hand off my blade. If I couldn't be civil, then I was no better than the rest of them. Alex, though, used his words like a weapon. "You're perpetuating this! You're making it worse. You should all be ashamed of yourselves. How much money are you making off of all this?" He smirked, but it wasn't a look of amusement. "There's got to be a money angle. There always is."

"More money than you can dream of... *boy*," Wyndham said, and his smug smile *was* amused, quite so. I don't know how I kept from getting up to wipe it right off of him.

"It's not quite how it sounds," Cen offered in his even-tempered way. "The Army fights within itself, and the people... Well, the people have been panicking. Something had to be done. Right at the beginning, a few of us pooled our resources to make most of the Army listen to reason and do what's right. You two were recovering, so nothing was ever said to you. That's my fault, and I'm sorry."

"Do what's right? Do you even hear yourself?" Alex's words seemed to make Cen flinch. "You know, you might have been my father's friend, but I'm really starting to wonder why he trusted you."

"Alex, if you would just listen..."

"You know what? Go fuck yourself. So what is this? Why are we all here? Planning for pay raises for the men who do the most looting and raping, then? Or are we just here to threaten small children? I mean, Lord Edin, do you even know what a regent is?" As Alex turned to the throne, his expression turned from raging to hollow, questioning.

The chair was empty.

*Where did he go? Was he really that fast and that quiet?* The face of the Lords gradually began to share that same look of confusion and wonder. They looked around, started to murmur to themselves and each other. *Idiots – no one's going to do anything?* Apparently not. I got up and approached the throne, peering behind it to find nothing in the shadows. "Where is he? What trick is this?" I asked Torven, who had been standing literally a few feet away.

"I can't say," Torven said, shaking his head. "I... didn't see him go."

That was a lie and we both knew it. But I didn't have time to debate with him – every moment we waited was another moment Edin had to run and hide. The Palace was his home, and he surely knew its depths well. A scared little boy could squirrel himself away almost anywhere here, but that was just asking for trouble. I considered Alex for a moment, and I could read his thoughts in his swirling quicksilver eyes.

*Go find him. I've got this under control.*

I bolted out the back door without a second glance.

# CHAPTER THIRTY-SEVEN

## Dominance
*10 Spring's Green, 1272*
*Alexander Vestarton*

Tristan was faster, and tougher, and armed. Why didn't I bring a weapon? I didn't even think of it. Then again, did I *need* one? Did *he*? Well, Tristan could handle himself alone regardless, and he could find the Prince – the King... whatever he was called these days. So why did I feel such a sense of dread as he darted out the room? Something was very wrong here, and it wasn't just that eight grown adults had apparently lost an eight year-old.

Strike that – *seven* adults lost the boy. The eighth one, I had a feeling, knew exactly what he was doing. I got up and approached Torven, who was still standing there with his stone-faced expression. The fucker. That self-important look on his face wiped away any pain still tugging at my side and my back. It was his fault that happened in the first place, and looking at him just fueled anger and annoyance. Then I glanced back at the table full of confused old men in various states of argumentation, every last one of them rats and scoundrels. I had never been ashamed of my place in the world before this day, not once. I was fortunate – I was wealthy, privileged, part of the ruling class. But if this was how I was expected to conduct myself, lining my pocket while others bled, I wanted no part of it.

"You know where he went," I said to Torven, not loud enough for anyone else to hear. Not that they were paying attention, anyway.

Torven just stood there, ever the consummate soldier, a man who could slaughter another without even a grimace. "He was here one minute," he replied, "and gone the next. I wish I had more to tell you, Lord Vestarton."

"Cut the bullshit. What's going on?"

"It's for his safety." Again, Torven never even missed a breath, but his eyes did give him away. They darted past my shoulder, reflecting the nearby torch glow in a strange way. Where was he looking?

I turned just in time to face a most unusual sight: a heavy length of wood, slender and simple, with feathers arranged neatly on one end and the other with a barbed tip, like the kind they put on arrows meant to rend flesh going in and out. Of course, this *was* one of those very same kinds of arrows, so it made sense, didn't it? Why was it there? Where did it come from? Why was I thinking about these things when it was bearing straight down on me at incredible speed?

The thing froze in flight about three inches from my left eye. Behind me, Torven's calm demeanor shattered in a sharp intake of breath.

"Well, this is all very interesting," I said under my breath as I reached out and plucked the arrow from its course. And it was a wicked one, too. This was the sort of thing you used to assassinate someone you really, really didn't like. I turned on Torven, whose face had gone ashen. "Care to explain this, General?"

He didn't. He had nothing to say. He remained speechless as I heard another arrow whisper through the air – I made it stop short of its goal without even a second look. I could hear it, of course, because the room had grown very, very quiet. The Lords at their table were still... for once.

"You know," I said to Torven, tapping that first arrow against his chest with each word as I spoke, "I'm not one much for fighting. Oh, well you did know that, didn't you? I think I was once evaluated in the Academy as being 'undone by simple maneuvers and without technique.' Something like that. The thing is, I'm not like you. I don't even have to lay a hand on you to kill you, you know. I can just sit here, and watch you die, bit by bit, heartbeat by heartbeat, every one slower than the last." The magic crawled and burned under my skin, through my veins, but for once, it wasn't an unpleasant feeling. It was refined and yet powerful all at once, something I could extend and retract – like claws – at a moment's notice. It was almost like I had tapped into something new, some different source within myself, or maybe even beyond. I didn't understand all that, and frankly, didn't care. All I knew was that I was so sick of all the fighting, all the politics, all the posturing, all the lies. Yet, I had the power to do something about it, didn't I?

Time to put it to work.

I made the magic reach out, just a little, not so much as to stop but to slow things down. The very air around me seemed to thicken, and the General's breath came slower and slower, as his eyes grew bigger and bigger. At any moment, I could make it stop all together, and he knew it – I held his very life force in my grasp. This was something I might have done on Peaceday, but I was too scared, too confused. Here, I was in control, and I was also angry. Oh, so *very* angry. It welled up inside me, not so much unlike the magic itself, an outpouring of rage and something not unlike the distinct desire for vengeance. These people had been manipulating everything that made this city the pit of despair it had become. Hell, maybe it was always like that and I had just been too distracted to notice. Or, it had all just been wriggling around too far under the surface to see.

"Do you feel that?" I asked. "I can make it stop, if you want to explain yourself. Or, I can make it just... *stop.*" His nod took almost half a minute, in real time. In my distortion of time, it might have felt like a year. I didn't know – I didn't care. I was past that point.

When I let the magic go, he wheezed and clutched his heart like he had just run seventeen miles uphill. Behind me, I heard stirring and noticed the real reason why the Lords had all gone so quiet. They had soldiers in Royal Guard armor standing around them, weapons drawn. The Guards were alert, keeping an eye on both the table and on their General. None of them dared approach the man who could stop arrows and hearts with his mind, though. From the table, only Cen was looking in my direction, and even across the room I could see the worry etched in his gaunt face. For a split second, I felt bad about what I'd said to him... just a little bit.

"Alexander, you weren't even supposed to be here," Torven said through deep, pained breaths. "You don't understand."

"Yeah? Everyone tells me that, lately. Make me understand."

"You and I are on the same side."

I cut him off with a laugh that sounded half-crazed. "Ha! Are you fucking kidding me?"

"Alexander, you care about this city, am I right? So do I. All my life, everything I have done is for Zondrell. Kelvaar has done no good for this city. The Lords will do no good for this city. The boy... time may tell, but not while controlled by them."

"They made *you* the regent. So what else could you ask for?"

Torven shook his head. "Come on, you know that's just in name only. A way of controlling me, and Edin, through that table over there. It's time to be done with the ways of the Great Houses, Alexander."

"So you asked for peace and all that nonsense, agreed to this meeting, all so you could bring us here to ambush us? That sounds like the General Torven I know. You know what? Fuck you." With that, I spat right on that fancy jacket of his, right between some triangular medal of valor and one of many silver falcon insignias.

Surprisingly, he ignored the affront. "Your power is immense, Alexander. I know that, and so do you. Think of what we could accomplish together, without their backstabbing politics to get in the way of what is truly important."

As I searched his eyes, I knew he believed everything he said. Just like he believed that killing Kelvaar was the right course of action, he believed that he was the solution the city needed, that he was Zondrell's savior. Who was he to decide when and how this city needed saving? I glanced back at the table and the tense scene there, a dozen or so loyalists with weapons at the ready, waiting for the General's cue. "And just what is important these days, General?" I asked without turning back to him. "I'm a bit confused on that."

"Lend your power to the throne and we'll begin to understand. We'll put things right, the way they should be."

The way things should be. What did that even mean anymore? What did it ever mean, for that matter? Everyone in this room, myself included, had been complacent for a long time. We went along with the day to day. We lived in the past while making decisions about the future, never considering what was actually happening right before our eyes. For just a second – a tiny split in the fabric of Time – I saw it all, past, present, future. We got here through greed, through inaction, through looking the other way. Zondrell rested now on a precipice built on poor intentions and apathy, and the future? It didn't look so good. Sure, Zondrell could stay powerful, but power isn't everything. Power alone doesn't command respect or foster loyalty. The world might cower in fear of the great City by the Seacliffs, but it would sneer behind its back at every available moment. And in the end, it would be the people who suffered – common folk, nobles, the royalty, everyone. I saw a flash of a man, looking far older than his years, slumping in the Great Throne, surrounded by opulence and servants and soldiers ready at his beck and call, and yet the man himself was miserable. Tired. Worn. He wanted nothing more than to leave that place, maybe jump off of one of those cliffs and let the Sea of Stars have its way with him. Someone else would just come to take his place. No one would go to rescue him; no would care to see him gone. They all knew he didn't really run things, anyhow.

In another flash, the image was gone. The man on the throne? Edin, of course. Edin, all grown up and hating everything about his life. I didn't want that for him. I didn't want that for Zondrell. As fucked up as it was, it was my home, and I wanted better for it.

I took a deep breath and stalked over toward the Council table, ignoring Torven's pleas to get me to come back and talk to him. As I passed, I looked beyond the soldiers, to the walls where all of our family seals stood emblazoned on centuries-old tapestries. The Great Houses of Zondrell, all eight of them, Blackwarren included. How long had they wrestled amongst each other and with the world around them for wealth and power? Maybe things had gone on the same way long enough. Without paying anyone any mind, I took the Vestarton tapestry from its hallowed place on the wall, draping it casually over my shoulder as I went over to Miller's stonecutter arch, positioned to the right of the royal Blackwarren falcon. I pulled it down, tossed it to the floor, and hung the Vestarton sword and pick in its place. Miller's banner was then placed back on the hooks where my family's had once been, way back at number six in the line of succession.

The armed men then parted for me as I strode up to Andrew Miller. His already pale face grew even more so as I grabbed the fat man by his collar and hoisted him – with considerable effort – to his feet. I wanted him to look me straight in the eye, so I held him close enough to me that I could feel his wine-soaked breath come in short, hitched waves. "There's a new Head Councilor as of today. Right now. Do we understand each other?" Miller started to shake his head, blinking, then wisely nodded instead. There would be no arguing this. It was already done – the damned tapestries said as much. Can't go fucking with those, now, could we? Tradition... I would argue with Torven on that one point. Tradition had its place, its way of exercising its own form of control where it needed to. Not all control was a bad thing, when used the right way. And this situation? It needed a different kind of control.

"What are you doing, Alex?" Cen said, his voice weak. Behind him, a soldier jumped at the sound, his weapon shuddering in his grasp.

"I'm doing something that needs to be done," I said, matter-of-fact. Then I looked to the soldiers, without letting go of Miller's jacket. If he was angry at how rumpled it'd gotten, he kept it to himself. "Who pays you your gold, gentlemen?"

At first, no one spoke. Then, the tall fellow near me cleared his throat. "We answer to General Torven."

"Yeah? All of you?" Around the room, heads bobbed. I turned back to the spot near the throne where Torven hadn't dared move an inch from his at-attention stance. "General, will you kindly adjust your orders?" Torven blinked, pale and confused. "Let me offer you some assistance. These men need to stop answering to you, and start answering to the throne, and the throne alone. They are, after all, the *Royal Guard*. Is that clear enough?"

Torven considered, and his hesitation did nothing to improve my mood. I felt magic well up in me at an alarming rate, so much so that I could reach across the room and change Time for any individual here. And I did just that, directing a wave of slowness at the General and all of his men in turn, giving them the distinct feeling that their hearts might give out at any moment. Eyes widened in panic everywhere, and some pulled away from the table, away from the bizarre silver-eyed Lord who seemed to suddenly hold their lives in his hands. "I… yes," Torven said at last, raising his hands in a gesture of surrender. I tried not to smile as I released the magic. "Lord Vestarton is correct. You should not answer to me. You answer to Edin, to your new King, and only to him. At ease, men."

With that, the Guards relaxed. Swords went back into scabbards, and some turned away from the table entirely. A collective sigh of relief drifted across the Council table.

Cen stood, addressing me. "Alexander, what you've done, I…"

A massive crashing noise, causing the very stone around us to shake, ended his thought for him. What the hell was that? A number of starts and yelps popped up all around, from the Council, from the soldiers, everywhere. It felt as if the whole building had been hit by some massive force – a lightning strike? It wasn't supposed to storm tonight, and even if it had, when was the last time lightning struck the Palace instead of one of the elegant metal spires that guarded it from such things in the first place?

Wait.

Lightning.

No.

I rushed toward the door leading out into the Council antechamber faster than I'd ever moved before.

# CHAPTER THIRTY-EIGHT

## Fire of the Will
*10 Spring's Green, 1272*
*Andella Weaver*

We had no trouble getting into the Palace – in fact, we walked right through the front door. I could hardly believe it. Why wasn't anyone around?

"Be careful," Larenne said as I followed her through one gilded chamber and then another. The decorations and artwork were stunning reminders of how rich the Zondrell royalty really was. The Palace made the homes of people like Tristan look like hovels by comparison. "Just because they're not at the gates doesn't mean they're not hiding out somewhere. I heard Torven sent all the servants and guards home, but he's got his own people."

"The Royal Guard, right?"

Larenne snorted out a derisive laugh. "Most of them. At least you can usually hear them coming."

We stopped at a crossing, where the hall split into three routes. Larenne considered her options, holding her hand up to keep me quiet. Somewhere off in the distance, I began to hear what she heard – voices, punctuated by metallic sounds. The Princess cursed.

"Are they coming this way?" I whispered.

"No, they're in... the throne room?" Her scowl was not a flattering one, and she didn't elaborate as she started off down the path straight ahead of us. The hall opened up into a wider, circular entrance, with two massive double doors at the end. Mosaics of inlaid glass and jewels covered the walls, depicting an intricate series of scenes of men in battle, of kings receiving tributes, and of people worshipping Catherine, praying at the Great Temple. The images of doves with outstretched wings circling over this latter scene reminded me of the ancient, stylized artwork in the small church my family owned outside of Doverton. I wondered how long this Palace had been here – even though every surface appeared polished and new, this kind of art spoke of a much older, more simplistic kind of style.

The doors swung open with little more than a creak, even though Larenne had not treated them in the most ladylike manner. As soon as she thrust the doors inward, no fewer than ten men in silver armor leapt to attention, some with weapons coming to bear. They hovered in something of a semicircle before the massive, gold-laden throne at the end of the room, the place where the King must have held court on a daily basis. My heart skipped a beat.

"What the... Princess Larenne?" one of the men said, a somewhat handsome, clean-shaven young man with a falcon design etched into the plate of armor on his right shoulder. He motioned for the others to relax, which they did.

The Princess was not nearly so pleased to see him, though. Her teeth seemed to grind with every word. "Jessip. What are you doing in here?"

"We're on standby," the man called Jessip replied, as if that explained everything.

"For what? Where's my brother?"

Jessip looked behind him at one of his companions, and the other man seemed to shrug, though it was hard to tell with all of that armor on. After some consideration, he turned back to Larenne, clearing his throat. "I believe he's at a Council meeting."

This was all Larenne needed to hear, as she started to go back the way she'd come, nodding for me to go with her. I would have, except there was a tall, barrel-chested man in my path, giving me a rather peculiar look. "Excuse me," I said, moving to go around. I didn't get very far.

"Wait a moment," Jessip said to us, voice harsh and biting. I didn't much like his tone. "What do you expect to do, Princess? I don't believe you were invited to this meeting."

Larenne huffed, hand resting on the hilt of her sword. I really wished she hadn't done that, since as soon as she made the gesture, any weapons that had been put away were out once again. The brute in front of me just narrowed his eyes – far intimidating enough. "Since when does a Royal Guard third captain make decisions about who does and does not attend Council meetings?" Larenne demanded.

"Since I started taking orders directly from the General."

"Your General can rot in hell, along with you and the rest of the traitors." With that, she did something very unprincess-like, spitting a wad of phlegm onto Jessip's steel boots. Even though I didn't think it a very wise decision, I folded my arms across my chest and stared at him and the others with as much venom as I could muster, joining my companion in trying to intimidate these men into submission. What else was I supposed to do?

A moment passed, and then another. No one moved. The captain did nothing but make a face that was half-smile, half-sneer. Finally, Larenne huffed and turned away from him again, and Jessip put up his hand. I bristled, but instead of seeing men rear back ready for an attack, they all stepped aside on cue, even the big brute. Weapons were sheathed, and no one said another word.

I breathed again once we got back out to the hall. The doors shut behind us with a soft thud that seemed to echo through the circular chamber, and Larenne cursed under her breath. "I can't believe him," she said.

"Who was that? Someone you know well?" To me, she seemed too upset for this Jessip to be just any soldier, even if he had been serving in her father's personal guard.

"Well enough to know that he should be better than that. They should all be better than that. They're animals."

"Would they have hurt us?"

"I don't know. I don't doubt it, but they saw you. You're a mage. Even those idiots aren't stupid enough to tangle with magic."

"I'm not so sure about that."

She almost smiled at me as we turned to the right and down a longer hall, this one just as dark and silent as all the others. The closer we got to the end, the quieter it got, and with the silence came a looming sense of... something. Dread? No, not quite, but I got the sense that the room beyond the next set of doors was not empty.

And I was right. Larenne pushed open this ornate set of double-doors to reveal a tall, airy chamber, resplendent with tapestries and statues and mosaics. It didn't have that much in the way of furnishings, though, not even more than a bench or two to sit. Whether it was some kind of museum or a waiting room or just a passageway to something better, I couldn't tell. On the end opposite another set of doors lay an open-air balcony overlooking the sea beyond, and I could smell a hint of salty air even from where I stood. The sky outside was grim, and provided little light, but here the sconces along the walls were lit, sending flickering light throughout the room and reflecting off of the armor of even more soldiers. There were more here than in the throne room – fifteen, maybe? Twenty? I stopped counting after one stalked up to us, a large sword in his hands.

"Princess Larenne?" the soldier asked in a gruff voice that reminded me of an old dog's bark.

"My brother is in the Council Room?" she asked, though it was more of a demand than a question.

"Yes, m'Lady, but..."

"But nothing." She pushed past him without another word, but this one didn't put up a fight. In fact, he seemed fine with the idea of her going to the Council Room, though some of his friends did not. A few among the gathered men raised weapons, some swords, an axe or two, and some wicked-looking thing with a hook at the end. I felt my throat constrict just thinking about that weapon coming down on me, or Larenne, for that matter. Why were these men on such high alert? What could possibly be going on in that Council Room?

"You can't go in there," one of them said as Larenne reached for the handle. At her side, I could feel her tense.

"I will do whatever I wish," she said, brazenly raising her chin. "This is my house, not yours."

Hesitation. Men exchanged glances. Why? Were they hiding something? In the room beyond, I couldn't hear much save for faint muffled voices, and though I couldn't make out any words, they didn't sound very pleased. Was Tristan in there? Alex? I wished I knew, wished I could push past all this and find out, but that didn't seem to be a viable option.

"The fate of this house is yet to determined," another of the men said, and there was some kind of sick cheer in his voice. Larenne just shook her head at him and moved to open the door again, but was stopped by a hook-pointed sword hovering inches in front of her face.

"Can't let you do that," its owner hissed.

"Like hell." The Princess might not have been large compared to these men, and she wore nothing but basic leathers compared to their full armor, but still, she had no qualms about drawing her weapon. The hook-sword reared back for a blow, but given its heft and its reach, it wasn't a quick movement. I grabbed at Larenne's free arm and hauled her backward, out of reach of the awful thing.

The maneuver landed me square on my rear end, though Larenne kept her footing. She narrowed her dark eyes at me, but only until she felt the rush of the sword bearing down into the place where she once stood. A weak sound escaped my lips.

All around us, weapons began to clash as the men joined sides and began to hack at each other. From the floor, all I saw were limbs and silver armor and swinging steel, which made no sense. Why were they fighting each other? Did they not all answer to the General?

Apparently, they did not. Some barked out the name of King Kelvaar as they bashed into their former comrades, while others laughed at the idea of serving a dead man. I scrambled to my feet just as a heavy-set man with an axe stepped backward to defend against a wicked blow. Both boot and blade nearly missed me.

Good Lady in Paradise, why did I wear a dress today, of all days? My skirt seemed to do nothing but get in the way as I put my back up against the wall, trying to figure out what to do. I could try to run, but that would leave Larenne alone. Only a handful of the men seemed concerned about her, including the man with the hook-sword who seemed to want nothing more than more royal blood spilled. He struck with vicious fury at her, though she was able to dodge and defend, agile where he was nothing but a big lout.

A few feet away, the gruff-voiced soldier fended off two men at once, quite the feat for someone who appeared to be at least twice the age of his opponents. Their weapons clashed against each other with deafening rings that echoed in my head and through my whole body. The whole place was nothing but echoes... I put my hands to my ears for a moment, willing the ringing and the noise and the chaos to just stop, but it wasn't much use.

Then one of the younger men in the tangle before me got a strike on the older one, and he grinned an awful, evil sort of grin that I'd never seen on anyone, ever. It turned my stomach. His blade came away with blood on it, and the old soldier reeled back, leaving himself open for another strike.

"How dare you!" I yelled. Why did I do that? But yet, the words escaped before it was too late to shove them back in. Not only that, but I was stepping forward, like I was going to do... something. What, I didn't quite know. Though on the other hand, they didn't know either. They saw an unarmed woman who might have been a mage standing there, getting ready to do something to them, and they had two choices – fight or flee. One of the two attackers stepped back a few paces, while the one with the bloodied blade just continued to smile. That weapon tore into my dress, right above the waist, before I even knew what was going on.

Searing pain ripped through my whole body. Great Lady, was this what it really felt like? This was nothing like a little cut from a dagger. This was pure, agonizing torture! I lurched forward, grabbing for something to break my fall.

What I found was relief. It washed over me like a dream, and the pain in my stomach melted away, replaced with a peaceful warm tingling. I enjoyed it for about a half a second, until I realized that the man whose arm I clutched at for balance was howling like a lunatic. And the skin beneath his armor was... smoking?

Dear Catherine! I let go and he collapsed in a heap, writhing in pain. The man who'd fought alongside him a moment ago now bolted away, and the old soldier just looked between me and the screaming pile on the ground, a mixture of shock and relief on his features.

I took a deep breath, and it felt good, much better than it might have since the front of my simple blue and white dress now had blood all over it. Noting the way the older man clutched at his shoulder, I directed magic toward him, something to ease that pain. He couldn't even express his thoughts to me, though he tried.

"What are you... I don't understand. Madam, you are..."

"You're welcome," I said, looking back toward Larenne and her struggle with Hook-Sword. "Please help the Princess." The old soldier was a good man – I could tell. He fought for the King, and he shouted as much as he bore down toward Hook-Sword.

I watched he and Larenne flank the big man and strike at his sides, and even though they should have had an advantage, that sword was creative in its deadliness. He thrust out toward Larenne, and though he missed, he drew back at an angle so that he caught the back of her left arm with that hook, ripping through fabric and flesh as if it were paper. I found myself transfixed by the sight of blood seeping out of her, unable to see or think about anything else. It was hideously fascinating.

Her shout of fury and pain snapped me back into reality. The hook pulled her forward, into the man's reach so that he could grab at her throat with his other hand. The old soldier, though, was not about to let that happen without a fight. He darted in, sword first, but his attempt to cut that hand off was met with a surprisingly quick dodge.

Magic, however, wasn't so easy to dodge. He never even saw me as I took a deep breath and did the first thing that came to mind. Did I even really think about it? No, if I had, I wouldn't have done what I did.

A ribbon of violet light shot forth from my hand toward Larenne, surrounding her in an aura that grew brighter and brighter until it took on a new form and reached out toward the man with the hooked sword. All the pain it had stored up from the wounds it had already healed became a weapon of its own, one without steel edges, but with a white-violet glare that still cut nonetheless. Maybe it was worse than any blade, because the ensuing screams were deafening. I could barely hear as others began to yell at each other, retreating and reforming their ranks.

Hook-Sword was on the ground, still. By the Goddess, was he... I couldn't imagine it. Couldn't even think the word. Luckily, I didn't have to. Larenne kicked him hard in the stomach and he flinched a little, curling further into a fetal position. "That was quite the spectacle, Miss Weaver," she said to me, rubbing at her newly healed shoulder.

"Are you all right?" I asked, and my voice sounded strange and hoarse to me.

"Better now, for the moment." Her hand tightened around the hilt of her sword as she noted more men filing in from behind us, the way we had come in. Captain Jessip led the charge.

"Great Mother of... I knew it," Jessip said, sounding sad, or maybe disappointed as he drew his blade. Those behind him did the same.

The old soldier that I'd healed a few moments ago stepped forward. "Jessip, what are you doing?" he demanded. "What is this?"

"What does it look like? And that's Captain Jessip, to you." He then turned to the Princess. "Nicely done, Lady Larenne. I believe you've made my job considerably easier."

"What do you mean? What the hell is going on here?"

Jessip bowed, but somehow, the gesture didn't seem humble. "My apologies, Princess, but you have to know there are some misguided souls yet in the Royal Guard."

"Misguided? Are you trying to joke with me? If none of you were misguided, we wouldn't be having this conversation!" With every word, Larenne's voice rose in pitch and volume.

"That might be, Princess, but without us, who would ensure the future of this city went to the right hands? Certainly not this one." With one quick movement, Jessip's sword thrust straight into the chest of the old soldier, in the small spot in the middle where the plates met. That poor man, who had seemed so loyal, so good-hearted, fell first to his knees, holding the sword as if to pull it out, but his strength went too quick. He wilted, and blood pooled around him as he slid onto the marble floor.

I screamed.

# CHAPTER THIRTY-NINE

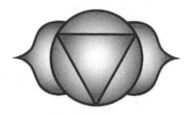

## Gathering Storm
*10 Spring's Green, 1272*
*Tristan Loringham*

I ran through the hall until I hit a cross-section. *Where would I go if I were a scared eight year-old?* Getting away from people wasn't hard – there was no one here. The Palace was about as empty as a tomb, no servants rushing around, no guards, no one. I wondered if they'd all been sent home, or they left on their own. I didn't think Torven had it in him to have the servants executed, although then again, I didn't think he'd kill Kelvaar in front of thousands of people, either.

On a whim, I turned left down a shorter hallway that opened up into a wide kitchen area, smelling of warm baking bread and some sort of vegetable stew. Well, at least someone was keeping up with the day-to-day around here. The strong aroma of rosemary and sweet flour made me realize that I had skipped both lunch and dinner today – I might have even grabbed something had I not realized I wasn't alone.

A stooped, heavy-set figure in a white apron and a flour-dusted brown dress pulled out another loaf of bread from the massive wall hearth, holding the golden circle out on a wood-handled metal paddle. It almost didn't make it to the counter though, for the cook jumped, startled to see me standing there.

"Good Lady's grace!" the old woman yelped, righting her paddle and deftly laying out the bread before raising the device up in a defensive posture. "What are ya doing back 'ere, son? Scared me 'alf to death, y'did." She had a strong "South Streets" accent, as they called it, a way of drawing out vowel sounds and cutting off certain consonants that was common among the so-called "lower-born" citizens of Zondrell.

I held my hands out to the sides, empty and open. "Sorry, I didn't mean to sneak up on you, m'lady," I said in a calming tone. "I'm looking for Prince Edin. Have you seen him?"

"Seen the Prince?" Her weathered face grew pensive. "I 'aven't seen 'im in a week or more, yeah? Aren't you that Lord's son what won that fancy Academy medal a while back?"

"Yes, ma'am." I offered a low bow. "Tristan, Lord of Loringham."

"Right, right. I knew it by that yellow mop on yer 'ead. Lord, eh? So you're with the fellows up with Lord Torven down the 'all?"

"Yes, ma'am. Prince Edin might come by here. If you see him, can you tell him to go back to see the Lords?"

"Them Lords didn't ask for a meal – too bad. I've got some good stew going. Tell 'em they can 'ave some if they want it. You know, I've been serving Kings for some forty years, you know that? I served Kelvaar and his papa, and now the General. Well, 'e don't call 'imself King. I don't know. I just make the food."

*Forty years?* I wasn't even sure I could imagine doing the same thing day after day for that long – that was almost two of my lifetimes. But wait, what did she say…? "He doesn't call himself King, does he?"

"Nope. 'e sent all the servants off, told them to go take a 'oliday. That's rich, eh?" She laughed, but there wasn't much happiness there. "I don't 'ave anywhere to go, so I stay 'ere, and I cook. Not getting any complaints from the General's lot, I'll tell ya that."

Whatever she really thought of Torven, she kept it to herself. Or maybe she had little feeling one way or the other about who she served. She clearly didn't care much about titles, because she turned away from me then, to the stewpot to add a little more salt. Our conversation apparently over, I moved to go back the other way and keep looking for Edin, when I saw a small movement out of the corner of my eye, behind the big center counter where that bread lay cooling.

Just as a small hand reached up to snag a bit of crust, I darted forward and peered over the counter. "Well, well, just the man I was looking to see," I said with the most non-threatening smile I could muster.

Little Edin looked up with brown eyes like dinner plates. "Lord Loringham!"

"Your Majesty, do you want to tell me why you ran away?"

The almost-King continued to stare, not sure what to do – he was frozen in place. Behind him, the old cook snickered. "Told ya this is a bad spot to 'ide. I did try. Lord Tristan or whatever yer name was, don't get 'im in trouble, will ya? 'e's a good boy."

"No trouble. I just want to talk for a while." This prompted Edin to stand up, though he still wasn't that much taller than the countertop. He continued to eye the bread, and after a nod from the cook, he tore off a big piece for himself.

"Do you want some?" he asked me in between bites.

I really did. I had no trouble tearing off my own hunk, resting my elbows on the counter as I tried not to inhale it all in one gulp. Fresh bread right out of the oven like this was, it was argued, solid evidence of the divine. I had a hard time contesting that as I reached in for another piece. Between the two of us, the loaf was half-gone in minutes, but the cook didn't seem to mind – she already had another ready to go into the hearth.

"I'm sorry I ran off, Lord Loringham," Edin said after a while. "Were you worried about me?"

"Yeah, I was. That's why I came out to find you."

"Lord Torven told me to go."

My brow furrowed, and I tried very hard not to look angry. "Really? He told you to run away and hide?"

Edin nodded, but he looked down at the countertop as he did so, fingers tracing lines in stray bits of flour there. "He told me to go see Essie, and stay with her. So I did. I don't trust him, though. Maybe I shouldn't have listened to him?"

"I don't know. He didn't tell you why?" Edin shook his head. "That's okay. Don't worry about it. We can go back when you're ready. I'll protect you."

"I don't want to go back."

*Don't blame you there, kid. Neither do I.* "Why not?"

"I don't want to be King."

"I understand. It's not an easy job."

The lines of flour began to get more intricate, swirls that formed the shape of a flower. "Can I ask you a question, Lord Loringham?"

"Of course. What do you want to know?"

He looked up from his artwork, eyes no longer filled with fear but with curiosity, touched with a hint of sadness. "Did you, um, did you cry when you father died?" *Way to throw out an easy one there, kid.*

I took a deep breath and nodded. "Sure, I did. I still do sometimes."

"You do? I do, too. My sister Larenne says I shouldn't cry."

"I know your sister, and I know she cries sometimes. So I think it's okay if you do."

"She does?"

"She does — I've seen it," I said with a slight smirk. This made the boy smile, too.

"She says you're a good teacher."

"That's nice of her to say. She's a good student."

"She's my favorite sister. I think she should be King. Can't she do it?"

I had to laugh at the thought of brash, loud-mouthed Larenne Blackwarren on the throne of Zondrell. Most certainly, she would rule with an iron fist. "I don't think so. At least, not right now. Maybe someday."

Edin seemed pleased with this, as if the hope that he didn't have to be the King forever was good enough. "Lord Miller said that I had to let Lord Torven help me be King. I don't think he was very good at helping my father. I mean, I used to like him, and I used to think he was my friend, but then…"

"I know," I said, not letting him complete that thought. "A lot of us used to respect Lord Torven."

"I'm scared of him. I'm scared of Lord Miller, too. Do you know what he says?"

"What's that?"

Edin leaned in, voice lowering to a whisper. "He says you and Lord Vestarton are stupid little boys that don't know anything and you can't be trusted."

*Why was that not surprising?* That portly old man was much more wily than I had once thought. He defended the idea of turning the Army against each other to sort out the "conflict" in the city, and yet *I* was the one who couldn't be trusted? Interesting. "He told you that, did he?"

"No, he said that to Lord Wyndham. I was listening, you know, when I was staying with him? They said that, but you're not very little. And you don't seem very stupid. But if he doesn't like little boys, well, I'm a little boy. So, maybe he doesn't like me?"

"I don't know, m'Lord. I can't say."

"You know what I think? I think he doesn't like you because you have magic, you and Lord Vestarton. You're... *awesome.*" The way he said it, with such reverence, I almost wanted to laugh. There was no way we were *that* awesome, and I modestly told him so. Still, he continued to prattle on. "No, you and Lord Vestarton did all of those amazing things on Peaceday – I saw! And Father used to say that you brought back something incredible from the border but wouldn't share what it was. He said it was too bad you were such a stubborn ox like your father because you would be really valuable. He said it just like that, too. What's a stubborn ox?"

I had to smile at that one. "Someone who doesn't listen to your father or Lord Miller, would be my guess."

"Oh. Does that mean I can be one, too, and not be the King?"

A thought struck me then, and though I wasn't exactly sure where I was going with it, I walked around the counter so I could kneel in front of Edin, putting us more or less on the same level. "Tell you what, Your Majesty. If you come back to the Council Room with me, I'll make sure they listen to what you have to say. Maybe we can make them change their minds about a few things."

"You'll help me?"

"Absolutely." I bowed my head in reverence. "I live to serve, Your Majesty."

Edin popped one more piece of bread into his mouth, and I did the same. After a nod to Essie the cook, I let him lead the way, back down the hall toward the Council Room door. At the intersection, however, he paused. "Lord Loringham?"

"Yes, Your Majesty?"

"Can we go the other way? Through the front? It takes longer. I have to think about what I want to say."

"Whatever you wish." I couldn't say I was in much of a hurry myself. Of course, he knew the Palace well, and led me along a series of winding passages, many of which were dark save for one or two lit sconces. Edin asked questions all along the route – everything from my favorite color to my favorite sword stance to how I got so tall. I didn't always have a good answer, but it was enough to satisfy his apparent need for knowledge... and a friend.

About halfway down what I thought was our last hall, he stopped and turned to me. "Lord Loringham? Do you hear voices?"

I did, and I immediately took the point position, urging him to follow close behind. I thought about making him stay put, but I didn't want him out of my sight, either. This became especially important the moment I heard the clash of swords, then shouting. Then, a woman's shrill scream – Edin grabbed onto my hand and held it like a vise.

Still, I couldn't stop. In fact, I moved faster. As we moved into the Council antechamber, I noticed it had more Royal Guards in it than the last time I was here – a lot more. There were twenty-one, all told, and was that... Larenne? And *Andella*? My breath caught in my throat, my blood going instantly cold. *What the fuck are they doing here? How did they get here? Better question – why were there six other Guards dead or dying on the floor nearby?*

*Stay in control. Don't panic.* I refused to give them the advantage by speculating and second-guessing – there was no time for that. One hand went to my weapon while the other freed itself of the boy's grip and motioned for Edin to stay back. "Shield your eyes, Edin," I said, not daring to take my eyes off of the cluster of Royal Guardsmen.

"Stay your hand, m'Lord," one of them said, stepping forward. They were all in Royal Guard plate, but this one had a captain's badge etched into one pauldron. Though his bearing was strong, like he'd seen some fighting in his day, he couldn't have been much older than thirty or so. His face was still too boyish, too lean and freshly shaven. A lot of soldiers, as they got older, grew beards to hide scars, but this man had nothing yet to hide.

"What's going on here?" I barked so loud he actually froze in place a few feet before me. The sword he held pointed at the ground at his side spilled a few crimson drops onto the pristine white marble.

"Now, Lord Loringham, you of all people must understand the problem of renegades in your ranks? I assure you, we're rooting them out, slowly but surely."

I did not appreciate his veiled commentary. "Who do you work for?" I asked, lunging in toward him but stopping short of the attack. He stepped back into a defensive posture.

"Excuse me?" the man asked, incredulous.

"I said, who do you fucking work for? Are you Torven's men, or the Council's?"

"Name's Jessip, Captain in Lord Torven's army, Sir. The Council doesn't have an army, last time I checked. Unless you know something I don't?" He cocked his head at me, as if looking for more information, but his dark eyes told me something else – I wasn't supposed to be asking a question like that.

"But surely those men didn't work for Torven?" I pointed toward the still, dark masses littering the floor. Whatever fighting had happened here, it looked fresh and fierce, and when I caught Andella's gaze, this was confirmed. She looked terrified.

"I believe these men worked for themselves, m'Lord," Jessip said, though something about the way he spoke seemed awkward – he found his words too fast. "I was just explaining to the Princess here how misguided they were. You know how allegiances are these days."

I knew all too well, and I was losing my patience with this whole thing. "You know, it doesn't matter. Andella, Larenne, come with me. We're leaving." The two women started to move on shaky legs, but Jessip's outstretched sword stopped their advance.

"I'm sorry, Sir. I can't let that happen." Captain Jessip glanced over his shoulder, then turned back to me. "Orders, you see, are orders. You've made things a little more complicated, but I'm the ranking officer here right now. Can't very well disappoint General Torven."

Larenne's sword danced in the air as she used it to punctuate every one of her words. "And what exactly *are* your orders, Jessip?"

"Eliminate those who stand in the way of progress, of course, Princess. It's not supposed to start yet, but now is as good a time as any." Close behind me, I felt Edin tense, a tiny whimper escaping his throat as the Captain turned his attention back to me. "I was told you weren't even supposed to be here, Loringham. But, I would rather have you out here, than in there. You've actually done us a favor. Doesn't the Academy always teach that it's better to divide your enemy to conquer it?"

*Holy hell, it's an ambush.* I could hardly believe it, even though it made nothing but sense. Torven wasn't beaten, or looking to create a peaceful pact of some kind. No, he was seeing this war through to the end, and behind that door, who knew how many more Royal Guards were getting ready to execute their orders? I'd seen a good number of them by the door. *Why didn't you pay more attention, you idiot?!* Slay the Council, wrest the last reins of control away – it wasn't anywhere close to brilliant. It was simple, *so* simple, and we all walked right into it. Oh, maybe the Head Councilor thought he had things under control. Hell, maybe he thought all of these men were his, and it turned out that only a small number were loyal to his coin in the end. If Miller had never hired from within the Royal Guard ranks to begin with, we might not even be here now. So many possibilities, so many mistakes and assumptions... time would only tell which were the most fatal.

*Alex, my Brother, stay alert.* He was so close, just on the other side of the Council Room door, probably oblivious to what was happening here. But I was confident – he had magic on his side, after all... just as I did. It still seemed so alien, but there it was, surging within me the moment my sword left its scabbard. I fought to hold it in check as I stepped backward and reached for Edin's arm with my free hand, though my gaze never left the Guards, and Andella and Larenne, held in check within their lines. Even if I could get them all to run somewhere, where would they go? And who would be waiting for them around the next corner in this maze of a Palace? These men had no respect, no allegiance, no honor – if they were willing to attack a Princess, they'd kill a boy Prince and anyone that stood in their path. I couldn't let that happen.

"You have no right to call yourselves Zondrellian," I said as more began to draw in, falling in behind their Captain.

Jessip chuckled, dropping much of his formal officer's air. "That's rather odd, coming from *you*, Loringham." His men fanned out in a wide arc, and there right in their path was Larenne and Andella, pinned near the wall. Larenne clutched her blade, ready to attack, while Andella seemed to be trying to convince herself to stay calm. I noticed the front of her dress was torn and bloody then, and the heat of anger grew in me that much more. She didn't seem hurt – anymore, anyhow – but that wasn't the point. *How dare they touch her! Fucking animals.*

"Use the door! Get out of here!" I shouted at them. They were close. They could dart into the Council Room unhindered, and if someone gave chase, well, I had a plan for that.

"But what about you?" Andella called back, her voice at a fever pitch. Larenne had no such questions, though, and she was good at following orders. I didn't have to tell her twice. She pulled on Andella's arm, fighting with her as she flung open the door and dragged Andella through. The door didn't shut but it didn't need to – with a thought, Light spiraled out of the heavens, shooting through the ceiling and sending a few bits of stone tumbling to the ground below, where they bounced harmlessly off a shield now encasing the doorway. Nothing would get in or out, at least for a while.

While this gave some of the advancing Royal Guard some pause, no one retreated. My stomach turned in on itself as I weighed my chances against twenty-one well-armored, trained men, while also trying to ensure the safety of a small child. Maybe I should have kept Larenne in the fight. The gilded Council Room antechamber was large, but nearly devoid of furniture, leaving little to use for cover. And at my back, getting closer with each step, was the balcony overlooking the sea – no exit there.

*Damn it all. There was no choice, was there?* "Stay back, Edin," I bade, and he did as he was told. Then as the first and most enthusiastic of them stared to move in, I brought another shield of Light down in front of the boy. Again, stone and dust tumbled out of a new hole ripped into the ceiling by lightning, and one large piece struck one of the first advancing Guards in the head. The lucky shot put the man on his knees, and his nearest comrade hesitated. The other two could have cared less about my magic tricks, though – they had orders, and wanted blood.

An electric tingle shot from my core and through my limbs, warming me, empowering me. With a swipe of my sword, I brought the Light forth, but it did not gently spread out to provide cover. That was what I imagined, what I pictured in my head, what I tried to will into reality. The power had been building so fast, and what was once a targeted, simple burst of energy had become a storm as powerful as the ones that swept in off the coast and blanketed the entirety of Zondrell in thundering darkness.

It was beautiful yet horrible, at once fascinating and terrifying. Three great strikes shook the floor beneath our feet, tearing a hole across the ceiling wide enough to allow in the misting rain. The images of the men advancing on us faded into blinding white light, just vague shapes holding arms and shields up to block the glare. Screams of pain were drowned out by other calls to fall back. Not everyone listened, though.

My vision cleared just in time to see a hulking mass of silver armor bearing down on me. I wheeled out of the way of his axe and attempted to strike his flank on my way, but my blade skittered clumsily off of his plate. Not a problem – I was behind him now, and he would be too slow to get that big weapon up for a block. The idea of impaling him through the back might have given me pause, but Zondrell citizen or not, if the tables were turned, he would not hesitate. I could see it in his eyes as he tried to lumber around to face me again. *If you want blood, my brother, you can have it.*

My father's gem-handled blade found a spot between the plates that wrapped around his side, near the kidneys, where they butted up against the greaves. It slid in easily, and with it came the horrific sounds that came with such an action – the familiar squelch of blood and bone, followed by a surprised, angry howl. I withdrew and let him collapse there to cradle his axe and consider what his Royal Guard career had truly been worth.

I turned just in time to feel the wind as a longsword swung out to find my throat, missing by mere inches. The surprise sent a surge of white-hot electricity through my whole body. I may or may not have had control over that power, but it was there to serve me, and I needed it as another Guard tried to sneak in from the left. Lightning arced out to meet him, an extension of my blade that I then brought forward to slam into the one with the poorly-aimed sword. An acrid smell unlike no other filled the air as pure electric magic met with flesh.

"By the fucking Lady, pull back!" I heard someone – probably Captain Jessip – call out over the chaotic din. Again, he got only partial compliance.

The fellow to my left had a shield, and while he seemed addled, he had his wits about him enough to charge me with it, putting his full weight into the heavy steel. With no armor at all, it hit hard, knocked the wind from my lungs, and I found myself airborne for a second or two until my right side connected hard with the floor. Outrageous pain shot through my shoulder, stirring up old memories and older injuries. I let out a groan. *Damn fucking barbarians.*

I had to fight it, though – I couldn't stay there. If I did, I was dead, Andella was dead, Larenne was dead... the King was dead. This could not happen. The magic crackling through my veins helped me find the strength to get to my feet, though it didn't do much to make my sword feel less heavy. It felt like it suddenly weighed two hundred pounds.

"If you surrender, Lord Loringham, we can make this quick," came Jessip's voice to my ear. I looked to find him not a few feet away. "I'd say you've earned it." I merely growled and shook my head, fighting through the pain to bring my weapon up to bear.

A tiny voice said something behind me, and I realized the light surrounding Prince Edin was no longer there. On the other side of the room, the light protecting the door to the Council room had faded as well, and I caught sight of Andella's auburn hair near the wall. She was speaking, too, but I couldn't understand her. I couldn't hear any of them anymore. All I heard was the surging buzz of electricity, rising faster and faster, drowning out everything else.

This had to stop, and there was only one way. The magic had to come out.

I counted five strikes – *boom, boom, boom, boom, BOOM!* – each one bathing the chamber in light brighter than the sun, just for an instant. The closest man to me, Captain Jessip himself, appeared to be writhing on the floor, and I could just make out his shrieks of pain... something about burning. I wished I could make out his face beyond the wall of Light that had sprung into being before me.

I raised my sword to summon another wall on the other side of the room, thinking to block in the soldiers and force their surrender. It was the best thing I could come up with under the circumstances, since my true aim was to protect, not to kill. I thought I had accomplished exactly that.

How very wrong I was.

I heard a very loud, "Get back!" from one of the soldiers. It was followed by another, and another, and a cry from Andella. People began to pull back toward the other end of the room. If I hadn't been so busy preparing a shield and watching them all try to figure out their next move, I might have noticed what they saw more quickly, might have seen the real reason for the sudden retreat.

The floor began to shake beneath us. With the ceiling above already compromised, there wasn't much to hold the room together after the latest strikes of Light had cut clean through the marble floor, as sure as a knife into fresh-baked bread. *This place wasn't built to withstand lightning, was it?* No, of course it wasn't, because that kind of crazy shit did not happen in nature. Kelvaar's newly constructed Council antechamber jutted proudly out over the ocean cliffs, never once threatened by raging weather – or raging magic – until this fated day. The floor beneath us buckled, violent in its intent to break loose from the rest of the Palace.

*Think fast.* I dropped my sword and rushed to the boy King, huddling by the balcony. "Your Majesty, you've got to trust me," I said, looking down into two tearful dark orbs. There was nowhere to go, and we both knew it. Edin's arms reached out and held to me as tightly as they could.

*This is insane, totally insane.* Indeed, but we had no choice. I chanced one look back, hoping to see Andella, but saw nothing but a blur of shimmering Light.

Then, there was a tremendous rush as the floor began to give out from underneath, my organs sliding up while the rest of me fell downward. Magic coursed through my veins at almost as alarming a rate as our freefall, and the sound... the sound was deafening. I heard nothing but the roar of wind, the crack of rock, then the rush of water, drowning out all else.

# CHAPTER FORTY

## Ascent
*11 Spring's Green, 1272*
*Alexander Vestarton*

The tower had been sheared in two as easily as a butcher cuts through a piece of good meat. A sour, overpowering smell hung in the air – burned stone? Flesh? A bit of both, actually. And at the edge of what was left of the perfect marble that had once been King Kelvaar's beautiful balcony antechamber overlooking the sea was one lone girl in a torn, bloodied dress. I started toward her through the surreal scene of men checking the vitals of the fallen, of Lords yelling at Royal Guards and each other, of the world's most pissed-off Princess this side of the Sea of Stars shrieking at the General and some officer.

"...you and *that* witch... get her the fuck out of here. I should have you executed where you stand." The Royal Guard with the officer's badge on his right shoulder was ranting and raving, despite Princess Larenne's sword waving dangerously close to his face. The Guard's short dark hair and youthful face made him look too young for that badge, but he was otherwise a mess. His armor looked... scorched? Violent black streaks across the arm and his chestplate made him look like he'd reached into some kind of fire. Of course, it wasn't really a fire, now was it? He was lucky to still be alive as far as I could tell.

"Captain, you need to stand down," Torven said to him in that far-too-calm tone he had.

"Sir," he started, huffing and puffing to catch his breath, "you didn't see what they did. That one, I don't know how she did it. She almost killed Vaughan there. Sucked the life right out of him or something."

"That doesn't change the fact that you failed to follow orders, Captain."

The Captain – well, only a third or a fourth, judging by the level of the badge – slumped his shoulders. "I did nothing of the sort, Sir, I..."

I stopped and turned on him, no longer able to ignore him. "Soldier, do you know who I am?" The man blinked. "Then tell me, how did *that* happen?" I gestured toward the end of the world across the room. "How do a bunch of men die and a room just get sheared through the middle like that?"

The officer spoke through clenched teeth as if fighting back pain, or annoyance – I couldn't tell which. "Sir, our contingent met..."

I cut him off, getting closer, leaning into him so that he could see – really *see* – my magic-filled silver irises. "I fucking *know* how it happened. Do you think I'm an idiot? I'm fucking right here! You were setting up your little ambush for the Lords. You found one you could pick off easily, or so you thought, right? How many did you start with in here? How many men did you set upon a lone, unarmored man and a little boy? Oh, not to mention a couple of women, and then you dare to stand there and insult them?"

"Sir, I..."

"*Answer. My. Question.*"

His voice faltered as he hurried over his words, his bravado all but crushed. "Sir, we had over twenty troops. I lost eight men to that... magic. It was like nothing ever seen before."

"Yeah? What's your name, soldier?"

"Jessip, Sir. Third Captain."

"Well, *Third* Captain Jessip, let me show you something else you've never seen before." In my pocket, I still hung onto that little hunting knife that Brin had given me, the one that was once Jonathan Loringham's. I had forgotten about it for a few days, then thought I'd give it to Tristan tonight, after we were done with our business here. Stupid me, I should have known better than to assume there would be always be a "later," a "better time." Later might not come for a while yet, but it *would* come. I clung to that. In the meantime, the people who made this happen needed to understand that what they did was unacceptable – starting with this Jessip.

I took that knife out, pulled it from its sheath in a swift motion, and drove it directly into the meaty part of the officer's neck. He let out a surprised sound, something not unlike a growl mixed with a gurgle, and blood began to seep from the wound. "Now, Captain, see, that's just to distract you. You have a bigger problem right now. Do you know what it is?" The man just stared at me through anger and fear and pain. "See how the blood doesn't really come out all that fast? It should be pouring out of there, don't you think? But I can keep that from happening, just by *thinking* about it. If I think hard enough, who knows? I might even be able to just reverse the whole thing, like it never happened. Or, I can make the blood flow faster, like a fountain, and pour your whole life into the fucking ocean. Now wouldn't that be appropriate? Blood for blood, as they say?" I had to admit, I was taking to this magic-threatening business rather well – if I were in another state of mind, I might have been concerned about that.

"I never laid a hand on Loringham," the soldier croaked.

"Right, because otherwise why would he try to protect himself from you and twenty of your best friends?"

For the first time, Jessip made direct eye contact with me, and I swear he was terrified by what he saw there. He swallowed hard. "I was just following orders."

"That's not what I hear. Your orders now are to get the fuck away from me, then leave this Palace and find a hole to go crawl into until you're needed again. I don't want to see you, or even know you exist. Do you understand me?"

I ripped the knife from his neck then, and pushed my magic a tiny bit further on that wound, slowing down the blood loss to a mere trickle. He'd be fine with a bandage and some treatment. Though I was done with him, he didn't seem done with me, and that was fine. I expected it as his hand went to his sword. It never went any further, though, as the General grabbed him by the arm.

"Jessip, one more move and I will execute you myself," he said. "That man is your King, and deserves your respect."

What? That was insanity. I didn't hear that right. I turned to Torven as Jessip stalked off. "You just said I'm the King."

"Yes, Sir." Torven paused, regarding me with steel-colored eyes set in tired, creased sockets. "You're the Head Councilor. By right of succession, when the last of the family line is... no longer on the throne, the family of the Head Councilor takes control."

"And you're not the least bit worried that I'll haul off and have *you* executed?" I asked, no hint of mirth in my voice. Couldn't very well have him mistaking it for a joke.

"If it comes to that, my Lord, I am prepared."

Brave words. I snorted and leveled my gaze at him, seriously considering whether I could successfully toss him off the side of the broken tower. But then again... I gestured toward the curly-haired Princess, still looking for Guardsmen to berate and threaten. "On second thought, General, I'm not the one you need to answer to."

"Indeed, Sir. Do know that I sent men to the docks a few minutes ago. They'll be out there shortly for the rescue effort." The way he said "rescue" made me cringe. He didn't believe they were rescuing anyone alive, and why would I blame him? Who could survive a fall into the cold sea with ten tons of stone on top of them? Tristan Loringham, that's fucking who. I knew it, I felt it with every fiber of my being. How long he could survive might be another story. I had half a mind to jump down from here myself. Who had time to wait for these idiots to find boats, for Catherine's sake?

"Do it faster."

"My Lord, I assure you, we have every man on this." His bow was low, his posture stiff. Was the great General actually worried and fearful just like me? I couldn't quite get past his formal veneer to tell for sure.

I looked over to the other half of what was left of the antechamber and realized Andella was now sitting, unmoving and looking down into the abyss of swirling sea below. She was threateningly close to the edge. "Have them save a boat for me. I'll be down there in a moment. Then go answer to the Princess."

To my surprise, Torven went and did exactly as I said – he barked something at some men, then went to Larenne Blackwarren, bowing to her just as he had to me. I didn't catch what he said to her, but her reaction was both expected and priceless. She reared back and punched him square in that perfectly manicured beard of his. It took another to drop him. If she was satisfied, I didn't care, because I didn't stick around. I had things to do.

I pushed past other huddled Royal Guards until I sank to my knees at the open maw of the broken antechamber, looking down at a dark mass of rubble and churning sea and...

"Do you see it?" Andella's voice was soft, but not quite sad. Hopeful, perhaps.

I did see it – Light. Deep down below the sea's dark surface, a glimmer of a falling star peeked out from in between layers of rock. "Brother, I let you down. I should have been there." I didn't say it to her, or to anyone – anyone but him.

"It all happened so fast." Tears began to fall from whirling purple eyes, spilling down her cheeks. She made no attempt to wipe them away, but she did start to lean further in toward the void below, straining through her sobs to see.

I caught her by the arm. "Be careful. He'll fucking kill me if I let you fall."

Andella sniffed back whatever she wanted to say, and the flash of anger in her eyes was replaced with fear. "But Alex, we have to go down there."

"I know." Taking a deep breath, I got to my feet, still watching the swirling waters below. It seemed so far down, like staring into a portal to another world. "Come on, let's go get a boat," I said, and offered my hand to help her to her feet. Though trembling like a leaf, her hands felt warm, almost too much so considering how cold it was with the wind and drizzle whipping around us.

Sparks of white and orange – yes, orange – danced in her eyes, like the color of embers in a fire just starting to go out. "Hurry. He can't hold on much longer," she said, breathless, as if trying to hold in a swarm of magical energy. I knew that feeling well; in fact, the more I thought about the implications of her words, the more I felt the exact same way.

We started out down the hall that would take us to the lower gates, the fastest way to the massive array of docks and shipyards set into the cliffs near the Palace. Even running, we couldn't seem to move fast enough, and when we finally got there, despite random soldiers acknowledging my sudden new title, it was Andella who directed the crowd. She barked at them, told them where to go, hurried them along with encouraging words. If they listened to her because they needed to, or because they were scared of the way the magic energy seemed to flare in her eyes and around her whole being, it didn't matter. All I knew was that she was far better at this than I – Tristan would have been proud of her.

Me, I just wanted to get them all the fuck out of my way and do what needed to be done to help Tristan – my Brother, who I refused to believe was anything but perfectly fine, but just... wouldn't necessarily stay that way for too long. I had to dig down pretty deep to not snap at every soldier who called me "My Lord" in that nervous, unsure tone. King... was I really their King? Talk about surreal. The very thought sent feelings even worse than the skin-crawling sensation of the magic to fester and burn beneath my skin. Yet, I did my part. I talked to them like I thought a leader should. I pretended to forget about the fact that many of them had been on the wrong side of a violent ten-day civil war. I focused on what needed to be done, and on that faint streamer of light within the roiling sea before us.

I might not have deserved respect, but I *would* command it – I had to. It was the only thing holding me together.

# EPILOGUE

## Beacon
*10 Spring's Green, 1272*
*Brinnürjn Jannausch*

*M*agic, you see, is directly correlated to emotion. It is no wonder, then, that those mages who spend their time in deep thought but never feel the true passions of their art rarely excel in anything. It is also no wonder that those who give in to baser "feelings" like anger, grief, and even joy wind up being rather a danger to themselves and to others.

From *The Research of Archmage Tiara Chandler: Lectures and Essays*

I was too late. I knew it before I left for the streets, and perhaps I should never have let them go in the first place. That was assuming I could stop them. I doubted I could – Tristan and Vestarton had been determined.

And now they were... I was not sure. The outpouring of magic had been so intense, so violent that I felt it even from a block away, down by the rocky seashore. It shook the very ground, tearing the Zondrell Palace apart as though it were a child's plaything. In some ways, I felt glad that I had taken the shorter route through the streets, instead of trying to climb the walls into the Palace itself. Maybe here, I would have time to do something.

A star fell out of the shattered piece of the Palace and tumbled to the water below, and as it did, my strength seemed to fail me. Too late, indeed. But then again, what could I have done in the face of that? What could anyone have done?

There was a time when I felt little for the loss of a comrade. Men died around me every day – to feel every one would rend my soul in two. It didn't take long for me to figure that out. Later, I would meet people who did feel every death, who shed tears even for men they never knew. Jade Saçaille, the girl some people called a Saint, was one of them.

I remembered sitting with her once, toward the end of a battle, looking out over a sea not like the vast Sea of Stars, but a sea of the dead. Trapped in a small valley at Hals des Drachen, the battle had been fierce, fast, gruesome – just the way I liked it – and both sides took heavy losses.

"You are hurt so bad," Jade said to me, holding my hand as she inspected my arm, broken in two places after using it to stop the advance of a cavalryman.

"There will be pain later. Right now, I am fine," I told her. When the thrill of battle faded, I would feel that one, healed or not. "You should not waste time with me. Safaa is still out there. She may have fallen to the *Zondern*."

Jade's brow furrowed and her swirling eyes began to fill with tears. "*Os de Chantal,* no. What about Monsieur Sturmberg?"

"He is with Vremya, up on the ridge. They have good protection."

"Safaa..."

"She sent me and half the squad to the other side, by the gorge. I lost track of her after that." Yet, we needed her. Jade knew it, I knew it, everyone in our elite Eislandisch squad knew it. Perhaps I should not have left her behind, but at the time, there was little choice. Among us, only she alone could drive the enemy back, and she alone could serve as Keis Sturmberg's best shield. Without her, the mountains at Hals des Drachen would be lost.

Jade's ribbon of healing warmed my arm, strengthened it, knit the bones back together well enough to go back into the fray. I started to move again, despite her protests that she was not yet done, then watched as a gout of magic fire engulfed the valley below. It lasted only a moment, but it left scorched rock and burning bodies in its wake. Men screamed, but still they pressed on, still they fought through the endless sea. At my side, Jade began to cry softly.

Then Light, a great flash from the heavens that left a pillar of pure white brilliance in its wake. It was more than a weapon – it was a symbol. All around, I could hear battle cries and the cheers of the Eislandisch, and years later, men would tell the tale of the day the War ended with a great storm. It became the stuff of legends, the kind of things old veterans shared in taverns over one too many drinks, while younger men refused to believe it ever happened. Who would ever accept that someone could command lightning from the heavens? It was simply not possible.

Now, I looked out over the Sea of Stars, toward the shadow of the Palace of Zondrell, and I could almost hear Jade again, muttering her strange Lavançaise curses through her tears. I could almost see the battle playing out amongst the churning waves, and then... then I thought I saw Light shine down from sky, turning into a thin beacon much like the shape of a great sword.

Hope.

"*Os de Chantal.*"

I didn't look back, not at first. It was just remembrances of Jade on the wind, after all. But then the smooth, singsong Lavançaise voice said it again, this time louder, and nearly in my ear. I whirled around, hand instinctively ready for Beschützer.

"Onyx." The darkness of her being seemed to blend into the night. How she was even standing there was a mystery, until I realized the small skiff bobbing at the nearby docks must have been hers – the familiar green and yellow of Doverton were prominent on the sail.

"Is that what I think it is?" Onyx Saçaille snarled as she pointed up to the broken Palace and the weak Light stretching up toward the heavens. There were hints of her sister there in that black stare of hers, yes, but there was no compassion, no concern, only demands. "Is it, Brin? Answer me."

I had no desire to fight with her, of all people, in that moment. "Consider your 'prophecy' fulfilled." I began to turn away, back to the mission at hand.

"Who? Who is it? It is not you." She said it with such surprise that it made me pause.

"*Nein*. Why would it be? It is my nephew. And unless you are helping me, we have nothing to talk about."

"Take the boat." I did not have to be told twice. We rushed to the dock together, and four Doverton Honor Guards took up oars to take us toward the Palace. Not fast enough, but I said nothing. The waves, after all, were difficult to fight, as tons of fallen stone and a chill wind had invoked the sea's anger. As long as the Light was still there...

"Brin, you..." Her voice trailed off as she reached into a pocket under her heavy cloak. "Here. I am to give you this."

She offered me a tattered, crumpled piece of paper, but I just shook my head. "Not now."

"The author was very insistent. You may wish to see this." Did she not know there were more important things at hand? And yet, the look on Onyx's sharp features was so... sincere. She looked more like Jade in that moment than I might have seen her.

So I took the thing, unfolding it to stare at it through the evening gloom. Sketched onto the page in colorful charcoal was a picture of Beschützer, my own weapon, resting against a fence with grass and flowers around it. Every detail was perfect, down to the scuffs in the hilt and the play of sunlight against its blade. It was... an impossibility, a thing from another place and time.

"It would appear that the girl misses her father," said Onyx, emotionless.

An image of a girl filled my mind's eye, a waif with strawberry blond hair, a bright smile, deep blue-green eyes. No, that couldn't be right. "You could not have traveled so far. Quatremagne is weeks away. Where did this come from?"

"Jade is in Doverton, Brin. She has been for some time. She asked me to tell you this, if I ever saw you again." She paused, a hint of a smile on her lips as she watched me with her limitless black gaze. "An interesting thing about the little one – she has lightning in her eyes. Imagine that."

Somewhere off in the distance, men had already poured out of the Palace, rushing to find their own boats. Perhaps they saw, too, how the pillar of Light grew fainter with each moment. Soon, it was little more than a shimmer – it could have been a mere trick of the moon. There was little time left. I tucked the drawing into the safety of my cloak, then handed the cloak and Beschützer to Onyx.

"There is no prophecy, Onyx – there is only magic," I told her, ignoring her attempts to interrupt. "Right now, that 'lightning' is the most important magic in this world." Then, I took a deep breath and dove into the icy waves.

The End

Tristan and Alexander will return in *Enlightenment,* Book Three of the Chronicles of M'Gistryn!

In the meantime, please check out Halsbren Publishing LLC's other great fantasy titles available at Amazon.com, or anywhere fine books are sold.

www.AuthorJayErickson.com
or
www.zelda23publishing.com

If you enjoyed this novel, please take a moment and review it favorably. Every bit helps.

# Thank you.

# Anastasia M. Trekles
# Author

# ABOUT THE AUTHOR

Dr. Anastasia Trekles is a clinical professor at Purdue University. She also works with several professional non-profits to support educators and writers in Indiana and the Chicagoland area. Dr. Trekles has an extensive background with education technology, including design and pedagogical strategies as well as the effective integration of various technologies into teaching. She has taught a wide array of undergraduate- and graduate-level courses in these areas, both in classrooms and via distance education. While she might not have graduated from the Zondrell Magic Academy, she has spent a fair amount of time around schools.

Dr. Trekles has a personal passion for all types of fantasy fiction. The world of M'Gistryn is a world completely her own, but she can trace her inspiration of it to everything from Final Fantasy to Star Wars, from Harry Potter to the Sopranos, and from Ancient Rome to feudal Europe. To Dr. Trekles there is more to M'Gistryn than magic and prophecies – it's a world full of real people, struggling with real situations and real emotions.

In her debut novel, *Core*, she explores issues of war, coming of age, and the fulfillment of our life's purpose. As the story continues, her characters continue to struggle in a world where philosophies clash and questions abound.

Dr. Anastasia Trekles currently resides in Northwest Indiana.